"Jennifer Haymore is an up-and-coming new writer who displays a skillful touch in her erotic tale of a woman torn between two lovers."

—SHIRLEE BUSBEE, *New York Times* bestselling author of *Seduction Becomes Her*

"Recommended for readers who enjoy steamy Regency-era romance...there's a surprising lightness and tenderness to the love story."

—Historical Novels Review

"A story of life and death, revenge and true love...filled with passion, intrigue, and suspense...I look forward to reading much more historical romance from Jennifer Haymore."

—ArmchairInterviews.com

"Sweet and satisfying...refreshingly honest...a gripping read."

—LikesBooks.com

"A new take on a historical romance...complicated and original...the characters are well crafted...surprisingly satisfying."

—TheRomanceReadersConnection.com

"The characters in this book are easy to love...I can't wait to read the next book!"

—TheBookGirl.net

"What an extraordinary book this is!...What a future this author has!"

—RomanceReviewsMag.com

Also by Jennifer Haymore

A Hint of Wicked

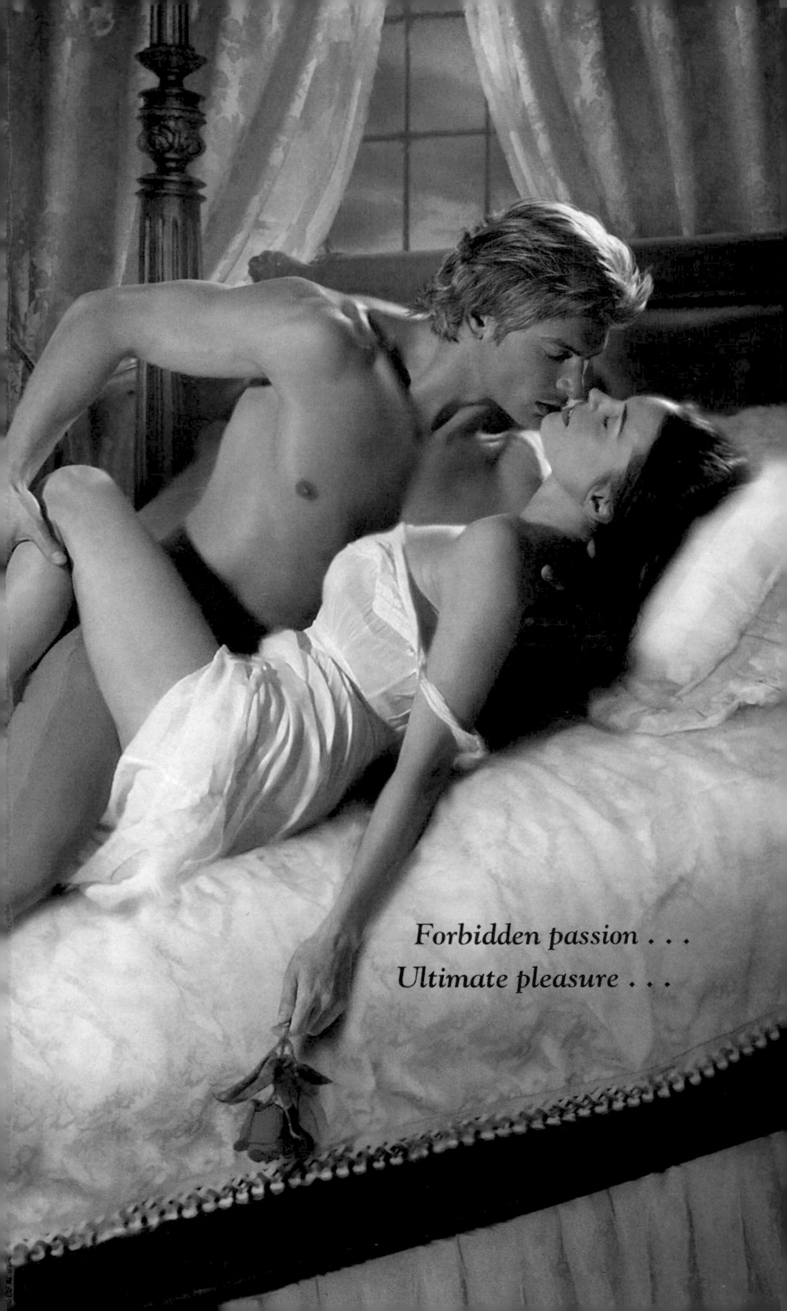
Forbidden passion . . .
Ultimate pleasure . . .

A Touch of Scandal

JENNIFER HAYMORE

FOREVER

NEW YORK BOSTON

Cover design by Diane Luger
Book design by Giorgetta Bell McRee

Forever
Hachette Book Group
237 Park Avenue
New York, NY 10017
Visit our website at www.HachetteBookGroup.com.

Forever is an imprint of Grand Central Publishing.
The Forever name and logo is a trademark of Hachette Book Group, Inc.

Printed in the United States of America

First Printing: April 2010

10 9 8 7 6 5 4 3 2 1

This book is dedicated to my husband,
who chases after our children, brushes their teeth, and
has even been known (albeit only in extreme circumstances)
to cook a meal or two so I could meet my deadlines.

Acknowledgments

Thanks to my super agent, Barbara Poelle, who has more energy than all three of my children put together (and if you knew my children, you'd know what a feat that is!).

Thanks to my editor, Selina McLemore, who always amazes me with her skill and insight.

Special thanks to all the people who read *A Hint of Wicked* and took the time to e-mail me about the book.

Thanks to the people who read this story before I turned it in: Tessa Dare, Evie Byrne, and Kate McKinley for their critiques; and April Morelock, Amanda Brice, Cindy Benser, and Maya Banks for beta reads. I appreciate your helpful suggestions more than I can say!

And thanks to my patient and ever-supportive family: Alex, Nicholas, Natasha, and Lawrence—I love you all!

A Touch of Scandal

Chapter One

Kenilworth, England

September 1823

A bothersome heat crept into Kate's cheeks as she hurried through the narrow, dimly lit passageway. If only she could learn how to hide her thoughts.

Taking a deep breath, she forcefully slowed her step, squared her shoulders, and lowered her eyes. She was simply a servant, finished with her duties for the day, ready to take the three-mile walk home. Not a flustered woman rushing out to a secret secluded spot to watch a strange man—no, a *god*, more like—bathe in the nude.

Kate paused at the threshold of the parlor. "Pardon me, my lady?"

She bobbed a curtsy as her mistress looked up from the novel she was reading. Lady Rebecca always kept her head firmly tucked in a book. A pang of sympathy shot into Kate's heart when the younger woman's haunted blue eyes met hers.

"Yes?" Lady Rebecca lowered the thick volume to her lap.

Lady Rebecca was the sister of a duke, and her breeding showed in her expression, in her bearing, and in her mannerisms. Today she wore a plain white muslin gown with a gauze fichu tucked into its rounded neckline, but neither the simplicity of her dress nor her relaxed position on the sofa diminished the evidence of her nobility. She'd kicked her shoes off and settled on the plum-colored velvet with her legs tucked beneath her. With her slender build, her coal-black hair, and her midnight-blue eyes, Lady Rebecca was one of the most beautiful women Kate had ever laid eyes on, but there was a sweetness about her, a vulnerability, that drew Kate, that made her want to protect her, even to share secrets.

No, Kate reprimanded herself. A shiver skittered down her spine. Some secrets were best left unspoken. *Forever*.

Had circumstances been different, she and Lady Rebecca might have been friends. *Sisters*. But Kate was merely a servant, albeit an unconventional one, given that she slept apart from the rest of the household. Still, she wished she had the freedom to sit beside Lady Rebecca and engage in a lively discussion about whatever it was she read with such passion.

"What is it, Kate?" Lady Rebecca gazed at her without really seeing her, but Kate was accustomed to it. It was how aristocrats always looked at her—as an object rather than a human. She couldn't blame them, for they didn't know any better. It infuriated Mama, though.

"Might I be dismissed, ma'am? I've prepared your bed, brought up fresh water, and set out your nightclothes for Annie." Kate's smile wobbled. The knowledge that she might see *him* again had butterfly wings tickling her insides. She fought not to squirm, but the mere thought of the handsome stranger made her skin prickle.

Lady Rebecca frowned. "Is it your little brother? Is he very unwell?"

The lady knew Reggie was the sole reason Kate walked home every night. Her younger brother was a sickly boy, and while Mama cared for him well enough during the day, she didn't like her sleep interrupted, so Kate was there for him through the long, sometimes difficult nights.

"Well..." Kate was a horrible liar, but she needn't exaggerate in order to answer the question. It also wasn't necessary to explain that her reasons for wanting to leave early today had nothing to do with Reggie's health. "He has been coughing quite a lot."

"Oh, the poor thing." Lady Rebecca waved her hand. "Of course, Kate. Please do go—I know you've a distance to walk, and"—she squinted at the drab chintz curtain covering the single square window—"it's near dark, isn't it?"

"I think so." *Oh, please, Lord, let him be there today. Let me not be too late.*

"Yes, well..." Lady Rebecca glanced across the room at the door that led downstairs. The hope in her eyes was unmistakable. "The master should be home soon."

Kate nodded. Her elder brother, William, was Lady Rebecca's husband, and he liked Kate to be gone before he arrived. He found it awkward to be with his sister and wife in the same room, and he feared Kate would betray them both. Kate didn't blame him. First of all, it was horribly awkward to her as well. Second, deception was not her forte. From the beginning, she'd felt the worst part of this whole arrangement was the duplicity inherent in it. She understood why it must be, but it still twisted her stomach.

Lady Rebecca turned back to Kate. "Of course you may go."

"Thank you, ma'am. I'll be here when you wake in the morning." Kate dipped into another curtsy and tried not to break into a run as she crossed the room to the opposite door. Even so, the clack of her shoe heels on the wood floor announced her hasty departure, and from the corner of her eye, she saw Lady Rebecca's brow tilt in bemusement as she watched her go.

The cottage was elegant and expensive, but certainly neither as elegant nor as expensive as a duke's sister was accustomed to. Willy was in financial straits and only employed four servants—Kate, the cook, the maid-of-all-work, and the manservant, John. The other female servants lived in the small room in the attic and John slept in a loft above the stable, but Kate walked back and forth to her home at Debussey Manor daily.

It was far less help than someone of Lady Rebecca's breeding expected. Yet she never complained. Kate admired her for that.

Her cheeks flaming despite all her efforts to douse the fire in them, Kate descended the last step and emerged into the drawing room. Glancing up, she stopped in her tracks, stiffening. John lay on the tasseled chaise longue, his stockinged feet crossed atop the cream-colored silk and his arm flung over his forehead.

He cracked one lid open to gaze at her with a green eye, and Kate pursed her lips in distaste.

"Leaving?" he asked.

"Yes," she answered curtly. Untying her apron, she spun round and strode to the closet behind the stairwell.

Feeling John's reptilian eye on her, she pulled off her apron and cap, hung them, and after a moment of consideration, decided to leave her cloak here overnight. It had been a warm day, so surely it wouldn't be too cold to walk without it in the morning, and it would be a nuisance to carry both ways.

"You look pretty today, Kitty. That color becomes you."

She cast a look down at her dull pale brown work dress. How pleasant to know that brown was her color. "Thank you," she pushed out.

He chuckled but Kate didn't look in his direction. John was negligent, arrogant, lazy, and, with his greased hair and pointed beak nose, unappealing. Whenever Willy was near, John's manner was obsequious to the point of inducing nausea, but when Willy wasn't home, he strutted about the place as if he owned it, even going so far as to be disrespectful to Lady Rebecca. Nothing raised Kate's ire more than to see that man's disdainful behavior toward her mistress.

She turned from the closet and strode to the front door. Opening it, she stepped into the pleasant late-summer evening. As she closed the door, John's voice drifted lazily out. "Tomorrow, then, pretty Kitty."

Her lips twisted, and when the door met its frame, she shoved it hard. The tiny slam brought her a small measure of satisfaction.

If John thought to seduce her with false flattery, he ought to think again. No man had seduced her yet, though a few had tried. She'd promised herself long ago to never go down that particular perilous road. And with a man like John…not a chance.

Still, it was best to stay away from him and make certain to avoid being alone with him. He didn't strike her as the kind of man who'd take her rejection to heart.

Kate paused on the tiny landing and took a deep breath. Was she a hypocrite? She shook her head, thinking not. *Watching* was a wholly different action from *doing*, after all. And John the skinny, lazy manservant was a wholly different creature from the bronze god at the pool.

Kenilworth's gently curving High Street was deserted for the moment. The setting sun cast an orange glow across the rooftops, and the houses and shops abutting the road shimmered in the haze.

She turned and strode down the street with purpose, her shoes scraping against the hard-packed dirt. Ahead, the shoemaker's widow, dressed in black with a dark shawl draped over her shoulders, emerged from one of the pretty neighboring cottages. Kate bobbed and murmured a polite greeting when they passed each other. The woman wished her a good evening as the clatter of wheels and the sound of hooves heralded a coach and four coming from behind. Kate glanced over her shoulder to see the carriage, a closed, lacquered black beast, approaching, tossing up a billow of dirt in its wake.

She picked up her skirts and hurried across the street in front of it, slipping through a broken slat in the old wooden gate and stepping onto a narrow path in the field beyond just in time to avoid a choking spray of dust. Through the gold-tinged trees loomed the tall, ivy-covered ruins of Kenilworth Castle. Keeping the castle to her right, Kate followed the overgrown trail that led along the bank of the brook. She skirted fallen branches and dead leaves, and before long grime caked her shoes and dampness seeped through her stockings.

Her heart thudded with a dull cadence, heavy in her chest. Under the coarse wool of her dress her skin flushed with excitement. Would he be there today? He wasn't yesterday, but she'd seen him four times in the past week, swimming in the small lake created by the ruin of a dam that had once formed the castle moat.

The air grew warm and close. Branches cracked under her feet, and leaves rustled. The faint drone of insects hummed in the air as twilight approached. She'd taken the long way, and it'd be full dark by the time she arrived home, but she cared about that just about as much as she cared about her wet feet and mud-soaked hem. Not a whit.

She slowed as the creek turned northward, and with her lower lip trapped between her teeth, she concentrated on placing her footfalls so her steps would be quiet.

A splash sounded in the distance, and Kate halted and looked up. Beyond a thick copse of greenery just ahead, the pool glimmered in the gathering dusk, its surface rippling.

Someone had just dove in. *He* had just dived in.

Kate swallowed hard and crept forward, crouching so he wouldn't see her behind the clusters of brambles and bushes. She ducked behind a particularly dense bush at the water's edge and peeked around it.

Just as the waves on the pool's surface began to settle, he emerged from the depths with his back to her. He rose until the water lapped eagerly at his narrow waist. For the tiniest fraction of a second, she wished she could be that water.

His thick shoulder rippled with muscle as he reached up to thrust a hand through his glistening blond hair.

Surely this man couldn't be human. He was perfectly built—like one of the gods she'd learned about when she spied on Mama reading to her brothers. Tall, muscular, his skin bronzed from the sun, as hard and beautiful and intimidating as Apollo himself. He shook his head, sending blond shoulder-length curls flying and a cascade of golden drops showering into the water. Then he dove again, his taut—and quite shockingly bare—backside emerging from the water before his entire body disappeared beneath the surface.

A pleasurable shudder coursed through Kate, leaving a low burn to simmer deep inside her.

The god-man swam like a fish. Perhaps he wasn't Apollo at all, though he rather looked like she'd always imagined Apollo. Perhaps he was Poseidon—a young, clean-shaven Poseidon. Perhaps this time when he emerged, he'd be carrying his golden trident. She held her breath, waiting, frozen.

Kate had been born at Kenilworth and raised at Debussey Manor, and she knew without a doubt this man didn't hail from these parts. What was he doing here? And why did he come here—this place that had been her secret spot for so many years—to bathe? The sight of him, and his very strong, very *naked* body, was so far removed from her realm of reality that it didn't seem all too farfetched to think that a lightning bolt had deposited him straight from Olympus.

He rose from the water again, this time farther away but facing her. She stared in fascination at the jagged scar near his waist, and when her gaze traveled up his solid torso and over his rugged face, she saw the second scar, a terrible knot glaring red just above his left eyebrow.

The imperfections on his otherwise perfect form emphasized the fact that this was not a god, but a very human man indeed. A man who'd seen, experienced, and ultimately survived terrible things.

He rubbed the water out of his eyes and opened them. His sky blue gaze settled directly on her.

She jerked her head behind the bush, gulping back a gasp. Her heart thundered in her ears. A bead of sweat trickled down the side of her face. Controlling her breaths, she froze in her crouched position and squeezed her eyes shut. She couldn't move, because now he'd surely hear her. Her best option was to remain still and quiet, keep herself hidden behind the bush, and pray he hadn't seen her.

She should fear this giant, intimidating man, but that wasn't why she prayed he hadn't seen her. No, she prayed he hadn't seen her because if he had, she wouldn't be able to watch his sculpted nude body anymore.

She let out a long, silent sigh through pursed lips. It was the undeniable truth. As much as she'd fought against it, she was hopelessly and thoroughly debauched. If not in body, at least in thought. The man could be a murderer or a lunatic, and all she cared about was spying on him.

Not only was she debauched, she was an idiot.

Perhaps he hadn't seen her. He had just opened his eyes after being submerged in water, and surely it would take a second or two for him to focus on an object as far away as her. And with her brown hair and brown dress, she blended into the landscape like a chameleon.

She'd remain hidden for a few moments longer, then make a hasty, as-quiet-as-possible retreat.

Keeping her eyes closed, she hugged her knees to her chest and counted to a hundred. All was silent for a while, but when she reached sixty, she heard splashing from the direction of the pond. Clearly he'd resumed his sport.

Ninety-nine. One hundred.

She released a relieved breath and raised her lids.

And found herself gazing into his rugged face.

She blinked several times in disbelief, trying to clear her vision as he stared at her with narrowed blue eyes from his position on his haunches an arm's length away. A frown creased his handsome features. Rivulets of water streamed from his golden hair and plastered a white shirt to his broad, imposing shoulders.

He'd been watching her. Spying on her in silence—probably throwing rocks into the water to mislead her.

With a squeal of fright, Kate stumbled to her feet. Her legs caught in her skirts, but she kicked them free. Brambles clawed at her dress, ripping the fabric as she lunged away.

She'd gone no farther than two steps when he clapped an arm around her waist and yanked her back. She stumbled and would have fallen had his hard body not ensnared her like a net.

Kate trembled all over. Small, pathetic whimpers bubbled from her throat as she futilely tried to twist away.

His warm, damp torso pressed against her back. He smelled fresh and clean, like hay drying in the sunlight, with an underlying almond scent she instinctually recognized as purely his.

His arm crossed over the front of her chest, pinning

her against him. The lock of his embrace rendered her utterly helpless.

"Who are you?" he demanded. He bent his head, and the trace of beard on his jaw scraped against the shell of her ear. "And why are you watching me?"

His voice, low and rough, stroked over her body like a coarse towel, causing every inch of Kate's skin to explode into flame.

Panic wouldn't help her now. She must stave it off, be as brave as a knight battling a rampaging dragon. For several moments, trapped in the steel of the stranger's arms, she worked to control her gasping breaths and to stop her limbs from shaking like autumn leaves in a gale.

Finally, she sucked in a lungful of air. Staring straight over the pool, now glowing purple in the twilight, she said, "My name is Katherine, sir. I'm very glad to meet you. Lovely evening, isn't it?"

Chapter Two

Garrett nearly dropped the vixen. He'd expected the shivering and the fear, and he had already concluded she gave a fine performance.

When her trembling had abated, he'd readied himself for a struggle—or perhaps she would yank a dagger or a pistol from the folds of her skirt and try to kill him. He didn't expect polite conversation.

Her words shocked him so thoroughly, he loosened the hand he'd clamped around her bodice and followed her gaze to the horizon.

She didn't take advantage of his mistake—another surprise. Instead, she remained as snugly fitted against him as if she belonged there.

Layers of clouds drifted across the horizon and the dipping sun lowered behind them, infusing them with red, oranges, pinks, and purples, and sending streams of color out over the pond he'd used as his bathing spot for the past week.

He reapplied the pressure round her waist. "Who are you?" Even to himself, he sounded menacing as hell. He clenched his free hand, prepared to clamp it over her mouth should she attempt to scream for help from her accomplices. "Why are you here?"

She glanced over her shoulder at him, sparks lighting her dark eyes. Her lips twisted into a rueful expression. "Must I answer that?"

"You must."

"Can I...?" Her chest rose beneath his forearm as she took a deep breath. "Might I look at you while I do so? I daresay this is a rather awkward means of conversing with a person one hasn't properly met."

He considered for a moment. "Very well. But I'm not letting you go."

"Of course." Slowly, she turned within the circle of his loosened arm until she pressed against him from chest to groin. She tilted her head to look up at him. "That's better."

Theoretically she should complain that this was still an awkward way to converse with someone who wasn't even an acquaintance, but Garrett didn't point out the inconsistency. He was somewhat more concerned with stifling his body's reaction to her. As if he were a long-dormant volcano flaring to life, blood boiled in his veins, and his skin heated from the inside out.

He took a deep breath, trying to calm his raging blood. It made no sense. Few women had this effect on him. The two who instantly came to mind possessed elegance and beauty in spades, while this woman didn't possess either of those attributes. Katherine was brown and drab, with pale lips, coffee-colored eyes that seemed too big for her face, and shoots of dark hair poking out haphazardly from her cap. Her body was tall and thin—too tall and too thin, perhaps—and her dress plain. All in all, her outward appearance reminded him of England in the dead of winter. Dry and somber. Lifeless.

And yet…she was *alive*. Somehow beneath all that dullness, she sparkled. She was radiant. He couldn't tear his eyes from her face. From those luminous eyes. Her glow must be infectious, because in such close proximity to her, something he'd thought dead deep inside him sprang to life.

"I…"

Her voice trailed off, and he lifted a brow. "You… what?"

She licked her lips. "This is embarrassing, sir. I'd really rather not tell you."

"Embarrassing?" He didn't understand. Either she was spying on him with the intention of relaying his activities and whereabouts to his enemies, or…He couldn't think of an "or." There was simply no other reason for the woman to be alone in this lonely, abandoned place.

"Well…yes. Quite embarrassing."

When he didn't respond, pink tinted her pale cheeks.

"Perhaps we could just shake hands and I'll continue on my way?" She bit her lower lip in anticipation and gazed at him from beneath her lashes.

Garrett stiffened. It wouldn't be so easy to manipulate him. Once, maybe, but not anymore. "I don't think so."

She released her breath in a whoosh. "Oh."

He tightened his arm around her, wedging her against his body. A pretty rose color suffused her cheeks, and she'd plastered her arms to her sides as if she were afraid to touch him—or didn't know how—and he considered the possibility that she'd never been this close to a man.

He ground his teeth. "Tell me."

"I... I was watching you," she breathed.

"I know that much," he bit out. "Why? Don't lie to me."

"Because..."

He held her close, every muscle in his body braced to hear his enemy's name. *William Fisk*. The man who had made his life a living hell for the past eight years.

"Because... well, because you're quite interesting," she finally said. "And..." Again, she began to tremble.

"And?" he growled.

The column of her pale throat moved as she swallowed hard. "And... you're... you're so beautiful."

Her flush deepened. Garrett stared at her with narrowed eyes, searching for signs of guile. He found none in the wide brown eyes that gazed up at him, nor in the flush that now bordered on crimson, but God knew he was no expert at discerning treachery and deceit.

She must be lying. He was damn ugly, inside and out. Ruined by the violence of war and betrayal and heartbreak, and of too many years of living a lie.

She studied him with eyes that widened minutely as she interpreted his expression. "No. No, you're wrong," she whispered with absolute conviction.

"What are you talking about?" he snapped.

"You think I'm playing you false, but I'm not. I am very bad at telling lies. I've abandoned lying altogether, for I'm discovered every time."

He shifted his stance. His instincts told him she was innocent of treachery, but his instincts were invariably wrong in such matters. And yet, he couldn't ignore them. Was he playing the fool yet again?

"Please forgive me. It was horrid of me to invade your privacy."

"Yes."

"But you see, this is my pool."

He raised a brow. "Is that so?"

She nodded. "I come here often." She gestured with her chin in the direction of the castle ruins. "People often visit the castle to explore and have picnics and such, but they never come out this far, and the pool is rather secret, hidden as it is. I never encountered another soul here until I saw you."

He believed her, despite himself. Against his will, his anger faded and his muscles relaxed. "When was that?"

She hesitated, then answered, "Eight days ago."

He'd arrived at Kenilworth eight days ago. He'd set up camp in an abandoned, ruined cottage near the castle, and he'd found the pool during his exploration of the area. It had been a fine, summery day, and the cold, clean water had lured him. He'd stripped off his clothes and dived in to wash the grime of travel from his body. He'd returned often since.

"And how many times have you spied on me?"

She broke her gaze from his eyes and dropped her chin to stare at his chest. "Four times. I..." Her voice dwindled.

He reached up to press his palm against her cheek, forcing her to look up at him. She blinked, and for the first time, he saw that her lashes were long, thick, and dark, gracefully framing her vibrant eyes.

He trusted her. He might regret it later, and he thought

that likely, but he couldn't continue to intimidate a woman he innately trusted. But he didn't let her go. *Not yet.*

"What is your name?" Katherine asked softly.

He sucked in a breath. Best not to get too specific. "Garrett."

"It's good to meet you, Mr. Garrett."

"No. Just Garrett."

She nodded. "Where are you from, Mr.... uhm... Garrett?"

He shook his head slightly. "Where are *you* from?"

"Kenilworth," she answered readily enough, but her lips twitched. "Well, I suppose you'll insist upon being mysterious." She scowled as she studied him. "You almost have a London gentleman's accent... but not quite. There's a touch of something else there, something I've never heard. Something foreign." She shrugged. "Which means that until you inform me otherwise, I shall be forced to stand by my first theory of your origin."

"What was that theory?"

"I concluded you must be from Olympus."

He choked on a laugh. "Olympus? Why?"

She groaned, and the flush bloomed over her cheeks again. "My mama is right. I'm a silly chit who shouldn't speak at all."

"I like the way you speak." The words flowed out of him before he could check them, and he snapped his mouth shut.

Her lips spread into a wide smile. It lit up her face, infused her lips with color, and made her eyes sparkle and dance with mischief. Holy hell—she *was* beautiful. Incredibly, devastatingly so. She stole the breath from his lungs. Stunned, he dropped his arm, freeing her.

She stepped back, still smiling. "Well, I have the unfortunate quality of being too blunt, I'm told. But I see you and I suffer from the same malaise."

She hadn't turned and sprinted. In fact, she seemed to have no plans—or desire—to escape from him.

"What malaise is that?" he asked stupidly. He couldn't get enough air. His brains had turned to porridge.

"You didn't intend to compliment me about the way I speak. The words escaped your mouth before you could stop them. It happens to me, too. Incessantly."

He answered that with a wry smile of his own. "It seldom happens to me. Perhaps your condition is contagious."

"Perhaps it is. Perhaps you should run away from me. I could be detrimental to your health."

It felt so odd, so foreign, to smile. The realization was enough to flatten his lips.

Her smile faded, too. "What's wrong?"

He paused, studying her. Why not speak the truth? If she was honest, she'd understand. If she was up to something, it would serve as a warning. "I cannot be certain you're to be trusted."

"Oh." She cocked her head, and her eyebrows squeezed together. "Is that why you're alone out here? Because you don't trust anyone?"

His jaw tightened. "Something like that."

"Sometimes it can be difficult to trust others, but I do believe most people are good. Though goodness can be near impossible to detect sometimes. Don't you think so?"

Once he might have agreed with her, but now... "I don't know."

She looked down, kicked at the dirt with her mud-caked shoes, then looked back up at him with shining eyes. She opened her mouth to speak, but as if she thought better of it, she clamped her lips. Her tongue darted out to lick them.

"What is it?" His voice was a gruff whisper. He couldn't tear his eyes from her lips. Plump. Enticing.

"Who betrayed you so terribly that you cannot trust a simple countrywoman?"

Her voice was soft, sympathetic, and nearly compelling enough for him to respond with the truth. He nipped the compulsion in the bud, quickly taking a different tack. "How old are you, Katherine?"

"Will you call me Kate?"

"Kate."

"Thank you."

He liked the sound of her name, so he said it again. "How old are you, Kate?"

"Two and twenty. How old are you?"

She wasn't as young as he'd thought. Still, she was far too young for him. Too sweet for him. Too innocent. Too... different. He had no intention of selecting a bed partner anytime soon, but when he did, he'd make certain the woman was experienced. And as jaded and cold as himself.

"Far older than you," he said quietly.

She smiled again, and his blood surged. Tamping down his lust, he pushed his hand through his wet, tangled hair. He resisted the urge to command her to stop smiling.

"How old?" she demanded.

"Thirty-four."

She released a breath through tight lips. "*Pfft.* Hardly too old to befriend someone such as me."

"Befriend?" he asked with a raised brow.

The suggestion in his tone escaped her. "I don't have

many friends." She clasped her hands together in front of her brown skirt. "But I believe I should like to be a friend of yours."

"You're too trusting," he said in a low voice. If he were any other man, her virtue would be in peril. Hell, her virtue *was* in peril.

"Am I?" She studied him, her eyes seeming to dive into his soul. Surely if they could do that, she would see the blackness residing there and flee for her life.

"Yes."

Slowly, she shook her head. "No, I don't think so. You won't hurt me."

His lips twisted. "You think not?"

"I know it," she said in a low voice.

"You are too naïve."

Her eyes darkened at that, and they flickered away. "You're wrong about that."

He clenched his hands into fists, stifling the protective instinct that overcame him at her words. He wanted to demand to know who'd caused that shadow to pass over her face, and then he wanted to go beat the hell out of that person.

It had been a long time since he'd felt much of anything. Surely these sudden, strange emotions weren't natural, nor were they logical. Garrett felt as if he was awakening from a months'-long slumber and was struggling to reassimilate into the world of the living.

She had done this to him. As they spoke, she brought him to life. How was it possible?

He pushed out a measured breath, reined himself in, and tried to conjure the response of a gentleman from his fractured memories.

"You don't understand," he said as gently as he could. "You cannot sneak up on a man, watch him bathe, speak to him the way you've spoken to me..."

"I wouldn't," she said. "I wouldn't sneak up on any man, nor would I speak to him the way I've spoken to you. I'm not stupid."

"I could be dishonest. I could be a criminal, a murderer." He said the words through clenched teeth as a shudder of revulsion slithered down his spine. "A rapist."

"But you're none of those things." A frown line appeared between her eyes as she gazed at him. "Are you?"

"I could be."

"You aren't."

The thought of this guileless woman stepping into the path of some predator made him want to grab her and shelter her. He might possess some honor, but not many men would resist this kind of temptation. Out at twilight beside an abandoned pool, a beautiful woman blatantly flirting with him...

He ground his teeth. "How can you know?"

"At first...I wasn't sure. Or maybe I was. I think maybe I always knew, deep inside. But now, after having spoken to you—" She shrugged. "—I just know."

"You shouldn't be out here alone, ever. It could be dangerous."

"I've come out here alone for my entire life, and I've never been in any sort of danger whatsoever. Not once." She tilted her head at the pool shimmering silver-orange in the decreasing twilight. "This is my private place. My thinking place."

He swallowed, imagining her stripped bare, swimming

in the pond. Imagining swimming with her, touching her, making her shudder in his arms…

Damn. He rubbed his temple to expel the images. Those thoughts were wrong. Depraved. Hell, the ink wasn't even dry on his divorce and he was already debauching a maiden in his dark fantasies.

"I apologize," he said tightly. "I didn't mean to intrude."

"I'm glad you did." She shifted from foot to foot. "As I said, I think you're very…interesting."

"You should stay away from me." He took a step closer to her, close enough to feel the sweet heat cascading from her body. She smelled of cinnamon and pine.

She stood her ground. "I don't fear you."

"I'm dangerous."

"Perhaps," she breathed. "But not to me."

"Associating with me will only bring you pain."

"How can you say such an awful thing?"

"I have that effect on people."

She reached out and brazenly placed her hand flat on his chest, scorching him through the thin linen of his shirt. "So be it. But no matter how much pain associating with you might bring me…" Her words dwindled as he pressed his palm over her hand.

She stared at his hand engulfing hers on his chest. Raising his other hand, he touched one finger to the soft skin beneath her chin and pressed upward.

"Tell me what you were going to say."

Her eyes shone, and she blinked. "I'll never regret it."

Bending his head, he touched his lips to hers.

Chapter Three

You seduced this poor man. You're a wicked, wicked woman.

The words flowed through Kate's mind like the cod liver oil Mama had always tried to force down her and her brothers' throats.

The good thing about cod liver oil was that once swallowed, it was gone, leaving only a fishy residue, which could, in theory, be ignored. Or obliterated completely by a spoonful of honey.

That's what Garrett's kiss was like. The softest, sweetest, smoothest, warmest honey that had ever crossed her lips.

Kate's eyelids fluttered shut. Tiny shudders began at the tips of her toes, worked through her legs, and spread up her torso. She raised trembling arms and grasped his shirt, curling her fingers in the damp white linen and fitting herself against his body. His big, warm hands cupped her cheeks, holding her face tilted up so that their lips aligned perfectly, his callused fingertips gently scraping her skin. He sipped at her lips as if he were the bee and she the nectar.

It was unfathomable that such a large, hardened man could touch her so delicately. As if she were fragile, precious, something to be revered.

Kate gripped his shirt even tighter and released a shaky breath. His nose bumped hers gently as he adjusted position, and his tongue brushed the inside of her lip in the tiniest of caresses.

Slowly, he pulled away. Keeping his hold on her face, he tilted her head so that they were nose to nose, their foreheads touching.

"Kate."

Kate opened her fists and flattened them against his shirt. The muscles running up and down his sides vibrated against her fingers.

She couldn't talk. All the places her body made contact with his tingled.

She *wanted* this man. How could it be?

Mama would say she was silly and wanton. Willy would be horrified—he'd probably duel Garrett for her honor. Protocol demanded she slap Garrett for his forwardness, then flee for her life and pray no one would discover her depravity. For if any outside observer saw her at this moment, he would cast one glance at her and denounce her as a brazen whore.

Yet she didn't care about any of it. All she cared about was how Garrett made her feel. Unbelievably safe, warm, comforted. She wanted to explore him. Remove his breeches and shirt, and taste every single hard inch of him. Crawl right into his body, curl up and stay. She never wanted to let him go.

"You must go home now."

"No," she breathed. "I want to stay here . . . with you."

"You cannot."

She didn't want this impossible, beautiful dream to end. She didn't want to return to the harshness of her life. Not yet.

Every evening for the past eight days, she'd hurried to the pool to see if he had come, and if he was here, she'd watched him raptly, silently. Later at night, she'd dreamed of touching him, of those big arms closing around her body. Holding her.

The reality of him, however, was so much more than her fantasy. When he spoke to her, when he looked at her with those sky-blue eyes, all the muscles in her body melted like butter, and when he touched her, every one of her nerves sang with pleasure.

The pads of his thumbs stroked over her cheekbones, and her cheeks warmed. She clutched him tighter.

"You must go. It's almost dark. Your family will worry."

He pulled back. His hands dropped away from her face and gently disentangled her fingers from his shirt.

She opened her eyes, tasting the bitterness of his rejection. But one glance at his face told her the decision cost him as much as it cost her. Maybe more. He didn't want her to go, either.

She forced a smile. "Why are you such a gentleman? I almost wish you were as bad as those men you tried to warn me about."

His face darkened, and a muscle ticked in his jaw. "No. You don't."

He was right, of course. From the beginning, something had told her he wasn't a bad man. It was that duality in him, that rugged body and those scathing blue eyes contrasted with an innate honor that shone around him like a nimbus. She felt as if she already knew him, but she wanted to know him better. Understand how he could be so hard and scarred, and yet remain so tangibly gentle, so honorable.

She gave a rueful shake of her head. She hadn't known him long enough to be so confident in her assessment of him. Yet she trusted herself. As willful and as lacking in common sense as she'd been, she truly wasn't as stupid as her behavior might lead one to believe. If she'd sensed danger, she would have run the first time she'd seen him, and she wouldn't have returned.

"I just..." Her voice dwindled. She licked her lips nervously. "I wish to let you know...I'm usually not so...uhm..." She pushed out the last word in a whisper. "Ardent."

"Is that so?" He seemed mildly amused. She stole a glance at him from beneath her lashes and saw a lightness in his expression she hadn't seen before. She relaxed a little.

"It's true," she confirmed. "It's just that you're... you're..." She swallowed down the lump in her throat and gazed down at the muddy toes peeking from the mud-crusted hem of her dress. "Well, as I said before, you're interesting to me. I...like you."

A knuckle grazed her cheek, but she couldn't look up at him. Her cheeks burned with mortification, but it seemed important to let him know she wasn't prone to gallivanting about in the woods and kissing every stranger she met. Not that she'd ever encountered a stranger out here before.

"I find you interesting, too."

That made her look up at him in surprise. She was the least interesting person she knew. "Truly?"

"Truly."

His voice and expression were solemn, but Kate released a shaky laugh. Happiness unfurled in her chest like a bright, blooming flower.

"Will I see you again?" she asked breathlessly.

His pause was infinitesimal, but she sensed it nevertheless. "Yes. Perhaps once more."

She let out the breath she'd been holding and resisted the compulsion to jump up and down like a child being offered the sweetest, most delicious sugary treat in the world. "Here?"

"Yes. Tomorrow."

To prevent herself from emitting a squeal of joy, she bit down hard on her lower lip and gave him a crooked smile. Quick as a flash, he reached out, grabbed her hand, and pulled her against him. He pressed his lips to the top of her head.

"Go."

He released her just as quickly. With her teeth still clamped on her lip, Kate raised her hand in farewell, collected her torn and muddy skirts, and turned toward Debussey Manor.

Garrett watched her hurry away until she disappeared behind an oak tree with leaves just beginning to darken into bronzes and golds.

He felt lighter than he had in months. Years, maybe.

He strode to the bank of the pool where he'd left his jacket, his weapons, and his dinner—a jug of ale, a loaf of bread, and a generous chunk of hard cheese. His most recent injury—a bullet in the thigh—had healed well during the warm summer. He rarely limped, and as he lowered himself to sit on a flat rock, he hardly felt a twinge. It only pained him late at night, when the air was at its most cold and damp.

He tore a piece of bread from the loaf, alternating between bites of cheese and bread and swigs of the warm, frothy ale as he watched the sunset and thought of beautiful, vivacious Kate who hid behind her disguise of drabness. How just about every word that emerged from her mouth surprised him. How she reminded him he was a man, that he was alive.

Did she know what she'd done to him? Surely she was aware of the sheer audacity of her behavior, of the blatancy of her flirting, but he didn't think she comprehended the power she wielded. Any man would see it once he looked past her outward severity. And when she smiled, he'd be lost.

Garrett scowled at the darkening water, crumpling the cloth that had held his dinner in his fist. The thought of another man wanting her—touching her—disturbed him.

He pushed out a breath. Christ, he didn't even know who she was, really. It was foolish, not to mention ridiculous, to be having these proprietary and protective thoughts after having known the woman for less than an hour. She hadn't even told him her surname.

The sun dipped beneath the horizon once and for all, and Garrett rose as more dark thoughts put an end to the surprising pleasantness of the evening.

Ultimately it didn't matter how Kate made him feel. He was nearly finished with his task in Kenilworth, and once it was over he'd return to Calton House to see his daughter. After Christmas, he planned to travel to Belgium. He had some unfinished business there to attend to. Kate, as beautiful and potentially addicting as she was, had no place in his plans.

Garrett gathered his things, strapped on his pistol and sword, and trudged toward Kenilworth Castle where his horse awaited him.

His enemy was close. Living in a cottage at Kenilworth, where he kept Garrett's sister locked like a prisoner away from the public eye. Nevertheless, Fisk's reappearance in the town of his birth had sparked gossip. Garrett doubted he'd stay much longer, for rumors of their presence here would soon spread, and Fisk knew Garrett was after him.

The man was slippery as an eel. For three days in a row, Garrett had prowled Debussey Manor from late morning to early evening—he'd been informed Fisk visited his mother there daily. But Fisk never showed. Last night, Garrett had covertly watched the inn where Fisk usually ate before returning home to the cottage he shared with Rebecca, but Fisk had never come.

Garrett hated the thought of having to confront the man in his sister's presence, but it was beginning to look unavoidable.

He could only pray Rebecca would someday forgive him for what he had to do.

"You're late," Mama announced as Kate dragged herself into the kitchens of Debussey Manor. After one glance at her mother, it was all Kate could do not to spin around and rush back to Garrett. She didn't, only because Reggie sat in the frayed brown armchair beside the fire, and he needed her.

As Kate took each step farther from Garrett, it seemed a rope tightened between the two of them, tugging at her, pulling her back to him. Yet she had resolutely trudged onward, removing her cap and her pins and letting her hair go free and wild. When she'd reached the arched alcove at the side entrance of Debussey Manor, she'd paused to kick off her mud-caked shoes and remove her dirty stockings, which she now held dangling from her fingers.

"Sorry, Mama." The apology emerged sounding small and false. But how could she even pretend to be repentant for her tardiness today, because goodness, she certainly wasn't!

Mama's lips tightened in disapproval as she took in Kate's unkempt state.

"Katie!"

Kneeling, Kate gathered her little brother into her arms as he jumped from the chair and scampered to her. "Oh, sweetheart, you know you shouldn't run. How did you breathe today?"

A harsh paroxysm of coughing made him double over, preventing him from answering. She held him, looking over his head at Mama, but the older woman's face was still pinched into a frown. "You are filthy."

Kate sighed. "I know. I'll sew the tear and brush out my skirts before bed."

"I don't see how you'll have time. Reggie is exhausted. Now you shall embarrass yourself before your brother's lady wife tomorrow."

"Lady Rebecca will hardly notice my dress, Mama," she murmured as she thumped Reggie gently on the back. "She hardly notices me at all."

"Honestly," huffed her mother. "I doubt that. She is merely too polite to point out your shortcomings, Katherine."

"Whereas you are not." Kate winced and clamped her lips shut so no more disrespectful, petulant words would emerge.

"I cannot fathom what is the matter with you," Mama sputtered. "You're twenty-two years old, and yet you refuse to respect your superiors. You still tramp about like a low-bred hoyden."

Kate *was* a low-bred hoyden. She'd always been. She'd learned long ago that there was no point in denying it.

"I raised you to be a lady, in hopes you could someday be respectable despite the position in which we've found ourselves. I've prayed you could be as respectable as William. Perhaps you could have made a decent marriage. But no, you insist on being a *nobody* and a *nothing*."

Mama spat "nobody" and "nothing" as if they were terrible curses.

"I'm sorry, Mama." She buried her face in Reggie's soft blond hair, still stroking her fingertips up and down his little back. This time, her apology was heartfelt. Kate had tried all her life to make Mama as proud of her as she was of the twins, Willy and Warren, both officers in Wellington's army. But nothing she'd ever done was good enough. And it seemed the harder she tried, the farther she fell in her mother's regard.

The ever-present wound had begun to fester when Willy returned home smelling like lavender and married to the Duke of Calton's sister. As happy as Kate was that her dear brother had returned after so many years, little had she known that Willy's excellent match would only highlight her own failure to marry anyone at all.

"Reginald cried for you for hours."

Kate's heart clenched. "Oh, Reggie. What's the matter?" She tugged him away from her and ran her thumb over the dried tear streaks running down his pale, thin cheeks.

"It hurt," he said somberly, tapping his chest. "Bad."

"Oh, sweetheart. I'm sorry I was late. Did you take another dose of the medicine the doctor gave you?"

"Yes, but it was so awful. I was scared, Katie…I thought it wasn't going to help…"

"Shhhh. I'm here now, and it sounds like you're breathing easy."

"Better now," he agreed.

She glanced around the quiet kitchen, looking for the sole other servant now that Lord Debussey had passed away and the rest of the help had been relieved of their duties. The vast grounds of Debussey Manor remained old Bertie's responsibility, but he was so ancient and frail, he scarcely was capable of making a dent in all the work that needed to be done. The groundskeeper lived in his cottage near the edge of Lord Debussey's lands, but he always dined with them before collecting his lantern and hobbling home for the night.

"Where's Bertie?"

Her mother released a breath through pursed lips. "Bertie didn't come tonight. Likely he went into Kenilworth to sup at the inn."

"Oh." Bertie did that sometimes, when he grew lonely for company other than theirs. Kate gazed at the long, planked table in the center of the room, but it was bare. "Have you already eaten?"

"Of course," her mother snapped. "I ate your portion myself since you were nowhere to be found."

Ignoring the low, rumbling complaint in her stomach, Kate took her brother's hand. "Come, Reg. I'll read to you for a while and we'll go to bed, all right?"

"Yes, Katie," Reggie agreed in his breathy voice.

Reggie didn't fare well when he slept without her. It was why she'd agreed to work for Willy on the condition he allow her to return to Debussey Manor nightly. If Reggie woke, Mama was more inclined to leave him crying than to soothe him. The truth of it was that the bulk of Mama's maternal nature had been bestowed on her two eldest children—her twin sons—which left little remaining for Kate and Reggie.

Kate didn't mind that Reggie needed her, nor did she mind the six miles she walked every day so she could be with him at night. They shared a special bond, she and Reggie. They were the children Mama lamented. Kate could never measure up to Mama's ideal vision of a daughter, and Reggie... well, the fact that he was the old Marquis of Debussey's son was little consolation in the face of his illegitimacy.

Mama lived and breathed for Willy and Warren. War heroes, both of them. Everyone thought they had perished eight years ago at Waterloo, but Willy had recently returned home. Kate had never seen Mama so blissfully happy as when she'd first reunited with her long-lost son. Even when she'd believed Lord Debussey madly in love with her, Mama's happiness was nothing compared to the discovery that Willy still lived.

And Mama had glowed with pride when she heard Willy had married the Duke of Calton's sister.

Never in a thousand years would Kate achieve what her brother had. She was proud of him, too, and she understood completely why he'd disassociated himself from his family for so long. He'd been making his way in London as a gentleman. He would never, ever have made so fine a match for himself if society learned he was the son of a mere housekeeper. Lady Rebecca remained ignorant that Kate was Willy's sister—Willy and Mama had agreed that their deception was for the best.

Kate also understood why Willy couldn't risk employing anyone from Kenilworth—if he did, gossip about him and his new wife would spread like wildfire, and no doubt Lady Rebecca would soon learn Kate's identity. After so long a separation, Kate and her mother wanted Willy to remain close for as long as possible. Lady Rebecca required a servant, so the reasonable solution was for Kate to take on the duties of lady's maid.

Kate understood all of it, truly she did, even if the deceit made her ache inside. Although Willy would never say he was ashamed of her, the mere fact that he took such pains to hide her identity told her he was.

Garrett hadn't seemed ashamed of her, though, and she was fairly certain he was a true gentleman. Perhaps an impoverished, foreign one—as his clothes were well-made but rather shabby and his accent not quite purely English—but he spoke and held himself as only a true gentleman did.

Nor did he seem to think she was inadequate. He seemed . . . taken with her.

It was really rather unbelievable.

"Yes, go," her mother snapped. "Enough dilly-dallying. And don't dribble mud all over the steps on your way down, if you please. I just swept them today."

Kate bit back a retort. Perhaps, after twenty-two years of living with her mother, she was finally learning. "Yes, Mama."

Reggie dutifully kissed Mama good night as Kate took a lantern and a warm brick from beside the fire, and then she led him down the narrow back stairs to the cellars. Mama had always slept in the fancy bedchamber designated for the housekeeper on the third floor, but most of the servants had slept in the cellars. These passages had once bustled with activity, but now Kate and Reggie occupied the first chamber at the bottom of the stairs, and the corridor and rooms beyond had grown cold and dark. Kate didn't like to venture into the other rooms, and she especially avoided the wine cellar at the end of the passage and the series of dungeons leading from it. Originally built in the sixteenth century, the dungeons had last been used to imprison Roundheads nearly two hundred years ago. Warren and Willy had rediscovered the dank chambers as boys and had often played in them, bringing their discoveries of ancient weapons and torture devices upstairs to show Mama.

In their small, windowless chamber, Kate changed her brother into his nightgown, then watched him say his prayers and tucked him into the narrow bed they shared. She stared at him for a long moment. He looked so pale and tiny with the patchwork quilt up to his chin.

His colorless lips turned up as he watched her study him. "Fables?" he asked hopefully.

"Just one or two. It's late, and you need your sleep if you're to get better."

But poor Reggie never got better. From birth, his lungs had been weak, and with every year that passed, they seemed to grow weaker.

"Katie?"

"Yes, sweetheart?"

He plucked the thoughts straight from her head. "I don't think I'm ever going to get better."

She smiled at him. "Of course you are. You're going to grow big and strong and you'll never be ill again."

"Do you really think so?"

She prayed to God it was so. "Of course I do," she said quietly.

With the fables book lying on her chest, she lay beside him, staring at the uneven white plaster ceiling. Already, her encounter with Garrett seemed far distant—an impossible dream. She could scarcely believe it had happened.

"Katie?"

"Sorry, sweetheart." She opened the book to the page she'd marked. "Do you remember where we were?"

"*The Lion and the Mouse*," Reggie said sleepily. "The tiny little mouse saved the great big lion from the cruel hunters."

She smiled, thinking of Garrett and his blond, shoulder-length hair. *The lion*. Today he'd elected not to eat her alive, though she'd all but served herself upon a silver platter. Yet she couldn't quite imagine herself a mouse. And how on earth could she ever conceive of coming to the rescue of someone as powerful as him?

"That's right, Reg."

He drifted off soon after she began reading. She finished "*The Countryman and the Snake*," in which a simple, trusting man saved the life of a near-dead snake.

The man took the snake into his house and nursed it back to health, but as soon as it recovered, it struck out at the poor man's family, nearly killing them all.

Kate glanced at Reggie, assuring herself that he was asleep. She closed the book and set it aside, her thoughts troubled. Was she the simple countryman putting too much trust in a stranger? Would Garrett be the snake that would terrorize those she loved?

She shook her head wryly. She was relating her own life too closely with the fables. Yet wasn't that what one was meant to do? Still, the more she tried to convince herself to be cautious, the less she believed Garrett could have anything in common with a deceptive snake.

He was simmering heat and honor, darkness and light, and goodness and roughness all bound together inside one man who fascinated her as no one ever had. He exuded danger and power, possessed a crushing strength, and yet, miraculously, she'd never felt safer with anyone. Even now, the memory of how he looked at her with those soulful blue eyes sent skittering warmth through her body. She was enamored of him—had been since the first day she'd seen him. But conversing with him, touching him, and kissing him today had taken her infatuation to greater heights than she ever could have imagined.

By the light of the lantern, she carefully sewed the tears in her skirt. Then she brushed out her dress as best she could, which wasn't very well—there were some stains that simply could not be removed without soap and water.

For a long while, she watched Reggie sleep. Beyond that first coughing fit, he'd breathed well tonight. Perhaps he *was* getting better.

Finally, she snuffed the light. She lay on her back, thinking about what had happened to her, how radically she had changed in the space of one evening.

When she did fall asleep, it was to dream of a shimmering man swimming like a fish in the crystalline waters of Kenilworth Castle's abandoned moat.

Kate woke Reggie early. They ate breakfast in silence in the kitchen, and Kate took two bowls of porridge and doubled the amount of butter in them to compensate for her missed dinner last night.

As she shoveled the hot cereal into her mouth in a most unladylike fashion, her stomach growling in thankful pleasure, she praised heaven Mama was nowhere to be found. Her brother, as usual, looked a little yellow as he poked his spoon into the steaming bowl. The poor boy never seemed much interested in food, but Kate had always possessed a hearty appetite. Watching him, she sighed, wishing she could bestow some of her love for food upon her brother. Even more, she wished she could give him some of her bodily strength and health.

Unfortunately, most things in life simply didn't work that way.

She stirred another dab of butter into her porridge, and as it melted, she remembered the sensation of her limbs melting when Garrett held her in his arms. She adjusted her bottom on the hard kitchen bench and licked her spoon, contemplating whether she had fallen asleep behind the bush and dreamed the whole scenario.

She thought not. For one thing, she'd never experienced such tactile sensations in a dream. The hard clasp of his arm around her waist. The rough bristle of his cheek abrading her skin. The soft, warm brush of his lips against hers.

She wanted more of his kisses. She wanted him to kiss not only her lips, but her neck. And her breasts. The insides of her thighs...

She rose abruptly and went to wash their bowls, her skin prickling with warmth. Reggie cast an alarmed glance in her direction, and she smiled at him. She swiped the bottle of prussic acid off the countertop and held it up. "Are you ready for your medicine, then?"

His face pinched in an expression of disgust. "Must I?"

"Yes, you must," she said firmly. "You slept well last night, and I think it is finally helping you. Just hold your nose and swallow it as quickly as you can."

He grimaced and scrunched his nose, but he nodded.

"Good." She gave her brother a spoonful of the medicine, held him as he gagged, and once she was certain the awful stuff wouldn't come up, she tucked him underneath a quilt in the chair beside the fire she'd stoked to wait for Mama to come down.

The weather had grown cool overnight, and as the sun rose over the eastern hills, she shivered all the way to Kenilworth, promising herself to never again leave her cloak at Willy's cottage, no matter how warm it seemed to be.

She wondered how she'd endure the day. It would be hours upon hours till she'd see Garrett again. Kiss him again...

If he came to the pool today.

And if he still wished to kiss her.

She wrapped her arms around herself. It couldn't have been a dream. But how on earth could a man as alluring as he was seem so attracted to someone like her? All her life she'd been told she was too tall, too plain. A hoyden, not overly intelligent, too impulsive, and altogether common. How could the attentions of such a man be anything but the result of an overactive imagination?

When she arrived at Willy's house, she trudged upstairs and entered Lady Rebecca's bedchamber only to find the lady lying motionless in her bed, facing away from the door.

Kate retreated, but as she pulled the door shut, sniffling sounds came from beneath the bedclothes, and she froze, staring at the huddled figure of her mistress.

"My lady?"

"Good morning, Kate," Lady Rebecca said after a pause. She spoke lightly, making a valiant attempt at normalcy. Still, she hugged her knees closer to her chest and her shoulders shook.

"Is something wrong, ma'am?"

Lady Rebecca turned to stare at Kate. Her face was pale, her eyes stark with pain and glistening with tears.

Kate clenched the door handle. "Oh! My lady, what has happened?"

After a long pause, Lady Rebecca murmured, "He didn't come home last night."

"What do you mean?"

"Mr. Fisk. He...never came home."

Kate frowned. That was unlike her brother. "Are you certain?"

Lady Rebecca nodded. "I think...I believe he must have a mistress."

"Oh, no!" Kate gasped. "That cannot be." It made

no sense. Willy always spoke of Lady Rebecca with the utmost fondness.

"He hates me," Lady Rebecca whispered.

Kate shook her head fiercely. "No, that is impossible—nobody could hate someone as sweet and beautiful as you are. There must be some explanation."

Lady Rebecca stared at her with blue eyes so dark they appeared indigo.

Hearing a shuffling movement in the corridor—probably that awful manservant, John—Kate stepped fully into the room and shut the door so she could speak privately to her mistress. "He doesn't hate you, my lady. I'm certain of it."

Lady Rebecca shook her head. "You know nothing about my husband...our past. You don't know the truth of it." Her plump lower lip trembled.

Kate's jaw tightened as anger crawled through her. Willy had spent the night away from Lady Rebecca, had frightened her, hurt her...

"I fear my brother and sister-in-law were right. I was too besotted to see reason, but they were right." She covered her face with her hands. "Oh, I've been such a fool!"

Kate took heavy steps toward the bed. "How do you mean, my lady?"

"You have a brother, Kate. But yours is younger..."

"I have an older brother, too." Kate barely caught herself from choking out the response a part of her so longed for Lady Rebecca to know: *And he happens to be your absent husband.*

Lady Rebecca sighed. "Then perhaps you might understand. My brother is quite...well, he's an intimidating man. I feared him, truly I did. He was gone for many years, and because we hardly knew each other, and because he was so frightening to me, I was certain he didn't—*couldn't*—have my best interests in mind."

Kate lowered herself onto the edge of the bed. She reached out to take Lady Rebecca's hand, then stopped herself and dropped her fingers, playing with the embroidered strands of the coverlet. "My older brother was gone for a long while, too. He went to war."

"So did mine," Lady Rebecca said.

Kate pictured Willy in her mind's eye. He didn't scare her really, but his dark, assessing eyes sometimes rattled her nerves. He had been absent for so long and had only just returned, and Kate was still working to reacquaint herself with him. "Well, in a way, it's much as you say. Sometimes I'm not sure he has my best interests at heart. Though I'm certain he does, in the end."

Lady Rebecca smiled sadly. "He is my half brother, and he is sixteen years older than me. I was so afraid of him... Oh, Kate, I think I've done a truly wretched thing."

"What have you done, my lady?"

"He was... having a difficult time of it, and I shunned him. I believe I hurt him."

All Kate knew about Lady Rebecca's brother was that he was the Duke of Calton—a powerful duke from faraway Yorkshire. Kate could hardly picture a delicate creature like Lady Rebecca causing hurt to such a man. It seemed impossible that someone so grand could be hurt by anything, much less the small, vulnerable woman lying beside her. "How do you mean?"

"Well... William—Mr. Fisk—and I..." Lady Rebecca

hesitated, pushing a stray strand of hair off her cheek. "You see, we eloped."

Kate froze so as not to embarrass herself or Willy with a conspicuous reaction. Even though she successfully bit back the gasp at the top of her throat, her insides fluttered, and she was certain all the blood must've drained from her face, for her pores tightened and stung.

Willy had told Kate and Mama that he developed a deep bond of friendship with the Duke of Calton after he'd served as a lieutenant in the duke's regiment at Waterloo. He'd said he'd spent much time as an honored guest at the duke's London home, he and Rebecca had fallen in love, and the duke was thrilled with the match.

The truth of it crashed through Kate with stunning clarity, shocking her into silence. Her smooth-talking brother had lied. He'd eloped with Rebecca, an heiress with a no doubt extremely large dowry. Hardly the prestigious marriage he'd led Mama to imagine. No wonder he kept Lady Rebecca alone. No wonder he'd brought her here rather than languish with all his renowned "friends" in London.

The bitter fact curdled in Kate's gut. Willy had lied to them. But why? Surely he could have entrusted them with the truth.

"At the time," Lady Rebecca continued, "I was so happy, so contented, so excited about what the future might hold."

"And you're not now?" Kate immediately regretted her words. It was not her place to ask such things. If only she could take a moment to think before allowing words to spew freely from her mouth.

"I'm trying so hard. But he—" Lady Rebecca's voice

cracked, and on impulse, Kate reached out to take her hand. Lady Rebecca's fingers curled gratefully around hers. "He only grows colder," she finished.

Kate stared at Lady Rebecca aghast for a long moment, her mind unable to connect this behavior to her brother. Willy? Cold? Why, he was a gentleman through and through. Always warm, always considerate. When he'd walked into Debussey Manor's kitchen for the first time since he'd left for Waterloo, he'd been overcome by as much emotion as Kate and Mama had. They'd all held one another for hours, alternating between laughing and crying as Reggie had watched them in bemusement.

But then Kate closed her eyes, remembering a time years ago when she'd spied on Willy and Warren at the edge of the forest near Debussey Manor. They'd captured a gray rabbit, tied it so it couldn't move, and had tortured it with knives they'd stolen from the kitchen, using the sharp tips to score the rabbit's skin.

For a long moment, she'd just watched them. Willy and Warren were both such kindly, sweet boys, such young gentlemen, and so well-behaved compared to her, that their actions stunned her. Primal rage had built within her as she watched the poor creature suffer. Finally, she couldn't stand watching a second longer. She'd walked right up to Warren and punched him in the face. Willy pulled her off him, but she'd twisted out of his arms, grabbed the rabbit, and run into the brush as the poor creature bit her in terror. Willy, busy attending to their sobbing brother, hadn't bothered to come after her, but before she fled, she'd seen a coldness in his eyes that had frozen her to the bone. He'd been utterly furious at her—not for saving the rabbit, but for harming his twin.

She'd released the rabbit and had sat in the bushes for hours with her legs curled to her chest, sucking the bite on her finger. When she finally went home, Mama whipped her with a belt and locked her in a closet without meals for a full day for blackening Warren's eye...and for lying. She hadn't believed a word when Kate told her what she'd seen. Kate hardly believed it herself.

She opened her eyes and looked at Lady Rebecca. Was it possible that the icy rage she'd seen so long ago in her brother's eyes wasn't just a fleeting brotherly loathing? Had some of that coldness remained and was it now directed toward the sweet lady lying in misery on the bed?

It didn't seem likely. For heaven's sake, they were all adults now. Yet a fierce, angry protectiveness rose in Kate. Lady Rebecca, with her big, glistening dark-blue eyes, reminded Kate of that poor rabbit. Kate curled her fist into the counterpane, but she'd far rather be using it to throttle her brother.

"When we fled to Scotland, my family chased after us," Lady Rebecca whispered. "My brother and my sister-in-law Sophie and my cousin Tristan." She licked her lips. "Sophie ranted to me that Mr. Fisk had done horrible things, that he'd manipulated me for my dowry. I thought they'd all gone mad. But now I realize it most likely they all thought the same of me, and they were merely trying to protect me."

"I'm very sorry, my lady," Kate murmured.

"We escaped from them... though not without a struggle. They nearly caught us, and Mr. Fisk was injured."

"Injured?" Kate gasped. "How?" Willy had said nothing of this!

"He was shot in the shoulder. I wasn't present, but Mr. Fisk believes...well, he said my sister-in-law shot him."

Kate stared at her wide-eyed.

"I know. I was—am—so angry with her. I couldn't believe that she'd be driven to such lengths to keep me from marrying the man I loved."

"I can't imagine." Kate truly couldn't imagine it. A duchess had shot Kate's brother in an attempt to keep him from marrying Lady Rebecca? The duke and his family must possess a very deep hatred for people not of their class.

"Fortunately, the injury was far less severe than I originally thought. The doctor said it was the cleanest bullet wound he'd ever seen. Though Mr. Fisk was still recovering, we traveled all the way to Gretna Green, where we were married right away. And now we have been married for four months, and he's already decided he doesn't love me." Lady Rebecca clutched the counterpane to her chest and looked at Kate with pleading eyes. "What have I done wrong? Where have I gone astray?"

"You have done nothing wrong. Nothing." Kate squeezed her hand. "It cannot be your fault. You have been nothing but a perfect wife to him."

"Perhaps this is my penance for betraying my brother."

Though she wasn't certain of the integrity of the man in question, Kate could not encourage Lady Rebecca to continue to spurn her family. Clearly the lady's actions thus far had caused her a great deal of anguish. "Perhaps you should write your brother to ask for his forgiveness for running away. Doing so might ease your guilt."

For a long moment, Lady Rebecca gnawed on her lip.

Then she nodded. "I'll do that, Kate. Thank you. You are very wise."

Kate laughed out loud. It emerged from her nose and sounded more like a snort—a sound Mama certainly would have been horrified to hear in the presence of a true lady like Lady Rebecca. But no one had called her wise in her entire existence on this earth, and it struck her as funny.

Lady Rebecca squeezed her hand even harder, then pulled away. "Don't laugh, Kate. That was an excellent suggestion. You *are* wise. And very kind as well. Thank you for allowing me to confide in you. And not only will I write my brother, but I shall write my sister-in-law, my niece, and my cousins, too. Will you help me to dress?"

Kate slid off the edge of the bed. "Of course."

As she dropped a peach-and-ivory-striped day dress over Lady Rebecca's head, bleak thoughts crossed her mind. What if the duke and his family were right? What if Willy had married Rebecca solely for her connections and her money? Why hadn't he troubled himself to come home last night? Could Lady Rebecca's suspicions really be true? Had he taken a lover? A mistress?

If it were any other day—any day she hadn't planned an illicit tryst with the most impossibly exciting stranger in the world—Kate would remain with Lady Rebecca tonight to make sure Willy returned. If he never arrived, she'd support her mistress in her time of need. If he did come home, she'd offer her brother a piece of her mind.

Maybe she should do that, she mused as she fastened the score of pearl buttons running up Lady Rebecca's back. She could meet with Garrett, go home to fetch Reggie, and then walk back with him, and they could both comfort Lady Rebecca.

It wouldn't work. Reggie was too exhausted at that time of day to walk all the way to Kenilworth, and if she didn't come at all, he'd cry for her, and Mama would be furious. Still, she despised the idea of leaving Lady Rebecca alone.

Kate picked up the tortoiseshell hairbrush and began to pull it through the lady's silky, jet-black locks. She made a poor lady's maid. Her knowledge of fashion was nearly nonexistent, after all. She'd spent her whole life at Debussey Manor, and before Lady Debussey had died five years ago, she had been bedridden for years and hardly needed to dress in the height of fashion.

In any case, Kate had served as a chambermaid back then—Lady Debussey's maid was a woman whom she'd brought from London when she'd married and who ran straight back to London upon her death.

Kate slid her fingers over Lady Rebecca's shoulder, smoothing a light wrinkle from the silk. The colors, the textures, and the rich, varied fabrics of Lady Rebecca's wardrobe intrigued her—even though the lady had complained that she hadn't been able to bring all the "requirements" from her home in Yorkshire. Now, Kate understood why that was the case.

She crossed the room to set the curling tongs over the fire, for the smooth black strands of Lady Rebecca's hair were quite straight and required daily curling. On her return to the dressing table, Kate retrieved a comb and flipped it over in her hands, drawing two lines down Lady Rebecca's head to divide her hair. She divided one of those sections into another three parts, grasped the strands, and folded them end over end, creating a tight braid.

"My lady?"

The lady had been staring balefully into the mirror, but when she heard Kate's voice, she looked up to meet Kate's eyes in the glass. "Yes?"

"When you eloped with my br—" Kate gulped in a breath. *Think about your words before you say them, girl!* "—Mr. Fisk, did you slip away in the dead of the night?"

Lady Rebecca's lips curved upward in a wistful smile. "We did. I was asleep, and Mr. Fisk, who was a guest in my brother's house, came flying into my room just after midnight. He clutched my shoulders and said he couldn't bear it anymore. He said they were going to make us wait to be married, but he burned for me, he wanted me now, and he couldn't wait another second for us to be together forever."

"Oh...my goodness," Kate murmured. How strange to think of Willy as being so amorous. He'd never much been the devil-may-care sort, either. What could have possibly prompted that behavior? Perhaps he truly was madly in love with Lady Rebecca, and there was a plausible excuse for his absence last night. For the lady's sake, Kate wished fervently for it to be so.

She finished wrapping the silky strands of the lady's hair, thinking of what she'd do if Garrett spoke to her in such a passionate way. She'd likely turn into a gelled pudding and puddle up on the ground, boneless and with no control over her muscles.

She smiled at her own foolishness. As much as Garrett seemed to like her, there was a strong hesitance in him. He'd nearly said no when she'd asked if they could see each other again.

In fact, Kate was quite sure that he would disappear as quickly and as mysteriously as he'd arrived. That thought made a bleak cloud of gloom gather within her. She knew it was true. He wouldn't stay in Kenilworth. He didn't belong here.

"We climbed from my window... Truly, I felt like Juliet with her Romeo. Never had I experienced such devotion." Lady Rebecca sighed, and her eyes swam with sudden tears. "He hasn't spoken to me like that since we were married."

Willy was ambitious—he always had been—but before today Kate had never considered the possibility that he might be manipulative and conniving as well. Now that he had shackled the duke's sister to him, perhaps he felt no compulsion to express any sort of devotion to his young wife—sweet, beautiful, and likeable as she might be.

No, it couldn't be true. Kate felt wretched even entertaining such a disparaging thought about her own brother. Lady Rebecca simply *must* be wrong.

In any case, Willy clearly hadn't seen a cent of Lady Rebecca's dowry—likely the duke was keeping it from him. Yet Kate's brother still struggled along, trying to support his wife in the manner to which she was accustomed. Surely he did that out of love. There had to be some reasonable explanation for last night.

A tear streaked down Lady Rebecca's cheek, and the need to comfort surged within Kate. "You were a very lucky bride indeed," she said. "I could never imagine being the recipient of such devotion."

"It was the most beautiful, most memorable, and most exciting night of my life," Lady Rebecca murmured. "I shall never forget it."

Both women were silent, lost in thought, as Kate finished pinning the coil of hair at Lady Rebecca's nape and curling the strands left around her crown. The lady took a deep breath and squeezed Kate's hand for strength before wandering to the parlor to compose her letters. Kate descended to the kitchen as she did every morning, to see whether she could help Cook and to give Annie her instructions for the day, for the girl wasn't capable of undertaking any task on her own. Even if an inch of dust coated the stair rail, Annie would require specific instructions before she cleaned it.

Sure enough, when Kate entered the back room, she found Cook chopping vegetables and a big pot boiling over the fire, where Annie sat idly, her fingers twisting in her bright red hair.

Kate sighed. Well, the banister hadn't looked as bright as it should... "Annie!" she said sharply.

Annie jumped a little and swiveled in the wicker chair to face her, her round cheeks rosy from the heat of the fire. "Good mornin', Miss Kate."

"Good morning. Will you please take a rag and some polish and scrub the banister till it shines?"

"Yes, miss."

Kate cocked her head at the servant. "And the moment you are finished, report back to me, do you understand?"

"Yes, miss."

Annie rose, took a rag and bottle of polish from the cabinet by the narrow back door, and cheerfully headed off to do as she was told.

Kate sighed. "She's so slow."

"Aye, that 'un's not quite right in the head."

Kate glanced sharply at Cook. "Really? Do you think so?"

Cook didn't take her eyes from the carrots she hacked at, but her cap bounced up and down as she nodded. "Oh, yes, indeed I do. Her mam used to tell her she'd got plum pudding for brains."

Kate glanced in the direction the girl had gone. "That is so cruel. Poor Annie."

Cook snorted. "She's done fair enough for herself, though. Got a position with a fine gentleman and lady."

"I suppose," Kate murmured. Of course, neither Cook nor Annie knew of Kate's relation to Willy. Willy had hired them in Birmingham before bringing them here. She had no idea where John had come from, but she assumed Willy had brought him all the way from London—which meant, she realized, that he knew all about her brother and Lady Rebecca's elopement.

Kate spent the remainder of the day scrubbing and cleaning, and daydreaming about Garrett. She thought about his lips, his expressive blue eyes, the square line of his jaw, and she imagined his hard, battle-ravaged body stroking hers in places she'd never imagined being stroked before.

As the hours passed, a chasm grew inside her, an emptiness only seeing Garrett again could fill. She ached for him. To be close to him. To touch him. The rope that had stretched between them last night as she'd walked away tightened and pulled at her chest.

Kate sat in a chair beside an upstairs window, hemming a frayed cuff on Lady Rebecca's spencer jacket, but her gaze kept wandering out at the pine trees edging the back of the property. Puffy gray clouds blotted out the sun, casting dark shadows across the land.

Her movements slowed, then stilled altogether.

A man—even a gentleman—didn't agree to meet a young woman alone in a secluded forest unless he wanted something from her. Something *carnal*. Any woman with an iota of sense knew this as undeniable, irrevocable fact. She would be an utter fool to believe otherwise.

Yet Kate couldn't bring herself to care.

Her hands dropped helplessly onto her lap.

She wanted something carnal. More than she'd ever wanted anything in her life, she wanted to be his, if just for one night. She'd promised she'd never freely offer herself to a man, but he wasn't just a man to her. Her attraction to him was too fierce. If she didn't go to him, she'd burst into flames. Or die of loneliness. Perhaps both.

Inexplicable, but true. There was no denying it.

Anything lasting between them could never be. He was separate from her real life. Like her private pool, Garrett belonged to the deepest, most secret part of her, and she suspected she'd never see him outside of that particular place.

Nevertheless, she wanted to make the most of the time they had together, as limited and temporary as she knew it must be.

She would come home late again tonight, and Mama would complain to Willy, and they'd find a way to prevent her from seeing him again. Tonight might be her last chance to see him.

Once more, he'd said.

If he hadn't changed his mind—if he actually went to the pool tonight—she would offer herself to him. Wholly and fully, without any foolish expectations of anything beyond. Just tonight, just once. She'd take what she could, give what she could, and she'd enjoy every single second of it.

Some time later, when Kate looked at the clock and saw it was nearing five o'clock, her heart jumped into her throat, making it so tight she could hardly speak when she entered the parlor to ask Lady Rebecca if she could take her leave.

Lady Rebecca had sequestered herself and written letters the day long, scarcely pausing to eat. She looked up from her writing desk, stared at Kate for a long moment, then looked away. "Of course you may go, Kate. Have a nice walk home."

The lady's words were thick with emotion, though, and regret stabbed through Kate. Lady Rebecca wanted her to stay. Truly Kate did wish to remain at the lady's side, but she could no more stop herself from going to Garrett than she could stop breathing for the remainder of the night.

"Thank you, my lady," she murmured. "I hope..." *I hope Willy comes home to you.*

Lady Rebecca dipped her pen in the inkpot and waved her away. "I'll see you tomorrow."

Kate curtsied, and before she could glance at Lady Rebecca's face again and be persuaded to stay, she turned from the door and hurried down the corridor.

Downstairs, she glanced at the chaise longue where she'd discovered John yesterday. Despite hearing him tramp about earlier, she hadn't seen the manservant all day—perhaps he'd gone wherever Willy was.

Drat them both. If she was a man, she'd challenge

them both to a duel—Willy for his thoughtless treatment of Lady Rebecca, and John for his . . . She paused to think, and then nodded when she came to her conclusion. She'd duel John for his sheer impertinence.

Once she stepped into the fresh outside air, Kate glanced at the clouds turning purple in the sunset, took a deep breath, gathered her skirts, and sprinted toward her pool.

Chapter Four

Something had compelled Garrett to bring her dinner. Perhaps because she was so thin. All day long, he'd imagined watching her eat. Watching her eyelids close in appreciation as she sipped the wine he'd bought. Watching her lick the sweet almond tart filling from her fingers and the crumbs from her lips.

She'd consumed his thoughts throughout the day, thrusting his black obsession with revenge into the background. Tonight, he wanted to please her. To see her smile.

He might as well be a green, besotted youth wooing her, he thought wryly. Of course, wooing her beyond today was impossible. Garrett simply wished to enjoy her as he had last night—enjoy watching her, enjoy how she made him feel. Yet he knew he must keep his hands off her. A woman of her innocence and vivacity deserved temperance.

Before they separated, he would clarify that he was not

available. Not as a lover, a husband, or even a friend. He would leave the area tomorrow, and he never intended to return. Later tonight, he planned to go to the cottage in Kenilworth and lie in wait for William Fisk. And when the blackguard finally showed his face, Garrett would kill him.

Just as the harsh light of day began to descend into twilight, he saw her. She hurried over a distant rise from the direction of Kenilworth—the opposite direction from the one she'd disappeared in last night—her skirts raised so high in her hands he could see the ivory-colored ribbon garters at her knees. She wore the same dress she'd worn yesterday, and even from this distance he could see the mud stains that had smeared her skirt when he'd caught her.

He hated that she wore the same dress. He despised that it was dirty, knowing he was the one responsible for making it so.

He could buy her a dress. He could buy her a house full of beautiful, bright silk and satin and lace. Deep reds and bright golds and rich forest greens—colors that would complement her subtle beauty. Colors that would make her smile.

No, he couldn't do any of that. Nor could he allow his mind to wander in such fanciful directions.

She slowed when she saw him. Dropping her skirts, she pushed her hands nervously down her front as if to smooth out the fabric. Then, holding her head high, she walked toward him. For the briefest instant, he glimpsed something in her. A hint of regal elegance. The subtlest touch of the lady.

Even from this distance, she resonated with energy.

Again the blood came alive in his veins. If he were the superstitious sort, he might think she'd cast some kind of spell over him. Rising from his perch on the blanket, he smiled half at her, half at the absurdity of his own thinking, as she drew near.

She paused at the edge of the blanket he'd laid out, her eyes widening at the straw basket that contained the food.

"Good afternoon." Her voice was low, almost sultry, and it washed over him like a warm, sparkling waterfall.

"Good afternoon," he responded. "I brought us some dinner."

She sucked in a breath. "That was very kind of you."

"Not so kind." He found himself giving her a rakish grin. "I'm hungry." As if to prove the statement, his stomach growled.

She seemed to relax a little. "Well, in that case..."

He gestured at the blanket. "Sit. Please." But she didn't move. "Why do you hesitate?"

She glanced at the blanket, at her skirts, and then back to him. "I'm not hesitating."

"You're lying."

Her lips twisted. "I told you I was a wretched liar."

He frowned at the wool blanket. It had been costly, but it was the most comfortable-looking blanket he'd been able to find, limited as he was by the dearth of shops selling blankets in Kenilworth. Did she think the blanket too fine for her and her worn dress? What a ridiculous notion. Reaching his hand toward her, he said, "Come."

Her cool fingertips touched his. He stepped forward and enveloped her hand in his, tugging her closer. "Sit beside me."

She sat, perhaps only because he hadn't given her a choice.

He opened the basket and withdrew the wine bottle. As he opened it, he watched her from the corner of his eye. "You're reticent today," he observed.

She gave a little shake of her head. "It all seems so...unreal." Her brown eyes studied him seriously. "You're not like anyone I've ever encountered, and this is like nothing I've ever experienced." She gestured at the basket. "It's a dream."

"Not a dream," he corrected. "Only wine and roasted chicken. Though the innkeeper's wife assured me the pastries will taste like a dream, I'm inclined to think they're real, too."

He took out the chicken and unwrapped it, then set it on the porcelain plate he'd purchased and placed it between them. Next, he removed the cups he'd bought—for he had none of his own, he drank from his flask—and poured wine into them. He handed her a cup, and she inclined her head. "Thank you. But...well, if you wish to get me drunk, I'm not very accustomed to wine, and—"

He held up his hand. "Wine goes well with roasted chicken."

A flush darkened her cheeks, and she took a sip. "Oh. I'd rather hoped...well...I was going to say I'd better not have too much, because I'd like to recall this evening after it is over."

She met his eyes, ensnared them, and he couldn't have looked away even if he'd wanted to. Her teeth closed over her lower lip.

He gestured at the plate of chicken. "I hope you don't mind eating with your fingers." He grinned ruefully.

"I forgot about eating utensils. They are not something I usually consider."

She smiled, and his gut clenched.

"I don't mind in the least. It's fun to pretend to be a barbarian. Especially when one is outside, sitting on the ground, and breathing fresh air. It would be rather awkward to eat with knives and forks in such circumstances, don't you think?"

He laughed gruffly. Tearing a piece of chicken from a drumstick, he offered it to her. "Here. Eat."

"You're anxious to feed me."

Was he so obvious? "I..." His voice trailed off. "Well, yes."

"Why?" She plucked the chicken from his fingers and popped it into her mouth as she waited for his answer.

"The idea of feeding you appeals to me." He shrugged. "Perhaps it appeals to the barbarian in me."

Humor sparkled in her eyes as she returned the wine cup to her lips, studying him over the rim. She lowered the cup. "You must know I'm capable of feeding myself."

"No doubt," he said dryly. "But indulge me."

"Only if you eat, too." Her lips twitched. "Eating is certainly *most* important in keeping up a physique such as yours."

He responded by taking a big bite from a thigh and making a show of chewing it and swallowing. Then he tore off a small piece of white meat.

"Open." He raised the meat to her lips and brushed it over her bottom lip.

Staring at him, she opened her mouth and took the morsel from his fingers. Her pink tongue stole over her lips.

He watched her chew and swallow, and then she moved the plate out of his reach. "If you can feed me, I can feed you."

She removed a piece dripping with juices and held it to his lips. He took hold of her wrist and guided her hand as he took the meat from her fingers. He chewed and swallowed, thinking Kate herself far more delicious than any roasted chicken could ever be. Without breaking eye contact with her, he licked the residual juices from her fingertip.

They settled into the moment, and as he'd known he would, Garrett took great pleasure in feeding her and observing her appreciation for the food. Speaking of lighter topics, they ate and drank until the sun dipped behind the treetops.

Kate set her cup aside and raised her arms overhead in a relaxed stretch, smiling at him. "Do you know," she said casually, "I promised myself I'd never offer a man anything outside of marriage? Well, possibly a curious kiss, but nothing more."

He managed to maintain a noncommittal expression. "Wise promise."

She returned his grin. "That's the second time I've been called wise today. The shock of it might make me swoon."

"No one would ever call a woman's choice to guard her virtue anything but wise."

She leaned back on her hands, and he tried not to observe how the gesture made her breasts thrust out. He raised his cup and took a deep swallow of wine.

"It was more than my virtue, I think. It was my soul that I wished to protect. I was determined not to sacrifice what was most important to me." She gazed at him with the most curious expression on her face. "But that changed yesterday. When I met you."

"Don't allow one short meeting to change your principles. You don't know me."

"But I do."

"You don't."

Her brow furrowed. "I do, though. Something changed inside me when I met you. I feel as though I've known you for far longer than the two days of our acquaintance."

He could do nothing but nod. After all, he couldn't deny feeling the same about her.

"And now I know what I want." Crimson flooded her cheeks, and she leaned forward, clasping her hands round her wine cup and staring into it. "I want you. All thoughts of guarding anything have vanished—for it feels as though there is nothing left to guard." Her frown deepened, and she shook her head in confusion. "It's the oddest craving. It's like... a hunger."

A hunger. Yes, that explained it well. It was a feeling he'd never thought to experience again.

His body hardened, and the compulsion to lay her bare on the blanket and take her, here and now, ravaged him. He closed his eyes for a long moment to fight it off. When he'd gained a semblance of control, he took a deep breath and opened his eyes. "I'm sorry, Kate. It cannot happen."

She raised her cup to her lips, studying him over its rim. "Will you at least... kiss me again?"

"That I might be persuaded to do. But no more. It wouldn't be fair to you."

"Why not?"

"Because... Kate, look at me." Reaching forward, he

took the wine cup from her hands and set it on the blanket. He curved his palms over her cheeks and tilted her face so her eyes met his. His fingertips pressed into the dark brown strands of her hair, slicked back severely into a roll behind her head. "I cannot stay here. I have nothing to offer you. I must leave this place soon, and I cannot take you with me."

"Are... are you... married?"

A muscle spasmed in his jaw. "No."

She cocked her head, reading into the tightness of his voice. "But you were."

"Yes. I was."

"I'm sorry." She clearly thought the obvious—that his wife had died. He wasn't prepared to correct her. He hadn't revealed the truth of his marital status to any acquaintance since the divorce. Yet it seemed sacrilegious to let anyone believe that Sophie was dead.

"It's complicated," he said in a low voice.

"Did you love her?"

"Yes."

She seemed unsettled by the promptness of his response. "You still mourn her."

"In a way." His insides were so tied up in knots, he could scarcely breathe. "There's far more to it than that, though. As I said, it is complicated."

"Do you have children?" Again, she discerned the truth, if not the complexity behind it.

"Yes. A daughter."

"Oh. I'm sure she's beautiful."

Before he knew it, he'd withdrawn the tiny portrait from his coat pocket and handed it to her. Its frame was now somewhat tarnished from much handling, but the image of his sparkling blond-haired and blue-eyed daughter was clear enough. Miranda's essence still shone through.

"I was right." Kate cradled the portrait in her palm, smiling at the likeness. "She looks like you."

That was what Sophie always said. Garrett couldn't force an answer through his tight throat.

"How old is she? She looks about my little brother's age."

"She'll be eight in a few weeks. That was painted some time ago, I think."

"Ah. A little older than Reggie, then. She is lovely." Kate handed him the portrait. "Thank you for showing her to me."

He shrugged.

"You care deeply for her."

"She's my daughter."

She reached up to brush a fingertip over the ugly scar on his forehead. The scar that frightened all but a select few—Kate among them. "What happened?"

"War," he murmured.

"When?"

"Eight years ago. Waterloo."

"Oh." Her expression filled with compassion. "Two of my brothers fought at Waterloo. We were certain they were both lost, but in the end one of them finally came home."

"I was one of the lucky ones," he said quietly. He didn't add that it had been nearly eight long years before he found his way back to England, only to find Sophie married to Tristan, his cousin and heir. He'd tried—and failed—to win her back.

"Did it hurt?" she asked.

"Yes."

Then he realized she spoke of the scar on his forehead. "There were other wounds that hurt more. It's just that one is the most obvious."

Her jaw tightened, and she spoke through thinned lips. "I hate that you were injured. I like you the more for it, though. That, and your feelings for your family both. You've been through much, and yet you're still so honorable. I've never known anyone like you."

"Kate—"

"You think too much." She leaned forward and her voice turned husky as she stared at him. Her dark eyes speared through him, leaving him hot. Ready.

He forced himself to breathe. He would not—*could not*—take this woman's innocence. "I can't...touch you. I wish I could, but I won't make you promises I cannot keep. I cannot risk hurting you."

"I told you before I didn't care about any of that."

"You should care. I could hurt you...not only physically. I won't use you and then abandon you to fend for yourself."

She took her wine cup again, as if holding it comforted her. "One night with you would be worth a hundred thousand with anyone else."

No one could be more wrong. He dropped his hands, curling his fingers at his sides. "That's not true," he said, his tone hard enough to scare away any tenderhearted soul. Not hard enough to scare away Kate.

"I'm twenty-two years old. There might never be another chance for me." Her voice was very soft, and she stared into her cup as if something fascinating swam in the wine.

"You're a beautiful young woman and there will be many chances for you," he said with conviction. "Chances far superior than any you might have with me. Chances with men who will offer you so much more than I can." Even as he spoke the words, the thought of another man offering her anything made possessive rage spark under his skin.

"I'm not beautiful."

He looked at her sharply. How could she say that? But then he remembered his first impression of her, before he'd looked deeper. Surely he wasn't the only one on the planet to have been stunned by the revelation of her beauty.

He let out a harsh breath. "You speak as if no man has ever shown interest in you."

"Never one who interests *me*. Not like you do."

Taking her hand in his own, he kissed the soft flesh on the inside of her palm and tugged her a little closer to graze the delicate skin on the inside of her wrist. She tasted so good. As sweet as sugared cinnamon.

Leaning forward, he held her arm as he kissed his way toward her shoulder, regretting the interference of the coarse fabric of her sleeve. Carnal images rolled through his mind. Of him unlacing her dress and her stays, lifting her shift up over her hips, taking her on the blanket, under the cool twilight sky. His cock throbbed and ached beneath his breeches.

He reached the lace at her neckline and kissed her collarbones, nibbling at the soft, delicious skin.

Her fingers brushed up his shoulders, exploring him through his shirt, tracing the tendons of his neck and then sifting through his hair and grazing erotically over his scalp.

"Garrett." She arched her neck for him, offering herself. So trusting. Far too trusting.

Gently, he curved his hand around her elegant swan's neck and tasted the sweet flesh there, alternating between suckling and nibbling until his lips met her jawline. He swiped his thumbs from her chin along her jawbones, scraping the skin with his calluses. She sighed as he trailed soothing kisses over the scrapes he'd made.

"I want you, Kate," he whispered when his lips reached the juncture of her jaw and earlobe.

One of her hands slid down the back of his neck and bunched in his shirt. She trembled in his arms, innocent and yearning. "I...I want you, too."

His body shuddered in response to her plea, and his cock turned to steel, but he gritted his teeth to rein in the base impulses threatening to consume him whole.

Kisses. Only kisses.

"No."

"Please, Garrett." Her body vibrated like a plucked violin string. "Please."

"I'm leaving tomorrow."

She turned and pressed her lips to his hairline. "I know...but we have this night. It is ours."

"No," he whispered again.

"Trust me...please trust me. My eyes are wide open. I understand and accept the terms. Please give me this one gift before you must leave me forever."

She sounded desperate, close to tears, and something inside Garrett shifted and flared to life.

Some things he would not risk, and he wouldn't fully compromise her, no matter how she begged, no matter how desperately his own base desires demanded fulfillment.

She was too innocent to fully grasp the repercussions. But there were other ways to bring a woman pleasure. Ways that didn't lead to ultimate ruination.

As much as he wanted to lose himself in Kate, it was more important to bring her pleasure. He wanted to be the first man to bring her the pinnacle, to make her lose herself in ecstasy, to feel her body succumb to it.

He pulled away from her so he could look into her eyes, and he cupped his hands over her shoulders. "Do you trust me?"

"Yes." Her response was automatic.

He pushed the basket onto the carpet of fallen leaves beside the blanket. "Lie down."

Bunching his coat, he used it to pillow her head as he helped her onto her back. Settling beside her, he nudged her cheek so she turned to face him. Her dark eyes seemed nearly black in the diminishing light, and her breaths were short and shallow. From the expression on her face, the trust in her eyes, he knew she didn't offer herself lightly. This meant everything to her. Warmth surged deep within him.

"You are so beautiful," he murmured.

She blinked, but didn't respond with a denial this time.

He traced her brow, then the ridge of her nose. "Your face lights up when you smile. Each time you've smiled, since that first time you smiled at me yesterday, I've ached for wanting you."

He brushed her lower lip with his index finger. "You have the most erotic lips. I can't focus on them for long without the most carnal images invading my mind."

Those lips parted, and her warm breath puffed out from between them.

"Kissing them," he continued, "is so sweet. It's like nothing I have ever experienced."

He spoke absolute truth. Though he hadn't touched a woman since before Parliament had begun its proceedings on his divorce bill, he'd kissed a few women in his occasional bouts of debauchery over the past eight years. Never had a kiss resonated through him as hers had.

"Please," she breathed. "I need you to kiss me."

He touched his lips to hers and then cupped the back of her head with his hand, tugging her closer to him so the line of her body pressed against his from his legs to his lips. His aching arousal prodded her hip, but she didn't seem to mind. Gasping, she turned fully to him and threw her arm around his waist, pulling him even closer.

He took her mouth. Plundered it. She tasted good—like the dinner they'd shared, but with that subtle sweet cinnamon essence just beneath. He couldn't get enough of her.

Touching her teeth with his tongue, he moved his hand downward, skimming her round breast, her nipple prominent through the layers of material. He curved his palm over the small mound, wishing he could strip the fabric away, take her into his mouth. But if he stripped her, no telling what else he might feel compelled to do. So he contented himself with brushing his thumb over the taut peak until she squirmed beneath his touch.

Traveling lower, he learned her body. The dip of her waist, the subtle flare of her hip. The slender leg beneath her skirts. He gripped the fabric and nudged it upward, and to his surprise, her arm left his torso, and she completed the task by yanking her skirts over her hips.

He stroked his hand up her thigh over the material

of her drawers, and then, nibbling her lower lip, gently insinuated his hand between her legs.

She didn't stiffen as he'd expected. Instead she parted her thighs, and he found the slit in her drawers, groaning against her mouth when he found her already slick with desire.

She jumped at the contact, then returned his groan as he pressed his fingers between the lips of her sex.

"Garrett," she whispered against his mouth. Tremors rolled through her body, against his body, and she whimpered as his fingertips found the sensitive button between her legs.

He kissed her again, gliding his fingers over her, and she bucked beneath him. He pulled slightly away but she wiggled, searching for his touch, and so he touched her, painting circles around the spot. She wrapped her arm around his neck, kissing him as if she was starved for his lips, as if she'd devour him alive, and she ground her sex against his fingers.

"God, Kate..." He gulped, and his heart galloped like a stampede of horses in his chest. Damn, damn...He couldn't lose control.

He slipped a finger inside her, and she wrapped around him like a vise. She went rigid. He stiffened, fearing he'd scared her, or, God forbid, hurt her.

"Oh," she whimpered. "Oh." But she didn't move. Her tight, wet heat remained clamped around his finger, and he feared he'd hurt her even more if he withdrew.

He pulled back so he could see her expression. She stared at him with glassy, wide eyes.

"Am I hurting you?"

She shook her head. "Please..."

"Do you want me to stop?"

She shook her head again.

"What then? Tell me what you want."

"I want..." She shifted a little, causing his finger to move within her, and she gasped. "That."

He frowned, not really understanding what she meant. He nudged his finger a tiny bit, pushing in a fraction of an inch, and she threw her head back. "Yes," she panted. "More. More...of...that..."

Ahh...He could certainly oblige her. Imitating true sexual congress, he pulled out until his fingertip nudged at her opening, and then pressed fully inside. She convulsed against him, and her channel pulsed around his finger.

"Yes," she whispered. "Oh, yes."

"Sweet Kate." He leaned forward because it was simply impossible not to taste her again. "Sweet, beautiful Kate."

He thrust into her over and over, and then, when he was certain she was ready, he inserted a second finger. He worked her body until she shivered and gasped with every thrust, and then he curled his thumb to brush over that most sensitive spot. At the first touch, she arched up, her body bowing. At the second brush, accompanied by a deep thrust of his fingers, she cried out, and her body undulated on the blanket. She tore her face away, and he opened his eyes to watch her.

"Come for me."

Her lips rounded in an O as she gave a silent scream. Her channel rippled, clamping down over his deeply lodged fingers.

He gentled in his motion as the spasms loosened their

grip over both of them, and she sank onto the blanket, her eyes half-lidded. Slowly, he pulled out of her and cupped her sex with his palm.

She turned to him and gave him a lazy smile.

He grinned back and rearranged her skirts over her legs. "Did you like it?"

"Mmm."

"Tell me."

She chuckled softly and murmured, "You arrogant man. Surely you know I did, but you're going to make me say it, aren't you?"

"Yes."

The smile left her face. She reached up to gently touch his cheek. "I did. I've... never felt anything like it."

He couldn't deny the male pride that puffed his chest, satisfying him even as his body continued to demand release. "Good."

Her fingertip drifted down his arm, then between them where it scraped over the ridge of his arousal. "But we're not finished yet, are we?"

He gripped her wrist, pushed her hand away, and threaded his fingers through hers. "We're finished."

The languid satisfaction instantly left her expression. "But... I haven't fulfilled you."

He laughed. "What do you know about fulfilling a man?"

"Nothing," she said seriously, frowning at him, "but I am a fast learner. And you will teach me."

"No. Not today."

"Tomorrow, then?"

He shook his head.

She scowled. "That's not very fair."

"What do you mean?"

"It's not fair that you can bring me..." She broke off for a moment, considering. "That you can bring me to such heights, and I can do nothing for you in return. Please, I don't deserve to have..."

"Stop it!" he snapped, more harshly than he'd intended. "You must stop undervaluing yourself."

She opened her mouth, then closed it, and her eyes filled with tears.

Deuce it, devil it, and damn it to hell. Groaning, he gathered her against him. "Don't cry. Please."

She buried her face in his chest. "I'm not crying," she sobbed. "I'm not."

"Well..." He inhaled deeply as a sob racked her body. "I'm glad you're not crying. I haven't any idea what to do with ladies who cry."

"Good," she sniffed. "Because I'm not the kind of person who cries." She hiccuped. "I never cry, and I won't start now."

He stroked her hair. His fingertips found a pin, and he pulled it, releasing a curling brown lock. Intrigued, he found another pin, and another, continuing as her sobs diminished, until her hair fanned around her head in deep mahogany waves.

He threaded his fingers into the thick strands, marveling at the softness of her hair, at how it glimmered and shone. "Your hair," he murmured. "God, it's beautiful."

She pulled away and looked up at him, and though the tears had cast a shine over her eyes, they were now dry.

"You must stop this nonsense." Impatiently, she tugged a lock of hair behind her ear. "You're going to turn me into the vainest woman in England."

"I doubt that."

"I—" she glanced down, then back at him, "—I wasn't crying...not for the reasons you might think. I'm not sad or angry or upset. I still understand and accept our arrangement, and I still expect nothing from you. I'm just...ever so grateful for what you've given me."

"I'm grateful for what you've given me, too," he said softly. The knowledge that he could feel alive again—be a man again—was the greatest gift anyone had ever bestowed upon him.

"I can't imagine what that could be..." She took a deep breath. "But I'll believe you. And I'll simply be glad that I've given you something, as mysterious and intangible as that something might be, in return."

"Good." Leaning on his elbow, he reached beyond her for her wine cup and handed it to her. Then he brought his own cup to his lips and tossed back the remaining contents.

"Tell me something." He wiped his mouth with the back of his hand, knowing she wouldn't think him unforgivably rude for doing so.

She grinned. "Anything."

He propped his chin in his hand. "You said you're from Kenilworth. If that's true, when you left yesterday, why did you go that way?" He gestured toward the northeast. "Kenilworth is in the opposite direction." He reached above her head for the plate containing the chicken. Fumbling a bit, he tore off a piece.

"My employer is in Kenilworth, but my mama and little brother live at Debussey Manor."

Garrett froze in midmotion. Then he dropped his hand

in front of him, the chunk of meat lodged between his fingers.

God, no.

Rolling onto her back, she linked her hands behind her head and continued blithely. "I walk to the manor every night because my brother is a sickly boy, the poor thing. He won't be comforted by Mama, and he won't sleep with anyone but me." She shrugged. "I love the walk and I like being outside, and at dawn and twilight I can experience the most beautiful times of day. Of course, during winter it might not be as nice, but then again, I might not be employed anymore when winter comes. My employer says he and his wife might be returning to London soon, and of course I won't be able to go with them."

"Why is that?" Garrett pushed the words from frozen lips. Debussey Manor, since the death of the marquis, had maintained a very limited staff. If Kate lived at Debussey Manor with her mother and younger brother, she could be none other than William Fisk's sister.

Hell... she'd even mentioned one of her brothers had survived Waterloo and the other had not. Garrett was so smitten, he hadn't put two and two together.

Fisk's sister. He stared at her, now recognizing the subtle similarities between them. Both dark-haired and dark-eyed, with wide mouths and similarly shaped faces. Kate must be near Fisk's height, though, if not taller, and she was much thinner than her brother.

"I cannot leave due to my little brother's poor health," she said. "He needs me too much. I could never leave him."

Hell, she knew nothing of any of this—his enmity with Fisk, his intent to kill her brother. He couldn't tell her, couldn't destroy the trusting, open way she spoke to him. How could he hurt her now, after what had happened between them?

His stomach twisted into a knot, and he forced words out through a tight throat, hardly understanding his own question. "What will you do, then, once you are no longer employed in Kenilworth?"

"I suppose I'll work with Mama at Debussey Manor for the time being." She flipped over onto her stomach. Propping herself on her elbows, she tore off a piece of chicken. "Lord Debussey died in the summer, and we've no idea at all what the new marquis plans to do with the house. But even if he decides Mama and Reggie and I must leave, we will be all right, because Lord Debussey left Mama an annuity." She popped the meat into her mouth and shifted so she faced him. "We'd likely move to Kenilworth and I'd look for a new opportunity. If Lady Rebecca leaves me with a good character reference, I am sure I will find a very good job. She's the sister of a duke, after all."

"Lady Rebecca?" he choked. For the love of God. Kate wasn't only Fisk's sister, she was employed by Fisk and Rebecca. He swallowed, trying to infuse moisture into his parched throat.

"Yes. In theory I am her lady's maid, but my master doesn't employ very many servants, so we share the duties."

In his peripheral vision, he saw her narrowing her eyes at him, discerning his discomfort. "What is it?" she whispered. "What's wrong?"

He yanked the basket onto the blanket and burrowed into it to find the box of pastries. "I brought dessert."

She paused. He felt her studying him, and he knew she

was debating whether to ask him to reveal the reason for his change in behavior. Finally, she asked quietly, "What did you bring?"

Relief flooded him. Thank God she knew when not to push. "Almond tarts. The innkeeper's wife said they're her best."

He still couldn't meet her eyes, but he heard the smile infuse her voice. "I've never had one, but they're quite famous in these parts. I've heard they dissolve in your mouth like little clouds."

"I suppose we shall see for ourselves." He took one of the puffs from its wrapping and glanced at Kate.

"You first. Open." He raised the tart to her lips.

She opened her mouth and took the morsel from him, brushing her lips over his fingers as she did so. She made a noise of sheer delight.

"Good?"

She swallowed. "Oh, yes. So very good. I'm glad you only brought a little box—I could eat a cart full of these. Especially after..."

Even in the gathering dusk, he could see the flush darkening her cheeks. Again, despite all that she had just revealed, that primal male satisfaction flooded through him.

She scrambled up and snatched the box from his lap. "Your turn." She unwrapped a tart and held it to his lips. "What do you think?"

"Mmm. Delicious."

They took turns feeding each other until the pastries were gone. Then they lay in silence on their backs, staring up at the stars popping out one by one in the evening sky.

Eventually Kate shifted her gaze from the stars to him. "Can I..." turning to her side, she moved a little closer, "...kiss you again?"

They would need to part soon, and this would be their last kiss. Garrett wanted to forget about Fisk when he kissed her. He wanted to make this kiss one they'd both remember forever. He slid his arm around her waist and lifted her until most of her weight settled over him.

She lowered her lips to his, but just as the soft warmth of her breath fluttered across his lips, her eyes opened wide in shock, and she was yanked off him.

"What...?"

Kate cried out. A loud, piercing scream that made Garrett bristle like a feral creature guarding its mate, intending to kill whoever harmed her.

As Garrett surged up, he saw the blunt edge of the cudgel an instant before it slammed down over the scar on his forehead. Agony rocketed through his skull. And then there was nothing.

Chapter Five

Finding strength she didn't know she possessed, Kate tore herself from her captor's grip and leaped toward Garrett to stop the man from hitting him again.

"No!" She curled her fists and slammed them into the side of the giant looming over Garrett. It was like punching steel. Ignoring her attack, he raised the club again. With smarting knuckles, she grabbed his arm, but he shook her off as a cow might flick away a bothersome fly.

"That's enough," snapped a familiar voice.

Nausea surged in her belly, and she spun round. Dressed as smartly as ever, her brother stood behind them, his hand raised at the tall, sneering man who'd attacked Garrett.

"Katherine, come here."

She stared at her brother's outstretched hand in horror. "Wha-what are you doing?"

Willy kept his narrow-eyed focus on Garrett. "Did he hurt you?" he snarled.

"No."

The tall man moved away, and she sank to her knees beside Garrett, studying the quickly rising lump beneath the scar on his forehead. She pressed her fingers to his wrist and found his pulse beating quickly but regularly. A sob of relief burst from her chest.

Willy's hand closed over her shoulder. "Katherine, stay away from this blackguard. Dear God, for your own safety. You don't know what this man is capable of."

What on earth was he talking about? "I won't."

Releasing a harsh breath, her brother knelt beside her. He glanced up at the tall man who still hovered behind them. "Leave us."

"Aye, sir."

The man strode off and joined another on the pebbled bank of the pond. She recognized that second man: John. For a second, his glittering green eyes met hers. The corners of his lips twisted into a smirk as both men turned to gaze out over the water.

"Katherine." Willy's voice was sharp as a whip. "Look at me."

Kate turned back to her brother. "What are you doing here?" she asked. "Why did you hurt him?"

"He compromised and debauched you. I saw everything." Willy gestured toward the two men standing on the bank of the pool. "They did, too."

Oh, no. No, no, no. Please, no...

"That in itself is enough for me to kill him," Willy said, his lips so tight, they'd turned white.

"No," she whispered.

"God, Katherine," Willy groaned. "Dear God. Why didn't I come in time? What have you done? Why didn't you try to fight him?" Clenching his hands into tight balls, he stared down at Garrett's inert form. "I know this cur. I've been searching for him for"—Willy's voice broke and his dark eyes glistened with sudden emotion—"a very long time. He knew I was after him. That is why he was so eager to leave town."

"No," she said again, feeling more confused by the second. She clung more tightly to Garrett's wrist, taking comfort from the pulse she felt beating strongly beneath the skin. She stared at Willy in confusion. If he honestly believed Garrett had debauched her, if he'd seen their entire encounter, why hadn't he endeavored to stop them before anything happened? A truly protective brother would have come between them the moment Garrett invited her to sit on the blanket.

"Trust me." Willy's expression darkened. "I shall explain everything once we have him safely home."

"Home?" Kate repeated stupidly.

"We will take him to Debussey Manor, and we'll keep him there until I summon the authorities in London. He is guilty of murder."

"You're lying." Her denial was instantaneous. Garrett, a murderer? Never.

"Unfortunately, I'm not," Willy said grimly.

She swayed slightly, blinking away the film covering her eyes. This couldn't be happening.

"Hayes!" Willy roared. The tall man turned and strode back to them, John at his heels.

"Aye?"

"Get him into the cart."

Willy unpeeled her grip from Garrett's wrist. Hayes grabbed Garrett by the armpits and John grabbed his ankles. Grunting, they dragged him over the dirt until they disappeared behind a cluster of trees. Rising to her feet, Kate tried to follow, but Willy clasped her arm and kept her back. She was too stunned, too confused to fight him. Instead, she watched dumbly, her mind churning.

"There must be some mistake."

Willy's fingers grasped her arm hard enough to bruise. "Good heavens, Katherine, do you make a habit of this? Tupping strangers in the forest? Is this what happened to you when Warren and I left? Did you lose all sense of decency? Of propriety?"

Kate's eyes stung as if he'd rubbed soap into them. Blinking, she gazed at the trees where Garrett and the tall man had disappeared, unable to meet her brother's gaze.

Willy released a harsh breath and asked in a low voice, "Did he pay you for your services?"

Kate stiffened. Never in her life had another's words made her feel so mortified. So dirty. So insulted. She stood still, as unmoving as a statue. "Stop it," she pushed out through her closed throat. "It wasn't like that."

Fingers clamped around her chin, forced her to face him. "Look at me."

Pressing her lips together, she gazed at her brother through her blurry eyes. Willy's expression was pained, dark with disappointment.

"How could you, Katherine? Our mother will never tolerate this behavior. She will disown you if she hears what happened here tonight. She'll throw you out. She won't be able to bear the sight of you."

"She hardly does now."

"She'll separate you from Reginald."

The stiffness melted from Kate with her exhalation of surprise. "She wouldn't," she gasped. "She can't."

Willy's eyes glistened in the darkness. "She will, and you know it." With an anguished groan, he shook her arm. His other hand came up to push through his hair, clenching the brown strands at the top of his head. Tears glimmered in his eyes. "Deuce it. Why didn't I come earlier? Why haven't I protected you as a brother should? Why haven't I been here for my family? Bloody hell, this is my fault."

"It has nothing to do with you, Willy."

"Reginald is the son of a marquis on his father's side, the great-grandson of a baronet on our mother's. Do you honestly think Mama would accept your influence on the boy if she were to learn how low you've fallen?"

"I haven't..." She stopped herself from saying any more. In her estimation, she'd never climbed so high. But she wasn't stupid enough to believe anyone else would feel the same about it.

This night was never supposed to intersect with her real life. Her relations with Garrett were never meant to extend beyond the dream world of her pool.

Willy's expression softened and his grip on her loosened. "Listen to me, Katherine. God knows I feel responsible enough for this. I should have been here, looking after you more closely... I don't want Mama to place the blame on you for this. I know your life with our mother hasn't been the easiest."

She was silent.

"I want to help you."

"How?" she whispered.

"Mama mustn't know."

Kate shook her head.

"I won't reveal what you've done. In fact, I will convince Mama to forgive—even approve of—your tardiness tonight. But you must cooperate with me. Trust me. Please, Katherine. You will soon learn what that man has done to our family, and you will understand my actions are entirely justified."

Earlier, Garrett had touched her, kissed her, asked if she trusted him. She'd said yes, and she'd meant it with all her heart.

Kate loved Willy—she always had. She respected him—how could one not? He was her family. Family loved one another. They stood beside one another in times of need. Kate would never dream of betraying him.

Nevertheless, in light of what Lady Rebecca had revealed to her earlier today, how could she trust everything that Willy told her? What he said about Garrett went against the very core of her intuition. How could she ever believe that Garrett, the man who touched her so gently and passionately, who gazed upon her with such desire, who listened to her so raptly, and who spoke to her with such respect—even admiration—was a murderer running from her brother? It made no sense.

Yet when she thought of Mama learning the details of the private moments she'd shared with Garrett, she did not doubt that Willy was right. Mama would be sickened by Kate's behavior. She'd toss her out. She would separate her from her little brother forever, and Reggie would not survive it.

Kate gazed at Willy for a long moment. He stared back, his dark eyes crowded with pained compassion and disappointment. Finally, she gave a short, decisive nod.

He released a breath of relief. "Good. Now we'll go home. Don't worry about anything, Katherine. I'll take care of all of it. Allow me to do all the talking, all right?"

"Very well." She looked away from her brother to the slight impression in the fine wool blanket where Garrett had lain.

When the cudgel slammed down on his head, it had made such a loud noise she'd expected to see his skull cracked wide open. But it hadn't even bled. Still, what if he was bleeding internally? A hot tear slid from one of her eyes, but she brushed it angrily away. She'd told Garrett she wasn't a crier, and that was the absolute truth.

She owed it to him to get to the bottom of this.

A hammer pounded the inside of his skull. Garrett cracked his lids to blinding light and squeezed them shut again, groaning. He lay on his side on a hard surface, and his hands were stretched awkwardly overhead, weighted as if by steel. Cold metal clamped his wrists, and when he tried to adjust his position, he couldn't separate his arms.

He stiffened, his body instantly coming alert.

He opened his eyes into a squint and found himself looking into the flickering flame of a lantern set in an alcove in a wall streaked with dirt. Gritting his teeth, he yanked his heavy arms over his head and stared at the thick, corroded iron manacles binding his wrists together.

He'd dropped his guard. Kate had shattered his defenses, and Fisk had found him first.

Had she done it purposely? Was she in league with her brother? Garrett's instincts screamed that no, that was impossible. But then again, God damn it, he had once thought the very same of Fisk. If Garrett had learned anything when Fisk had tried to take everything from him, it was that his own instincts were not to be trusted.

Not Kate. His gut rebelled against the idea. His soul resisted it. His head revolted most strongly, sending pain zinging straight from his scarred forehead down to his chest, where it expanded and spread slowly outward, like poisoned syrup.

She had seemed surprised when Fisk yanked her off his chest. Had she been playacting? Had she manipulated him from the very first moment he'd caught her watching him?

Breathing heavily, Garrett surged to a seated position. After he took several deep breaths to stave off the dizziness, he found himself on a narrow cot pushed against the wall of a small, low-ceilinged room. Irregular clumps of plaster spotted the streaked and stained brick-and-mortar surface of the walls. The room was unfurnished save for the cot, and the lantern provided the only light, for there were no windows. An arched wooden door marked the only possible exit, its planks emitting the scent of newly cut wood to mingle with the resident odors of mildew and rot.

Someone had removed Garrett's boots and stockings, and a shackle was clamped over one of his legs, its rusty surface scraping the bare skin of his ankle. A heavy chain led from his ankle to a shiny metal loop bolted to the wall.

Where had Fisk brought him? A long-abandoned dungeon at Debussey Manor seemed the most obvious answer. A dungeon thoughtfully prepared for his occupancy, with the inclusion of the new bolt and door, the lantern, and the cot.

All the evidence strengthened the theory that Kate was involved.

Garrett examined the manacles. Though corroded, speckled with green and red flecks of rust, they were strong, impossible to remove by muscle alone, and clamped on his wrists and ankle tightly enough to eliminate all hope of sliding loose. The same went for each link of the chain, and the loops attached to the manacle and the wall. He'd require either a hacksaw or a key to free himself.

Why in hell hadn't Fisk just killed him and been done with it?

Hearing a soft noise outside, Garrett cocked his head and listened to the sounds of people speaking. He couldn't discern the words, only that the voices were male.

A bolt was thrown, and the door glided open on its new hinges. Garrett leaped to his feet at the clank of the chain against the dirt-spotted flagstones as he moved.

Fisk stood in the doorway in a casual stance. He raised a small, silver pistol until it was aimed squarely at Garrett's chest.

"I won't hesitate to use it," Fisk said pleasantly.

"I don't know why you haven't already."

Fisk chuckled. "A fast, nearly painless death—no, that's simply not for you, Your Grace."

The man was insane. To think he'd tried to pin that insanity on Garrett, and he'd done it so effectively, half of London still believed Garrett was mad. The people called him *The Mad Duke*. They'd waited for him outside Parliament during the proceedings for his divorce and then heckled him as he'd walked to his carriage.

"What are your intentions, then?" Garrett asked.

"Oh, I'll kill you, eventually. I just intend to do it in the way you deserve, you understand." Fisk's facial muscles tightened. "You must suffer. As Warren suffered."

"I didn't kill your brother, Fisk," Garrett said through clenched teeth. "Damn it, you've already destroyed my life. Is that not sufficient vengeance for the death of your brother?"

Fisk's lip curled, and he blinked hard. Garrett thought he detected a slight tremble in the hand clutching the gun. "No. I will never have Warren back, will I?"

Raising his bound hands, Garrett rubbed his forehead with his knuckles. Warren Fisk, a lieutenant in Garrett's regiment, had lost his life on a June day eight years ago. Garrett's men were defending the château of Hougoumont against the French. The French nearly overwhelmed them, but Garrett wasn't the only officer convinced that the loss of the château would mean ultimate victory for Napoleon. And though the day ended in victory, that victory came at great cost. He had lost many fine soldiers—Warren Fisk among them—and he'd lost eight years of his own life.

"In the army, that is the risk you take." He recognized the futility of argument. Fisk had gone too far. He'd never give up, not until one of them was dead.

The pistol in Fisk's hand vibrated, and he pressed his lips into a thin, pale line. "You killed him."

"The enemy killed him."

"No." Fisk swung his head back and forth, blinking hard against the sheen covering his eyes. "I saw it all. An Englishman's bullet killed him."

Garrett ground his teeth. He didn't know the circumstances—he'd hardly known William and Warren Fisk. He had interacted only infrequently with the lower-ranking officers.

"An accident, then. Those things happen in the heat of battle. It's over now. It was over and done with eight years ago."

"And yet you are here."

"I'm here for my sister."

Fisk sneered. "Not for *my* sister?"

Garrett's jaw went rigid. He didn't answer.

Four months ago, Fisk had been his closest companion and confidant. But then Tristan and Sophie had unearthed the truth: Fisk possessed a consuming hatred of Garrett, and he'd been obsessed by his need for vengeance since Waterloo.

Garrett had lost his memory when Fisk attempted to kill him on the battlefield. After Waterloo, Fisk had hidden him from the people who'd searched for him. Stripped of his identity, Garrett spent seven years in Belgium. During that time, he'd worked as a field laborer from dawn to dusk every day. Not knowing he was a married man, he'd taken women into his bed until he'd met Joelle, the last and most enduring of those women.

When his memory started returning to him, when Garrett had finally come to terms with the knowledge that he was a married man, a father, and a duke, Fisk had wheedled his way into his confidence and proceeded to strip him—again—of everything, this time targeting Garrett's family and wealth.

Fisk had attempted to murder Sophie. He'd stolen the innocence of Garrett's young, beautiful sister. For those transgressions alone, Garrett would kill him.

Holding the pistol steady, Fisk studied the bluntly cut nails of his free hand. "I heard that last bit, you know, when you and my sister were talking. Well, I heard it all, but the last was the most delicious. When Katherine revealed her identity to you. I saw your reaction, and... ah, it was rich." He looked up, a small smile curving his thinned lips. "Your whole body went as rigid as if it had been stretched out on the rack. Katherine did well, didn't she? Sheer perfection, if you ask me. I could scarcely have performed it better."

"It appears a knack for deception runs in your family," Garrett said dryly.

"Looked to me you were quite taken with her."

Garrett remained silent. He would not reveal how Kate's betrayal cut him to the quick.

Fisk's lips flattened. "You're far too proud, duke. You'll be begging me for mercy by the time I'm finished with you. And I won't give it, because you are a murderer, and you deserve no quarter. Death will be your only mercy."

"You'll find your threats ineffective, Fisk. I don't fear you." And he didn't fear death.

"You should." Dark eyes narrowed at him, so like Kate's and yet so different. So much colder and harder. From the seething hatred in those eyes, it seemed unfathomable that Garrett had once thought Fisk his closest friend.

"I understand exactly how you must be punished for your sins," Fisk said quietly. "You shall reap what you sow. As you destroyed the one I loved, so I must destroy those you love. And I happen to have two or three of the members of that select category at my disposal."

Garrett's fists, held together before him, clenched. Rebecca was in danger. Who the hell else could Fisk be talking about? Garrett's ex-wife and daughter were safe in London, surely. *God, please*, he prayed. If Fisk hurt either of them...

No—his cousin would keep them safe. If Garrett could trust anyone in this world to keep Miranda and Sophie safe, it was Tristan.

"This is between you and me, Fisk. There is no need to involve anyone else."

Garrett never took his eyes from his enemy. He watched for an opening, a chance to lunge at him, to knock him down. But Fisk wasn't a fool, and as casual as he attempted to appear, he remained out of reach of the chain attached to Garrett's leg shackle, and his focus was sharp. He was prepared for any sudden move Garrett might make. Garrett didn't doubt that he'd shoot to cause the most pain possible rather than to kill.

Fisk shook his head somberly. "Of course there is a need to involve others. You're already primed for a painful death. You wouldn't even fight it much. You wouldn't even feel the pain."

"So you would sacrifice an innocent to see me suffer?"

Fisk released a breath. "You don't understand. Sometimes there must be sacrifices made for the greater good."

"As in war?"

"There was no greater good in Waterloo," Fisk snarled. "Warren's death...*No.* I would gladly have offered Napoleon the United Kingdom on a platter to save my brother."

"You would have sold your soul."

Fisk didn't blink. His response was instantaneous. "Yes."

A light somewhere in the antechamber beyond cast the shadow of another person across the threshold. Was it the same tall man who had shot Garrett in the leg months ago in Brough, the man who had cudgeled him hours ago? Or maybe it was Kate, gloating over her success. His chest tightened.

"You're mad."

Fisk cast him a bitter smile. "You're *The Mad Duke*, remember?"

"Praise God you are all right."

Mama plunged her flour-covered hands into the dough. It was a rather late hour to be making bread, but Kate understood her mother's need to stay busy in the midst of the uproar. At this very moment, there were unfamiliar men in the house she'd lived in for twenty years. Including one villainous stranger who'd attempted to compromise her daughter's virtue.

Mama shuddered. "Surely it was your screams that kept him from overcoming you in a most wretched, vile fashion."

The story Willy had told Mama—which Kate knew was contrived for her own good but instead made her feel like the lowest form of humanity—was that Kate had been walking home in all innocence when the horrid man had accosted her. The man had grabbed her and tried to ravish her. But poor Kate had screamed, fought, and then fainted in sheer terror. The commotion had scared the wretch off, and moments later, Willy had found her. In a fit of righteous brotherly rage, he and his men had gone after the villain, cudgeled him until he lost consciousness, and dragged him here to keep him under guard until the authorities could be summoned.

"I'm fine, Mama. Really." Lowering her gaze, she stared down at Reggie, raising her thumb to stroke his soft little cheek. Exhausted from a difficult, cough-ridden day and from worrying over her coming home so late, he'd fallen asleep in her lap soon after they'd arrived.

Kate still trembled inside, but she hid it from everyone. She knew she must look quite pale and shaken, which only added credence to Willy's fabrication. She had to give him credit, though. She never would have had the gumption to lie so thoroughly or so easily to Mama. It seemed he'd perfected the art, and the lie came out as smoothly and believably as if it were God's true word.

"I'm so proud of you, my dear." Mama pushed the heels of her hands into the dough. "You behaved as a lady should."

For once. The unspoken words hovered in the close, warm air of the kitchen.

Even though she *hadn't* behaved as a lady should. Of all the times in her life Kate had tried to make Mama proud, she was finally successful when Willy invented her actions for her. Yes, tonight she was quite the heroine. Quite the lady.

In truth, she was the opposite of both. Even now, her thoughts swirled around the man locked in the old underground dungeon.

Kate tucked Reggie closer to her chest. Her baby brother's welfare must remain her priority.

Her mother grimaced. "Katherine, you look exhausted.

I shall heat some milk for you and then you must go directly to bed and sleep off this distressing experience."

"Thank you, Mama," she murmured. She couldn't look at her mother, though. Mama would never be proud of her. Not of *her*, not of the true Katherine Fisk. No matter what course of action Kate took, if she chose it herself, she would disappoint her mother.

Instead of looking at the woman who bore her, Kate stared at Reggie's sweet, pale face. Reggie loved her for who she was. For a brief moment in her life, there had been Garrett, too. She'd never felt pushed to pretend to be someone she wasn't in his presence. From the beginning, he seemed to like her for herself. But had it been real?

They'd stowed him in the dungeon, so close to the room she shared with Reggie. Would Willy and his men allow her to go to him? To question him?

Wearily, she rubbed the bridge of her nose. She was tired and confused. Her ability to think logically had begun to shut down the moment the cudgel had struck Garrett, and now it had ceased to function altogether.

Just as Mama set the kettle over the stove, Willy strode into the kitchen. "Ah, good." The bench scraped the stone floor as he pulled it from beneath the table. "I'm glad neither of you has gone to bed."

He didn't acknowledge Reggie's presence, but then he scarcely ever did. Kate knew it was because he hardly was aquainted with Reggie, but a part of her thought Willy might be jealous that their brother possessed more aristocratic blood than they did. Though they were legitimate and Reggie wasn't, Reggie's father was the late Marquis of Debussey, while Willy and Kate's father was merely a lowly commoner who'd abandoned them when Kate was still in swaddling clothes.

Mama returned to plunging her fists into the dough, but her gaze fixed on Willy, and deep lines creased her forehead. "Is everything all right, William?"

Willy gave Mama a small smile, but he looked tired. "All is well, Mama. He's manacled, and I'm keeping an armed man at the entrance to the dungeon in the event he tries to escape. A pointless endeavor, given he's chained to the wall. I am the only soul with the power to release him."

Her brother pulled a shiny key from his coat pocket and clapped it onto the table. Kate stared at it. For a blink of a moment, she considered laying Reggie down, grabbing the key, then sprinting to the dungeon to release Garrett. She released an inward groan. Her inclinations were so impulsive, yet she hadn't had a chance to work anything out. Freeing Garrett might be the worst possible thing she could do. How could she be certain?

"But I truly don't believe he'll attempt escape," Willy continued. "He's resigned to his fate."

"What fate is that?" Kate whispered.

"Why, the gallows, of course. I did tell you he's wanted by the authorities."

Mama gasped, and her hands froze, buried to the wrists in dough that matched the shade of her cheeks. "*What* did you say?"

Willy's shoulders tightened. "Yes, Mama. I told Kate part of the story on our way home, but I thought I ought to reveal the bulk of it to the two of you together." Willy clasped his hands together on the tabletop. The key to Garrett's freedom shimmered beside his knuckles. "That man's name is Mr. Garrett Longmire. He was a soldier under Warren's command."

Clutching her little brother's warm body against her own, Kate regarded her older brother steadily. Garrett seemed so much more than a common soldier. He exuded power. Strength. Confidence. Leadership. She couldn't imagine men like Willy and Warren as superior to him in any way.

Jerkily, Mama began to knead again. The poor lump of dough was like a band of rubber. The bread wouldn't be any good at all, if Mama truly intended to bake it.

Willy continued. "He never saw eye to eye with Warren and argued with him at every turn—challenged his authority."

Kate could well imagine that. A man like Garrett would never be sycophantic toward a man like Warren. Or toward anyone, for that matter.

"Our colonel, the Duke of Calton, had planned to court-martial him for insolence to an officer. Mr. Longmire knew he was in trouble, and during the battle of Waterloo…" Willy took a deep, shaky breath and looked up at Mama. "Sorry, Mama. Sometimes the memories of that day are so fresh…" His voice lapsed as he struggled against the remembered grief of that day.

Mama's eyes filled, and she reached across the table to take Willy's hand. "I know, William. I know. I wasn't even there, and I shall never forget the horror of Waterloo."

"He killed Warren," her brother whispered.

Mama's flour-covered hand flew to her mouth. "Oh, no!"

"No!" Kate gasped. "You're…" She was going to accuse Willy of lying, but his grief-darkened eyes turned to her, and the words died in her throat.

Garrett could not have killed her brother. She could not have felt such strong emotion for a murderer. Especially for a man who'd murdered her own brother. Never. It was simply not possible.

Realizing she was clutching Reggie too tightly, Kate relaxed her arms and shifted her weight. Reggie slept soundly, though his chest still labored, and he was quite warm. She hoped he wasn't developing a fever.

"I saw it all," Willy said quietly. "Longmire shot him in the back as Warren fought off the French."

Willy spoke as if Warren had fought the entire French army singlehandedly. No doubt he truly believed it was so. Her brother had always idolized his twin.

"No," Mama whispered again, her hand still over her mouth.

Willy rose and stumbled around the table. He reached for Mama, and she sagged into his arms.

"Yes, Mama, I'm afraid it's true." His voice shook as he patted her back. "Garrett Longmire is a murderer, and he's plagued my life ever since that terrible day." Willy's voice cracked, and he bowed his head to press his forehead to Mama's shoulder. His own shoulders shuddered with emotion.

Kate's eyes smarted. Lord, it appeared as though he truly believed what he was saying.

But it couldn't be true. It just couldn't. Willy had to be lying. As he'd lied about his marriage to Lady Rebecca. As he'd lied to Mama about how he'd captured Garrett.

Willy was a liar. An expert one, at that.

Still, he was her brother. Her blood. They'd grown up together here at Debussey Manor. She loved him. And right now, the emotion that racked Willy's frame was utterly genuine.

Kate's throat went dry. Garrett didn't murder Warren. It couldn't be true. It just *couldn't.*

"Why is he here, then?" Kate said in a gritty voice. Two dark, shining sets of eyes riveted to her, but her mother didn't release her hold on Willy. "Why did he come to Kenilworth?" Kate asked.

"He's out for revenge, Katherine. I've been vocal against him in London. He has come after me to kill me, I think." Willy's Adam's apple bobbed as he swallowed. "It seems he found you first. Thank God he didn't truly harm you."

It was a grand, giant lie. It simply had to be. But two things were clear: The first was that Willy had known Garrett before today, and the second was that Willy hated Garrett more than anything. In spite of his romantic behavior toward Lady Rebecca at the onset of their elopement, Willy had never been a man prone to powerful love or powerful hate. In fact, it seemed to Kate that Warren's death was the only thing capable of rousing such intense emotion in her brother.

Which meant Garrett truly did kill Warren.

But no. *No, no, no.* That, of all things, couldn't be true. Maybe Willy was wrong—maybe he only *thought* Garrett had killed Warren.

Mama trembled in Willy's arms, and he muttered soothing words to her.

"Are you certain?" Kate asked in a quiet voice. "Are you *positive* he murdered Warren?"

Her brother straightened his spine. His voice vibrated with intensity, with utter conviction. "I am certain. Make no mistake, Katherine—that villain is responsible for our brother's death. I'm as sure of that as I am of the sun rising every day."

"He must pay," Mama whispered.

Willy turned back to Mama, and a glistening tear slid down his cheek as he said, "Never fear, Mama. I intend to make him pay. He will pay with his life."

Chapter Six

"I want you to keep an eye on him," Willy said.

Kate had just carried Reggie downstairs and tucked him beneath the quilt. Utterly exhausted, she sat perched on the edge of the bed brushing her hair when Willy had opened the door.

Kate rounded her eyes at him. "Me?"

"Yes. Mama's too overwrought. If she goes within striking range, she just might go so far as to attack him with one of the kitchen knives." He frowned at her. "You wouldn't want our mother accused of murdering a man, would you?"

At least this meant that Willy had no intention of murdering Garrett himself. Thank the Lord, because if he truly believed Garrett had murdered Warren, she expected Willy would try to kill him singlehandedly.

"No, of course not," she murmured. "I wouldn't want Mama accused of anything."

"You must be the one to see to his needs."

She'd see Garrett again! She'd be close to him. She'd talk to him...Her heart leaped into her throat at her traitorous excitement, and she struggled to order her thoughts. "But Willy, I must be at your house just after dawn."

"You may come later. I'll warn Rebecca."

"But..." She looked at him, knowing her eyes pleaded for the truth. "Willy, you saw us together earlier. You saw what we...what happened between us. How can you possibly ask me to go to him now? Wouldn't it be safer for you—for everyone—if I stayed away?"

In truth, this wasn't the way to approach her brother if she wanted to see Garrett—and she did want to see him, more than anything. But as usual, she couldn't contain herself. Couldn't stop her confusion from pouring out.

"He manipulated you, Katherine. I know him, and I know the truth of it. Don't you see? He was using you to get to me." Willy's lip curled. "And trying to get a bit of skirt in the interim. He chose you because you're my sister. He wished to twist the dagger in my gut."

Pain flooded through her. Garrett had seemed so genuine. If that was all a performance, then she was the most gullible, most stupid woman on the planet.

But even as the unconfident part of her cried out in humiliation and shame, the stronger part of her denied it. The stronger part of her believed with all her heart that the tenderness in Garrett's eyes and the gentleness in his touch were genuine.

Willy lowered himself on the side of the bed next to her. "John or Hayes will protect you from him, Katherine. Please, help me. You're the only one, do you understand?"

She gazed at the door. Garrett was beyond it and at the opposite end of the passageway. She could feel his proximity. "I suppose..."

Reaching down, Willy took her hand and squeezed it in his own. "Listen to me. He is a master of manipulation. He will coax you, try to make you believe grand untruths. He'll assume airs of importance and pretend he's someone he's not. He'll deny murdering our brother. He'll talk smoothly to you, he'll offer false flattery, and he'll try to seduce you. But you must be strong. Think of us, Katherine." His hand tightened over hers. "Think of Warren. Think of our family. I shall depend upon you."

Like your wife depends on you, Kate thought, for once keeping her words to herself. Willy had just handed her the opportunity to solve this mystery. If Garrett was innocent, she'd help him escape before the authorities arrived.

How could he be anything *but* innocent? She closed her eyes. The thought that she might have allowed the man who'd murdered Warren to touch her curdled her stomach.

"All right," she whispered over the thick mixture of emotion and confusion welling within her. It was very late, it had been the strangest day of her whole life, and she was so tired.

Willy bowed his head. "You always come through for me, and I know you will once more. Thank you." He placed a gentle, fraternal kiss on her temple.

"You're welcome."

"Now, I'll have John or Hayes guard him during the day, but he's sufficiently restrained, and with the door locked, I believe no overnight guard will be required."

It seemed strange, even illogical, that he'd employ a guard for the daytime hours and not for the night, but Kate was too exhausted to argue. In any case, no reasonable argument could emerge around her aching need to see Garrett again. To make certain he was all right. To draw the truth from him—for certainly no one could draw it from Willy.

"You will bring him his meals. Water to wash, a chamber pot, et cetera." He took a breath. "But for goodness' sake, don't do anything foolish. You must never approach him unless John or Hayes is on guard and watching out for you. Do you understand?"

"Yes."

"Thank you, Katherine." She nodded, and he gave her a faltering smile. "You're tired, aren't you?"

"Yes. Very."

"Sleep, then."

As he rose from the bed, she climbed beneath the covers and cuddled up to Reggie.

"Don't forget." Willy leaned down so close to her, his breath puffed against her cheek. "Longmire is a murderer. He's mad, and he's dangerous. He killed our brother in cold blood. He is responsible for Warren's suffering, and for our grief in his loss. No matter what he says or does, never forget the truth."

Kate squeezed herself tight, flinching when she pressed against the tender spot on her upper arm where Willy had bruised her earlier.

"Good night, then. I shall tell Lady Rebecca you will be there to wait upon her at nine o'clock sharp."

He shut the door behind him, and his footsteps receded down the corridor.

Garrett woke to biting cold. He'd slipped from wakefulness to sleep and back repeatedly in the past hours.

The lamp burned low, and its light flickered bleakly, casting long, arching shadows over the gloomy walls.

He hoped his horse was all right. Surely Fisk had found it, and even he wasn't cruel or negligent enough to let such a valuable animal starve.

Odd that when he'd slept under the stars it hadn't seemed this cold. Then again, he'd slept in his coat and beneath a heavy woolen blanket. All he had now was his shirt and a thin cotton sheet to cover him.

Maybe he'd freeze to death before Fisk put his family in peril.

He had no intention of freezing to death, nor of Fisk getting to his family, damn it. He was going to get the hell out of here. After he took care of Fisk, he was going to Calton House to be with his daughter through the winter holidays. And then he was off to Belgium to see Joelle.

Escape would be impossible, however, if Fisk intended to keep him locked in darkness for eternity. And it damn well already felt like an eternity, although reason told him it must be morning, so he couldn't have been locked up much longer than a full night. A full night in which he'd pondered how he'd come to be caught, and his mind kept circling to the same point: Kate.

She had approached him so similarly to the way Fisk had first approached him. With such open, innocent friendliness, no one would ever think the behavior hid a sinister intent. He'd continued to believe Fisk was his closest friend, even as Fisk was slipping him drugs, causing him to believe he was losing his mind. He'd become suspicious and distrustful of everyone during those dark days. Except his closest, most trustworthy friend, the gregarious, guileless, and ever-so-honest William Fisk.

Kate possessed the same innocent exuberance as Fisk, but with a feminine allure Garrett had found impossible to resist. She'd effortlessly struck down his wall of defense and left him vulnerable.

Now Fisk was in a position to hurt Garrett through his family, no doubt starting with Rebecca. Guilt tasted bitter in his throat. If anything happened to his sister, it was because of him. He was responsible. He'd fallen into the Fisk trap yet again. He was a damned fool.

A scraping noise came from outside the door, followed by the low murmur of voices. He raised his body to an upright position, swung his legs over the edge of the cot, and stood. Chilled to stiffness, the still-healing wound in his leg rebelled, and he shifted his weight to his healthier side.

He heard a sound—a feminine voice—and his jaw went rigid. *Kate*. She was just outside, speaking in low tones to someone.

The heavy wooden door swung, and he blinked against the brighter light coming from beyond the threshold. Whoever had opened the door stopped in midmotion, and when his eyes adjusted to the glare, Garrett saw Kate peeking in, holding a bowl clutched to her chest, her expression wary. Dark circles ringed her eyes as if she hadn't gotten enough sleep.

Of course she was tired. She'd probably sat up all night with her brother discussing their nefarious plot. Her wariness didn't surprise him either. He now knew what she was. A villain. No better than her brother.

"I—" She paused to suck in a breath. "I brought you some breakfast."

"Bitch," he growled.

She recoiled as if he'd struck her, nearly disappearing as the door swung shut. But her foot intercepted it, leaving it cracked open. Now he could only see one wide brown eye and a slice of her body leading down to her foot, shoddily clad in a leather shoe. That was one marked difference between her and her brother: Fisk used his ill-gotten funds to dress in the height of fashion.

"Why—?" She shook her head, seemingly unable to finish.

He narrowed his eyes. His fists clenched tight. "You manipulated me. You were in league with him. You had this all planned."

She gasped. "No!"

For a split second, he read anguish in her eyes, and he believed it. Then he hardened. It was exactly how Fisk had deceived him for so long. He'd wheedled his way into Garrett's family, into his confidence, until Garrett was ready to hand over everything to the man. Including Rebecca.

He was too damned gullible.

"What do you want?" he ground out.

"I-I brought you breakfast."

"Bring it, then. And then go away." He held his manacled hands in front of him. They shook visibly. The frigid cold in his bones disappeared, replaced by a burning, killing rage as she stepped closer and the door clicked shut behind her.

She paused. "Garrett?"

Slowly, he looked up at her, blinking through the red tingeing his vision. "What is your game?"

She clutched the bowl tighter to her chest. "I...don't know. Willy—my brother—said to bring you breakfast. He said terrible things about you. That you...that you murdered our brother Warren at Waterloo."

"You're a liar," he ground out.

"No!" She shook her head from side to side.

"You're in league with him." He allowed all his anger to resonate in his voice.

She stared at him in stunned silence for a long moment. When she spoke, emotion bled into her speech, making her words emerge like the choppy waves of a storm-struck sea. "Before last night, I didn't know that you were acquainted with him. He told me you were a terrible man. He said you're a master of manipulation. That you'll lie to achieve your ends. That you're mad and dangerous. He says you killed our brother in cold blood and are now trying to kill him. He said that you chose me because I'm his sister, and you used me to hurt him." She took a step deeper into the room. "Tell me he's lying. Please, Garrett. Tell me you didn't kill Warren. Tell me you're not a murderer."

He shook his head.

"Please," she whispered. "Tell me you didn't use me to..."

He pushed out each word through clenched teeth. "I...did...not...kill...Warren. I...did...not...use...you."

Her shoulders seemed to deflate. Staring at him, she murmured, "Thank God. Thank the Lord."

His lip curled. "Do you believe me?"

"I-I think so." Her teeth raked over her lower lip. "Do *you* believe *me*?" she asked in a low voice.

"No." But at least part of him—a part he wanted to crush like a bug—did believe her.

She flinched. "I didn't plan anything. I swear it. I had no idea you and Willy knew each other. How could you not believe me...after all we talked about, after all we...did?"

"I've been known to be too trusting."

"Please," she whispered. "Trust me."

Garrett peered into Kate's eyes, shining with unshed tears in the dim light of the lantern. "I placed my family in jeopardy because I trusted your brother. And now you ask me to trust you? How can I?"

"Because...because we nearly"—her throat moved as she swallowed, "—engaged in...in..."

He released a breath. "Usually, for a man, that is more of a reason to distrust."

"But surely that doesn't apply to you!"

He stared at her in silence for a long moment, and then he shook his head. "No. Not me."

"What...what did he do to you? What happened between the two of you? What happened to Warren?"

Garrett closed his eyes. "You must already know."

"I don't know anything." Her voice rose to a desperate pitch. "I don't understand anything."

What the hell was going on? Each time she spoke, the part of him that believed her grew. Now, it bellowed that she was innocent and he was treating her unfairly.

"He tried to destroy me," he said in a low voice.

"Why?"

"He blames me for Warren's death. I was there, with your brothers at Waterloo. But I didn't kill Warren."

"Who did?"

"I don't know."

"Warren was everything to him. They were twins, inseparable, closer than I have ever known any two people to be. If he truly believes you killed our brother, well..." She drew in a deep breath. "He won't stop until you are dead."

"Exactly."

She shuddered, whether from the cold air in the dungeon or from Garrett's icy response, he couldn't be sure. "It's so cold in here. You must be near frozen."

"Not anymore," he mumbled, but she seemed not to hear.

"I'll return shortly."

Before he could blink, she'd disappeared. He stared at the rough planks of the door as the bolt slid behind her.

He must face this logically. Raising his weighted hands to his head, he pressed his fingers against his aching forehead, trying to think. Last night, he'd convinced himself she was as guilty as Fisk, but in her presence...Again, she'd shattered his defenses. What was it about this woman?

She was Fisk's sister. He didn't want to trust her. Hell, he didn't even want to like her. But he both trusted her and liked her, and that made for a damn dangerous combination.

He must tread carefully and not give anything away. But he couldn't threaten her, nor could he harm her. Not until he possessed proof of her guilt.

Minutes later, she opened the door again. Her arms full of blankets, she strode in, less fearful of him now. She set down the blankets and placed two heated bricks near the foot of the cot.

"Thank you."

"I'm amazed that you didn't freeze solid overnight."

"I thought about it," he admitted. "More than once."

She flicked a glance at him. "I'll be right back."

She disappeared, but returned within seconds this time, carrying a basin and bucket filled with steaming water, both of which she set on the floor.

Standing, she tentatively stepped closer to him and sat on the edge of the cot in an obvious gesture of peace. She motioned to the bowl beside her. "I brought you a bit of porridge, and I doubled the butter like I do with my own breakfast sometimes when I'm very hungry."

He just looked at her.

She gave him a wobbling smile. "The lump on your forehead looks better than it did last night. Do you have a horrible headache?"

"Yes."

"I imagine you do." She took a shaky breath. "I thought for a moment that he'd killed you." She glanced at the manacles, and her expression darkened.

He lowered himself to the other side of the bowl. He could smell the sweet butter, and his stomach rumbled in response. "Tell me something."

"Anything." Her gaze descended to his bare ankles and followed the chain traveling from them, winding on the floor until it reached the loop in the wall.

"Look at me."

Her gaze snapped to his. A red flush spread upward from the scooped line of the bodice of the brown dress she always wore. Why did she blush? Because she was appalled at seeing him in this state? Embarrassed by her brother's deeds? Or because she'd seen his bare ankles? He sucked in a breath. *Focus*.

"If you knew nothing of your brother's hatred for me, and if you knew nothing about his pursuit of me, then why are you here?"

She considered his words for a long moment. "I am the only person available to feed you."

"So he allows you to come see me? Alone, without anyone to protect you from my so-called violent tendencies?"

"Well, he did warn me to be very careful. I spoke to Mr. Hayes before I came in. I asked if I could speak with you alone, and he said it would be all right but to shout if I required any help."

Garrett shook his head. "It's a dangerous plan, don't you think? After seeing us together and knowing that we're…friends, how can your brother be certain you'll remain loyal to him? You and I could collude, plan my escape, plan his demise."

She glanced at the door and lowered her voice. "You must know that no matter what happens, I'd never willingly plan my brother's demise."

"Why not?"

A horrified expression crossed her face. "He's my brother!"

Garrett studied her. Fisk said he had witnessed their encounter last night. If that was true, then he had certainly deduced how Garrett felt about her.

She continued. "My brother has been gone for eight years and has only recently returned to us. Since his return, he has treated me with kindness and understanding, which I daresay is more than just about anyone has ever given me." She clenched her hands in her lap. "Most important, though, he is my family. My family is all I have in this world."

So that was it. Fisk planned to use Kate as a pawn in this game of vengeance. It made Garrett's gut churn to think that any man could be so callous, and it was something a woman as innocent as Kate would never believe of anyone, much less her venerated older brother. His jaw clenched.

"In any case, if I wished to set you free, I couldn't, because I don't have the key to free you," Kate said.

"Do you know where the key is?"

"No. Last night Willy had it. Now...I haven't any idea."

He couldn't ask for her aid. If Fisk truly intended to use his own sister against Garrett, God knew what Fisk had in store for her if she helped him escape. It should come as no surprise that this was one of Fisk's perverse games. He'd try to manipulate Kate into "helping" Garrett and then use her betrayal as justification for making her, and ultimately Garrett, suffer.

Garrett's chest tightened. It seemed he was finally beginning to understand the twisted inner workings of Fisk's mind. Yet there was one thing Fisk didn't understand—Garrett had no intention of putting Kate at risk.

"Even if I were to find the key and free you..." Anguish shimmered in the dark eyes studying him. "I fear you'll murder my brother. It's why you came to Kenilworth, isn't it? To kill him?"

He sucked in a breath. He couldn't lie to her. *Hell.* "Yes."

"Why?"

After a long pause, Garrett said, "Your brother is a very bad man."

"That's what he says about you."

Garrett didn't respond.

Kate stared at her hands clasped in her lap. "We already thought he'd died after Waterloo. If he did perish by your hand, we would be devastated all over again. My mother...she couldn't bear it." She clenched her hands together so tight, her knuckles whitened. "He's my blood. I cannot betray him."

"I understand that, Kate. I do." Family loyalty was a force that went deeper than emotion and beyond instinct. He remembered the killing rage he'd felt when he'd seen Tristan for the first time after so many years. Garrett had mistakenly believed he was abusing Sophie. Yet he couldn't bring himself to kill his cousin, even then.

Kate sucked in a breath. "I believe you didn't murder Warren, but you did come here to kill Willy. Perhaps my brother acts only in self-defense."

"That's not true."

"Then, please. Tell me what happened between the two of you."

Garrett released a breath through his teeth. "He believes I am responsible for your brother Warren's death. He feigned to be my closest friend, but all along he sought vengeance."

"How?"

"In—" He nearly choked. God, how to explain to her the depth of her brother's evil? "In nearly every way you could imagine."

"But Garrett, Warren died so long ago. Eight years have passed since Waterloo."

"He trapped me in Belgium, forced me to live in poverty for the first seven years."

"Not Olympus," she breathed. "Belgium. That explains so much. Your behavior. Your accent."

He raised a brow. "Accent?"

"You don't exactly sound like a London gentleman." She shrugged. "What I mean is, you do, but you don't. I suppose seven years on the Continent would account for it." She looked from her hands into his eyes. "What did you mean when you said earlier that you placed your family in jeopardy by trusting him?"

"When I returned home to England after so many years, I took him into my confidence. I didn't know it was because of him that I was trapped in Belgium for so long." Garrett took a breath. "He...shot my wife."

She leaped to her feet, staring at him in wide-eyed disbelief. "Willy killed your wife?"

"No. He didn't kill her. She nearly bled to death, but she recovered."

She slapped her hand to her heart and closed her eyes. "Oh. Thank God. I thought for a moment that you were going to say Willy was the one responsible for your poor wife's death."

"You believe everything I say, don't you, Kate?" Garrett asked quietly.

Opening her eyes, she stared at him for a long, silent moment, and then she said, "Yes. I trust you. Against all reason, I trust you. I cannot explain it, but I do." Her shoulders drooped. "I don't know what to do."

Standing, he stepped toward her and reached up to brush her cheek with his fingertip. "You must do as he says."

Ever so slightly, she leaned into his touch. "Willy is my brother, and I won't betray him. But I cannot betray you, either."

"Can't you?"

She shook her head somberly. "I like you too much to willingly cause you harm."

"I don't want you involved in this, Kate. You must stay away from me."

"I cannot. He's commanded me to come to you."

"Ask him to rescind that command. Tell him I'm too dangerous. Say you don't want to see me anymore."

"But I *do* want to see you."

"No. It's too dangerous. You must go, and you shouldn't return."

"You're always telling me to leave you."

"Because you're safer when you're not with me."

She bowed her head. "My mistress is waiting for me. She's been . . . melancholy. And Willy—" She swallowed. "—He said I must be there by nine." She raised her head, and her brown eyes sparked with that vivacity he'd seen by the pool. "But I'll return tonight."

It struck Garrett that she still didn't seem aware of the fact that Rebecca was his sister. Why hadn't Fisk informed her of his identity?

Garrett himself saw no reason to tell her he was the Duke of Calton. If she tried to go to Rebecca or fetch help from Tristan . . . *no.* They would only be putting themselves at greater risk, and Garrett didn't wish to be responsible for any more bloodshed than he already was.

Ultimately, he'd much rather Kate continued to think him an equal, or rather, somewhat closer to an equal. She would change once she discovered his identity. She would withdraw from him. That was what servants did—they hovered and bowed, flattered and fawned, but they rarely revealed their true humanity to people of his status.

It was one of the reasons he believed people of his class considered them a few notches below human. It had taken Garrett seven years of living among the lower classes to discover that most people, regardless of their rank, were more human than himself.

She slipped her hand into his. "I won't let them take you away."

"What do you mean?"

"Willy plans to summon the authorities in London. He says you're headed for the gallows."

Garrett arched his brows. "Really?"

She nodded.

He squeezed her hand, grazing her knuckles with his callused thumb. "I assure you, the authorities aren't after me, Kate."

"You're in danger, though. You cannot deny that."

"Always looking out for others, aren't you?" he murmured. "You need someone to look after you for once." He wished he could be that person, but he couldn't. Not now, shackled in an underground dungeon. And later—he couldn't later, either.

He disentangled his hand from hers. "Go now."

She reached for him, and her hands closed around his wrists, over the iron bands. "I want to set you free," she whispered impulsively. "I wish I could. Right now."

She'd already set him free, last night and the night before. She'd given him hope. He would overcome Fisk. He'd do it without compromising this woman's sense of honor. He wouldn't hurt her knowingly.

Yet ultimately, he would, because he would kill her brother. For the first time, he regretted what he must do.

Reaching up, she threaded her hands in his hair, her

fingertips pressing against his scalp. "You have scars here, too," she whispered as her fingers passed behind his ears.

"Yes." He closed his eyes. Her brother had done that to him. "The injuries...they made me forget who I was."

"But you remember now?"

"I do."

She pulled him toward her. Then she tugged him closer, angling her head first one way and then the other. Their noses brushed, and then her lips pressed against his, inquisitive at first, tentative, then slowly taking command. Her hands tightened over the back of his skull, locking him to her.

Her mouth moved sensuously, softly, over his, and Garrett's anger and despair faded away, singed to ashes by the fire that spread through his veins, beneath his skin, and into his loins. The sudden, overwhelming need for her, the compulsion to make her his, even shackled and chained, made him groan aloud.

He yanked back. He stared at her, thoughts tumbling about in his mind. Fisk's sister. How could this be?

She pulled his head back to hers, but she didn't kiss him again. Instead, she pressed her cheek against his unshaven jaw. "Thank you," she whispered.

For a long moment, he couldn't bring himself to say anything intelligent, so he remained silent, focused on the feel of her warm, soft skin pressed against his own.

Finally, she turned to his jaw and kissed it hard. Releasing him, she stood. "You should eat. Cold porridge is awful."

He gazed up at her. Red dots speckled her cheek where it had rubbed against his stubble. "I will."

"Good."

Pausing at the door, she turned back to him. "I'll come later to bring you your dinner. I'll bring you some books, too, so you won't perish from boredom."

He nodded. God, he hoped to hell he'd have escaped by dinnertime.

Kate couldn't stop licking her lips. She could still feel Garrett's touch on them. She could feel his tongue and the rough growth of his overnight beard prickling over them.

What on earth was she going to do? Why had Willy given her the task of taking care of Garrett? He'd witnessed their encounter by the pool, so surely he knew she and Garrett could scarcely keep their hands off each other. Was this a test of her loyalty?

She understood Willy now less than she ever had, but Willy was no fool. Whatever course of action he took, he did so with purpose. She must be wary... it was up to her to discover Willy's true intentions when it came to her and Garrett, and poor Lady Rebecca.

Her mind busy with untangling her brother's motivations, she hurried down the overgrown lane leading from Debussey Manor to the main road. It was terribly, embarrassingly overgrown. Where had Bertie been for the past few days? She hadn't seen any sign of him, and that was quite odd, since when he wasn't asleep or working, he invariably hovered over the kitchen fire to "soothe his weary bones." She glanced at the sky. If she hurried, she could take the detour to his cottage, just to make certain everything was all right—and to remind him to cut the weeds back from the lane.

She broke into a jog as she turned down the path leading to his cottage, which was built in the same Tudor style as Debussey Manor, with white walls and dark timbered beams. Behind the cottage, hidden in a gully behind a row of trees, a tiny stream led from the man-made lake situated beside the manor. The lake, created by an earlier marquis, was the one-time jewel of the estate, but it had fallen into disrepair after Lady Debussey's death and now sat putrid and foul. Its green, mossy banks bordered a body of water that looked like pea soup and smelled rank.

Approaching the cottage, she heard a soft noise. It sounded like a whimper, as though an injured animal were trapped inside.

Kate slowed, fear tightening her chest. Swallowing, she trudged closer. She should call Bertie's name, but she couldn't conjure the voice to do so. What if Bertie was ill? What if he'd had an apoplexy and was suffering?

This approach led to the side of the cottage, and she moved to peer through a clean spot in the pane of the smudged window, her heart thudding like a drum in her chest.

It took a moment for her eyes to adjust to the dim interior light. When they did, her fist flew to her mouth. But she couldn't look away.

Willy and a woman were inside, both utterly naked. All she could see was her brother's pale backside, and beyond that, a tangle of limbs. It took a long while to make sense of it.

Willy was standing. The woman was on hands and knees on the bed, and Willy was gripping her hips as he penetrated her from behind. Both of them were making odd, guttural noises of pleasure.

The woman wasn't Lady Rebecca. Her body was

voluptuous, with generously curved limbs and rounded buttocks, unlike Lady Rebecca's slender form. Her bright golden curls shimmered, bouncing and full, and nothing like Lady Rebecca's sleek black locks.

Willy muttered obscene, lascivious words to the woman, and she seemed to like them, for she responded with phrases like "ah, yes" and "give more to me, William" in an accented voice.

As Kate watched, petrified with horror, Willy took a fistful of the woman's hair and yanked her head back so Kate could see her profile. The woman wiggled wantonly and cried, "Yes, yes! More, harder!"

Kate peeled her eyes away from the horrible scene and forced her frozen body to turn around. Rigidly, resolutely, she pushed her legs forward. For the first two miles, the only emotions she could feel were overwhelming sympathy for Lady Rebecca and utter loathing for her brother.

She'd never known Willy at all. Not really.

Since his return to Kenilworth, he had been so kind to her. So calm and caring. But was he evil, deep inside? Had war and Warren's death turned him into a monster?

Dear Lord, how could anyone—especially Kate, who was so very flawed herself—place such a horrible judgment on one's own brother? *Judge not, lest ye be judged...*

She couldn't do it. She wouldn't.

But then there was Garrett, trapped in a cellar and shackled, waiting for her brother to see him punished for a crime she was convinced he hadn't committed. In turn, he wanted Willy dead for forcing him into a life of poverty in Belgium and for nearly killing his poor wife.

And then there was Lady Rebecca, whom Willy had

seduced into an elopement, and who pined for Willy's love while he tupped another woman in Bertie's cottage.

How could Kate do anything without betraying her own family? Without causing pain and misery for one or more of them? How could she know what was truly right? And once she knew for certain what the right path was, how could she, of all people, be trusted to travel it? How could she be responsible for so many people without botching everything?

By the time she reached town, she had come to a series of conclusions, and her resolve had hardened to marble. Reggie came first. He needed her, and she would die before causing him harm. Second, she couldn't allow Garrett or Lady Rebecca to suffer, for they were both innocents, she was sure of it. Third, Mama couldn't learn about her carnal relations with Garrett—not only would that knowledge destroy what little affection Mama had for her, it would tear apart their family. Finally, Kate must retain Willy's trust, because she had no idea what he was capable of, but she feared what he might do if she angered him.

There had to be a way to keep everyone safe and happy. To keep her family intact while releasing Garrett and Lady Rebecca from certain misery.

By the end of the day, Kate had written and secretly sent a letter to the Duke of Calton, begging for his assistance on behalf of his sister. Perhaps the duke could help.

Chapter Seven

Kate took a generous helping of mutton stew from the big iron pot on the stove. She'd just returned from delivering dinner to Garrett. They'd fallen into conversation, and then John had opened the door to announce that he must leave for the night, and Kate must go, too—Willy didn't want her there when there was no guard present to protect her. She'd loitered in the dungeon for nearly an hour, and Mama and Reggie were waiting for her, so Kate had regretfully retreated upstairs.

She thought it rather odd that while Mama seemed appalled by the idea of Kate encountering Garrett on a road out in the open, she expressed no reservations about allowing her daughter to visit him in the dungeon. Kate wondered how Willy had negotiated that with Mama. Perhaps he hadn't negotiated at all—perhaps Mama felt whatever was done to her daughter in the confines of

Debussey Manor was negligible compared to something that might occur on such a public venue as a road.

With her soup bowl cupped in her hands, she turned to her mother, who sat in the armchair by the fire. "Mama, where's Bertie?"

Mama didn't look up from the book opened in her lap. "William has sent him to his family in Birmingham."

How convenient, Kate thought bleakly. She set her soup on the table, pulled out the long bench, and unfolded her napkin. Now Willy would have unlimited use of Bertie's cottage for his liaisons with the plump blond woman. "But why has he gone to Birmingham? Who will care for the grounds while Bertie is gone?"

Mama shrugged. "William said it was unimportant, for now."

"But—"

Mama thrust a hand in Kate's direction. "Hush, Katherine." She cast Kate a scowl. "Where is your common sense? There is a vulgar criminal belowstairs, and naturally William doesn't wish for anyone besides our immediate family and his own men to be involved."

Kate glanced at Reggie, who sat beside her, his face bent to his bowl. He always remained quiet and never interfered with their altercations. Kate didn't blame him in the least.

"But, Mama...*Bertie*?" The old groundskeeper was utterly harmless.

Mama slapped her hand on the arm of the chair. "Don't be a fool, girl. Why must you always argue, even when something is done solely for you? For the sake of your good reputation?"

"Sorry, Mama."

"It is just like before. He thinks of you first, Katherine, just as Warren did."

"What do you mean?"

"Do you remember that awful boy? What was his name? Peter?"

She blinked at her mother. Peter's name hadn't been uttered at Debussey Manor for over eight years. She'd been fourteen years old, and Peter, a youth four years older, had set her in his sights. He'd scared her a little, because he was ruthless in his pursuit of her. He'd waited for her outside the kitchens of Debussey Manor, he'd followed her daily, and once he'd pulled her behind a tree and given her a sloppy kiss that had made her feel dirty for days afterward.

Peter had gone to her brothers for their permission to publicly court her, but when they discovered he was the illegitimate son of a coal merchant, they rejected his suit and ordered him never to approach their sister again. Peter didn't bother her after that, and a few months later, he'd joined the army and had gone to Waterloo. He hadn't returned.

"Yes, Mama," she said quietly. "I remember Peter."

"Your brother protects you now just as he did then. He hasn't forgotten the importance of family."

There was no doubt that Willy truly believed Garrett to be a villain, so she couldn't blame him for wanting to protect her from Garrett. But Willy was also an adulterer. If protecting his family was so important to him, how could he deceive his new wife?

Chewing her lip in indecision, Kate gazed at Reggie. John was gone—he'd followed her upstairs after she'd brought Garrett his dinner, and she'd heard the door to the servants' entrance slam shut as he left the house.

She brought Reggie down to their bedchamber, and while Garrett's nearby presence consumed her thoughts, she followed their routine and prepared her brother for bed. After five fables, Reggie still hadn't fallen asleep, so she sang a lullaby to him as she rubbed his back over his thin nightshirt.

He finally slept, and she brushed her hair, watching his chest rise and fall, each breath a struggle. She couldn't tell if the awful-tasting prussic acid the doctor had prescribed was helping him at all. He wasn't improving, but a multitude of things could be causing his symptoms. Winter was coming, and Reggie always seemed to do worse when the weather was cold and dry.

Even as she gazed at her little brother, she felt the pull in her chest, that rope stretched taut between her and Garrett, leading her down a thin, curving golden path straight to the last cell in the dungeons.

It was foolish, the strength of feeling she'd developed for him, and she'd certainly never thought of herself as foolish before. She was a sensible sort of girl. So why, then, did Garrett make her toss aside the sensibility in which she'd always prided herself?

She could forget herself completely in Garrett's presence. Give in to her feelings for him. Abandon all sense of restraint. All these were frightening thoughts that should scare her to death. Instead, they strengthened the compulsion to go to him.

What would it feel like to lose herself with him?

It would be pleasure like nothing she'd ever known, she thought. It would be the most glorious experience of her life. She'd felt this always, even from the beginning when she'd watched him in the pond and he wasn't aware of her existence. Deep in her soul, she'd known that of all the men on Earth, this particular man could become her world.

What was it about Garrett Longmire? His perfect beauty with those scars that reminded one of his unrefined humanity? Or his gentlemanliness, his restraint when it was clear he wanted her and when she so brazenly offered herself to him? Was it the fact that he made no demands on her to help him escape?

Despite her uncertainty about her older brother, she had responsibilities to her family and even to Lady Rebecca. Responsibilities she bore like heavy sacks of grain weighting her shoulders, but that she'd never toss away, nor forget.

Garrett had told her that anything lasting between them was impossible. He'd told her to find someone else; a man who would take care of her in a way he could not.

In truth, he'd offered her nothing. So why, then, did it feel as if he'd given her everything?

How quickly she'd become wrapped up in this man, with so much at stake. Her own brother wanted him to hang, and he wanted her brother dead.

Kate truly understood her brother's need for vengeance. She'd grown up with Willy and Warren, had watched them together, had envied the strength of their bond. As a small child, before she'd understood anything about individuality, Kate had thought of them as two parts of a whole.

Perhaps, in the end, there was something to her childish observations. When Warren had died, had he taken half of Willy's soul with him? Had Warren's death robbed Willy of those traits that he exhibited outwardly, but that she'd recently discovered he lacked? Honesty, sensibility, reason? The ability to love?

Had Warren's death driven Willy to madness?

She squeezed her eyes shut, banishing the thought.

Regardless of Willy's state of sanity, it made perfect sense that he would go to any length to avenge his twin's death. Kate would have expected no less of her eldest brother.

She dropped her brush to her lap. During her walk home, a kernel of a plan had formed in her mind, and yet she was hesitant. Willy's words from last night came back to haunt her: "No matter what he says or does, never forget the truth."

Would it be her family or Garrett? Whom should she trust? How could she choose?

If she were to carry out her plan, would it be a betrayal to her family?

It certainly would. It would be a terrible, wretched betrayal, and if they ever discovered what she had done, Mama and Willy would hate her.

She rose abruptly to return her brush to its place on the table at the foot of the bed. With clipped movements, she bent to kiss Reggie's pale cheek.

Guilt tightened her shoulders and stiffened her legs. She might hate herself for what she was going to do, but her mind was made up. She would deceive her own family for someone she'd known for only a few days. Someone whose surname she'd just learned last night, whose origins were still a mystery, whose past was as muddy as the dirt road leading to Kenilworth.

She would betray her family for a man she'd begged to debauch her.

With stinging eyes, she left Reggie. Instead of turning toward the dungeon, she trod in the opposite direction to the narrow staircase. Forcing her heavy legs to mount each stair, she reached the ground floor, where she plodded through the servants' hall into the public passageway. She paused at the main staircase and stared up into the heart of Debussey Manor.

The deep mahogany staircase curved darkly before her. Without making a noise, she mounted the stairs on her bare feet. At the top, she turned down one passage and then a second. Halfway down the back corridor of the house, she halted at one of the doors. She turned the handle and slipped inside.

It was dark, but she had lived in this house ever since she could remember, and she'd never been the sort to remain passive about her whereabouts. She knew every nook and cranny of Debussey Manor, and even if it was dark as pitch, if someone spun her around a hundred times and then led her to any room, it would take her seconds using only her senses of touch and smell to discern her exact location.

It wasn't pitch dark in the armory, but it was close. The waning moon glowed beyond the tightly drawn curtains, casting a small measure of shadowy light through the two tall windows set in the back wall of the long, narrow room.

Oak cabinets lined the facing walls. Pistols, swords, and daggers occupied the cabinets on her left. On her right side stood the cases holding the collection of armor and ancient torture devices taken from the dungeons and restored in loving fashion by her brothers and the marquis. A faint scent of grease seeped from the glass cabinet doors.

Kate strode past the cabinets to the tapestry draped across the back wall between the windows. The darkness muted the details woven into the tapestry—which she knew from daylight study depicted a disgustingly gory battle of long ago.

She reached behind the heavy wool, and her knuckles brushed against the keys, making them clank softly. Lifting the ring from the peg, she moved to the window and used the dim moonlight to aid her in selecting the key she required.

The very first time she'd visited the armory, she must have been near eight years of age. That afternoon, she'd found her brothers here, but they'd hidden whatever they'd been playing with and shooed her away, saying this was no place for good girls. Their words had encouraged her rather than warned her away, and she'd returned that night and explored every square inch. She'd found the keys, and driven by curiosity, she'd matched a key to each lock, opened all the cabinets, and touched the weapons and tools in awe, speculating how much destruction and pain each one had wrought over the centuries.

She remembered which key to use. The smallest key on the ring unlocked the cabinet containing the smallest weapons: the tiny pistols and the daggers.

Using her sense of touch more than her sight, she fitted the key to the lock and opened the glass door. The long-pent-up odor of aged, corroding metal burst from the small enclosure.

Feeling along the lumps of metal in the center shelf,

she found a small gun beside a powder horn and a bag of ammunition. Sliding the items into her pocket, she methodically locked the cabinet, hung the keys on their peg, and returned downstairs. She looked in on Reggie to make certain he still slept, then she walked to the opposite end of the passage. She crossed through the wine cellar, now sparsely stocked with bottles of ancient wine, and ducked through the low doorway leading to the antechamber of the dungeons.

On silent feet, she slipped past the two chairs that had been brought down from the drawing room and stood at the entrance to the last cell in the row. She drew the shiny bolt and opened the door.

She'd brought a fresh lantern down earlier with Garrett's dinner, and it cast a bright yellow glow through the room. He lay on the bed staring at the ceiling, his hands laced behind his head. His hair was damp—he must've used the water she'd brought earlier to wash. As soon as he saw her, he rose clumsily to his feet. Ever the gentleman, even in shackles. No man had ever risen for her before she'd met Garrett.

"I hoped you'd come back," he said gruffly.

She drew the gun from her pocket, and gripping it by the barrel, held it out to him. His gaze narrowed when he saw it.

"One condition," she whispered.

His eyes met hers, and he raised a questioning brow.

"Use it only to protect yourself from my brother. If you must defend yourself against him, injure him and run from this place. Promise me not to use it to kill him. Please."

His lips flattened. "You needn't do this, Kate."

She shook her head. Stupid man. Of course she must.

He took one step toward her, then another. The chain scraped against the floor. He raised his hands and gently unpeeled her fingers from the gun. Taking it from her, he turned away and set it on the floor beside the bed. Then he returned to her, raised his shackled hands high, and enfolded her in the circle of his arms.

Comfort. Complete acceptance. Confusion swarmed through her like a mass of angry bees, and she could do nothing but close her eyes and cling to him, her breaths harsh and shallow.

His big hands pressed against her back, threading through her loose hair, crushing her against his chest, holding her safe in his embrace.

She began to shake. It started in her core and spread outward, through her limbs, all the way to her fingers and toes.

"Shh." He stroked her hair, her back, the outsides of her arms. "Beautiful Kate, sweet, honorable Kate..."

"Not...honorable," she choked out.

He was so warm. His body so hard, so real, against hers. The rigidness of his muscles, so strong, pressed against her cheek—muscles she'd given him many chances to hurt her with, but he wouldn't dream of hurting her. She knew it now, as she'd known it in her heart from the moment she'd first seen him at the pool.

She wanted him.

She shook harder. He made her feel so safe. So beautiful and whole and warm. She craved more, much, much more.

He planned to kill her brother, and she still wanted him. She was impulsive and impertinent and disloyal, but none of that mattered. She wanted this man desperately. She wanted to give everything to him and take from him in return. It was a fierce craving, an undeniable, painful, aching need, comparable to nothing she'd ever desired in her life.

They could never be together. He'd been clear about that. As much as he seemed to care for her in return, he'd never claim her as his own. Not as a wife. Not forever.

Never forever.

"Please," she whispered into the soft linen of his shirt.

They both knew what she asked, and Garrett's hands stalled, resting against her lower back.

"Make love to me, Garrett." *Because I need you. To feel safe. To feel whole.* "Just tonight. Then..."

"Then?" His voice was gruff.

"I will release you. I'll steal the key from Willy—I'll find a way—and I will set you free. I want you to escape."

"Kate."

"I want you to live, Garrett. I want you to be safe and happy. I know there can be nothing between us. I know I cannot ask for more. But tonight, I want you."

He shuddered hard against her. "You don't understand—"

"I do."

"No, my innocent Kate. You don't."

Clenching her teeth, Kate grabbed fistfuls of his shirt and yanked upward. "Don't I?"

She flattened her palms against the hot, bare flesh of his back. So hard, so smooth. She whimpered at the feel of it. She moved around his waist, tugging his shirt from his breeches. Plunging her hands under the fine worn linen, she touched him all over. Her hands ranged over his torso. Her fingers brushed over the scar on his waist, lingered over the edges of hard muscles of his abdomen, fluttered up his chest.

He stood frozen, his arms clasped round her, silently giving her leave to explore under his shirt. But when the heels of her hands brushed over his nipples, he groaned softly.

She froze. Realizing she'd been staring at his chest, she dragged her gaze upward until she met his eyes. His blue stare smoldered, sending warmth rocketing through her.

His arms jerked, and she glanced down. His muscles bulged as he strained against the manacles binding his wrists.

"I want to touch you, Kate. It kills me that I cannot touch you."

"*I* want to touch *you*."

A muscle spasmed in his jaw. "This isn't right."

She paused and stared up at him. "What's wrong? Is it that you're in shackles? That my brother wishes you dead, or that you wish him dead? Or is it wrong that I want to touch you? That you want to touch me?"

"It's wrong that I can't touch you the way I'd like. That I cannot bring you the pleasure I'd like—"

"Your *existence* brings me pleasure."

"That we aren't in my bed is wrong," he continued quietly. "That we're not free to love as we wish to is wrong. It's wrong that I can't make love to you all night long under a soft quilt, on a downy mattress, and it's wrong that we cannot sleep in the warmth of each other's arms when it's over."

"We cannot choose where we are now, or where we'll be tomorrow, but at this moment—perhaps in this moment alone—I offer myself freely to you."

His arms tightened around her. "Are you certain, Kate? There is so much you don't know, that you can't understand..."

"I know enough."

"You don't know who I am. What I am."

Reaching up to stroke his rough, unshaven cheek, she looked into those haunted eyes. "You're Garrett. You're a man. And I'm a woman."

He stared down at her. "Is it enough?"

He seemed to be questioning himself rather than her, but she answered nonetheless. "Yes."

His body molded against hers, and the rigidity of his indecision melted away. His hands dipped lower, just above the curve of her buttocks.

Still staring at him, she bit her lip to keep it from trembling. She plucked at the string at the neck of his shirt and loosened it, revealing the top of his bronzed chest. How on earth had his skin acquired such a deep, glorious color? Lightly, she traced the plunging vee of his neckline. His skin scorched her fingertip.

She wanted to see his bare torso more than anything, but in order to pass his shirt over his manacled wrists, she would have to tear it. And although everything about this night was impractical to the point of hopelessness, she wasn't utterly stupid. Garrett needed his shirt.

"I don't want to hurt you, Kate."

She dropped her forehead against his muscled shoulder. "You don't understand. Every touch is like a gift. How can you hurt me when each time your flesh touches mine, I feel...?" She paused, struggling for the words to explain. "Parts of me I scarcely knew were injured... well, it's as if you have the power to heal them. Tiny, open wounds cover my soul, you see, but your touch is the salve that cures them." She looked up, questioning him with her eyes.

His lips softened. "I understand, Kate. It's exactly how I feel when I'm with you."

Surely he didn't understand. Not really. How could he, when he'd only known her for such a short time? How could he know that she hid her insignificance behind the layered shields of pluck and cheer? That she faced life fearlessly simply because she possessed so little of value? How could he know that he tore down her barriers and offered her something she'd never considered herself worthy enough to experience? The sensation that she was worthwhile. Valuable, even. *Valued.*

"You are so good," she murmured. Powerful. Strong. Commanding. Everything she was not.

"Never believe that."

"But I do." She shook her head. "Nothing you can say or do will make me believe otherwise, so—"

His eyes hardened and flashed gray as his lips crashed down over hers. Hard and demanding. Roughly, his hands tore at the ties of her dress, releasing the bow in seconds. Kissing him back fervently, she pushed the sleeves from her shoulders. Her dress fell heavily to the ground and puddled around her calves, weighted by the powder horn and ball bag still in the pocket.

Next came her stays. He loosened them, and as she pulled them off, he lifted his arms over her head, releasing her from their enclosure.

She dropped the stays beside her. Now only her simple, shapeless cotton shift hid her nakedness.

Garrett stepped back. Color flushed his cheeks, and his chest rose and fell harshly with every breath he took. His gaze raked over her body.

Kate stared at his shackled hands held before him, above his shirt and covering the tops of his breeches. She bunched handfuls of her shift in her fists, using her fingers to pull it higher, studying Garrett as he watched her reveal her body inch by inch. When her hands couldn't contain any more of the material, she sucked in a breath, lifted the thin garment over her head, and tossed it aside.

Now she truly was naked. Cool air assaulted her body, and her skin prickled as the fine hairs rose on her arms and legs. Her breasts felt heavy, their tips tender. She pressed her thighs together and forced her hands to drop to her sides rather than wrap around her body to hide it from his gaze.

She stared at the dirty flagstones. At the battered wall above the cot, its stains glowing in different shades of gold from the light of the lantern. Anywhere but at him.

"You're beautiful." He hadn't moved, hadn't stepped forward, hadn't touched her in long seconds. "Beautiful and perfect. God, I don't deserve you."

At that, she raised her gaze to his, a denial on her lips. Before she could speak, though, he took one long stride forward and captured her in the circle of his embrace once again. She flung her arms around his neck, straining upward so she could kiss him. His fingers grazed down her bare back. Her sensitive breasts rubbed against the linen of his shirt, and although the material had once felt softly worn against her fingertips, it now felt coarse and rough, and tiny lightning bolts of sensation jolted through her body.

She gasped against his mouth as his hands lowered to cup her buttocks. He lifted her easily, and she wrapped her legs around him. As if from a distance, she heard the chain scraping over the floor as he carried her to the cot.

Chapter Eight

Though the action should have been awkward given his limitations in movement, Garrett smoothly lowered her onto the blankets she'd brought him. He slid his arms from beneath her, his fingertips scraping the satiny backs of her legs as he disentangled his arms from her body.

She lay on her back, pressing her knees together, and he gently pried them apart, dropping a kiss on the warm flesh inside her knee.

Kate rose on her elbows. "You've seen me bare, so now I want to see you."

Garrett's lips twitched. "You have seen me naked. More than once."

"You weren't close enough."

He forcibly dragged his gaze from the pink, puckered tips of her breasts as she continued, "I know you cannot remove your shirt. But..."

Her eyes flickered downward, and she reached forward,

pushing his hands and shirt out of the way so she had access to his falls. As she worked to loosen them, his ragged breathing mingled with hers, punctuating the release of each button. Finally, his breeches fell open.

"Stand," she ordered in a voice so low he had to strain to hear her.

He complied, and moving from the cot to kneel before him, she tugged the breeches down until they pooled at his ankles. He couldn't get rid of them completely, he realized—they'd loop round the chain.

His shirttails and shackled hands covered his cock, which happened to be in a rather uncomfortable position at the moment. At full stand, throbbing with need.

Kate smoothed her hands up his thighs, pausing at his most recent wound—the puckered, raw-looking gunshot wound in his thigh.

"What happened?" she whispered.

"Hayes," he said shortly. "Four months ago."

He saw her grind her teeth. "Does it hurt?"

"No."

She pressed her lips gently to the wound. Her hands stopped moving on the fronts of his thighs, and she tilted her head to face him. "Lie down."

Patience. As much as his body craved release *now*, he'd exercise restraint.

With a small smile, he kicked off his breeches as best he could and lowered himself onto his back on the cot. Staring down at him with dark eyes, she sat near his hip, in the same position he'd taken moments before.

Her lush brown hair tumbled in thick waves over her shoulders and down to her waist. In contrast, her skin was creamy pale and utterly smooth except for the dark triangle at the apex of her legs and the pink tips of her breasts. She was the goddess of beauty—of seduction—completely at odds with the initial dreary prospect he'd had of her at the pool.

The curl of her lips strengthened into a smile—the smile that never ceased to knock the breath from his lungs.

Gently, she moved his arms aside and slid her hands under his shirt, over his hip bones, nudging the shirt upward as her hands traveled in the same direction.

"I should fear you," she said as more of his body was revealed to her curious gaze.

"True." He watched her through half-lidded eyes. "For many reasons."

It was good he was shackled at this moment. His fingers itched to take her, to grasp her waist and heave her over him.

"But I don't." She didn't break her stare at the parts of him now exposed. "It's beautiful."

He nearly laughed. Though women had used various means of showing appreciation for this particular appendage of his, no woman had ever sought to compliment it. And "beautiful" wasn't a word he would have expected from anyone.

Kate glanced at him from beneath her lashes. "Can I touch?"

"Yes," he choked out.

He clenched his teeth as she ran a fingertip from base to tip.

"It's so soft," she murmured.

He cast a glance downward, but the folds of his shirt effectively hid his cock from his gaze. "Doesn't feel soft," he muttered. In fact, it felt hot and hard, and...*angry*.

She took him in two hands, fingers curling round his length. "You're right," she agreed. "Soft on the outside. Hard as steel inside." Her lips quirked. "Now I believe I understand all the sword and sheath references."

"And when have you had the occasion to hear such references?" he asked in a strangled voice. He closed his eyes as her hands slid sensuously up and down his shaft.

"Lord..." She inhaled deeply. "Lord Debussey has an extensive library. It can be a lonely life out here. We read heaps."

He groaned as her fingers brushed over the tip of his length.

"Does it feel good?"

He nodded, opening his eyes to slits. The way she twisted on the edge of the cot made her arm press against her breast, plumping it. Raising his hands, he took the inward curve of her breast in his palm and brushed the nipple with his thumb. Her fingers tightened over his cock.

He echoed her question. "Does it feel good?"

"It..." She paused a moment, thinking. "It makes me *want*. Deep inside."

He raised himself to a seated position. Keeping his hand cupped around the bottom curve of her breast, he lowered his head to take the taut peak into his mouth. She sucked in a surprised breath, then arched her back to give him easier access.

"Oh, yes," she breathed as he swirled his tongue around her nipple. "It does feel good."

"Now," he said against her ripe, warm flesh, punctuating his words with gentle nips and pressed kisses, "I would lay you down. I'd kiss you...everywhere. And then I'd take you. Gently, slowly, because it is your first time."

Her hands, still gripping his shaft, tugged on him hard enough to make him groan. "None of that is necessary."

His lips traveled to her collarbone, kissing across it as he brushed each of his fingers in turn over her nipple. Against her shoulder, he murmured, "It is necessary. I regret I haven't the full use of my hands. If I did, I could touch you more."

Her fingers loosened over his cock and began a slow, maddening glide up and down his length. She tilted her head as he nibbled his way up her neck and across the line of her jaw. "I don't think I could bear it if you did."

He pulled away slightly. "Why?"

"It would be too much. I'd surely explode." She released a trembling breath. "I'd become a brazen fool. As it is...it's taking every bit of strength I have to restrain myself with you. If you could have free rein in touching me, I'd be lost."

His hands, holding her thigh where it draped over the edge of the bed, tightened. "It takes every bit of strength I have to restrain myself with you, Kate."

"Then why must we exercise restraint at all? Why not set ourselves free? Allow us to do what is natural to us both?"

"It would hurt you."

"I don't care!"

"I do."

He touched his tongue to the corner of her lips, the soft edge that curled just before she broke into a smile. They changed places again, but this time he knelt between her slender legs. He slid his hands over the silky, smooth skin of her thighs, tracing the light definition of muscles. He'd already known she was an active woman, but the sight of her body—taut yet softly rounded everywhere a woman should be—made his blood race and his cock demand release.

Using a light touch, he stroked down the sensitive inside of her thigh.

"Garrett," she sighed. Her hands closed over his shoulders.

He sank onto his elbows as his fingers descended to the warm, wet heat between her legs.

She was slick for him already, and she let out a low moan when he touched the dark pink nub of her clitoris.

Lowering his head, he followed the gentle rub with a lick, and this time, his groan mingled with hers. Her taste tested the bonds of his control. He closed his lips around the small nub and slipped a finger inside her tight, slick channel.

"Garrett!" she gasped. "What...?" But her question faded into a whimper as he swept his tongue over her, tasting her. Sweet, beautiful Kate.

He moved his finger, slowly at first then increasing the pace until every thrust was met with a whoosh of Kate's breath. Then he added a second finger, working her, preparing her for his invasion. Cupping her rounded bottom with one shackled hand, he continued to thrust the fingers of the other into her while he circled her clitoris with light touches of his tongue.

She vibrated all around him. Her trembling hands clutched at his shoulders. Her flesh scorched his lips, the heat barreling straight to his aching cock.

Suddenly, she stopped breathing. She stiffened. Her

hands clawed at his shirt. Her thighs locked around his ears. Rings of muscles contracted and pulsed around his fingers.

He continued to thrust his fingers deep until the pulses weakened and then stopped altogether, and she went limp around him. Her breaths returned in deep, gasping sobs. He slipped his damp fingers from her body and kissed his way to her lips.

"Taste yourself, Kate." He kissed her gently, almost chastely. Her eyelids were squeezed tight, but she still held him, and after a moment's hesitation, she opened her mouth and touched her tongue to his.

As he kissed her, he braced his shackled hands over the top of her head and adjusted his position. She was so wet from her release, he wasn't sure if this would work, but he saw no other way. And hell, if he wasn't inside her soon, he was going to explode.

He tried to line himself up once, twice, and both times, he slipped down. Gritting his teeth, he made to try again, but she pushed her hand between them.

"Let me." She grasped his cock and guided it to the hot notch of her body. Her hand loosened, and she spread her legs wide. Her other hand locked around his hip, drawing him closer.

"Do it, Garrett." Locking her hands around his neck, she arched toward him. "Please. Take me. Make me yours."

"Kate," he groaned. "I'm not sure…I'm not certain…"

"I need this. I need you."

"I am so close…"

"I want to be close to you."

Damn, but he didn't want to lose control. Slowly, his jaw tight with restraint, he pushed in.

"Yes," she murmured. "Yes, yes. Yesss."

He felt the resistance. She stilled beneath him as he tested it, but it was too late. He shook from head to toe with the effort required to keep the slow pace—there was no way on earth he could stop now. So he pushed through it, slowly breaching her maidenhead and continuing until he was fully seated inside, wedged against her womb. She closed like a tight, hot fist around him, tugging him ever deeper inside.

Being inside her body was heaven.

She remained utterly still, and he opened his eyes to look down at her. Her eyes were closed, her body tense and unmoving.

"Kate?" he rasped.

Her eyes flickered open and stared at him, so dark as to be black in the light of the lantern.

"Are you all right?"

She gave a tight nod. "Move…I want to feel what it's like when you move inside me."

Slowly, he pulled out until the crown of his cock hovered at her entrance, and then he pushed in, faster this time.

"Hurt?" he breathed.

She nodded again.

"God, I'm sorry."

"Again, Garrett. Move. Please."

Again he pulled out, and then pushed back in. This time, she let out a puff of breath as he lodged deep inside. "Better," she murmured. "Again."

He did it again, stopping when the tip of his cock pushed against her womb.

"Again," she commanded almost immediately.

He groaned. "Kate, you're making me crazy."

She frowned up at him. "Does it feel so terrible?"

"It's—" He swallowed. "You feel like heaven. I don't think I'll ever be able to get enough of you. But I have to move, or I'm going to go mad."

"But...I've been telling you to move."

He smiled and dropped a kiss on her lips. "Is it hurting less now?"

She nodded.

"Then let me love you."

"Yes, Garrett," she whispered. "Love me."

He kissed her again, and as his lips clung to hers, he took slow, long drags out of her body, followed by deep, hard thrusts in. It wouldn't be long. She'd teased him since he'd wrapped his arm around her on the first day at the pond, and his body had craved this moment ever since.

He was losing himself. All he could feel were the places she touched him. Her lips, so soft, smooth, supple. Her legs wrapped around his waist, clutching him just as her hands clutched his back, pulling him forward with every thrust he took. And then there was her hot, tight channel clamped around him. A thrumming sensation began at the base of his spine and traveled through his lower extremities. He thrust harder, and below him, she made sweet little moans of pleasure, urging him higher, harder, faster.

All at once, the dam broke. At the very last second, he remembered he mustn't come inside her, and he yanked himself from her embrace, then pressed himself over her as he groaned and shook, releasing himself on the lower part of her stomach.

Fully spent, he forced himself to collapse to her side

on the narrow cot. She wiggled closer to the wall to make more room, then turned and snuggled against him.

Garrett closed his lids, but a deep foreboding pushed at the soft feeling of contentment, along with the certainty that he'd once again, perhaps for the last time, fallen into a trap set by William Fisk.

"I'll fall asleep if I stay here," Kate murmured sometime later. Wedged against Garrett's powerful body, held by his strong arms, she was altogether too comfortable. It was too safe here. Too peaceful.

"We both will," he replied drowsily. "A bad idea."

"Yes," she agreed. But still she didn't budge. She stared at the dungeon door, glimmering gold in the lantern light. Danger lurked outside, and she didn't want to leave this peaceful dream to return to it.

"Go, Kate." Gently, Garrett disentangled himself from her, and, sighing, she rose to a seated position at the edge of the cot. He slid off and went to the basin of water.

His chain scraped on the floor as he returned and knelt before her. He gave her a chagrined glance. "Another thing that is not right."

"What's that?"

"I should have warm water for this."

She frowned at him. "For what?"

"Brace yourself. It'll be a little cool."

He nudged her legs apart and gently swiped the cloth over her stomach, then lower to the sticky insides of her thighs and between them. He glanced up at her. "Are you in pain?"

She shook her head, and he released a relieved breath. Her cheeks heated, and she studied the bed for the telltale signs of blood. Except for a pink smudge on the cloth he used, there was none.

She gestured at the cloth. "Is that...common?"

He chuckled softly. "I haven't a great deal of experience in bedding virgins, but I'd say...yes. Quite common."

"Good."

"Too cold?"

"No," she breathed.

Pulling the cloth away, he turned and collected her shift from the floor. After she dropped it over her head, she cast a shy glance at Garrett, who fumbled with his own clothes. Pausing in midaction, he met her gaze. His features had softened, and she realized she hadn't seen such a look on his face before. He looked...happy.

"Good night." She gave him a hard kiss on his bristled cheek and gathered her shift and dress, leaving the powder horn and ball bag with the gun beside the bed. Certain she'd be compelled to stay if she looked back, she hurried out the door, bolting it behind her so as not to arouse suspicion.

She didn't breathe until she was in the room she shared with Reggie, and then she sucked in a deep lungful of air. Glancing at the clock, she saw it was a little before two o'clock in the morning. Reggie was sound asleep. Thank goodness on both counts. Spending so much time with Garrett was foolish, but what had happened was so overwhelming, and the warmth of Garrett's embrace afterward was like the most comforting lullaby.

She closed her eyes.

Today, she would find a way to steal the key from Willy. Tonight, she would set Garrett free.

* * *

Becky opened her eyes. Behind her, William shifted, and the bed creaked softly as he rose. She heard his footsteps as he padded across the floor, the slide of fabric as he donned his robe, and the gentle click of the door as he closed it behind him.

She swallowed a sob. He'd neither explained his absence last night nor joined with her tonight. His actions only strengthened her fear that he had taken a mistress. She wasn't a complete fool—as much as William pretended to fawn over her, she could read the distance and aloofness in his brown eyes. That distance and aloofness had increased a hundredfold since they had arrived at Kenilworth.

She'd spent an inordinate amount of time in the past weeks reflecting on her foolishness. In the last few days, she'd thought of nothing else.

She'd abandoned her family for a penniless man who didn't possess one ounce of love for her. And he was a liar, too, for he'd lied about his income. He'd told her a grand story about his two thousand a year, but he didn't have enough for more than this tiny cottage and four servants—one of whom walked six miles a day rather than sleep here.

Becky had searched William's personal papers through and through, and there was no mention of two thousand pounds, or a sum anywhere near that, in any of them. In fact, William's papers mostly consisted of bills and threats of retribution should he fail to pay.

Soon, she'd have to write to Calton House to beg for money. The thought made her ill, especially after she'd so confidently extolled William's virtues to her sister-in-law and listed his income at the very top of the list. Even if her recent letters won her some measure of forgiveness, she would still look extremely foolish.

Becky was even beginning to think there might be some truth to Sophie's accusations that William had tried to extort money from them, and when Sophie had discovered his nefarious plot, he had tried to murder her.

No. She still couldn't accept the last bit. William might be dishonest, but a murderer? After spending a few seconds entertaining the thought, she pushed it from her mind, hoping to quell the nausea building in her stomach.

As Aunt Bertrice would say, she'd made her bed, and now she must lie in it. Alone. She'd chosen a life with William Fisk, and there was no turning back.

Yet she must do something. She couldn't live in this way—pathetically needy and hopeful. Becky dreamed of being a powerful, strong woman. A woman whose every action exuded confidence. A woman who was well-respected and well-liked. She couldn't become that woman hidden in this little town, with no one to speak to but one kindly female servant—the only educated one of the four—who was ever anxious to be rid of her company.

Had William left the house? Or was he down in the parlor, enjoying an innocent brandy? If that were the case, she would serve him. Then she'd rub his feet—maybe her touch would rouse him from his lack of interest.

Becky rose and took her robe from where it hung on a peg in the closet. Wrapping it around her, she slipped out the door and walked down the corridor in search of her husband.

The parlor was dark. But...she cocked her head, listening. Low voices filtered up from the ground floor.

Slowly, carefully, tiptoeing so the boards wouldn't creak, she descended the narrow staircase. As she neared the bottom, she recognized the voice of William's manservant, John. She paused five steps from the landing, realizing they were most likely sitting in the drawing room, and if she descended all the way, they'd see her.

"Your sister, she seduced him right smartly."

"He fucked her?"

William's voice shocked her. Becky swallowed down a gasp, and her fingers tightened over the handrail. She'd never heard him use such crude language. The William she knew was utterly refined and unfailingly polite. And she didn't know he had a sister at all.

"Oh, aye, and very prettily too, considering he was all tangled up in them chains."

"Deuce it!" William's tone rose to a near-shout and then calmed. There was a slapping noise as his hand came down on something—probably the sidebar. "I knew I couldn't trust her."

"I've been wondering, sir—if she can't be trusted, then why'd you send her to him?"

"It was a test," William said, his voice clipped. "I was testing her loyalty to me and our mother. I wanted to see if she would do what was right. She failed."

"Ah. Right smart of you to test her, then, I daresay."

William grunted. "I shouldn't be surprised my sister has betrayed me." Becky heard him take a swallow of a drink. "It's so odd to think that she's as much my sister as Warren was my brother. Warren would have stood by my side through anything. But Katherine—she's fickle. She possesses absolutely none of his better qualities. Then again, she's a woman, isn't she? One who possesses all of the most unappealing qualities of her sex."

Katherine?

"She ought to be punished for betraying you," John said, taking on a menacing tone. "If I'd a sister and she turned from her family like that, I wager I'd beat her into a pulp."

"Yes. You're right, of course." There was a brief pause, and then William said, "I trust you won't fail me."

"Not to worry, sir. You can count on me."

"Thank you, John." William sounded tired, his voice full of pain. "Tomorrow night, then. When Katherine goes to the dungeon, you must 'interrupt' them. But don't kill her, understand? I want the duke enraged, but I need her alive."

Becky's body turned to ice. She stood frozen, holding her breath, too stunned to move.

The duke?

"I've half a mind to command you to kill her." Becky heard the slapping sound again, and then William sighed. "Well, she's somewhat of a help to my mother, what with her caring for the brat. In any case, when you're done using her, we'll take my wife out there. Day after tomorrow, I should think."

"Lady Rebecca?" John questioned. "Take *her* to Debussey Manor, sir?"

Debussey Manor?

"That's right. I haven't yet decided exactly what we'll do with her," William mused. "It must be something to taunt the duke beyond endurance. I will make plans and then execute them to obtain the maximum effect." He hesitated, and Becky heard the smile in his voice when he said, "Maybe you ought to help me with that, John."

"Oh, anything, sir." There was a pause. "And then we'll kill them?"

"Yes, of course," William said easily. "Eventually."

Glasses clinked. "To your health, Mr. Fisk."

"Yes, and to our upcoming prosperity and the impending end of my marriage to the most insipidly dull woman I have ever had the misfortune of meeting."

Emotionlessly, Becky's mind sifted through the facts. Debussey Manor was where Kate lived, where she returned every night to care for her young brother. Only Kate, her young brother, and their mother lived in the house now that the marquis had died.

Kate must be Katherine, William's sister. Kate had sided with Garrett against William. Had her lady's maid and her brother become lovers?

In the past four months, Becky had managed to glean enough information from the newspapers to know that her brother and Sophie had gone through a spectacularly publicized and scandalous divorce. The papers had flagrantly sided with Tristan and Sophie, and bandied gossip about the bitterness of the relations between them and Garrett. Becky was a duke's daughter, and she knew how the papers exaggerated scandals. She'd wondered how much of what they said was true.

Despite her knowledge of the divorce, it was difficult for Becky to imagine her brother with anyone other than Sophie. He had been solely committed to Sophie for as long as she had known him.

It was even stranger to think of him bedding her vivacious and seemingly innocent lady's maid.

The drawing room had been immersed in silence for several moments.

The two men were drinking, Becky supposed. Her mind, though it still busily computed the facts, was completely and utterly blank of emotion. She felt nothing but the stiffness in every muscle of her body.

She turned, and on wooden legs, crept back upstairs. She went directly to William's coat and withdrew the key from its inner pocket. Like any jealous wife, she'd searched his pockets as soon as he'd removed his coat for dinner, but she had found nothing save the innocuous-looking antique key.

She now had a rather good guess as to the key's purpose. She replaced it with one from her household ring. William would only have to draw it out to realize it was a different key, but it was a risk she'd gladly take.

She tucked the key into the hem of the striped spencer jacket she would wear tomorrow evening. When she would finally defy her husband's order for her to stay inside and would go for a "walk."

Like an automaton, she hung her robe and slid under the blankets. When William returned an hour later, she breathed deeply, feigning sleep.

Chapter Nine

Kate strode home nearly at a run, blood pumping angrily through her veins. Willy had stayed home all day and had kept her busy with tasks at Kenilworth. He'd told her Lady Rebecca had come down with a cold and didn't want to be disturbed.

Perhaps even worse, she hadn't been able to steal the key. When she first arrived at the house in the morning, she'd brushed against Willy's coat, and she'd felt the heaviness in his pocket. Just as she'd reached up to pluck it out, he'd jerked away from her with a knowing gleam in his eyes that sent a shiver of dread tumbling down her spine. Then he'd sent her on another errand in town. He'd kept his distance for the remainder of the day.

As she worked, Kate had contemplated other ways to set Garrett free. Fire? No, the heat would hurt him, not to mention that she was fairly certain she couldn't get it hot enough to melt iron. A very sharp, very small saw? Possibly...

Sent to fetch a set of new shirts for Willy, Kate rushed from the tailor to Mr. Gwynn's, the watchmaker's, where she explained that her mistress was a tinkerer obsessed with everything mechanical. Kate said Lady Rebecca had become enamored of one of the clocks in the house and was in the process of dismantling it when she determined she required a saw.

The bemused watchmaker had handed over the device, its small, jagged blade the same size as her longest finger, and a cylindrical wooden handle to double its length. Promising she'd return it soon, Kate slipped it into her pocket.

On the way home, Kate took the short detour to Bertie's cottage. It was clear Willy's mistress was inhabiting it, for when Kate peeked in the window, she saw lacy, feminine garments strewn haphazardly across the floor. But no one appeared to be inside, and when she knocked on the door, no one answered. She tried to open the door, but it was locked. For good measure, she tried each of the windows as well, but they were also locked tight.

She cut along the bank of the stream to take the shortcut to the manor house, but halfway there a sudden, terrible smell assaulted her nostrils, and she glanced around curiously.

It didn't take long to discover the source of the odor. She reeled to a halt, staring at a small clearing a few feet from the bank of the stream.

A body. Bertie's body, to be more precise.

Kate blinked hard, then blinked again, trying to rid herself of the awful vision. It was no use. Bertie was still there. Still horribly motionless.

He had been buried, but shoddily, and some animal had dug part of him up. His eyes were closed, and his bald pate glowed like a beacon in the dirt. And right in the center of his forehead was a black, gaping hole.

Kate's chest heaved. With a small cry, she spun round and fled.

She didn't stop running until she reached the main road leading to Kenilworth, and then her legs gave out. She sank to the muddy ground, clutching handfuls of her skirts in her hands, tears streaming down her cheeks.

Bertie was dead. Bertie had been murdered.

Much later, her tears dried but still battling the unsteadying sensations of grief and horror, Kate slipped into the servants' entrance. Night had descended over Debussey Manor.

She had mustered all her remaining control and used it to fortify herself. Now was not the time to crumble. Now was the time to be strong. If she wasn't strong, more people would be hurt. She was certain of it.

Her brother had killed Bertie—or, more likely, he'd ordered either John or Mr. Hayes to kill him. She was certain it was so. Further, Kate could think of no reason for Willy to wish Bertie dead save for a concern that the old man might interfere with his carefully laid plans. If Willy was willing to commit murder for so weak a reason, he certainly had far more vile plans for Garrett.

Catching her breath, she turned to walk down the corridor leading to the kitchen, but within a handful of steps, she stopped.

Voices came from inside the kitchen. Willy and Mama speaking in urgent tones. Reggie was probably with them, but as usual, he was silent.

On her guard, her skin prickling with something akin to fear, Kate crept closer. She couldn't decipher their words.

Her fingers closed around the door handle, and she shuddered as the coldness of the metal rushed through her. She uncurled her fingers and lowered her hand.

She couldn't face her brother or her mother right now. There was only one person she wanted to see. Whose embrace she wanted to bury herself within. Garrett would know what to do. With Garrett she would be safe.

Kate spun away from the door, and nearly tripping over her skirts, she sprinted downstairs. She skidded to a stop when John came into view. He sat tilted back in one of Lord Debussey's drawing room chairs. He'd placed the second chair across from him and had propped his muddy booted feet on the silk as if it were worthless.

He looked up, his pale lips twisting.

Pretending not to see him, she tramped past and drew the bolt to the dungeon. As she pulled open the door, John's hand closed over her shoulder.

Kate stiffened. The door swung wide, and Garrett glanced over the top of the book he'd been reading. When he saw John behind her, his gaze hardened. He set the book beside him on the cot and rose warily, chains clanking.

John's arm snaked around her middle. Kate twisted in an effort to free herself, but fingers dug into the side of her body, trapping her.

Garrett made a threatening sound low in his throat.

"What on earth are you doing?" she snapped at John. She grabbed his wrist and tried to yank his arm away from her body. "Release me, at once!"

"Not today, Kitty. I thought we might have a bit of fun,

you see. Just like you did with Mr. Longmire over there last night."

Panic flooded Kate, and she stared at Garrett, wide-eyed. "W-what are you talking about?"

John's breath puffed into her ear. "Ah, I think you know. I was here, listening. Watching. You spread your legs wide for him, now didn't you?"

Garrett's growl came to her ears as if from a distance. "Unhand her."

"Mr. Fisk promises it'll be my turn for a taste next."

"Let me go!" But fighting him was useless. The arm clamped around her was strong and thick as a tree trunk.

Suddenly, his eyes widened, and Kate realized his leg had brushed against the hard object in her pocket. "What's this?"

Kate squeezed her eyes shut as his hand burrowed into her apron and withdrew the saw. "Trying to free your lover, were you? Stupid chit."

He tossed it into the antechamber behind them, and it clattered onto the floor far out of Garrett's reach. And her own.

She'd been caught. He would tell Willy. Now Garrett would never be free.

John jerked her hands behind her, and before she could blink, rough twine bit into the flesh of her wrists. She twisted, strained every muscle in her arms to free herself from the looped rope, but he'd wrapped it too tightly. She couldn't move.

Garrett snarled something, but she couldn't decipher it. Metal scraped over the flagstones. He'd drawn the chain taut and strained against the bolt, but John was still out of his reach. Filled with foreboding, Kate glanced at

Garrett's face. Pale, drawn. Lips pulled tight and thinned in a grimace. Eyebrows snapped together, narrowed ice-cold eyes. Silver glimmered in his hand, and Kate whimpered. He held the pistol she'd given him.

John didn't see the weapon—he was focused on her alone. All of a sudden, he slammed her against the wall so hard the breath whooshed out of her lungs. She gasped for air, and spots appeared in her vision.

"Let...me...go..." Kate forced the words out as her tight lungs protested.

A hot puff of kipper-scented breath washed over her face as a sneering John loomed over her. Her stomach tossed like a paper boat in a gale.

Something flew through the air and connected to his skull with a thump. Garrett's book, Kate realized as it tumbled to the ground, its pages ruffling open. With a muttered curse, John turned, rubbing the back of his head, his forearm releasing some of the pressure on her chest.

"Get down, Kate!" Garrett bellowed.

Without thinking, Kate allowed her legs to collapse beneath her. She crumpled to the floor, sliding underneath John's grip.

The crack of a pistol overwhelmed her senses, reverberated inside her head.

Dimly, she realized John had collapsed beside her. And there was blood. It seeped over John's shirt, staining his sleeve a deep red.

Taking gasping, sobbing breaths, Kate crawled to her knees. She couldn't tear her eyes from John. His eyes fluttered, then rolled back into his skull, and he stilled.

"Kate!" she heard through the din in her head. Garrett. She turned, searching for him. "Kate, are you all right?"

She blinked and blinked again, trying to clear the haze in her vision. Garrett knelt, chain extended, moving something in his hands. The gun. His fingers fumbled with the powder horn as he worked to reload the weapon. She swung her gaze back to John. He didn't move.

"Did you kill him?" Her voice was a raw whisper.

"I don't know," Garrett said tersely. "I only grazed his shoulder, so it's not likely."

She stared down at the unconscious man, unable to summon any sympathy. She was glad Garrett had shot him.

Garrett's tone softened. "It's all right, Kate. Come to me, and I'll untie your hands."

She tried to force her body up, to go to him, but someone must've glued her to the floor because try as she might, she couldn't move. Had John really watched her and Garrett last night? Had Willy truly said John could take his turn with her? Still crouched on the floor, she began to shake.

"It's Willy," she whispered, staring at John's still form. "Willy is the snake."

"Kate—"

"Just like in the fable. We trusted him, and we opened our hearts and home to him, and he was the snake." She looked up at Garrett, frowning. "I wondered if it would be you, but it wasn't. It was Willy all along. Warren's death took his soul. If only I'd known, if only I'd seen it...I might have been able to stop it."

Garrett flicked a glance at the open door. "You must tell me who else is in the house."

"Willy," she responded automatically. "Mama. Reggie."

"Anyone else?"

She shook her head. "I don't know for certain. I don't think so."

"Damn it," he snapped. "We must hurry. Your brother is coming. I don't know if this is going to work. If it doesn't, you must run from here. You must hide from your brother. Promise me you'll do this."

"I promise," she whispered, staring at him.

Straightening, he aimed the pistol at the wall, where the bolt was attached to his chain, and fired.

The booming gunshot echoed in the small space, and clay, mortar, and dirt exploded in a cloud of dust by the wall.

Before Kate could tell whether the shot had freed Garrett, someone grabbed a handful of her hair, hauled her to her feet, and dragged her backward toward the door. Hard metal pressed against her face, making her teeth cut into the inside of her cheek, and she tasted blood.

She knew who had her from the sound of him, the feel of him, from the scent of lavender wafting from his clothes.

Willy.

Debussey Manor was a ramshackle pile of timber, and it had been a simple task for Becky to slip inside undetected. She'd just finished a surreptitious exploration of the ground floor when the first shot exploded through the house.

She paused, her foot poised to step forward, fear surging through her.

That could have been William shooting Garrett. Or he could have shot Kate. She swallowed hard. She might be too late.

Who cared if someone saw her now? All that mattered was her brother. And her sister-in-law, the only person who'd been truly kind to her since her marriage. Now Becky understood the sorrowful, lonely look in Kate's dark eyes—eyes so like William's, if only she'd paid attention. William had forced her to work as a servant for them, and he'd forced her to keep secrets. Becky didn't understand how Kate could have been involved with Garrett, but she knew that Kate didn't possess a cruel bone in her body. She was as much a victim of William's machinations as Becky and her brother were.

Kate or Garrett could already be dead, and Becky could be next. If William caught her here, he'd make her suffer.

But that hardly mattered—she already suffered. She would suffer more if either Garrett or Kate was hurt, if she failed to prevent William from hurting them.

Ruthlessly thrusting the paralyzing fear aside, she gathered her skirts and hurried back toward the side entrance she'd slipped through earlier. She passed it and jogged down a corridor that must be a servants' passageway, for it was dingy and barren of decoration. At a large, wooden doorway, she paused.

A child wept inside.

A woman's low, rich voice said, "Now, then, Reginald. Never fear. William is ever so strong and powerful. He will kill that bad man, and it'll all be over."

The crying child was Reginald, Kate and William's brother, whom Kate had spoken of with such affection. Becky's young brother-in-law.

Swallowing hard, Becky passed the door and continued down the corridor, nearly missing the narrow set of stairs leading down to the cellars. She was halfway down them when a second gunshot boomed from somewhere below.

She gripped the rail screwed into the wall, her knuckles white. *Not Garrett. Please, not my brother.*

She would not survive his death, not after all she'd done to him. It would be her fault. No different than if she'd pulled the trigger herself.

Following the sound of voices, she sprinted down the dim, gloomy passageway, turned into a wine cellar, and passed down the center row of sparsely populated wine racks toward a gaping, jagged hole cut from the opposite wall. A weak light shone from the hole, and the voices grew louder as she approached.

"I know that gun isn't loaded, but it'd be a wise choice to drop it regardless." *William.* Becky stopped in her tracks. "Unless you want my sister's face blown to hell," her husband continued in a conversational tone.

Surely he wouldn't do that. He was playacting. No one would shoot his own sister in the face.

"Willy," a woman choked, and behind the raw, fearful tone, Becky recognized Kate's voice. "W-what are you doing?"

Becky turned, looking for a weapon. Foolish girl that she was, she hadn't thought to bring one. What had she thought, that she'd just stroll in here, unlock Garrett, set him free, and be done with it? Why, oh why, hadn't she thought to bring something to defend herself—all of them—with?

"You needn't adopt that innocent tone with me, Katherine." William's voice dripped with venom. "I know everything. I know how you've betrayed me."

Why wasn't Garrett speaking? Was he injured? Already

dead? Becky drew in a sobbing breath and halted, trying to control her racing heart. If Garrett were already dead, who had William ordered to drop the gun?

William sighed. "Poor John. So eager for violence, but so utterly stupid about it, and altogether too enthusiastic."

This declaration was met by stark silence, and William continued. "It was a miracle I kept him alive as long as I did. I hope, at least, he was able to punish you a bit, Katherine, before you murdered him."

"I didn't—"

"Of course you did. How else could Mr. Longmire have acquired the gun? You gave it to him. You're responsible."

Becky scanned the room. Nothing but wine bottles, of course—what else would she expect in a wine cellar? Probably not the most effective weapon, but all she had at her disposal. Becky took one in each hand, her fingers curling over the dusty necks of the bottles.

"What do you want, Fisk?"

Garrett's hard, angry, *healthy* voice. Becky stumbled, nearly swooning with relief. She leaned against one of the supporting posts of a wine rack to steady herself.

"Have you been enjoying your elegant accommodations?" William asked.

Garrett didn't answer.

"Oh, come now. I heard you had a grand time with my slattern of a sister last night."

Becky trembled all over. She turned back to face the hole in the wall, gripping the slippery wine bottles tighter.

"I'll kill you," Garrett growled.

"Willy," Kate whispered. "Stop. You're... hurting me."

Becky tiptoed closer on rubbery legs. She'd never fought such paralyzing fear. But she must do this—she must protect her brother and Kate. If she had any hope of atoning for her sins, she had to save them.

"Isn't that the point? You must be punished for your treachery, Katherine."

Garrett said something in a low voice, but Becky couldn't decipher what it was.

"I had such hopes for you, hopes that you'd be true to me, to Mama and Warren, but you've betrayed us all. I should have known you would. I was a fool to give you the chance."

A hollow thump echoed through the small space, and Kate cried out. Becky flinched and bit back a gasp. William had struck his sister.

"God damn it," Garrett pushed out.

Becky's hands shook as she approached the last doorway—the only one with a working door, which was currently propped open. William was turned completely from Becky, so all she could see was the back of his jacket and the blunt cut of his dark hair. He had his arm around Kate, and she stood partly to his side, partly in front of him just inside the cell, her plain, muddy skirt a contrast to his clean, sharply tailored black trousers and maroon dinner jacket.

From the corner of her eye, Becky saw a metal object glinting in the corner of the small antechamber. At first glance she thought it was a dagger, but as she tiptoed closer, she realized it was a tiny saw. Not as useful as a dagger would be right now, but better than wine bottles, surely.

"Don't you see?" William's voice cracked with emotion.

"My own sister so quickly dismisses her blood ties. But Warren never would have. He would have stayed by my side till the end. He was the only one who was honest and loyal, the only one I could trust, count on, depend on. He was all I had. And now, no matter what I do, nothing will be enough. He'll never be by my side again."

Becky gently set one of the wine bottles in the corner and grasped the wooden handle of the saw. She had no idea who this Warren person was, and she didn't really care. All she cared about was helping Kate and Garrett.

A noise that sounded like a sob erupted from William's throat, and from the corner of her eye, Becky saw him twisting the barrel of the gun deeper into Kate's cheek. Kate groaned softly.

"Even this won't bring him back." William's voice brimmed with the agony of grief. "No matter what I do, he'll never come back to me. I will never be whole again."

Rising, clutching one of the bottles in one hand and the small saw in the other, Becky crept up behind her husband.

William was so intently focused on Kate and Garrett, he hadn't the faintest idea she was there, just behind him. Neither did Kate, for the gun barrel wedged against her cheek pushed her face away from Becky.

Slowly, Becky raised the bottle high, simultaneously aiming the saw blade at William's torso. Garrett's gaze flicked to her, then away quickly, as if he had seen her but didn't want to expose her presence.

William raised his thumb over the cock of the gun and pressed it down. A *click* resonated in the silence.

Becky held the bottle high... and hesitated. If she hit William over the head, would he shoot Kate?

No...not if she slammed the gun away. Not if she did this right.

With all the meager force she possessed, she brought the wine bottle crashing down atop the hand holding the gun. Simultaneously, she plunged the saw blade into the soft flesh at William's waist. Glass and burgundy liquid exploded over all three of them, and the gun flew out of William's hand. He careened forward, toward Garrett, his legs buckling, but he recovered quickly and spun around to face her.

His eyes widened as he recognized her, and his mouth dropped open in shock. But he didn't have a chance to react, for Garrett lunged at him, dragging him to the glass-splattered floor.

Kate collapsed weakly against the doorframe, gasping. Her eye was already swollen where William had hit her, and her cheek was red.

Becky still gripped the now-jagged neck of the wine bottle, but she'd released the saw, leaving it embedded in her husband's side. She tossed the bottle fragment away and turned to Kate. Only then did she realize there was another body in the small room—the motionless form of John, William's manservant.

The men rolled on the floor. The hollow sounds of groans and grunts, of fists connecting to flesh, the clank of chains, and the crunch of glass filled the sour, stale-smelling place.

Awkwardly maneuvering his bound hands, Garrett punched William in the face, using the shackles to his benefit. A sickening crack echoed through the room. William howled as blood spurted from his nose, and Garrett swayed back as William's flailing fists pummeled his torso.

"No," Kate whispered through chattering teeth as she watched them. "No, no."

William scrambled from beneath Garrett and leaped to his feet, making Garrett fall back, his head grazing the edge of the cot.

"Garrett!" Kate shouted. She lunged toward William's gun, which had skittered to a stop near the wall beneath the lantern. Garrett rolled in her direction.

Grimacing, William grabbed at the saw handle and yanked the blade from his side, releasing a yowl of pain as he did so. Blood gushed from his side. He swooped at Garrett, aiming the saw blade at his heart.

Garrett slid across the floor, forcing William to waste precious moments to adjust direction. Kate kicked the gun directly into Garrett's outstretched hands.

The silver barrel glittered as Garrett swung his arms up to aim at William.

Becky closed her eyes.

She'd loved William with all her heart. Loved him enough to walk away from her family, the only people who'd ever truly cared for her.

She'd been so wrong.

The hollow boom of the third gunshot was a balm to Becky's soul.

Chapter Ten

After Garrett pulled the trigger, the world seemed to slow and then stop moving altogether, as though everyone in the dungeon was mired in fast-drying plaster. And then, Kate lurched toward her brother. She sank beside him, her knees crunching on glass. Garrett winced. He was already bleeding in at least a half dozen places thanks to the shards from the broken wine bottle covering the floor.

Fisk still lived, he thought dispassionately, watching his enemy's lips move—but not for long. He'd shot him in the heart. His aim at Fisk was truer than his aim at the henchman who'd assaulted Kate had been.

Her wrists still bound behind her back, Kate leaned over her brother. Her eye was nearly swollen shut from his blow.

Garrett glanced toward the doorway where Rebecca stood, her legs braced, her hands clenched at her sides.

She met his eyes and gave a quick jerk of a nod, and Garrett's chest tightened. Rebecca had always been a delicate, bookish sort of girl. He'd never thought his young sister capable of the courage he'd just witnessed.

He crawled to Kate, trying to avoid the glass. Kneeling behind her, he untied the rough twine that bound her wrists. He clenched his teeth at the pink line of flesh encircling both her wrists as he peeled the twine away.

"I've been killed." Fisk coughed weakly, then groaned and took a shaky breath.

Kate took his hand and brought it to her lips. How she could do so after the way Fisk had treated her, Garrett would never fully understand.

"You'll see Warren, Willy. You'll finally be with our brother again."

"No." A single tear welled at the corner of Fisk's eye. "No, I won't see Warren. Ever."

Taking a stuttering breath, he closed his eyes, and the tear slid down the side of his face. Pink saliva bubbled from his mouth. Less than a minute later, he inhaled one final time. His breath slid out, and with it his life.

Still crouched beside Kate, Garrett took his pulse. Nothing. Dry-eyed, Kate bowed her head. Garrett couldn't look at her. God, he hated this.

Behind him, Rebecca began to cry. Squeezing Kate's shoulder, he rose and carefully walked to his sister, gritting his teeth at the sound of the chain scraping on the floor as he crossed the room. He'd have to search Fisk for the key—a task he did not relish. As he'd suspected, his shot hadn't completely freed the cemented bolt, so he stopped a few feet from the door, the chain pulled taut.

The last time he'd seen his sister she'd been convinced

he was insane, because Fisk had manipulated her along with just about everyone else into believing him a madman. She'd cringed away from him, terrified. As he stared into her tear-filled eyes, he saw the residue of that fear.

"Rebecca?"

With a sob, she launched herself at him and wrapped her arms around him, pressing his shackled hands between them.

He simply stood awkwardly, unsure what to say. Her body heaved as she buried her face against his chest and wept.

He glanced at Kate, who had turned to stare at them.

"You...know each other?"

Here it comes...

"She's my sister," Garrett explained in a low voice.

Kate shook her head. "No. No, that's not possible. That...that would make you the...the duke..." She swallowed, swinging her head back and forth in denial.

Clinging to his arm, Rebecca turned to face Kate, sniffing. "You knew, didn't you, Kate? This is my brother, Garrett...the Duke of Calton."

"No," Kate repeated. "That's...impossible."

He could see her stiffening, shutting down, slamming the remaining doors between them.

"Kate," he murmured. "It is all right."

She blinked at him once, stared at him blankly for another moment, then turned back to her brother.

Rebecca stepped back from him and withdrew a metal object from her jacket.

"I'll free you," she murmured. "Hold out your arms."

Struck speechless—she'd surprised him again—he obeyed. Her hands trembled, and it took her several moments to fit the key into the lock and turn it. Finally, the pressure on his wrists released as the clasp came open. He shook off the manacles and let them fall to the floor, and then he took the key from Rebecca and removed the clasp from his ankle, flinging it away when he was finally free.

He rose, rubbing his raw wrists. "Thank you, Rebecca."

"Please do not thank me." She gazed at Kate. "What happens now?"

He glanced first at Fisk and then at the henchman. Both bodies were still, but he didn't think Fisk's minion was dead. He had little inclination to check, however. If he found the devil alive, he'd be compelled to finish the job.

First and foremost, he must get the women out of here. Take them somewhere safe. "We will leave this place. We're going home."

Rebecca released a shuddering sigh.

He glanced at Kate. "Kate? Do you know where the rest of your family is?"

"Kitchen," she said in a small voice. She didn't look at him.

He'd never seen Fisk's mother, but he had visions of her marching into the dungeon like an Amazon, swords at her sides, guns raised in her hands. He knew nothing about the woman besides what little Kate had told him, but he must prepare for all contingencies. He crossed the room again, kneeling to retrieve the small pistol and the powder horn.

"What are you doing?" Kate asked dully.

"I'm taking you and Rebecca away from here."

Kate shook her head. "I can't leave."

"You must."

"No. I can't. I won't leave Reggie. Mama is going to be…" Her voice faded, and her shoulders shook with some repressed emotion.

Hell. He had forgotten about Kate's younger brother. Kate wouldn't leave the boy willingly. But there was no way Garrett would abandon her here. Not in this hellish place, not alone.

"Kate, we're leaving this place." His voice was hard, almost angry, and Rebecca shot him a quelling look. He clamped his lips shut.

He wouldn't let her out of his sight. The thought of leaving her at all made his gut clench into a lump of granite. She wasn't safe here. He clenched his fists. Damn it, he'd toss her over his shoulder and drag her to Calton House, if that was what it took. He'd chain her to the carriage…

Glass crunched under Rebecca's shoes as she crossed the room to kneel at Kate's side. She slipped an arm around her. "Come, Kate. We must go now."

Kate's slender throat moved as she swallowed and nodded. She rose on shaking legs and followed Rebecca to the door. Finished loading the weapon, Garrett pushed it into the waistband of his breeches and rose to follow them. At the door, he called them to a halt. "I'll go first."

She stepped aside, and he led the way through a wine cellar that led to a long corridor. He glanced back at Kate. "Which way?"

"To your left. The stairs are at the end of the corridor." She paused, and then spoke without intonation. "Once you reach the top of the stairs, the kitchen is two doors to the left."

He nodded and turned. He strode through the long passageway, alert for the approach of any more of Fisk's men. Finding none, he mounted the narrow stairs. He paused at the second doorway, listening.

He shook his head as Kate approached. "Nothing."

Kate brushed past him, wrapped her fingers around the door handle, took a deep breath, and opened the door.

"Katherine!" A woman with salt-and-pepper hair rose from a crouched position beside the fire. When she saw Garrett and Rebecca behind her daughter, she froze midstep. She stood there, mouth agape, glancing from Kate to Garrett to Rebecca, taking in Garrett's disheveled appearance and bare, bloodied feet, and his sister's silk primrose dress and smart, stylish matching spencer jacket. At least he'd had the presence of mind to hide the pistol beneath his shirt.

"I'm sorry," Mrs. Fisk said slowly. She looked back to Kate and cocked her head, clearly waiting for an explanation.

Kate's shoulders slumped. "Willy..."

"Ah, where is William?" She gestured at an armchair by the hearth. It wasn't facing the doorway, but Garrett could see part of a thin, pale arm. "Reginald and I have been waiting for him. He said he'd be back by now."

"Willy's dead, Mama," Kate whispered.

"No. No, he's not." Mrs. Fisk gave a determined shake of her head. "He just left a few minutes ago to take care of some unpleasant business. Why I was just telling Reginald what a brave soldier his brother was, wasn't I, Reginald?"

The boy remained silent.

"Mama, didn't you hear the gunshots?"

Mrs. Fisk's gaze whipped to Garrett and Rebecca. "Won't you introduce me to your friends, Katherine?"

"Mama—"

Releasing a harsh breath, Mrs. Fisk stepped toward them. "I'm so very sorry. My daughter is ever a disappointment. As much as I raised her to be a simple, God-fearing young lady, I fear she is merely a mannerless slattern. I am Mrs. Fisk, the housekeeper. And you are...?"

The dismissive way in which the woman addressed her daughter made Garrett too furious to speak. Beside him, Rebecca curtsied. "I'm Lady Rebecca," she murmured. "You are my mother-in-law, I believe. Pleasure to meet you, ma'am."

Mrs. Fisk's mouth opened and closed like a landed fish. "Lady Rebecca? But...but...how did you...?" She spun on Kate, giving her a murderous look. "Ah, surely Katherine's not telling tales again." She emitted a strange, strangled noise clearly meant to be a laugh. "But no, no...the foolish girl is always jesting, you see. I'm so sorry, my lady. We're from a different family of Fisks, of course. Not the same family as your esteemed husband."

"Mama, stop," Kate whispered. "It is too late for lies. Willy is dead, and they know everything."

The woman gave that painful-sounding laugh again. "William, dead? Of course he is not. You silly girl."

The child had turned and stared at them, his eyes dark and round in his pale face.

Rebecca stepped forward and gently placed her hand on Mrs. Fisk's forearm. Garrett tensed. He didn't know what the woman might do. Her reactions to this point had been odd, and the air around her seemed to crackle as though she were a stack of dry timber on the verge of exploding into flame.

"I'm sorry, ma'am." Tears welled in Rebecca's eyes again, but she blinked them back and motioned to Garrett. "This is my brother, the Duke of Calton."

Mrs. Fisk's eyes slid in his direction and then focused back on Rebecca. "That's simply impossible," she pronounced. "The Duke of Calton is safe at his residence in London."

Garrett coughed. "Forgive me, madam, but you are incorrect. I *am* the Duke of Calton."

Mrs. Fisk raised a disbelieving brow, no doubt because he appeared as different from a duke as a mongrel from a thoroughbred.

"Mama, Willy was shot...after...after he held a gun to my head," Kate whispered, a pleading quality to her voice that made Garrett's gut clench. "I...was at his side when he died. Didn't you hear?"

She hadn't cried when her brother died, but now tears streamed down Kate's face. Garrett stiffened further, resisting the nearly overwhelming compulsion to comfort her.

Shaking herself as a duck might shake water from its back, Mrs. Fisk turned and strode to the fire. "I was just stoking the fire for poor little Reginald. He's very easily chilled, you know."

"Mama..." Kate began helplessly.

Mrs. Fisk retrieved a poker, and just as she began to kneel, she seemed to change her mind. She spun back around to face Kate, who'd followed her a few steps into the room.

In the few seconds since she'd turned away from

them, Mrs. Fisk's face had changed, darkened. Her lips had thinned and her eyes had narrowed. "It was you, wasn't it? I knew you would tear us apart. I knew you would be the cause of our demise, you spiteful, wretched girl!"

"No, Mama," Kate gasped.

"Murderess!" Raising the poker, the woman lunged at Kate.

Garrett leaped forward, thrusting Kate out of the way. Dodging the weapon now aimed for his belly, he turned and grasped it, yanking it from the woman's grip. He tossed it aside, and it clattered to the floor as he grabbed her by the middle, for she was trying to lunge past him to get to her daughter.

"Calm down, Mrs. Fisk," he commanded. "She had naught to do with your son's death."

"Get out of here!" She lurched in his arms, looking past him to glare at Kate. "I knew you would be this family's downfall. I never want to see you again! You are none of mine!"

At that, Kate straightened. "No."

"No?" Mrs. Fisk repeated incredulously.

Angrily, Kate brushed a welling tear from her eye. "This isn't your house, Mama. You cannot command me to leave. I'm not going anywhere. I won't leave Reggie."

Again, Garrett glanced at the little boy. He seemed frozen in place, like a pale blond statue with wide eyes and a perfectly expressionless face.

"I want you out of my sight!" screamed Mrs. Fisk.

Clearly the woman was in shock. The sudden loss of her son had robbed her of her faculties of reason. He held her firmly in his arms. "Very well." He tried to keep his tone soothing despite the anger that swirled in him. "Your daughter will go away, but only if you allow her to take your son."

"No! William stays with me."

"William is dead, Mrs. Fisk."

Suddenly, she stopped fighting. She sagged in his arms. Tears streamed down her rounded cheeks. "I don't care what you do. Just don't take William. Please don't take him from me, Your Grace."

"We shall leave William's body, if that is what you wish."

"Go away." She pushed at him, then brushed past Rebecca as she stumbled from the room. "Go away, all of you. I must see to my darling William. My son."

They returned to Kenilworth on foot. Garrett had found his horse in the stables, and Reggie sat uneasily upon the creature, clutching the pommel for dear life as the rest of them walked beside the animal. Kate walked close to Reggie, prepared to catch him should he fall off.

Reggie had never sat on a horse before. Once upon a time, when Kate, Willy, and Warren were young, there had been a stable full of fine horses at Debussey Manor. Lord Debussey had even given the boys ponies of their own, and when they were thirteen, the twins took charge of the stables. But then Lord Debussey's wife had fallen ill, and the marquis, desperate for an heir, had taken Mama into his bed and stopped caring about everything but the conception of his heir. After Lady Debussey died, Reggie was born, too late to be passed off as Lord and Lady Debussey's legitimate son. Brokenhearted, Lord Debussey slowly declined. During the past five years, the entire span of Reggie's life, the stables had been abandoned.

Willy had ordered a stall cleaned out for Garrett's chestnut mare. She'd been well fed and seemed anxious for a nighttime ride. Kate had watched in silence as Garrett lifted Reggie onto the horse's back.

She should stop calling him "Garrett," even in her mind. He was the Duke of Calton. She should only think of him as "the duke" or "His Grace."

They passed the lane leading to Bertie's house. And Bertie... Kate swallowed a sob.

What would Willy's mistress do now? How long would it take before she discovered her protector no longer lived? Where would she go?

It didn't matter. It wasn't any of Kate's concern. The people who had composed her childhood universe were all gone. Lord and Lady Debussey and Bertie. Willy and Warren. Even Mama had gone someplace Kate could not reach.

Kate blinked hard and stiffened her spine. Not yet. She couldn't let go yet. She must stay strong for what remained of her broken family, for her baby brother. If she lost Reggie, she'd truly have nothing. She must keep her focus on Reggie and make the best decisions for him, for his health and happiness.

And at the moment, their well-being seemed inexorably linked to the people walking on the other side of the horse: the Duke of Calton and his sister, Lady Rebecca.

Kate had been raised in the house of a marquis, so she wasn't unfamiliar with the aristocracy. Granted, Lord Debussey was a reclusive man—some called him a hermit—but he was a peer of the realm, and he behaved the part.

Garrett didn't. He was so...earthy. Authentic. Open. Honest. Not tightly closed or as inflexible as Lord Debussey, and not like one of those pompous, preening, stuffy lords she imagined strutted through the streets of London.

He was Garrett, and she knew him as intimately as she knew herself. But he was also the Duke of Calton, and of him she knew nothing at all.

Lady Rebecca materialized beside her and captured Kate's callused hand in her soft, slender one.

"Thank you, Kate."

Kate stared at the lady. She spent several moments trying to gather a response from the shards that remained of her fractured sensibilities. "For... what? My lady."

"For being a friend to me. You knew you were my sister all along, but I only learned about it last night. I..." Lady Rebecca glanced at Garrett, who took long strides in his boots despite the glass cuts on his feet. They'd found the boots, along with Garrett's other personal items, in Lord Debussey's bedchamber—where Willy had evidently been sleeping when he wasn't with Lady Rebecca. Or his mistress.

Garrett murmured something encouraging to Reggie and reached up to adjust him in the saddle as Lady Rebecca continued. "I always dreamed about having a sister."

"Oh." Kate gave the lady a questioning look. She couldn't think what else to say.

"Please come with us to Calton House," Rebecca continued. "I..." She swallowed. "Please. I need you, Kate. Only you can understand."

Kate glanced at her, squinting through her blackened eye, then over the neck of the horse at Garrett—the *duke*. The Duke of Calton, who had killed her brother.

Hopeless misery filled her, and she shook her head. "I don't belong with you."

Once Garrett had said he was taking Reggie, she'd wanted nothing more than to leave Debussey Manor behind forever. If that made her selfish and slatternly, then so be it. Yet she couldn't comprehend what the duke and his sister would do with her and Reggie. She despised the notion of becoming dependent on either of them.

"But you do belong with us." Lady Rebecca squeezed her hand. "You are my sister by marriage, don't you see? You are family."

They'd finally settled into bed at the King's Arms Inn at Kenilworth long after midnight. Kate lay stiffly beside Lady Rebecca in the big, lush bed, and Reggie snored softly on a pallet by their feet. At first Kate thought the pallet was meant for both her and Reggie, but then Lady Rebecca had insisted Kate sleep with her.

Both women had lain awake and silent for hours, but finally Kate heard the lady's breaths deepen and turn even, and she knew her sister-in-law had fallen asleep.

Simply lying in such a soft, luxurious bed was enough to make Kate's eyes remain popped open the night long, but add to that all that had happened, all that had changed in the course of one day, and sleep was impossible.

Kate lay quietly, trying to sort out her tangled feelings and twisted emotions. Yet the more she attempted to calm her riotous thoughts, the more confused they became. The soft quilted counterpane turned heavy, the downy pillows puffed up around her ears, and her body sank deep into the mattress, stifling her. She couldn't stand it for another moment. She surged upright, but stilled as Lady Rebecca mumbled softly and turned over.

Carefully, she prodded her bruised eye. The innkeeper's wife had given her a cold cloth and a poultice, and the swelling had gone down. At least she could see again.

Kate slid out of bed, glancing at the crack in the curtain covering the room's single window. The barest grayish-pink blush of dawn tinted the sky, and since there was no use in trying to sleep, she pulled on her stays and petticoat. Then she took her dress from where it lay folded of the back of a chair and shook it out. She dropped it over her head and deftly reached back to tie the frayed ribbons at her waist and button the two large, saucerlike buttons above the ties.

Opening the door, she slipped from the room. In search of fresh air, she descended to the ground floor, down the corridor and past the unlit, shadowy front parlor.

When she swung open the inn's front door and stepped onto the landing, she nearly ran headlong into Garrett, who stood leaning against a wooden post supporting the awning, his back to her.

"Forgive me," she gasped, careening backward as he turned. "Er... Your Grace."

He reached out and clasped her shoulders to steady her. "Kate." He gave her a searching look in the dim early morning light. "You couldn't sleep?"

"No. Your Grace."

His expression betrayed a subtle flinch as she spoke, and he released her shoulders and dropped his hands to his sides. Kate couldn't help but admit to herself that when she'd said his title, the words contained an edge of venom. She truly hadn't meant them to come out that way, and yet...

"I'm so very sorry...about your brother," he murmured.

She swallowed hard. She didn't want to talk—or think—about Willy. Not right now. Not yet.

"Why didn't you tell me who you were?" she blurted.

Garrett shrugged and turned to lean against the pillar again, gazing out over the street. "Would it have changed anything?"

Of course it would have. If she'd known who he was, known that when he said they could have no future it was due to class and nothing more, she wouldn't have allowed intimacy between them. She would have kept herself aloof from the very beginning, and most important, she wouldn't have allowed herself to become enamored of him. She was no fool. When members of her class engaged in private interactions with the upper orders, nothing good could ever result.

Oblivious and ignorant, she'd almost become her mother, someone whose mistakes she'd counseled herself never to repeat. Kate had watched Mama through the years: the first giddy bloom of love when Lord Debussey had invited her into his bed, the growing dependence upon his continued affection, the disappointment of her son's bastardy, the misery of rejection after Lady Debussey's death, and the ultimate understanding that Lord Debussey had cared little for her beyond her potential ability to bear him a son he could pass off as his wife's.

Kate had lost all sense. With this man, all connection to everything she'd held sacred within herself had simply vanished into thin air. At least Kate's monthly flux had come late yesterday. Bringing a fatherless, illegitimate baby into this cruel world would have been the ultimate failure.

"Yes," she said after a long silence. "If I'd known who you were, it would have changed everything. I'm not a fool, you know. I know better than to become entangled with an aristocrat."

Garrett—*His Grace*—reached to touch her, but she stepped back. He gave her a sad smile. "I was selfish."

Standing at his side, she gazed out at the dark dirt street fronting the inn, the buildings on the other side shadowy and unlit. So quiet at this time of day. In a few hours the street would be bustling with early morning traffic.

She wanted to stay angry, but in truth, this was as much her fault as his.

"You tried to warn me," she finally said. "I chose not to listen."

"Forgive me, Kate."

"I would never have guessed," she said in a low voice. "Never in a thousand years."

He released a bitter laugh. "I know. I am not an ordinary duke."

"You are not," she agreed.

"I will always be different, a magnet for scandal."

"Why?"

"Waterloo," he stated flatly. "Your brother. And... the events that have occurred since I've returned to England. They changed me forever."

For the better? Kate wondered, but she was certain if she voiced the question, he would say no, rather for the worse. She could understand that. Surely before

Waterloo—and Willy—Garrett's eyes hadn't reflected the suffering they did now.

"There was more I didn't tell you," he said abruptly. "When I gave you the warning that I could offer you nothing, it was not due to the chasm between our social statuses."

She cut him a glance. "I know. You lied about being married. Lady Rebecca has mentioned her sister-in-law—your wife. Her name is Sophie."

A muscle twitched in his jaw. "I'm not married, Kate."

Tears pricked at her eyes. "It is no use lying to me anymore, Your Grace. If you truly intend to take me with you to Calton House, surely I'll learn the truth eventually."

She swallowed down the threatening tears and hardened her stare at the street. Across the way, the lines of the trees and buildings became more defined in the rising light of dawn as she waited for him to continue, braced herself for whatever he might say.

"I'm no longer married to Sophie. Our divorce was final last month."

His words seemed to echo into the dimness.

"Divorce?" she repeated stupidly.

"That is correct. Parliament has declared our marriage...terminated."

"Why?" she choked out. Garrett had already expressed his devotion to Sophie when he'd allowed Kate to think that she had died. Beyond sheer hatred, Kate couldn't imagine a single reason anyone would seek so final a separation as divorce.

"She...she loved. Someone else."

Kate turned to stare at him. His face was pale, his

expression stark in the dim light of predawn. How on earth could someone who possessed the love of this man possibly fall in love with someone else? Sophie must be the stupidest woman in the world.

"When I returned from Belgium, I found her right away. Thinking me dead, she'd married my cousin, Tristan. I tried to win her back through legal means, but"—he took a breath—"it wasn't to be. We'd been separated too long. She'd changed. I'd changed. I was trying to force something that could never be as it once was."

"But how could you have ended your marriage?" Kate whispered.

He leaned against the pole and looked out over the street. "I told the lawyers what was required and allowed them to manage most of it. In order to ensure Parliament would pass the divorce bill, my lawyer first brought an action of criminal conversation against Tristan." His lips twisted. "It was a farce. He was found guilty of 'misconduct' with my wife and ordered to pay a token amount in damages."

"Why was it a farce?" she asked.

His lip curled. "I was gone for over seven years. I was declared legally dead. How absurd to bring such action against someone whose intentions were so far removed from malice. Yet once I had returned to London and Sophie's marriage to Tristan was nullified..." He took a breath. "They'd lain together when Sophie was technically married to me. There were witnesses, and because Tristan made no effort to defend himself against the action, he lost."

"If you felt the crim.con. suit was wrong," Kate said quietly, "then why did you pursue it?"

"It was a necessary step in achieving what Sophie ultimately desired."

"What was that?"

"She wanted a divorce bill passed. She wanted a legal marriage to Tristan." Garrett still stared straight ahead. He hadn't looked at her in a long while. "Then I sued Sophie for separation on the grounds of adultery in the Consistory Court. Also a farce."

"For the same reasons?"

He nodded. "Yes. And the fact that the public and political tide had swayed to Tristan and Sophie's side. Theirs was a story of lost love, and the public wanted to see them joined again. The courts were eager to wash their hands of the matter, and then when I petitioned Parliament for a bill for divorce, they were equally eager to be done with it. They might have refuted it on the grounds of collusion between Sophie and me, but no one would testify with evidence of collusion." He shook his head. "The majority of men in the House of Lords are friends of Tristan. Once the bill was introduced, it took less than three weeks for it to pass, uncontested by Sophie. She remarried Tristan just before I left London."

Kate winced. Though he didn't say so, his ex-wife's eagerness to marry another had hurt him. His pain was written in the harsh lines of his face.

"It's all over now," she said quietly.

"Yes, it is."

"And here we are."

"Yes."

They stood quietly for several minutes, watching the sun's rays gain in strength and begin to burn through the thin cover of clouds. Finally, Garrett turned to her. "I won't leave you in Kenilworth alone. It's not safe here for you. Your mother…"

His voice trailed off, but she could guess what he was going to say. *Your mother blames you for Willy's death.* Or perhaps, *Your mother is as mad as a March hare.*

"It's too dangerous for you. I want you to come with me to Calton House, at least for a while. Until things calm down. I can guarantee your safety there. I understand that you might despise me for lying to you about my identity." His voice softened. "And for what happened with your brother."

"No." She paused, shaking her head. "No. I could never despise you. You never lied to me outright, you never promised me anything, and you offered me fair warning. As for Willy…"

He deserved the fate that befell him. She couldn't voice those words, though, because a part of her was certain God would smite her on the spot for saying such an awful thing about someone of her blood.

"I'm sorry, Kate," Garrett said in a low voice. "I'm so sorry for all of it."

She bowed her head. She was sorry, too.

Chapter Eleven

Kate sat across from Lady Rebecca in the carriage Garrett had hired to transport them to Calton House. They hadn't left Kenilworth for three full days, for there was much to do. While Kate and Lady Rebecca remained at the inn struggling with their emotions over what had happened, Garrett managed everything. He saw to Willy's debts, had Rebecca's personal items and books packed for travel, hired servants and a carriage to transport them to Yorkshire, informed Bertie's family of his death, arranged for the burials of Willy and Bertie, saw to Mama's welfare, engaged the services of a doctor to see to John, and sent constables to arrest both John and Mr. Hayes. He'd even ordered a new saw for the watchmaker, Mr. Gwynn.

When they left Kenilworth, the women rode with Reggie in the carriage and Garrett rode his horse alongside them. Lady Rebecca and Kate spent the whole of the first day hardly speaking beyond basic polite inquiries. Instead, they had sat stiffly, each lost in her own thoughts. The vast majority of their conversation had to do with ensuring Reggie's comfort, for the rattle of the carriage seemed to go directly to his lungs, and his cough had worsened.

On the afternoon of their second day of travel, Kate rested her chin in her hand as she watched the countryside go by in an endless scroll of deep greens and reds and golds of autumn. She could distinguish Garrett's horse's hoofbeats from those of the horses drawing the carriage, and the knowledge that he was close by comforted her.

She would never admit it to a soul, most especially not to Garrett himself—not now—but she felt safe with him near. His proximity made her heart stutter and her flesh turn warm. Last night at the posting inn, he'd slept in the room adjacent to theirs. After Lady Rebecca had fallen asleep, Kate flattened her hand on the wall and imagined him sleeping on the other side, his torso bare and glimmering bronze in the candlelight.

As much as Kate tried to think of other things, her mind kept wandering back to that night in the dungeon. To the hard, heavy feel of his body above hers. To the gentle way he'd touched her. He hadn't merely bedded her, he'd *loved* her.

She absolutely could not allow it to happen again. She told herself over and over that carnal relations between members of her class and members of his could never be simple. They were destined for heartbreak and misery. That knowledge, however, did nothing to stop her wicked cravings.

Across from her, Lady Rebecca took a deep breath. "I spoke with Garrett this morning. We spoke of you. Of your future with us."

Kate glanced down at Reggie, who dozed in her lap, then up at the lady.

"I told him how compassionate you were to me at Kenilworth." Lady Rebecca took a breath. "Kate, you are my sister now, in truth. I was married to your brother, and that raises you to a certain status in the world, do you understand?"

Kate turned to look back out the window. "It isn't necessary to attempt to mold me into a lady, truly. It would be impossible, in any case. My mother has informed me that I am to a lady as oil is to water."

"Yet she educated you."

"She tried."

"And Garrett told me at breakfast that your blood is not as common as your position might imply. That your mother was a lady in her own right before she eloped with your father. Your great-grandfather was a baronet. Your distant cousin is Sir Thornton Howell of Birmingham. Your brother is the son of a marquis."

"Reggie is illegitimate."

Lady Rebecca shrugged. "Still, a marquis's blood is nothing to sneer at. His illegitimacy should not relegate him to a life in service. Just as your mother's sins should not relegate you to such a life. If she'd married within her class, you'd be a lady, too."

"If she married within her class, I wouldn't exist." Kate winced at the bitterness in her words.

"Nevertheless," Lady Rebecca said quietly, "do you see what I am getting at?"

"Not really." Kate shrugged. "I'm sorry."

In truth, as much as she tried to wrap her mind around the future, it was ghostlike, elusive. How could she imagine living in close contact with Lady Rebecca and her duke brother? The duke who had killed her own brother. The duke whom she was madly, desperately besotted with.

Her world was Debussey Manor, with brief forays to Kenilworth, and, rarely, as far as Warwick. How could she comprehend a future in Yorkshire, a place so distant to her, it might as well be Ancient Greece? It might as well be Olympus.

It was hopeless. She shook her head again.

"He—I—both of us wish for you to be our guest at Calton House. As my sister."

The skin across Kate's chest tightened. Imagine, her, in her drab brown dress, a guest of a duke! The scandal and embarrassment it would cause Lady Rebecca and her family would be too much to endure.

Kate licked her lips. "Is this because His Grace feels guilty for what he has done? Does he believe he must compensate Reggie and me for the death of our brother?"

Lord knew she didn't want to be a charity case. Like it or not, though, she was one.

"No, I don't think so." Lady Rebecca paused, then amended her words. "Well, it might be part of it. He deeply regrets hurting you. But I also feel guilty. I hardly gave you a second glance, Kate. I didn't really see you for who you are."

"And now you do?" Again, the bitter words escaped from Kate before she had the sense to recall them.

"I..." Lady Rebecca broke off abruptly. "Well, I won't lie to you. In truth, I'm not certain. I should at the very least try to know you better."

So she *was* just a charity case to them. The duke acted on his guilt for killing her brother. Lady Rebecca acted on her guilt for treating Kate like a mere servant when she had an aristocratic bloodline and was a sister to her by marriage. And now they both thought to compensate her with attention not befitting someone of her status.

Still, Kate wasn't stupid. She had little alternative—there was nowhere else to turn. And she hesitated to allow pride to prevent her from learning what it was like to pretend to be a resident of a great house. Her and Reggie's bedchamber might have a window. Who would consciously reject the prospect of a room with a window? Perhaps someone who'd never lived without one, she thought.

"You are very kind, Lady Rebecca—"

"Becky. You must call me Becky."

"—but I still shouldn't like to bring scandal down upon you and His Grace. And certainly taking a mere maid and her illegitimate brother under your wing in such a way would create a feast of a scandal."

"Garrett has never been one to care about such things. Even less so now that he has returned from Belgium."

"And you?"

Becky's shoulders deflated subtly, a gesture nearly invisible to the naked eye. "I am only eighteen. Until this past summer, I lived a very sheltered life. I haven't faced much in terms of scandal." She shrugged. "But now, after my elopement, after *all* that has happened, I can't see bringing myself to care about what anyone should think of me. I'm already ruined."

"No," Kate breathed. "You were legitimately married. And now you are a legitimate—"

"—widow," Becky whispered.

Kate nodded.

"A widow at eighteen." Becky crossed her arms over her chest. "I never thought this was what my life would become. And now I return home in shame and disgrace. What a foolish girl I've been." She blinked hard, her jaw tightened, and for the first time, her expression reminded Kate of Garrett. "I shall hardly be touched by a scandal, Kate. I doubt there's anything—or anyone—who can touch me now."

"I don't wish to make this more difficult for you," Kate said.

"No, that is impossible." A wobbly smile crossed Becky's lips. "I feel stronger knowing you are near. That someone—another woman—understands."

"I do understand." Kate could feel Becky's despair and guilt as if it were her own. And in a way, it was her own. Her older brother was dead. The man she was trying desperately not to love had killed him.

Her motives were selfish—she wanted to escape from Mama, from Debussey Manor and the horrible things that had happened there. What shamed her and scared her most, however, was that she knew, deep in her heart, the foremost reason she came with Becky and her brother to Yorkshire was that she couldn't bring herself to say good-bye to Garrett. She came because she couldn't countenance any other choice.

"I shall be in mourning for the next year." Becky stared vacantly out at the tall brown weeds that wilted over the edges of the road. "I shall not be mourning inside. Does that make me evil, Kate?"

"I..." Kate's voice faltered. She'd wondered something similar about her own feelings for her brother. "I...don't think so."

Becky rubbed her forehead. "Four months ago I thought I'd perish if I were to live another day without him beside me. And now I know I shall never truly mourn him. I am fickle and immature. How can I be trusted with my own feelings?"

"Willy was a master of manipulation, and he forced you to love him before he showed his true colors."

"Did... did he manipulate you, too?"

"Yes, I... I think so." He had, Kate realized. He'd asked her to bring Garrett his meals and see to his comfort, suspecting all along that she would give herself to him, intending all along to use her as a tool for his vengeance.

"Kate?"

"Yes, my... Becky?"

"Are you and my brother... ?" She paused, cleared her throat, and tried again. "That is to say, did you and my brother... ?"

Kate tensed.

"I know he and Sophie divorced after William and I eloped, so I know he is free to... take lovers."

Kate pressed her lips together. Her face burned. She couldn't meet the younger woman's eyes.

Becky turned her gaze to Kate. "When I was a little girl, I hardly knew Garrett. Sophie was often at Calton House waiting for him to return from his military engagements. She was a combination of older sister and mother to me, for I never knew my own mother. She was a perfect example of a lady—so beautiful and elegant. But later, after Garrett was lost in the war, she suffered terribly. Tristan was always there for her. She has a bond with Tristan that she and Garrett never shared." Becky's gaze softened. "They have a true, pure love. She was right to choose him."

At that, Kate looked up. "But—"

Becky's lips twitched upward in a fleeting smile. "Garrett loved her, yes. But he'll be all right, I think."

"Does... does he still love her?"

"Oh, yes, I'm certain he does."

The certainty in Becky's tone hit Kate like a brick in her chest. Several moments passed as she battled the tears pricking at her eyes. The carriage sank into a muddy rut in the road then rattled as it came out, and she grasped the leather door handle to hold herself steady.

"I'm not one to give advice," Becky said in a low voice. "Lord knows, I cannot be trusted with my own actions."

Kate almost wished she could cover her ears like a child, because she had a feeling Becky was preparing to say something she didn't want to hear.

"I shouldn't like to see you hurt, Kate."

Too late, Kate thought miserably. She was a wanton fool to have fallen so hard and so fast. Garrett had warned her, and she had plunged into it headlong, as she always did. She was like her mother. No, she was worse, for she'd been the one to seduce Garrett while Lord Debussey had seduced Mama. He'd pretended to love her, and he'd even told her that once Lady Debussey was gone, he'd make Mama his wife. Now Kate knew he couldn't have done so, even if he wanted to. Mama was legally married already, to Kate's father, a man she couldn't even remember.

Becky speared Kate with eyes reflecting the soft purple fabrics that covered the carriage's seats and walls, making them appear violet. "I shouldn't like to see Garrett hurt, either."

The following afternoon, Kate sat stiffly on the squabs, her apprehension rising with every step the horses took, for they had made good time that day and expected to arrive at Calton House before dark. Even Becky, who Kate assumed would be excited to return to her grand home, grew quiet and pensive.

In the past days, Kate had accepted how Becky's attitude toward her had changed. Becky was terribly lonely and afraid, full of guilt for all the strife she had caused. Once she'd forged a bond with Kate, however fragile and unimportant, she'd latched on to her. To take the focus off the actions she'd taken with such poor judgment, she'd turned her attentions to Kate. Becky repeated over and over that Kate understood her. Kate and she would be great friends, she hoped. She couldn't wait to show her all the books in the library at Calton House.

Becky was determined to make Kate a lady, though she never admitted it outright after Kate had dismissed the notion. She spoke of visits to the dressmakers and milliners, of parties and other social gatherings. At Calton House, she said, they always had wonderful Christmas parties.

Kate just listened and nodded, and said the appropriate things when Becky expected them. She felt sorry for Becky in so many ways. She couldn't say no to all the things Becky proposed, because she didn't want to hurt her young sister-in-law.

Not to mention the fact that she'd always had a secret yearning to wear silk. A secret longing to dance a quadrille with a gentleman. And she had a mad, traitorous craving for Garrett to see her dressed in silk and to watch his reaction when he saw her dancing with a gentleman.

She was very bad, she knew, to have such desires. But she'd be stupid to fail to acknowledge them. Acknowledgment was the first step in eliminating a sin, wasn't it?

This wouldn't be easy—any of it. And, of course, there was Reggie, who wasn't faring well at all. His cough had continued to worsen, probably because she'd been a terrible sister and, in the flurry of all that had happened, had forgotten his prussic acid.

She glanced at Becky, who lay back on a pillow, her eyes closed. She didn't appear to be asleep, only resting. Then she looked over at Reggie, who sat beside Becky, his fingers toying idly with the fine lace on her cuff. He'd developed a little boy's infatuation with the lady. Fortunately Becky had taken a liking to Reggie as well and didn't seem to mind his fascination with her.

Reggie met Kate's eyes and gave her a smile. He was too pale, though, and his lips were tinged with blue. Lord, how she hated to see him this way. How would she keep him well now? She had no money to pay for a doctor. She didn't know anyone in Yorkshire besides Becky and Garrett, and she would hate to ask them for anything. But she'd have to. Reggie needed a doctor.

"Are you cold, Reg?"

He shook his head.

"Does your chest hurt?"

"A little." He turned to study the passing countryside out the window, a familiar evasive gesture.

Suddenly, the carriage rattled to a halt, and Becky straightened, opening her eyes. "What is it?"

"I don't know." Kate cocked her head, listening to the voices of Garrett and the coachmen as they spoke in low tones.

In a few seconds, Garrett himself pulled open her door. He leaned forward. "Would you mind if I joined you for the duration of our journey?"

Kate and Becky shared a glance. A sick fear had begun to rise in Kate in Garrett's presence—a fear that she would do or say something stupid and reveal herself for the besotted fool she was. And Becky had explained she never had felt entirely comfortable in her brother's company.

"Of course not," Becky murmured.

He gave them a poor semblance of a smile. "My leg is stiff. It's the cold. I thought it best to warm it—to build my strength before I appeared before the world in all my ducal glory."

Becky licked her lips, and Kate stared straight ahead. Neither acknowledged his sarcasm.

Oh, Lord, Garrett would be sitting beside her. Taking a deep, strengthening breath, Kate moved over to make room for him. He climbed into the carriage and shut the door, and the carriage lurched as the coachman urged the horses forward.

Dressed in buckskin riding breeches that clung to his thighs and a gray wool coat that did nothing to hide the broad width of his shoulders, he dominated the carriage's interior. He smelled of fresh air, grass, and that underlying almond essence that was uniquely his. The memory of his taste flooded her mouth, and she tried to swallow it away, to no avail. Though Kate scooted as far to the opposite side of the carriage as she could, his arm touched hers, and his thigh brushed her skirt. Both hard with muscle, both broad. The places he touched her erupted in gooseflesh.

"You make this carriage seem about a million times smaller," she murmured.

She couldn't meet his eyes in the ensuing pause, but the heat of embarrassment prickled over her chest.

Finally, he said, "It is only for a short while. We'll arrive at Calton House soon."

Becky braved a welcoming smile at him. "Do not think that you're invading our privacy. You are most welcome to join us, of course."

He inclined his head at his sister. "Thank you."

Kate squared her shoulders and sat stiffly. His voice did strange things to her insides, turned them all tingly and shuddery.

How on earth was she going to survive with this man—this *duke*—in the same house?

Then again, she'd surely perish if he wasn't near. His presence elicited an odd juxtaposition of soothing calm and agonizing agitation in her.

After another long pause, Garrett cleared his throat. "As soon as we arrive, I'll send word to London. I wish to have Miranda at Calton House through Christmas."

Becky patted Reggie's shoulder. "Oh, you'll adore Miranda, Reginald. She is the loveliest girl you can imagine. I'm certain you shall become bosom friends in no time at all."

Reggie chewed on his lower lip—a habit he had no doubt acquired from Kate—and he gave Becky a nervous look. "I've never had a bosom friend."

He'd scarcely seen children of his age at all, Kate

thought with no small measure of remorse. His illnesses had kept him secluded in the kitchens at Debussey Manor for most of his short life. He'd never ventured far outside the confines of the estate.

Still, could Reggie be expected to associate with the daughter of a duke? That pretty young lady Kate had seen in the tiny portrait? Kate was afraid to ask, but it seemed rather implausible.

"I know where you shall sleep," Becky declared. "In my old room right beside the nursery."

"Reggie sleeps with me," Kate said quietly.

Becky blinked at her. It was the first time that Kate had spoken with any authority to the lady. But there were certain things that must be made clear.

"Oh." Becky paused. "Of course." She glanced at Garrett, seeming to lose a bit of her earlier confidence. "I thought the Yellow Room would be perfect for Kate."

Garrett didn't answer for what seemed like an eternity. When he opened his mouth, Kate was sure he would banish her to the attic or the cellars with the other servants, where she belonged. So his response sucked the air from her lungs. "The Yellow Room is too small."

Becky seemed to contemplate this for a moment. "Yes, it is small, but—" She tapped her bottom lip with her index finger. "I wasn't anticipating Reginald's presence there with her."

Kate looked back and forth between the duke and the lady debating over the assignment of her bedchamber. What an odd conversation.

"The Ivory Room, then," Becky said. "It is much larger, and even better, it has an adjoining door to my bedchamber." Garrett nodded in agreement, and Becky turned to Kate. "I hope you will like it. I would have chosen it first, but you see, the Yellow Room is a corner room with beautiful windows and a most desirable prospect over the back gardens."

"I'm sure that whatever room you choose for us will be lovely," Kate murmured.

The pressure of Garrett's thigh on hers increased the slightest bit.

Reggie fortunately chose that moment to break into a paroxysm of coughing. Kate pulled him into her lap so he faced Garrett, cupped her hand, and rapped on his back as the doctor had taught her, to no avail. Becky—now familiar with Reggie's coughing fits—took some cold coffee from the bottle they'd brought into the carriage, poured it into a small cup, and handed it to him.

Still coughing, he gratefully took it from her and tossed it back. But just as he began to swallow, he broke into an even stronger cough and spewed the contents of his mouth all over Garrett's face.

"Oh!" Kate exclaimed. "I am so very sorry! Your Grace!"

Garrett took a handkerchief from his coat pocket and dabbed at his face. "It's nothing," he muttered, frowning.

Oh, Lord. *Strength*. Mortification heated Kate's cheeks, and she shifted Reggie in her lap so he no longer faced Garrett.

"Reggie couldn't help it," she said defensively over the sound of his continued coughing.

Garrett turned his narrow blue gaze to her. "I am aware of that. It just worries me that—"

Just then, one of the horses neighed, and the carriage lurched as the animals leaped forward, the sudden force pressing her back into her seat. Becky slid to Kate and Garrett's feet. Kate dimly registered the voice of the coachman shouting, trying to regain control of the horses.

The carriage swayed to one side as its left wheels crested a bump. Reggie and Kate slid on top of Garrett. He grunted but raised his arms to soften their fall. The horses slowed, but it was too late. The carriage righted itself but kept the momentum and swayed in the opposite direction. As if in slow motion, all four of them slid toward the window. Somehow—Kate didn't know how he accomplished it—Garrett prevented himself from crushing her and Reggie.

The body of the carriage slammed onto its side. The window beneath Kate's shoulder shattered. Instinctively, she curled her body round Reggie like a cocoon, protecting him from the impact as the jolt resonated painfully through her body.

The horses dragged the overturned carriage a few inches before they gave up and came to a straining halt. And then there was silence.

Chapter Twelve

Nobody moved or spoke. Kate squeezed her eyes shut, trying to remember how to breathe. And then sound erupted. Outside, the coachmen shouted and cursed.

"Damn it to hell," Garrett muttered, his words hardly distinguishable over Reggie's sudden, loud sobs.

Kate pried her eyes open to see Becky hunched on the door—now the floor—her bright blue skirts tangled with Kate's brown ones.

Becky moaned, and then she looked up at the ceiling—the opposite door—her face white. "Garrett . . . ?"

Still clutching her sobbing brother in her embrace, Kate forcibly turned her head to see Garrett hanging over her, Reggie, and Becky, somehow managing to keep his weight off them. He swung his legs down, looking for a foothold near Kate's head on the broken, muddy, window.

"Your Grace!" came a call from the outside. "Your Grace, is everyone all right in there?"

Still grasping the door handle overhead, Garrett hunched over her. "Kate?"

"I'm all right," she gasped. Using her hands, because she couldn't adjust her body to see him properly, she explored Reggie's small frame. He seemed unhurt, only terrified. His poor body shook like a leaf.

"Rebecca?"

Becky responded in a trembling voice. "I fell on my arm... It... hurts, but... just... please. I have to get out of here. Please get me out of here, Garrett."

Fumbling at the handle on the overhead door, Garrett assured the coachman that everyone was alive.

Garrett glanced down at them. "Close your eyes, all of you," he commanded. "And cover your heads. The glass on the door is cracked—it might break."

Becky found a woolen blanket they'd had on the seat, and using one arm, pulled it awkwardly over her face. Garrett quickly removed his coat and draped it over Reggie and Kate's exposed faces and arms. Kate held her shuddering little brother tightly, murmuring soothing words of comfort to him as Garrett levered the door open.

Kate winced when she heard the cracking sound of the glass. Seconds later, it exploded, raining down over Garrett's coat, and she flinched to think that he might've been cut by the razor-sharp shards.

Carefully, the coat was removed. "It's all right," Garrett said softly. Kate opened her eyes to Garrett's softened—and blessedly uninjured—face haloed by bright blue sky. Cold air washed over her face, and she released a breath of relief.

Voices came from outside the carriage, negotiating how best to help them out.

"Reginald first." Garrett reached for the boy, but Reggie clung to Kate, looking up at her with wide, dark eyes.

Gently, she pried him off. "Garrett's going to lift you out, Reg." She winced, realizing belatedly that she'd called the duke by his first name.

Garrett ignored her faux pas and held his arms out to Reggie. "Everything will be just fine. It's over now."

"No!" her brother cried. "I want Katie!"

"She'll come right after you," Garrett soothed. "I can't get to your sister until you're out, lad."

Becky whimpered, and Kate glanced down at her. Her face was pale as death, and Kate's heart gave an alarmed lurch.

"Go, Reg. I'll be with you soon, I promise." She thrust Reggie at Garrett, and he lifted the wailing boy into the arms waiting to deposit him on solid ground outside.

Garrett grasped Kate's hand, and she stumbled to a crouched position. Only then did she feel the warm wash of liquid over her shoulder.

A muscle leaped in Garrett's jaw. "You're cut."

"It's all right," she said, but she felt lightheaded all the same. She smiled at him gamely. "Doesn't hurt."

He inspected her as best as he could in the small space. "Will I hurt you if I lift you?"

"No."

He grasped her by the waist and hefted her. She ended up on the outside of the carriage in a crisp October breeze, where a small crowd of men, women, and children waited to help her down.

"Thank you," she murmured when her tattered shoes hit the mud. She glanced down the road and saw that they'd crashed as they'd approached a farmhouse. A cluster of cottages dotted the side of the road just beyond.

As soon as Reggie saw her, he ran to her side and, clinging to her skirts, promptly dissolved into a coughing fit. She patted him on the back, but the motion caused sharp pain to dart through her shoulder.

An older woman and an adolescent girl approached. The woman, who had a kindly round face and voluminous gray skirts to match her puffy silver hair, took over the task of pounding Reggie's back. The girl curtsied at her and glanced back at the carriage. "Are ye awright, miss?"

Kate recognized the girl's Yorkshire drawl. "Yes, thank you," she said. "But there's a lady inside..."

At that moment, a squeal came from inside the carriage, and Kate whipped her head round. "Oh!"

"No, Garrett!" cried Becky from inside.

He murmured something indecipherable in response, and Becky sobbed an equally indecipherable answer.

Moments later, she and Garrett emerged from the doorway. Becky clutched Garrett around the neck with one arm and looked even more pale-faced, if possible. "Careful of her arm," Garrett barked. "I believe it's broken."

Garrett and the crowd gently brought Becky down as she carefully guarded her right arm, which hung at an awkward angle.

"Why, it's Lady Rebecca," one of the younger girls gasped. The group clustered around Becky, murmuring at her and tending to her arm.

One of the men's eyes widened as he studied Garrett, his eyes lingering on the scar at his forehead, and then he drew off his hat and bowed. "Your Grace," he said. "We'd heard you was alive, but we'd heard nowt of when ye'd be back at Calton…" His voice trailed off, and he shifted his stance uncomfortably.

Garrett summoned a smile. "It is good to see you again. Smythe, isn't it?"

"Aye, sir."

The kind-faced woman drew Kate's attention away from the men. "Can ye walk to my house, lass? I've a mind to bandage that wound."

Kate glanced through the people gathered around Becky a few feet away and met the lady's panicked blue eyes. "I should stay with Lady Rebecca, I think…"

"Are ye the lady's maid, then?"

Becky glanced sharply in their direction, and Kate saw that someone had covered her shoulders with a blanket to fend off the cold. "No," she said coolly through pale, drawn lips. "This is my sister-in-law, Miss Fisk."

All eyes focused on Kate, and heat crept over her cheeks. She knew they wondered how on earth she could be Lady Rebecca's sister-in-law when it was so obvious from her attire and demeanor that she was a mere servant. No one dared to contradict Lady Rebecca, though, so everyone remained silent, staring at her.

Finally, the woman smiled kindly. "Forgive me, miss. I've crammed my foot straight into me mouth, now, haven't I?"

"Not at all," Kate reassured her. "There's nothing to forgive."

Still, no one had looked away from her, and her face felt as if someone had lit a torch to it.

Reggie hiccupped in her skirts, and she glanced down at him. "This is my brother, Reggie."

"The lad looks like 'e could use a bite. I've a meat pie

just out of the oven, and fresh milk." The woman turned to Garrett and curtsied. "Your Grace, might I take the ladies to our house? I'll endeavor to keep 'em comfortable till help arrives."

Garrett's icy eyes assessed the woman briefly, and he turned to Becky. "Rebecca?"

She nodded, her lips pressed tightly together and her eyes shining. Kate sensed it was all she could do to keep from moaning from the pain.

Garrett nodded. "Thank you, Mrs. Smythe."

A cold blast of wind whipped a strand of hair over Kate's mouth, and she brushed it impatiently away. She didn't want to go. She wanted to stay with Garrett, who was deep in conversation with Mr. Smythe and two younger men about the accident. But Mrs. Smythe and the girls herded her, Becky, and Reggie away.

Garrett was glad to see them go. Rebecca was in a great deal of pain, and the blood streaming from Kate's shoulder and staining her dress made him want to kill someone.

He watched the ladies until they disappeared into the Smythe house, and then he turned to the ruins of the carriage. The horses shifted restlessly, and wildness edged their eyes.

"Your Grace?"

Garrett turned to Franklin, the coachman he'd hired at Kenilworth. "What happened?"

"It was a snake, sir, in the center of the road." Sweat beaded over Franklin's forehead. "It rose up, and it hissed, sir, and the horses got spooked, and... I couldn't control them."

"Is it alive?"

"I don't know."

Garrett spun around and strode down the road. "How far?" he shot back over his shoulder.

"Not too far, sir." Franklin swallowed hard, hurrying to his side. The other two men—Smythe and a younger man, probably Smythe's son—followed.

As soon as he rounded a slight bend in the road, he saw the snake. Thick-bodied and long, it was silver with a black oval pattern running down its back. An adder. It lay dead, splayed over the packed dirt, flattened in its center. Garrett had seen one or two of them as a lad, though they were rare in this part of Yorkshire. Usually a fairly sedate animal, the adder could be deadly when provoked.

"We must have run over it," Franklin breathed beside him. "Forgive me, sir. I tried best I could, but the horses—"

"It isn't your fault," Garrett said wearily.

"*Willy is the snake*." How true Kate's words had been. William Fisk, outwardly docile and friendly, but underneath the placid façade, poised to strike. To kill.

"Dispatch a message to Calton House," Garrett said. "Tell them to send a fast carriage and call a doctor for Lady Rebecca. I want to be home as soon as possible."

The carriage bearing an ornate gold ducal crest and several men on horses arrived just before twilight. Garrett entered the Smythe cottage, his lip curling at the sight of Kate, but he didn't say a word.

Kate wondered if he was angry at her for something or whether he was simply upset by her injury—apparent from her bloodied dress and bandaged shoulder. She tried not to think too much about it—instead she gripped Reggie's hand as Garrett led her outside and handed her into the carriage before returning to the cottage to fetch Becky. He wrapped her in blankets and carried her into the small compartment, somehow managing to climb in while bearing Becky's bulky weight in his arms and make the exercise appear completely effortless. His cheeks were flushed from the wind, a shadow of a beard brushed over his jaw, but his lips were tight with strain. He was tense, his body taut, and he looked as if he'd rather be anywhere but here with her and Becky.

They rode in silence in the gathering dusk the remaining distance to Calton House. Becky dozed fitfully for the duration of the journey. By the time they arrived, the temperature outside had fallen below freezing, and though Mrs. Smythe had provided them with several blankets, in pure self-preservation, the four of them huddled together to share body heat.

If they were cold, Kate thought, she ought to be happy she wasn't outside on the servants' bench, the seat she'd always been relegated to on the Debussey carriages before Lord Debussey had sold them. She'd be an icicle. Surely the coachmen and the others riding outside must be nearly frozen solid.

They took a sharp turn, and Garrett shook Becky gently. "Rebecca? We're almost home."

Her eyes fluttered, and in the near blackness, Kate saw her struggle to rise to a seated position, flinching as a blanket brushed her broken arm. Mrs. Smythe had expertly bound it in a sling earlier, saying she'd raised four boys and had seen more than her share of broken limbs, but Becky's pain didn't seem to have diminished much at all, and her elbow had swollen enough to resemble a melon.

The carriage rumbled to a halt, and Kate glanced out the window. From her side of the vehicle, she could only see a vast lawn stretching from the curving drive. In the far distance, a dark line of trees marked the edge of the expanse of mowed greenery.

Garrett sucked in a breath, and she turned to him. Beyond him and through the window, she saw part of a façade and wide stairs, blazing white from the glow of a long row of tall lanterns.

"I haven't been home..." Garrett's voice dwindled.

"In eight years," Becky finished for him in a quiet voice. "You'll find it much as you left it."

Still staring, Garrett nodded, and then someone opened the door.

A very proper-looking liveried footman helped Kate out of the carriage, and as the others followed, Kate gazed at the house in awe. It was a vast, modern, beautiful building. In its day, Debussey Manor had been beautiful, too, but this house was simply lovely. A sparkling gem. A veritable palace. A house fit for a duke of the realm.

Towering Ionic columns flanked the wide staircase that led up to the largest front door Kate had ever seen. At the top, a small crowd of people assembled. Kate recognized more liveried servants and maids in mobcaps and aprons. One lady stood apart from the rest. She was an older woman, round in shape, dressed in a hooded, fur-lined cloak. She studied the carriage with narrowed eyes reminiscent of Garrett's.

From somewhere behind her, Becky whispered, "Aunt Bertrice. Did you know she was here, Garrett?"

"No, I did not," Garrett replied in a low voice.

This sparkling, daunting place was nothing like the comfortable home she knew. Kate swallowed back the childish words rising through her chest. *I don't belong here. I want to go home!* Raising her chin, she stilled the fearful tremors in her shoulders and waited for the others to alight. She couldn't embarrass Becky or Garrett. Not after all they'd done for her.

Reggie took her hand, and Garrett stepped to Reggie's side, looking as discomfited as Kate felt. Becky stopped at her other side and grasped Kate's hand with her good one. Kate cast Becky a surprised glance. The lady had been mired so deep in her personal pain and confusion for the past days that Kate hadn't thought her capable of detecting anyone else's anxiety.

"Don't worry about Aunt Bertrice, Kate," she murmured. "She's rather blunt, but she's soft as a pillow under that hard shell."

Side by side, the four of them mounted the stairs leading up to the landing where the servants and the lady waited. Sudden, unexpected power surged through Kate. With Reggie and Becky and Garrett flanking her, she felt indomitable.

Garrett's presence was the key. The powerful glue linking them and piecing together Kate's fractured sense of self-worth.

Becky's hand tightened over hers as they mounted the final step, and Kate glanced at her. The lady had carefully composed her features to rigidity, and she stared at the old woman who must be Aunt Bertrice as they stepped forward.

The woman spared a shrewd glance at Kate and Reggie and then dismissed them before turning to Becky.

"Rebecca..." Aunt Bertrice reached out to grasp Becky's hands, but finding them unavailable, she dropped her arms. "Thank God you have finally come home."

Becky burst into tears.

Garrett sat beside Rebecca in the salon staring at the round bald spot on Dr. Barnard's head as he bent over her arm. The doctor had cut off Rebecca's sleeve, and now the frayed blue silk dangled from her shoulder. Dr. Barnard looked up at her. His bushy gray eyebrows drew together, and his hook-shaped nose puckered at its tip.

"How would you rate the pain, my lady?"

"It is the worst I've ever felt," Rebecca said tonelessly.

"I see." Dr. Barnard turned to Garrett, his frown causing deep lines to bracket his mouth. "Your Grace, it is a very serious break. I must set the arm at the proper angle and wait for the swelling to go down before I apply a splint. The arm shouldn't be moved for several weeks. Even then, I doubt the lady shall ever have a full range of motion. Furthermore..." He paused, glancing from Garrett to Rebecca and back again. "It is likely to be somewhat... disfigured."

Rebecca took this news with stoic calm. Aunt Bertrice let out a hissing breath from behind Garrett's shoulder. Kate, who'd joined them after putting Reginald to bed in the Ivory Room, twisted her hands in her lap.

At least we're alive. It was a mantra Garrett had repeated to himself often over the years. The first time was when he was a small boy. His father had beaten him for bloodying his clothes after Garrett had fallen, struck his head on a rock, and lost consciousness. He'd opened his eyes to a sobbing six-year-old Tristan, who was certain Garrett had perished in the fall. Later, with every stroke of his father's switch on his backside, Garrett had inwardly chanted, *At least I'm alive.*

Even in those blurry, pain-filled days just after Waterloo, he'd forgotten everything else, but he'd remembered those words. *I can't remember who I am*, he'd whispered to himself as he'd stared up at the foreign strangers who'd cared for him during the ordeal, *but at least I'm alive.*

They could have all been killed in the carriage accident. It was a miracle no one had been more seriously injured. Garrett rose and walked to the window. Taking hold of the thick gold edging, he parted the blue-and-green-striped curtain and gazed outside. The salon looked over the vast lawn extending from the curved driveway to Calton House out to the main road. Light spilled from the row of lamps lining the front of the house over the silvery frozen grass. All appeared peaceful and sedate. There was no movement out there, no evil. No snakes. They were home, and it was safe.

Satisfied, he dropped the curtain and turned back to the occupants of the room, all waiting with bated breath for his response. "Do your best, doctor."

Rebecca closed her eyes.

"I shall require a burly man or two to hold her down."

Garrett nodded and motioned to the footman standing at the door, his livery blending with the blue-and-ivory wallpaper. The man immediately slipped away.

Dr. Barnard glanced pointedly at Kate and then at Aunt Bertrice. Aunt Bertrice glowered, but Kate stared at the floor, looking stiff and fearful. Something panged in Garrett's chest. Dr. Barnard cleared his throat. "Perhaps those with, ah, more fragile temperaments should exit the room until we are finished."

Aunt Bertrice spoke for the first time. "I shall certainly remain," she huffed. "Furthermore, I shan't permit any soul to accuse me of having a fragile temperament."

The doctor inclined his head. "Of course, my lady. I wouldn't dream of it. But please, be forewarned..."

"I shall scream," Rebecca put in blandly, her eyes still shut. "Loudly. I'm certain of it."

In fact, she looked on the verge of a scream already. She pressed her lips together so tightly they paled.

"I suspect your screaming won't have the power to send me into a fit of the vapors, Rebecca." Garrett's aunt paused. "The only thing capable of sending me into such a state, I daresay, is learning you eloped in the middle of the night with a..." She cut a sharp glance at Kate, to whom she'd been introduced earlier. Kate continued to stare at the floor.

"I am a stupid girl," Rebecca said, her voice tight. "Trust me, aunt. I shall never elope again. At any time of day."

"Then I will retain no fear of vapors for the remainder of my time on this earth," Aunt Bertrice said dryly.

Giving up on Garrett's aunt, Dr. Barnard glanced at Kate. "Miss?"

Kate chewed on her lip, and Garrett looked away as carnal images slammed through him. She chewed on her lip whenever she was worried or nervous. It was a habit he'd associated with her. With touching her. Kissing her. Bedding her.

God, had he ever wanted anyone so much? He'd craved particular women before—Sophie, who'd offered him comfort; Joelle, his lover in Belgium, who'd offered him release. But Kate...she was different from both of them. Everything about her drew him. Powerfully.

"May I stay?"

Garrett pushed away his thoughts. He couldn't think like this about Kate. What they'd had—as sweet and honest as it was—was over. It had to be. Hell, he'd killed her brother.

"Please," Rebecca whispered. "Please allow her to stay with me, doctor."

Dr. Barnard sighed. "Very well."

A knock on the door heralded two stout groomsmen. The doctor directed Rebecca to lie on the crimson velvet chaise longue, her injured arm aligned with its corded edge.

"Do you require anything else, doctor?" Aunt Bertrice asked.

The doctor, who was rolling up his sleeves, shook his head. "No, ma'am." He flexed his fingers, cracking the joints, and then held out his oversized, long-fingered hands for them all to see. "I've everything I require."

Kate stepped behind the chaise and took Rebecca's good hand in her own, squeezing tightly. Rebecca gave her a ghostly smile.

Dr. Barnard situated one of the men at Rebecca's feet and the other at her head with instructions to hold her upper arm at the shoulder. Garrett stood beside Kate, and Aunt Bertrice stood beside him, but Rebecca kept her eyes on Kate.

Very gently, the doctor took Rebecca's elbow in his

hands. And then, almost before anyone could react, he twisted her arm brutally.

As promised, Rebecca screamed. Her legs flailed, her body bucked. Just as the shrill sound began to die down, the doctor twisted again.

"No!" Rebecca screamed. "No! No, no, no!" She whipped her head back and forth as the doctor manipulated her arm once again. Dr. Barnard ignored her movements, her choking sobs, her begging, but Kate murmured soothing words to her, keeping her grip on Rebecca's hand. Rebecca clutched her like a lifeline.

"Shh," Kate crooned. "Only a bit more. Right, doctor? Only a bit more..."

"That's right," Dr. Barnard said impatiently.

"Oh, please stop," Rebecca groaned, her eyes bright and round.

Focused intently on her arm, the doctor twisted, pulled, and prodded until he was satisfied. And then, directing the men to continue holding her, he slipped on Mrs. Smythe's sling. Finally, he said, "There, it is done. You may release her."

Instantly, Garrett's sister curled into a shuddering ball on the chaise longue. Kate walked around to kneel beside her, stroking away the hair clinging to her damp cheeks. Aunt Bertrice crossed her arms over her bosom and scowled at everyone.

The doctor drew Garrett aside. "I've set the break as best I could, Your Grace, and I shall be back daily to check on it. However, I do fear for her freedom of movement in the future. And her elbow—"

"I won't discuss fears with you." Garrett said. "We

will face each problem as it arises. What can we do to ensure it heals as quickly and thoroughly as possible?"

"Keep it utterly immobile. First and foremost, the fracture must heal." He glanced over at the still-sobbing Rebecca. "She will be in a great deal of pain, Your Grace. I will give you something to calm her."

Garrett glanced at Kate, who still whispered softly to Rebecca. Her offer of comfort appeared effective, because Rebecca's sobs diminished to whimpers. Kate had a way of calming people. He thought of her brother, who struggled for every breath. Garrett had wondered at first why Kate had said Reginald needed her. Now he knew. The boy likely wouldn't have survived without her comforting touch and soothing voice.

Feeling his gaze on her, Kate glanced at him. She looked away quickly, returning her focus to Rebecca, but not before he saw the flush bloom over her cheek.

Could anything be done about the little boy's health? Garrett cast an appraising glance at Dr. Barnard. "Before you go, doctor, there is someone else I'd like you to see."

Chapter Thirteen

Garrett roamed the corridors at Calton House. It was late—almost three in the morning—but he couldn't sleep here. After the sleepless, nightmare-filled months Garrett had spent in London after his return from Belgium, living outdoors in the countryside had soothed him. Now he'd been back in a house for a week—his own house—and he couldn't sleep at all. Instead, he prowled the corridors nightly, remembering.

Garrett mounted the grand staircase, taking the steps two at a time, glancing up at the ceiling as he went. Plaster rosettes trimmed the white molding, and the ceiling was painted forest green, with a nude, pink-cheeked cupid aiming his arrow at whomever might dare to ascend the stairs.

It was one of the few changes to the house since he had last left it. For the most part, it was very much as he remembered. After nearly eight years of memory loss, coming home sparked a flood of recollections. He remembered his childhood in great detail now, especially the years after Tristan's parents had died from a fever and he'd come to live with them. Garrett had been eight years old; his cousin Tristan was five.

The most memorable events from his youth had taken place at this house. After his mother's death giving birth to a stillborn girl, Garrett had withdrawn into himself, become a somber, serious child. His father had never been one to offer familial affection. Aunt Bertrice had come to live with them, but she wasn't maternal by nature, and she hadn't any idea how to manage the scowling, brooding boy he'd become.

Garrett stepped onto the landing at the top of the stairs. So much life had been lived in this quiet house, in these dark passages. So many memories for him to mull over.

When Tristan had arrived, equally damaged by his own parents' deaths, something had sparked between the two boys. That spark had brought life back into the house, and Garrett and Tristan had clung to each other for the love and support they couldn't obtain from any adult.

And then they'd met Sophie. First they saw her only on Sundays at church, and then Aunt Bertrice had befriended her mother and they began to see her more often. She lived two miles away, and her parents were a loving pair who allowed their only child free rein to run wild with the older Tristan and Garrett. No doubt her parents hoped she'd eventually marry one of them. They probably hadn't predicted she'd marry them both, Garrett thought wryly.

As children, Garrett, Tristan, and Sophie spent many pleasant days at Calton House in the spring and summer months when Garrett's father and Aunt Bertrice were away in London. The three of them explored every dark corner, wreaking havoc on the estate, with no one but the servants to try to stop them.

Garrett slowed as he passed the door to Rebecca's room. His half-sister was born much later, when he was ending his time at Eton, and their age difference and the distance between them had prevented them from becoming close. Yet, for some reason, she possessed a strong sisterly affection for him—she'd proven it that night at Debussey Manor.

He blamed himself for her suffering. She'd been so young, so naïve, and he'd been ignorant, too focused on himself and Sophie to ascertain her well-being.

He had so much to make up for. He intended to keep her close, shelter her, care for her for as long as she needed him.

The door to the Ivory Room stood just down the corridor from his sister's room. Kate was in there, asleep. He stopped there and pressed his palm against the painted wood planks. All was silent inside.

Kate. Something in his chest surged toward her.

She'd changed in the past few days. Withdrawn even further. She'd become unreadable—polite but closed, like the servants who had continually discomfited him since his return from Belgium. So unlike how she'd been at the pool, when she'd speculated he'd come from Olympus.

He missed her.

Yet she was right to shun him. There were too many forces working to push them apart, and he still had nothing to offer her.

He lied to himself. He did have something to offer her: himself. He didn't give a damn that he was a duke and she was a housekeeper's daughter. She clearly did, however. By her aloofness, she made it clear that the difference in their social statuses was a chasm too deep for her to cross.

Somehow, he needed to build a bridge to help her cross that gulf. He hated being separated from her. These days with her so close yet so distant drained something from him, the part of him she'd brought to life at Kenilworth. He wanted it back.

Just then, the door behind him opened. He jumped back from Kate's door as if it had burned him and looked up guiltily to see his sister, dressed only in nightclothes that had been altered to account for her splint. No doubt a robe would have been too cumbersome to pull on over her broken arm, which she held guardedly against her body.

Rebecca had survived the past several days in a haze of pain and laudanum, but her arm was mending. Since the doctor had splinted it four days ago, she'd improved rapidly.

"Garrett?" She paused at her threshold, her dark brows raised.

"I couldn't sleep," he explained in a low voice so as not to wake Kate and Reginald.

He held his ground, resisting the urge to turn on his heel and stride down the corridor. But that would be running away, and his sister might require something.

"I couldn't sleep either," she said.

"Can I get you something? Are you in pain? Why didn't you call for your maid?"

"I just...I prefer to be alone. I thought I'd go to the library." She gave him a small smile. "I finished my book, you see, and I need another. My schedule is awry," she explained uncomfortably, her gaze skittering away. "I sleep all day and read all night."

"Perhaps it is the laudanum."

She looked thoughtful. "Or perhaps I'm finding it rather difficult to adjust." She met his eyes. "To being home... and alone again."

"Of course. I understand."

"In any case, it hurts worse during the day," she said, motioning to her arm. "I feel I require the laudanum more then."

She did seem cogent, and her eyes had cleared—they were no longer glazed with the silvery pain he'd seen so often in the last few days. "Are you certain you're well?"

She nodded.

"I will leave you, then. You know where you can find me if you require anything."

She slid a glance at Kate's door.

"In my bedchamber," he said pointedly.

Rebecca looked back at him, her expression innocent. "Of course, Garrett. In your bedchamber. Alone."

"They're coming, Your Grace."

Garrett surged to his feet, his heart pounding. His daughter was here. He hadn't seen her in two months. "How far?"

"They're coming down the drive as we speak, sir," the footman said.

Garrett strode past the footman and walked through the expansive entry hall with its gilded frescoes and spare Oriental furnishings. He pushed open the heavy front door just as the carriage came to a halt before the steps.

He took them two at a time, and when he reached the bottom, the carriage door flew open, and his daughter flung herself into his arms.

"Papa!"

He kissed the top of her blond head. "Miranda, my darling."

She squeezed him tight. "I missed you so, Papa." She looked up at him with rounded blue eyes. "The journey was quite wretched, for it rained every day, but today the sun is shining because the world is happy, and now so am I."

"I am happy, too," he said. "Very happy." As always in his daughter's presence, a sort of bemused peace flooded through him. He was glad Sophie had agreed that she stay with him for the next few months. Sophie herself would be arriving, along with Tristan, when the Christmas season drew near.

A footman handed a maid and Miss Dalworthy, Miranda's governess, from the carriage, and both women curtsied in his direction, murmuring, "Your Grace."

A blast of cold wind ruffled his hair, and Miranda shivered. Garrett took hold of her hand and led her up the stairs, eager to introduce her to their guests. He had no doubt that his daughter would be as healing to young Reginald as she was to himself.

"Come inside, Miranda," he said. "There is someone I want you to meet."

The door to Becky's bedchamber opened, and Kate looked up, expecting to see Reggie returning from the nursery with a new book to read. But it wasn't Reggie at all. It was Lady Bertrice.

Kate stiffened. Pages ruffled as Becky closed her book, Thomas Paine's *Rights of Man*, from which she'd been reading a passage to Kate, and set it aside.

Becky had reassured Kate that Lady Bertrice presented the same brusque demeanor to everyone, but even after several days, Kate still felt singled out by the lady's frigid gaze. Worse, perhaps, it seemed the woman could unearth all Kate's secrets with nothing but the shrewdness of her blue stare. She turned that stare upon Kate as Kate rose from the pink armchair. The green fabric of her borrowed dress swished with the movement, and she self-consciously smoothed the skirts.

She'd worn the dress every day, for though it was far too wide around the middle, it was the only garment to be found that could fit her with any semblance of decency. The blood from the cut in her shoulder had ruined her old brown dress. Becky had wanted to lend Kate one of her own, but Becky was half a foot shorter than Kate, and far too slight. Kate was thankful that one of the chambermaids possessed a dress that fit her without rising halfway up her shins.

She dipped a curtsy. "Good afternoon, Lady Bertrice."

The older woman inclined her head and then turned to Becky. "How is your pain, Rebecca?"

"Better." Becky glanced down at her splinted arm supported by several puffy pillows. "The doctor says I may walk downstairs to dinner tonight, so long as I guard my arm carefully."

"Excellent." Lady Bertrice made a grand gesture at a heavy wooden armchair upholstered in pink velvet with white bobs dangling from its fringes. The maid who'd trailed behind her as she entered hastened to drag it to

Becky's bed. But the chair was far too big and the girl far too small, and when she tugged at it, the chair hardly budged.

Kate caught herself gnawing on her lower lip, and she pressed her lips together. How was this meant to work? The girl needed help, but certainly Lady Bertrice wouldn't help her. Even if she wasn't injured, Becky wouldn't help her. Which left Kate, who truly should help her. Yet Becky would think it beneath her to move a chair, and Lady Bertrice would no doubt find it a reason to increase her scorn toward Kate.

She released a breath. The girl needed someone to assist her, and Kate would not sit here and dispassionately watch her grow more embarrassed by the second. It was sheer rudeness—cruelty, even—to do anything but offer help.

Kate rose, and feeling the blue gazes of Becky and Aunt Bertrice on her back, she strode across the room. "Here, I will help you."

"Thank you, miss," the girl murmured. Together, they managed to get the chair—which must surely have been built of solid iron—to an acceptable position adjacent to Becky's bed. But the room was warm—as ordered by the doctor—and the activity combined with the warmth and her unease caused beads of sweat to break out across her forehead. Kate tried to surreptitiously wipe them away with the back of her hand, but when she looked up, she saw Lady Bertrice's cool gaze on her.

The girl disappeared, and with a swish of her voluminous skirts, Lady Bertrice settled her plump body into the armchair.

Silently, Kate walked around the bed, gathered her

knitting, and resumed her seat on the opposite side. She knew what they were thinking. That it was odd, even unacceptable, for her to assist the maid in such a manner. And that it was vulgar that she had broken out in a sweat while doing it.

Well, she'd told Becky it was no use to try to form her into a lady. Perhaps Becky would finally begin to believe her.

Sudden, unwelcome emotion surged in her throat and pricked at her eyes. If only she could succeed, if only she could be that lady. For Mama, for Becky. Most of all, she wanted to be a lady to rival the beautiful Sophie. Then would she be worthy of Garrett?

She squashed that thought and plunged her needles into the stocking she was knitting for Reggie. Why did she torture herself?

She missed him so much. Having him so close but being unable to show her true feelings for him was about to drive her to utter madness.

Lady Bertrice glanced from her to Becky. "We received a slew of letters from London today, Rebecca."

Becky groaned softly. "I'd almost rather not hear what they have to say."

"Whyever not?"

Flushing, Becky looked toward Kate. Kate smiled at her, wishing her strength. Surely none of Becky's family members would speak too harshly to her in a letter.

The maid magically reappeared at Lady Bertrice's side, this time bearing a silver salver piled with letters.

Becky eyed the stack of stationery warily. "Who are they from?"

"Everyone." Lady Bertrice raised an imperious hand

and plucked the top piece of stationery from the pile and unfolded it.

"Well, it is no wonder I scarcely saw you those first few days I was home. You were writing to every single soul in London, weren't you?"

Lady Bertrice's lips thinned. "Not *every* soul in London, not at all. Only the select members of our family and friends who were hungry for news of you and your brother. In any case, Rebecca, it would hardly make any sense for me to sit by your bedside for hours on end. You were asleep half the time, and the other half incoherent from the pain."

"It doesn't matter, Aunt, for I had no need of you. Kate sat beside me during those hours."

Lady Bertrice cut a sharp glance at Kate. "Well. Surely there was something else she could have occupied herself with as well, something more useful."

Becky reached out with her good hand and Kate took it, appreciating the gesture of solidarity. They both turned to Aunt Bertrice. "I doubt that." Becky squeezed Kate's fingers. "I took great comfort from knowing she was here."

Lady Bertrice shrugged. "I shall never understand such frivolous sentiments." She glanced down at the letter in her lap. "This one is from the Countess of Harpsford."

Becky groaned softly.

"Very well." Without glancing up, Lady Bertrice raised her hand again. The maid quickly moved to place the salver beneath her seeking fingers, and she retrieved a second letter. She glanced at it. "This one is from Sophie. I recognize her handwriting."

Kate's chest tightened at the mention of Garrett's ex-wife.

"Oh, dear. I am certain she must hate me now." Becky looked tiny and fragile in her plain white chemise with the pink counterpane tucked around her lap. The vulnerable expression on her face did nothing to soften the effect.

"Oh, come. Of course she does not hate you," Lady Bertrice said.

"She should, after what I did. It was because of me that she nearly died. Garrett told me all about how she was shot, how she nearly bled to death. And all because I wouldn't believe her when she tried to stop me from eloping."

Kate squeezed Becky's hand and tried to give her friend a reassuring smile. She shouldn't feel guilty or responsible for her brother's actions, but every mention of his evil deeds still pained her to her soul.

"I have known Sophie since she was a baby. You'd best trust me when I say she does not blame you for William Fisk's sins." Lady Bertrice sent a dark look Kate's way as she said her brother's name.

"But for my own sins?"

"You've paid enough for those, I daresay," Lady Bertrice said. "You suffered a miserable wretch in marriage for four months, watched your brother kill him, and then endured a terrible carriage accident. Please recall that we're not papists, Rebecca. We do not mope about, obsessed by our guilt, endeavoring to create a means of penance by which to divert it."

"But what if there are actions we regret? That we would change, if only we had the opportunity?"

Kate dropped her head and stared at her knitting. Reggie's stocking was turning out wrong, she knew. It was longer than its match. But what else could she do? She had to occupy herself to keep from involving herself in this conversation. Certainly Lady Bertrice didn't want her to speak. Yet she was a hairsbreadth from opening her fool mouth.

"Too late," Lady Bertrice snapped. "It is too late for any of that. Time moves forward, not backward, and so should you."

"I will try, Aunt, truly I will." Becky sighed and nodded jerkily at Lady Bertrice. "Please read Sophie's letter."

"Very well." Lady Bertrice placed spectacles on her nose and raised the stationery to her face, but just as she opened her mouth to read, Reggie opened the door. He reeled to a halt at the threshold and stared at Lady Bertrice, looking uncertain. He was as uncomfortable in the lady's presence as Kate was.

The old woman let out a hissing breath and looked over the paper at Becky. "Must you have the child in here at all times, Rebecca?"

The question might have been directed at Becky, but Kate knew it was meant for her.

Becky gave a one-shouldered shrug. "He prefers to be near Kate. And he's not here nearly so much now Miranda has arrived."

Lady Bertrice's icy gaze slid toward Kate. Her lips pinched in disapproval as she directed her first words of the day at her. "Why do you insist upon keeping the child in a dank sickroom? Why isn't he outside being a boy"—she waved a dismissive arm—"doing as boys do?"

"Reggie is easily chilled and easily tired," Kate explained, impressed by the calmness of her voice. "And he isn't accustomed to being outdoors." She glanced back at Reggie, who still hovered on the threshold. "What is it, Reg?"

"Lady Miranda and Miss Dalworthy have asked me to play with them in the nursery. May I go?"

She frowned. He'd taken a liking to pretty little Lady Miranda as soon as they'd met—so had Kate, for that matter. Miranda was a sweet girl, bright, and extremely precocious. She'd taken one assessing look at Reggie and had seemed to understand him right away.

Still, it struck Kate as not quite right for Reggie to be playing in a nursery meant for the children of a duke, with a duke's daughter. She didn't want anyone to think she was foisting Reggie on them, so she'd kept him even closer to her than usual.

Nevertheless, she didn't like the thought of Reggie subjected to Lady Bertrice's judgmental glare, and she knew Miranda and Miss Dalworthy would be kind to him.

"All right," she said. "But be on your best behavior, do you understand?"

"Yes, Katie."

"And if your breathing begins to bother you, you must find me right away."

"Or send a servant to fetch her," Becky added.

Reggie glanced from Becky to her and nodded solemnly.

She smiled at him. "Go, then."

He scampered off, and she sat watching the door for a moment after it shut. He was moving more quickly now, and there was more color in his cheeks. She hadn't seen that blue tinge to his lips since they'd arrived. Maybe the medicine Dr. Barnard had given him was helping, but

Kate was more inclined to think Yorkshire was good for Reggie. Or maybe it was Garrett and his family who were good for him. She turned from the door, a soft smile on her face.

Lady Bertrice frowned, and her eyes slid from Kate to the door and back again. "William Fisk's siblings." She sighed dramatically. "There are certain things in this world I shall never understand. But since Rebecca insists—"

"I do," Becky interrupted. "You must understand, Aunt Bertrice, Kate and Reginald are nothing like William."

Lady Bertrice raised a brow, and heat shot through Kate's cheeks. "How can you be so certain? We know how he fooled us—all of us, but especially you. You were sheltered and young and naïve..."

"I am none of those things, Aunt. Not anymore. And Kate and Reginald are part of our family now."

Kate stared at the knitting lowered in her lap, knowing her face must be crimson. They were speaking of her and Reggie as if she wasn't there. She had to say something. Slowly, she raised her eyes to Lady Bertrice.

"Lady Rebecca and His Grace have been very kind to us, perhaps kinder than we deserve—"

Lady Bertrice snorted an agreement.

Kate continued, "But you must never fool yourself into thinking either of us would ever hurt you as our brother did. You shall find no soul on this earth sweeter or purer than my brother Reggie. And as for me—" She sucked in a breath and faced the older woman's narrow gaze. "I try my best."

She needed air. With deliberate movements, Kate set her knitting aside and rose, brushing down the ill-fitting skirts of the green dress. “Please excuse me, Lady Bertrice. Lady Rebecca. I believe I should like to go for a walk.”

Becky smiled at her, and Kate realized with a small shock that it was a smile of pride. “Very well, Kate. I shall see you when the dressmaker arrives.”

Kate nodded at Becky then turned to Lady Bertrice and curtsied stiffly. “I owe Lady Rebecca and His Grace a great deal. I promise you, I would protect them with my life.”

As Kate closed the door behind her, Becky said in a quiet voice, “She already has.”

Chapter Fourteen

Garrett sat at his desk in the library. With its dark mahogany furniture, rust-colored carpets, and the musty smell of old books, this place had rapidly become his sanctuary. Just as his study had become his sanctuary at the London house.

He spent a few hours daily with his daughter. They read together—Miranda was obsessed with Shakespeare, and they'd divide the roles and speak the parts aloud. Currently they were reading *A Comedy of Errors*, which made Miranda laugh so hard, tears welled in her eyes.

Sometimes they walked the grounds. Though she was a young lady through and through, Miranda impressed him with her knowledge of botany and her familiarity with even the most obscure plants in the gardens. She'd convinced him to accompany her on calls to some of the neighboring families next week—a task he knew he must perform eventually but would not relish. His daughter's presence would make it far easier.

He was busy. There was much to do, much to see to. Several quarries were located on his lands in Yorkshire, and there had been a recent turnover in leadership. Between yanking control of his properties from Tristan and his relentless pursuit of Fisk, Garrett had neglected his responsibilities to the quarries and their workers. He was determined to remedy his oversight, and yet he was continually distracted. Not by Kate herself, because she persisted in avoiding him, but by thoughts of her. He took her letter from his pocket, unfolded it, and read it again.

For His Grace, the Duke of Calton:

Forgive me for writing you, but I feel it is necessary in the circumstances, and I have nowhere else to turn.

I am employed by Mr. William Fisk, whose wife is your sister, Lady Rebecca. Through no fault of hers, the circumstances regarding Lady Rebecca's marriage have been revealed to me. For certain you are angry with Lady Rebecca, Your Grace, and rightly so, but she admits her folly and wishes nothing more than to reconcile with you and the other members of her family—most especially you.

I hesitate to reveal what I shall proceed to explain to you, Your Grace, but I have no other choice. I shall beg my employers' forgiveness for breaking their confidence at a later date, but for now, my sole concern is for my mistress, and upon weighing the unfortunate fact of my betrayal with the alternative,

I have concluded I must eventually suffer the repercussions of my failure as a dependable and discreet servant.

Here it is, Your Grace, the unkind truth as bluntly as I am capable of wording it: Despite the newness of his marriage, Mr. Fisk is finding entertainments elsewhere, and Lady Rebecca is perfectly wretched, not only because of her husband's lack of interest, but from the overwhelming guilt that comes with the knowledge of how much grief she has caused her family.

If you possess any remaining affection for your sister or her husband, I entreat you to come to Kenilworth and to speak with both parties. I beg you to encourage Mr. Fisk to give Lady Rebecca the honor and attention she deserves. For she is very gentle, Your Grace, and I fear for her well-being. I truly do.

Sincerely,
K. F.

She'd written it before she'd known who he was. Brave, beautiful, loyal Kate.

He missed her. His body ached for her.

He rose and strode to the window. Parting the heavy, dark damask curtains, he gazed outside. It was a clear autumn day, warm for the season. A gentle breeze fluttered over one of the box hedges in the back garden, sending a shimmering silver cascade over the green.

Created by the famous landscape gardener, Capability Brown, in Garrett's grandfather's day, the gardens at

Calton House were lush and vast, blooming with the deep reds, greens, and browns of the season. The south garden was arranged with paths radiating in a spokelike pattern from an octagonal gazebo designed like a Roman temple.

Movement drew Garrett's gaze to the gazebo. Clasping her hands behind her back, Kate descended the steps and stepped onto one of the paths. She walked at a sedate pace, stopping often to survey her surroundings. She was hatless, but she wore a dark coat that extended just beneath her knees, and her pale green skirts fell to her feet—the same pale green she'd been wearing daily since her return, the dress likely borrowed from one of the servants.

He stared at her for a few seconds, and then spun around, tucking her letter into the pocket of his waistcoat. He wished to be near her, and he could no more resist her pull than he could resist drawing air into his lungs. He hurried downstairs and thrust his arms into his coat. Jenkins, the aged butler, made no comment as Garrett snatched his gloves from the brown-spotted hands and waved off the proffered hat, but he raised his brow the slightest fraction—an enormous response given Jenkins's taciturn reputation.

Ignoring him, Garrett went out the back entrance, allowing the door to slam behind him. Ducking beneath the low lintel, he hurried through the wrought-iron garden gate.

She'd been walking near the chrysanthemums when he'd last seen her. They bloomed late this year, in a rainbow of colors that framed Kate's willowy form as she walked down the path. He turned a corner.

There she was. Startled by the sound of his feet on the

gravel, she turned. Instantly, she shuttered her expression, and her eyes transformed from open surprise to blankness, making her virtually unreadable.

"Good afternoon." Garrett forced his pace to slow despite the compulsion to run to her, gather her in his arms, and kiss her until she opened herself to him again. Until her expression became as fluid and readable as that first time he'd met her by the pool at Kenilworth Castle.

She inclined her head and curtsied. "Your Grace."

Her eyes darted from left to right, searching for someone else. A savior, perhaps. She didn't wish to be alone with him.

How could he blame her? This was his house, his land. She lived under his protection. He held all the control, and she held...nothing, in her estimation. He was the lion and she the mouse. He could take whatever he wished from her, and she would have no recourse whatsoever.

If only Kate knew the power she held over him.

"Kate."

She still wouldn't look at him. "I was just...exploring the grounds. They're beautiful."

"Yes," he agreed. "Walk with me."

It wasn't a question. His words were hard, and he infused the command into his expression. He gave her no choice but to comply, but not because he possessed some sinister intent. It was only because he feared her rejection.

"Your Grace." Her expression and tone were rigid, and he almost regretted his order. Any semblance of regret vanished from his thoughts, however, when she slid her arm through his.

His body came alive. Every part of him heated, reacted to her touch. The last time he'd touched her had been in the carriage en route to Calton House. It felt like eons ago.

She frowned, studying a spindly tree to their left, barren of leaves. In the spring it would explode with waxy green leaves and large pink blooms. "It's a rare kind of magnolia—a hybrid of Chinese magnolias. My father smuggled it from the south of France just before the Peninsular War."

"Really?"

Garrett twisted his lips. "The acquisition earned him much fame and caused his peers to try to outdo him by smuggling ever more rare and illegal botanical specimens." He remembered his father kneeling by this tree, coaxing it to survive, offering it words of encouragement he'd never troubled to give his son.

Kate's dark eyes studied him. "You didn't approve of your father bringing this tree from France."

He never talked about his father to anyone. Even Sophie. His ex-wife had always despised the old duke, and she avoided him because Tristan had told her about the punishments he'd inflicted on Garrett for every minor transgression.

When Sophie revealed that she knew his secret, Garrett was ashamed, furious with Tristan. He'd given Tristan a black eye that day, but in self-defense, Tristan had punched him so hard in the stomach, Garrett had been unable to eat for two days.

He stared at the gravel as they strolled down the path. "I dislike how the men of my class are prone to waste time with ridiculous wagering and pointless competition.

After my mother died, my father became the worst of them all, squandering half his fortune on women and gambling."

"I'm sorry," she said softly. She motioned to their surroundings. "Becky told me she is your half-sister. Was her mama one of those women?"

"Yes. She was a very young lady, an earl's niece. He debauched her." Garrett closed his eyes—he'd always suspected his father had done worse than merely debauch her. Rebecca's mother was so young, a pale, delicate flower of a woman, who'd seemed more a shadow than a duchess. Garrett flexed his fingers at his sides. There was no need to share his suspicions with Kate. He continued. "He'd been imbibing one night and bragged about his conquest to the gentlemen at his club. The scandal spread, and they married perforce. He died four years later."

"And what happened to Becky's mother?"

"She died as well, of consumption, soon after. Rebecca was six when Aunt Bertrice took over her care."

"Where were you?"

"I was scarcely ever at home to witness these events." He flinched. God, he had so much to make up for. In those days, he had been young, in love, obsessed with his military career. He'd hated anything to do with Calton House and his father. He'd altogether neglected his sister's childhood. "Busy with the army...and Sophie," he confessed through the thick wash of regret.

He gave Kate a sidelong glance, saw the white column of her throat move as she swallowed. But she didn't turn to him, nor meet his eyes. After a long silence, she gestured to their surroundings. "It appears your father didn't lose everything."

"No. If he'd lived long enough, he would have. But gluttony and drink killed him before it happened."

She shook her head. "So it was on you to restore your name as well as your fortune."

"For a time. Tristan took control while I was on the Continent."

"He did a fine job of it, looks like."

"Yes, he did."

"Now it is your responsibility once again," she murmured. "Is it one you desire?"

He looked around him at the gardens, back at the regal Grecian columns of Calton House and the gazebo glimmering white in the midday sun. He'd changed since the impetuous, angry days of his early twenties. He'd developed a connection to the earth, and a stronger bond to his family. He was born here. This was his home.

"My ancestors built this place. When I am gone, it shall go to Tristan, and then his son. I would like to leave it as my legacy, as a symbol of James pride."

"That's right, James is your surname," she mused. "Willy said your surname was Longmire."

"He lied."

"So you intend to leave everything in your cousin's hands?"

"Yes." He found himself bemused by all her questions. Her arm had relaxed against his, and it seemed she was returning to herself. That wasn't something he'd discourage, even if it was painful to answer her at times.

"Don't you wish for an heir? A son of your own?"

Her question startled him. He didn't respond for a long moment as he sorted it out in his mind. He hadn't thought of it for years. "In Belgium, I was too poor for a wife, much less a son. Before that..." He searched his memories of the years before Waterloo. "As a cocksure youth, I always assumed Sophie would give me many sons. But after we were married, we believed she was barren."

"But you have your daughter."

"Conceived just before I left for Waterloo, yes. She was a blessing. A surprise." He added after a silence, "I missed the first seven years with her."

"That is a long time to go without knowing your own child."

"It is."

"You accepted that you would have no sons long ago, then."

He glanced at her. She stared at the path unfurling before them. "Yes, I suppose I did."

She sighed. "I accept it, too."

"What do you mean?"

"I mean that I shall have no sons," she said simply. "No children, for that matter."

"Don't you desire to have children?" She would be a perfect mother. She was meant to be a mother.

"No." Her expression went still. "The life of a child is difficult, full of illness and suffering and uncertainty."

"It should never be that way."

"But your childhood was spent here, Garrett." She waved her hand toward the house.

"Class shouldn't matter. Childhood should be the most carefree time in anyone's life."

"I agree, and I did enjoy many carefree moments when I was a child at Debussey Manor. But since Reggie was born..." She made a helpless gesture with her hands. "You see, I try endlessly to make his life easier for him, and I fail at it, and it breaks my heart. I love him—I love all children." She smiled wistfully. "I once had dreams of becoming a governess for a great family."

It would have been a perfect position for her, he thought.

She continued, "I suppose if I could trust my life to retain some sense of stability, then I should wish to have a dozen children. But I don't believe my life will ever be stable, you see."

Garrett opened his mouth to say that she could have a stable life with anyone she chose, for any man in his right mind would be eager to make children with this woman. But the words stalled in his throat. Hell, he'd stripped Kate of her innocence. She belonged to him, and he'd kill any man who touched her now, much less married her.

She was his.

"What's wrong?" She was looking at him, a frown creasing her brow.

"Nothing."

"No," she said. Her fingers tapped his forearm. "Your arm—it just went hard as granite." Her eyes widened in horror. "Do you think I was implying that you should offer me that stability? Oh, dear, that isn't what I meant at all—"

"I know." He took a breath. "I just don't like to hear you speaking that way."

"Do you mean...that I will never have children?" She sounded surprised.

"Yes," he bit out.

She walked along slowly and silently, her face taking on that unreadable quality he'd grown to despise as she seemed to absorb what he'd said. He should tell her how he felt. Tell her how much he wanted her, how he needed her at his side.

Yet her dark eyes chilled him to the core. He had a sick feeling she would reject him, cite a hundred different reasons why it was impossible. His family would agree with her.

He must build the bridge brick by brick, not force her to leap across the chasm. God, the ink was not yet dry on his divorce papers. Less than a fortnight ago, he'd killed her brother. His mind knew these things, along with the dozens of other "reasons" for them to stay apart. Yet his heart and his body wanted her now.

He took a moment to steady himself, brushing his hand down the front of his coat. The parchment she'd written to him on crackled beneath his hand. "I came out here to thank you," he said.

She looked startled. "For what?"

"Your letter."

"What letter?"

He drew the stationery from his pocket and held it out to her. "The one you wrote to me from Kenilworth."

Pink washed over her cheeks. "Oh. That."

"It was brave and loyal of you to send that letter."

She stiffened. "Please. Never accuse me of being loyal."

He frowned down at her. Her reaction confused him—he'd never met anyone as unfailingly loyal as her. And then it struck him like a hammer to his temple. Of course—she saw all that she'd done out of loyalty to him and Rebecca as traitorous to her family.

He halted on the gravel, drawing her to a stop beside him. "Kate."

She looked up at him with shining eyes, and it was as

if she'd followed every one of his thoughts, knew exactly what he was going to say to her. "I shouldn't be out here with you."

"Of course, you should," Garrett said.

"No. It's...it's...dangerous." She began to draw away, but he tightened his arm, pinning hers against his body. He couldn't let her leave him now. He'd seen a hint of a thaw toward him, a subtle sign of the Kate he had longed for in the past few days.

"Stay with me. Just for a while."

From the look of anguish on her face, he knew he was torturing her. All those thoughts were running through her mind—reasons they should keep their distance from each other.

But he couldn't help himself. He *couldn't* let her go.

They stood there in a suspended, charged silence for a long moment. Finally, the tension slid from her shoulders, and she surrendered. "I can't deny you anything," she whispered. "I want to, I know I must, but I still cannot."

They began to stroll again in silence, now at a slower pace. They reached the end of the path and stepped onto the Palladian bridge that crossed the river bordering the geometric gardens. In the acres beyond the river, Brown had created a more natural effect, with tree-dotted rolling grass hills bordered by the forest. Far ahead, one of the three Roman-inspired gazebos gleamed starkly white from its position tucked into the forest's edge.

At the center of the bridge, Kate withdrew her arm from his. She leaned over the railing and looked out over the water.

"So lovely," she murmured. "It reminds me of how

Debussey Manor once was. It was so beautiful. It was tragic to see it fall into disrepair after Lady Debussey died."

She spoke of her home with such fondness, it sent a pang through him. "Do you miss Debussey Manor?"

She took a deep breath. "In a way. I do—" Her teeth came out to close over her lower lip, and Garrett fought not to reach up to loosen the suddenly too-tight cravat round his neck. "I worry about my mama."

"Do you?" he asked in surprise. From the way the woman had treated her, he expected Kate would never want to lay eyes on her again.

Kate slid her gloved fingertips along the bridge's handrail, swiping beads of dew from the smooth marble surface. "She didn't truly mean to hurt me with that poker. It was just her initial reaction of denial and anger. Willy was her life, you see. She loved him beyond measure. She was so proud of him."

"She couldn't have comprehended how far he had fallen."

"I don't think she did. Even if she'd been given proof of it, she never would have accepted it." Kate looked up at him, the pain of her mother's rejection gleaming in her eyes.

"I'm sorry, Kate." He could say that to her their whole lives and it still wouldn't be enough.

Kate smiled wistfully. "You ought to have seen Mama when she reunited with Willy for the first time after he'd been gone all those years. I've never seen her happier."

"She was misguided. She should have loved you more." Garrett tried to temper his tone, but his voice emerged sounding harsh and unyielding.

"No." Kate stared at her fingers gripping the curved

surface of the rail. "I wasn't a very good daughter to her. She wanted so desperately for me to be a lady, and... well, I cannot."

What was this? He cocked his head at her in question. "Why not?"

"From the time we were children, Mama taught us everything. She was determined to turn us into a true lady and gentlemen so that we would marry well and never suffer the shameful fate she did by eloping with a lowly tradesman. She taught us how to read and write, she taught us manners, how to speak and conduct ourselves. But I—" Kate's eyelids lowered, screening her emotions from him. "I was very bad at it. I preferred novels to the classics and French, I disliked learning comportment, I was terrible at music, I despaired of writing, and my manners were altogether atrocious. I would have much rather played with the animals and spoken like the local children."

"Ridiculous," he muttered under his breath. To her, he said, "I read your letter." *About a hundred times.* "You write well. Better than me, I daresay."

She seemed not to hear him. "I was a hoyden who preferred running wild outside to the more docile entertainments of a lady. I disrespected her at every turn. I could not contain my tongue, and I was far too tall and awkward." She gazed out over the trickling silver water. "But Willy and Warren were perfect. They were intelligent and conducted themselves as gentlemen, from the time they were very young. They won the favor of Lord Debussey while he never so much as spared me a second glance."

"Could that be because he was the one who coveted the son? Because he liked to pretend your brothers were his own?"

She shrugged. "Perhaps. But I always thought Willy and Warren caught his eye with their intelligence and demeanor. Lord Debussey gave them both their commissions."

"I'd heard," he said.

She turned to smile at him, but pain darkened her eyes. "So you see, Mama had no reason to love me, and every reason to love my brothers."

"I can think of many reasons for your mother to love you, Kate," he said in a hard voice. "Not the least of which is the fact that you are her daughter, as much a part of her as your brothers were."

Her smile remained fixed on her face, small and false. "I know that in theory. But in practice...I understand why she is the way she is."

"You are far too understanding," he muttered. He wouldn't hurt Kate by telling her what he really thought of her mother—that she was a selfish, conniving shrew on the verge of insanity, who had long ago decided that whenever it was time to place blame for anything that went wrong, Kate was the chosen scapegoat. The woman had hurt Kate, and Garrett wasn't sure whether Kate's wounds would ever heal.

"A part of me is glad to be away from Debussey Manor." She shuddered. "You see—that is just one example of my shortcomings. I wish to be separated from my own mama, who I know is beset with grief."

He shook his head. "It is not a shortcoming. It is a natural response toward someone who has inflicted pain upon you."

Kate turned back to the river. "Perhaps. It doesn't make me feel any more justified, nor does it make my feelings acceptable, Garrett." Her hands tightened over the railing. "Sorry. I called you 'Garrett' again. *Your Grace*. Forgive me." She offered him a rueful grin. "See what I mean? Hopeless."

"I prefer you to call me Garrett."

"I can't," she breathed. "Imagine if I did it in Lady Bertrice's hearing. She'd think—"

"She'd be correct," he said dryly.

"But she'd . . . she'd . . ."

He squeezed her arm. "I know, Kate." He ground his teeth. "This is impossible."

"Do you wish me to leave Calton House?"

"No," he said sharply. "You must stay."

"Why?"

Because I can't bear the thought of you leaving me. "Where else would you go?"

She shrugged. "I'm certain Becky would write me a character reference. I could go to London and find—"

"London? No." The thought of Kate alone in London made his skin crawl.

"Leeds?"

"No."

She sighed. "I should return to Kenilworth. I might find work there. Reggie and I could be close to Mama."

The thought of that woman opening her vile mouth in that innocent child's presence made Garrett grit his teeth. "No," he said flatly. "You will remain with me."

She narrowed her eyes at him. "You don't own me, Your Grace."

"No, I don't," he conceded. "But I wish I did."

Her jaw dropped, but then she snapped it shut and turned toward the stream.

Stiff and frozen, they both stared at the water. A male duck waddled to the bank and slid in with a small splash. It bobbed to the surface, preening as if to lure a potential mate, though there were no other ducks in view.

The river curved around into the distance. Barren trees dotted the dale, trees that Garrett and Tristan had dodged and climbed, trees that Tristan had buried "treasure" beneath when he convinced Garrett and Sophie to play archaeologist with him.

His gaze caught a brown blur high up in one of the largest trees, and he studied it. He, Tristan, and Sophie had built the tree house when Garrett had come home on holiday his first year at Eton. Now, the white paint had faded to brown, many of the planks were missing or rotting, and the walls balanced precariously within a triangle of branches.

In the distance beyond, the tree-dotted grass swept up a low-lying hill, blending into the forest at the top. Garrett gazed at the hill, his pulse quickening.

"Come with me." He took her arm. "I want to show you something."

"Becky is expecting me—"

"Becky can wait," he said, suddenly breathless with anticipation. He couldn't wait for her to see it. He herded Kate over the bridge and through the gate on the other side.

She glanced up at the rotting tree house as they passed it. "Did you build that?"

"Yes."

"How wonderful," she breathed.

"Sophie liked it."

"So she was a hoyden, too?"

Garrett chuckled. "Well, my aunt liked to call her one."

"But she isn't one anymore, I gather."

"You gather correctly," he said. "She's . . . well, I can no longer envision her climbing the rope ladder to our tree house."

A hint of rebellion glinted in Kate's eyes. "If it were still there, I'd climb it."

He grinned at her. "I know. That's why I like you."

She returned his grin with that generous, beautiful, open smile that he loved, and his heart skipped a beat.

Her gaze slipped away, and the smile faded. "Perhaps you should fix it for Miranda."

"Hm," he said thoughtfully. "I will. Reginald can play there, too. And Tristan's son Gary, when they come to visit."

"Oh, Reggie couldn't—"

"Of course he could."

She bit her lower lip, and all thoughts of children vanished from his mind. That unsure look she gave would never fail to remind him of holding her beneath him.

As they climbed the low hill leading toward the trees, she asked, "Where are you taking me?"

"You'll see," he said smugly. At the edge of the forest, he tugged her off the path at the stone marker he'd placed on its edge years ago. He felt young. Almost weightless. He knew she'd love it.

The tinkling sound of water was her first hint as he lifted her over a small rocky ledge.

"A river?" she guessed as he set her down.

"Something like that." He grasped her hand and led her onward.

They passed through a copse of trees and walked down a shallow slope into a glen cut by a narrow stream. The noise of rushing water increased, blotting out the trickling sounds of the water flowing beside them. The stones beside the riverbank were damp; covered with mosses and bracken glistening with dew.

With Kate trailing closely behind him, Garrett sidestepped a clump of ferns and followed the turn in the river as the slope of the small valley steepened to a sheer limestone wall draped from top to bottom with wild garlic. He remembered the smell that permeated the area in the summertime, when the violets and lily of the valley bloomed and infused the place with color. Since Garrett's childhood, the smell of garlic had reminded him of this place. Even when he'd lost his memories, he'd known some important part of his forgotten life was connected to the smell.

Garrett stopped, gazing across an oblong crystalline pool at the curtain of water. Kate came to a sudden halt behind him and gasped. "Oh!"

The waterfall roared before them in a tribute to nature's power. It towered a good twenty feet above the pool below and was about twice as wide as Kate was tall. The sleek limestone rock face of the fall shimmered through the stream of water in a vivid array of mossy greens. Barren, twisted branches framed the falls and towered above them. Rich mineral deposits in the river fed the trees, and in the spring and summer months, they grew lush, crowding around the falls and the banks of the river above to hide the sky, which now cast a blue-gray hue through the leafless branches. Directly across the pool and to the right of the waterfall, the stones opened to a low, false cave, but

Garrett knew from his childhood explorations that a real cave lay just behind the falls, hidden by its face.

"Oh, Garrett...it's...it's..." She gulped. It looked as if she was about to cry.

Garrett frowned at her, confused. "You don't like it?"

"I...I've never seen a waterfall before. It's... magnificent."

He released a breath and slid his arm around her, drawing her close. He nudged her chin until she faced him. "Then why do you look sad?"

She tried to smile at him, but her lips trembled at their edges. "Why did you bring me here?"

"I thought you would like it."

"I do. Very much."

He turned back to the waterfall, tucking her against his side, willing his errant body to behave. His cock was painfully stiff. It was her shining eyes that did it, the feel of her soft skin beneath his fingers, the curve of her waist.

He wanted her. The force of it nearly made him groan aloud.

"I've never brought anyone here before," he mused, tightening his arm around her.

Her brows rose in surprise.

"Like your pool at Kenilworth Castle, this was my place. I came here sometimes to escape from everyone and everything. To think. In the summer, I'd swim, but even in the dead of winter I'd come to sit or read. Tristan found me once, but he never bothered me again after that." Garrett shook his head thoughtfully. "I don't think he ever told Sophie."

"He is a good friend to you, isn't he?"

He paused a moment, then said, "Yes, he is."

"You've forgiven him for taking Sophie from you?" Her voice was tentative, as if she feared her words might anger him.

He turned to face her. "He and Sophie are best for each other."

He'd loved Sophie...but at this moment, his past feelings for her seemed unreal and distant, like a strange, disconnected dream. Unfathomable.

Kate was real. Kate was his. Standing before him now, connected to him body and soul.

He wanted her. He wanted to be near her. He could be himself with her. She didn't fear him; she understood him. She was honest and intelligent, and yes, loyal. Beautiful and desirable, too.

He wanted her to be with him. He wanted her to share his meals, his days, his bed. For the rest of his life. They could overcome all that stood between them. Right here, right now, it didn't seem so difficult.

"Kate," he said in a voice so low and gruff it emerged as a whisper. "I am sorry about William."

She blinked hard and nodded. He was surprised she'd heard him over the roar of the falls. "I know."

"I wish that things had been different. That he hadn't done any of the things he did, that you weren't his sister, that you didn't have to see—"

She turned away from the falls and into his arms, reaching up to cup his cheeks with her gloved hands. "He was mad, Garrett. He lost his mind when Warren died."

Garrett swallowed. "I'm sorry."

"You did what you had to do," she whispered, dropping her hands. "I understand."

"But you cannot forgive me."

"I forgive you in my mind. But he was my brother. He was a part of me. I don't know if my heart will ever heal from that loss."

"And yet, you came home with me. You continue to speak to me."

"Because I know you did what was necessary. If it wasn't him who died, it would have been you. And I couldn't survive your death."

She winced as soon as her words emerged, as if she regretted them, wished she could swallow them back into her body.

He bent closer to her. Close enough to take in her scent. Cinnamon and pine. Earthy and sweet. "I couldn't survive your death either."

He bent even closer. And then he took a great risk.

He kissed her.

Chapter Fifteen

His lips clung to hers for a full second before Kate remembered herself.

She jumped away as if his touch had singed her. And it had—it singed her to her soul. Her heel caught on her skirts, and she staggered backward, but Garrett lunged forward and deftly caught her before she tumbled into the placid pool and struck her head on one of the rocks rising up through the clear water.

She stared up at him. Safe. That was how she felt with his arms wrapped around her. God help her, she never wanted him to let go. Panic swelled in her chest.

"You are going to be the death of me," she said.

"No," he said in that husky voice, just barely audible above the sound of the falls, "I'm going to love you."

"You can't!" She gripped his forearms and tried to pull them off her, but it was like trying to bend steel.

"Why?" he demanded. "Tell me."

"Because..." Lord, there were too many reasons. All of them perfectly logical. And vital. Why, then, would none come to her? All she could think of was the intent in those blue eyes. The way they studied her as if she were the most important thing in the universe. The rugged face, strong nose, the way the fine wool coat hugged those broad shoulders...

Yes, she was thoroughly debauched. Her assessment of herself that very first day at the pool—the day he'd discovered her watching him—was absolutely correct.

"Kate."

Whenever he said her name as a single sentence, a low hum resonated through her body. It was the way he said it. How he infused her name with meaning. Importance.

"I...can't." She struggled to maintain hold on the thread she knew was keeping her from plunging into an abyss of desire, of *love*, that would lead to her downfall.

"Kate." Emotion glistened in his eyes, and he gathered her to his chest and bowed his head over hers. His lips glanced over the shell of her ear as he continued. "I promise you, I will never hurt you. I will care for you always. I will protect you and Reginald. Everything has happened so fast. Too fast. We need time to sort it all out. Just don't distance yourself from me. Please."

The past days had been hell. Keeping apart from him, trying to avoid him. *That* was what had nearly killed her. In contrast, his closeness at this moment was heaven. She slid her arms around him, holding him tight. Comfort seeped through her bones as it always did when she touched him.

"I need you," he murmured, gripping her as tightly as she clung to him. His fingers trailed through the strands of her hair that the wind had torn free from its pins. "I am only whole when I am with you. You bring me to life, beautiful Kate."

She laid her cheek on his chest. In her whole life, she'd never thought herself beautiful, but she felt beautiful when she was with Garrett. The dark wool of his coat scratched at her skin as she gazed at the waterfall. It was so powerful, like Garrett himself.

They stood there for long minutes, both of them watching the white wall of water cascading over the sleek green surface of the rock face. Kate didn't know how much time passed. All she knew was that she could stand here forever, staring at the waterfall, holding on to him like this.

Finally, Garrett's arms relaxed. She looked up at him in question.

"We should return to the house. You said Rebecca—"

Wrapping her hands around his neck, she tugged him to her. She kissed him. Like she'd never kissed anyone. Like she was dying and his lips were the only medicine that would save her. A delicious, welcome cure. One she'd sought all her life.

He responded in kind, his big arms tightening around her, lifting her. His tongue brushed over hers, over her teeth, over her lips. Soft yet firm, his lips moved over hers in a question, then a sensual caress, and finally a command. He swept through her and possessed her until she was a shuddering, boneless creature, with nothing but the sensations his lips wrought to sustain her.

She had no choice, for he demanded her submission, and every part of her cried that she must obey. She must touch him, skin against skin. She tore off her gloves and dropped them. Framing his face in her hands, she drew him closer, every nerve-ending in her palms reveling in the bristle-roughened skin and the powerful, square jaw. Her right index finger skimmed the smooth scar above his brow. She rubbed her thumb over the tiny cleft at the center of his chin, and she shivered.

His lips moved over hers, hard and commanding, but her lips weren't passive. They attacked him in kind, making demands equivalent to his. His hands roamed over her coat, over her body, sliding over her breasts until her nipples tightened and pushed against the fabric. Dipping lower, his big palms closed around her waist and then spread over the flare of her hips.

She dropped her own hands to his chest, pressing against the solid wall, finding the buttons of his coat and slipping them loose.

Suddenly, he lifted her off her feet, a movement that made her pause in surprise. But only for a second, for she couldn't survive for long without his taste on her tongue.

He carried her a few feet and then pressed her against a bed of green leaves growing on the sheer face of rock. He hesitated. "Does that hurt the cut on your shoulder?"

"No," she breathed. "It's all but healed." In truth, she couldn't feel it at all. She could feel only Garrett. Sinking her hands beneath the lapels of his coat, she groaned softly, the sound drowned out by the nearby roar of water, as her hand descended to the falls of his trousers and brushed over the solid length of his arousal. She curled her fingers around it.

That made him release her. Flattening his hands against the rocky face of the cliff, he pushed himself back. He tightened his jaw, and his arms, caging her body between them, shook with restraint. Again his eyes, now narrow and dark with need, searched her face, his question so evident there was no need to voice it.

It took her a moment to find the strength to speak. The air seemed to hang suspended around them, warm and damp, heavy with their mutual desire.

"Yes, Garrett," she said, her voice rough. "Yes." As if to punctuate her capitulation, she squeezed him. "Take me. I want—I want to be yours. Like nothing I've ever wanted."

Still, he didn't move. A muscle twitched in his jaw. "I...don't want to hurt you," he said.

"Impossible." She fumbled at his buttons and loosened them in seconds. Then she plunged her hands into his trousers.

He released an audible gasp as the fingers of both her hands curled around him.

"Tell me what feels good," she commanded. "Teach me what to do."

"Keep...doing...that," he said as she slid her fingers from the base to the tip. "God, your fingers are so warm. Tighter. Hold me tight, Kate."

She tightened her fingers. "That doesn't hurt?"

"You can't hurt me."

Her lips curled. "And you cannot hurt me. You see?" Squeezing tightly, she slid up and down again, feeling him grow even harder beneath her fingers.

He bunched her skirt in his fists, yanking it upward until his palms rasped over her thighs. He'd removed his gloves, too, she realized dazedly.

She leaned back into the soft green plants and slid her

hands up and down his shaft, glorying in the texture of him, that fascinating mix of hard and soft she'd discovered the last time she'd touched him.

His palm moved between her legs and, finding her center, he cupped her. Kate bit the inside of her cheek. It was all she could do to prevent herself from thrusting herself against him. And then his fingers pushed between her lips and slipped over that sensitive spot, and she cried out.

His hand left her suddenly, cupped her buttocks, and then moved lower. He lifted her off her feet a second time, spreading her thighs so they pressed against the outsides of his. The fabric of her skirts crushed between them as he pushed his body against hers, and she guided his erection toward her. When she'd positioned him against the opening to her womb, he lowered her a scant inch onto him.

"Move your hands," he ordered, his voice harsh. "Hold me."

She wrapped her arms around his neck and stared up into his eyes. He stared back at her, and she was suddenly...afraid. Not of what they did, but of the monumental meaning for her behind it. The enormous swell of energy—of love—pulsing between them. Surely she wouldn't survive this. Surely—

He surged upward as he pushed her down. She cried out as all air was sucked out of her body and transformed to a white-hot heat that swirled about them.

Perspiration broke out across her skin, dripped between her breasts. It didn't hurt this time, not at all. It felt glorious, wonderful. He pulled out and thrust in her again, hard. Spots exploded in Kate's vision. The sensation of his shaft stroking her deepest, most intimate parts, the friction. Oh, Lord, it was too beautiful to bear.

She gasped in a breath and clutched him harder.

He'd let himself go. He looked *primal*. His eyes were squeezed shut, perspiration had broken out on his forehead, the muscles in his jaw had tensed, his scar had deepened in color, and his lips pressed together. His entire focus had moved, centered to the part of himself that was joined with her.

He pulled out and thrust again, holding her body, working her over him. Sensation buzzed from her core down through her legs and up through her center, warm and vibrating. She began to shake, and her eyes drifted closed.

He seated himself deep, and the base of his shaft brushed that sensitive spot on the outside of her body. She jerked and cried out, but he pulled out and thrust in before she could grasp the exquisite feeling. Again his base touched that spot, and she wriggled as the white heat enveloped her.

He moved faster, thrusting in and out of her with excruciating precision, as if he knew exactly how to drive her to distraction. She trembled. She squirmed and twisted and shook, but he held her firm.

And then she exploded. The white heat condensed, clustered deep in her core, and then spread through her veins like wildfire, bursting into a thousand tiny sparks of light through her skin. Her body convulsed over his, and she sobbed as she erupted with pleasure and then simmered for long moments in the aftermath, her channel constricting and tightening over him just as her hand had tugged at him earlier.

Finally she slumped in his arms. But he wasn't finished. He was hard as a board, and she moaned weakly as the pleasure again escalated within her body. He grew larger within her, tighter and harder inside and out, and Kate opened her eyes just as he let out a low groan and yanked her off him. Pressing against her mound, he let himself go, pulsing against her, his release warm against her skin. She held him even tighter, wanting him to feel the same pleasure she had felt earlier.

His muscles relaxed, but he didn't draw away. Instead, she clung to him as he held her crushed against the crisp leaves. They stayed that way for long minutes, the harsh sounds of their breathing gradually diminishing behind the roar of the waterfall.

Finally, he raised his head. He buttoned his trousers and smoothed her skirt, and then he stared at her for a long moment, his expression unreadable.

"Did I hurt you?"

"Did *I* hurt *you*?

He shook his head, a faint smile curving his lips.

"No," she said. Just like the first time he'd touched her by the pool at Kenilworth Castle, emotion crowded her throat. But she would not cry. She swallowed hard. "No, you didn't hurt me. It was . . . very pleasurable."

"Did you come?"

She frowned. "Is that the word for . . . ?"

"For what?" His eyes softened, and he stroked his thumb across her lower lip.

"Well, for that . . . feeling?"

His smile turned sly. "What feeling?"

"I think you know."

"Describe it to me."

"It's like a surge. A spark—no, a million sparks surging

through my body, and then exploding like... like a volcano." She frowned, thinking she'd done a poor job of describing a sensation she found completely indescribable. It was like nothing she'd ever experienced apart from him.

He kissed her forehead, the tip of her nose, her cheeks, her chin, and then her lips again. "Yes, Kate. That's exactly it."

"Is that how it feels when... when you release your seed?"

"Yes. Something like that. I think it's similar for a man and a woman."

She shook her head in wonderment. "I never knew."

His lips descended to her neck. "You taste so good, Kate," he murmured against her skin. "I can't stop tasting you."

She turned her face, and her lips brushed his silky blond hair. "You, too."

She nuzzled into his scalp, inhaling him. Her lips pressed over the scar behind his ear, and he jerked back. For a moment, she stared at him in surprise, and then she shook her head.

"Are you shy about your scars?"

"No." The tightness in his expression relaxed into a grin. "Well... maybe a little."

"Don't be," she murmured. "Please."

She sensed something had shifted, erecting a thin, invisible wall between them. She knew he was remembering, as she was, that her brother had inflicted that scar. And Garrett had killed him for it.

Garrett took a breath. "We should see about some new clothes for you." He gave her a ghost of a smile. "You can't live your life dressed in green."

"Thank you, but Becky has already called upon a dressmaker from Leeds." She looked toward the waterfall, embarrassment flooding through her. "I told her it wasn't important, that I could alter something, but she seems to have an entire wardrobe planned for me."

"That was good of her." Garrett frowned. "But that was my responsibility, and I should have thought of it sooner. I'm sorry."

She shook her head vehemently. "No, of course it wasn't your responsibility, nor is it hers, though she is more than kind to offer. Neither of you owes me anything."

She glimpsed Garrett's gaze harden and his eyes turn the color of flint before he turned away. "Rebecca will be wondering what has become of you."

She sighed. He was absolutely correct, and she wasn't looking forward to Becky's questions when she returned to the house with her hair awry and her skirts rumpled.

"Let us go." Taking her hand, he led her between the ferns, over the mossy stones and grass, back the way they had come.

They walked in comfortable silence until they rounded a bend in the path and the southern side of Calton House appeared in the distance.

Garrett gently pulled his hand from hers, stroked a stray hair away from her cheek, and tucked it behind her ear. Then he dropped his hand to his side, and she knew he wouldn't touch her again, not with Calton House in view. Pain stabbed through her chest, but she sucked it down and tucked it away. She was stupid to think, even for a second, that he'd touch her in plain sight of the inhabitants of Calton House. She'd known what she'd walked into today. She'd submitted to him knowing exactly what to expect afterward.

It still hurt.

He'd said to give it time...maybe in time...

No. *No!* She clenched her fists at her sides. It was a farfetched dream, at best. She should know better. All she had to do was remember what had happened to Mama.

He tilted his head as they drew closer. "There are two carriages in the drive."

Kate's stomach dropped, and despair flooded her. "Oh, no. It's the dressmaker. Becky will be furious with me." She glanced at Garrett. "Would you mind very much if I were to run?"

"Of course not." He hesitated. "I believe I'll walk."

She nodded and blinked hard. And then she turned from him and ran hard all the way to the house, convincing herself that the sting in her eyes was due solely to the crispness of the wind.

Garrett watched her run. Her lithe body glided like a gazelle's down the path, through the gardens, and, moments later, into the house.

What to do? How to manage this? He wanted Kate, but he hadn't the faintest idea how best to go about winning her. He couldn't protect her reputation much longer by pretending indifference. Rebecca had seen him hovering at Kate's door a few nights ago. Surely it wouldn't be long before the entire household knew where his affections lay, because he couldn't live in the same house with her without spending every waking moment thinking about her. Which would make him careless. Which meant her reputation was at risk.

Marriage. The thought skittered into his brain and stopped, tentatively waiting for its reception. For the first time, he didn't chase it away.

He'd delayed because it would seem too impulsive so soon after his divorce, and there was still the matter of the unfinished business in Belgium. But in the face of his affection for Kate, of the need to protect her, none of that mattered. He must marry her, as soon as possible. There was no alternative. He wouldn't allow her to be disgraced, and he hated seeing her unhappy. He despised her thinking her life was a waste, that she wasn't worth a commitment from any man, much less him. She didn't comprehend her value, couldn't believe that it was he who wasn't good enough for her.

Everyone would agree it was too soon after his arrival home, after his divorce, after Fisk's death. The world would counsel him against this impulsive decision. But he didn't give a damn what anyone else thought. The thought of marrying her pleased him greatly.

His lover. His wife. Perhaps, one day, the mother of his children...

He would arrange for a special license from London. During that time, he'd woo her wholeheartedly, relentlessly, day and night. She'd realize they were meant for each other. He'd close the chasm between them by building the most solid, stable, and strong bridge in the history of mankind.

His stride lengthened and he gained speed. By the time he entered the house and walked through the back hall and into the front to discard his coat and gloves, his boot heels clicking on the parquet, he was grinning from ear to ear. He felt like a new man.

He was going to ask Kate to be his wife. And if she accepted him, he'd spend the rest of his life showing her how much she meant to him. How valuable she was. How she'd saved him, in more ways than one.

The butler met him in the entry hall, his face expressionless as usual. "Enjoyable walk, Your Grace?"

"Extremely, Jenkins."

"Excellent." Jenkins took his gloves. "Sir, you have a visitor."

Garrett paused in the act of unbuttoning his coat and looked at the butler in surprise. "Who is it?"

"She said her name is Madame Joelle Martin, Your Grace. She awaits you in the drawing room."

Garrett's body convulsed, and it took every ounce of his remaining control to stay upright. Unsteadily, he pressed his hand against the blue-and-gold-striped wallpaper.

Joelle Martin. God help him.

Chapter Sixteen

Garrett pushed open the drawing-room door. Joelle stood at the window. Her blond curls, piled high on her head with several strands tumbling down her back, shone gold in the light streaming through the square panes.

Slowly, she turned, and Garrett's mouth went dry.

Joelle was heavily pregnant—certainly close to her delivery. She wore a buttercup-yellow dress with tiny white roses embroidered down the front and a matching jacket that split open just beneath a puffy flower-shaped button to reveal her protruding belly.

What was she doing here when she should be in her confinement?

But he knew. A part of him knew, though another part screamed in denial even as his brain rolled through the calculations. The last time he'd taken her to bed...early March. Almost eight months ago.

"Garrett," she said in her low, velvety, French-accented

voice. The way she said his name—with the rolling French *r* and ending with "eet"—always struck him as carnal. The timbre of her voice in combination with the accent never failed to bring him to the heights of arousal. But at the moment, his body was too frozen with shock to react to anything.

"Where?" he asked. "How...?" His voice trailed off.

She took a tentative step forward. "I...knew I must find you." She motioned to her distended abdomen.

Garrett found his fascinated gaze fixed upon her stomach.

"The child is yours."

He searched desperately for something to say, but came up blank.

"Papa threw me away," she whispered, cupping her hands protectively around her middle and blinking back a sheen of moisture forming in her eyes. "I had nowhere else to turn."

Her father was a Belgian mine owner with four daughters—the oldest, prettiest, and most rebellious of whom was Joelle. She'd been married briefly but had lost her husband and their fortune to the war. Her family lived in a manor house near the farmhouse barracks where Garrett had resided. Four summers ago, as he'd worked tilling the fields, he caught her watching him. It was a hot day, and he had shucked his shirt and tucked it into the waistband of his trousers. As soon as he saw her flushed, curious face, her voluptuous body, and her lush blond curls, he'd been drawn to her. When he'd heard her husky voice, he'd been lost.

Six months later, they succumbed to their mutual lust, and he tumbled her in the fields. After that, they'd met occasionally at the inn in town. She'd claimed she had no interest in marrying again, not that Garrett was in a position to ask. She'd made an eager, willing, and entertaining bedmate. As the years progressed, they became more than occasional lovers—they had become good friends as well.

He hadn't said good-bye to her. Once Garrett remembered Sophie, he'd rushed to England. Later, in London, he had arranged for Fisk to send her a letter to apologize for his abrupt departure. Fisk had advised him to send her some money as well, and Garrett had agreed without hesitation, not only because he felt guilty, but because he knew she'd appreciate the gesture. Joelle liked money.

He'd scarcely thought about her since he'd met Kate.

Garrett swallowed. "How...did you find me?"

"I received your letter and your 'gift.' Thank you."

He nodded, but still he was surprised to hear Fisk had done something he'd promised.

"I begged Maman for the funds to come to England, and she purchased my passage and persuaded Papa to allow my maid to join me. Maman believed you would help me." She took another small step forward and cast her gaze at the floor. "Colette and I went to London first. But you were not there."

"I remained in London only for a short time." Since then, he'd been all over the United Kingdom in pursuit of Fisk.

After a long pause, she made a wide gesture with her arm. "My Garrett, a duke of England?"

He followed her gaze. Even after several months, the truth of it had hardly sunk in. He stepped inside and shut the door behind him, his lips twisting. "Evidently I am."

She gazed at him, her blue eyes glowing. "You must be very, very happy to hear you are rich. You struggled for so long." Her plump, pink mouth curved into a smile. "It does not surprise me. I knew you were more than a farmer." She assessed him with her gaze, and her breath caught. "You look very handsome in your duke's clothes."

Her voice was timid, but that was Joelle. Her crust was frail and sweet, like candied sugar. Inside, however, she was determined, passionate, and strong. And ambitious. He couldn't forget that about her. She would never have accepted a mere farmhand as a husband. Late at night, she'd whispered her hopes for her grand future, of a life in Paris society.

Now she was pregnant and unmarried, and that future was lost. Because of him.

He glanced down at himself, and a chill washed over his skin. His trousers were rumpled from his "walk" with Kate. Still, there was no denying that his clothing was far richer than anything he'd ever worn in Belgium, and even far richer than Joelle's fashionable muslin dress.

He made a loose gesture toward her stomach. "When is...the child...?"

"In a few weeks." She paused. "I should not have waited as long as I did, but I was so afraid..." She twisted her hands. "Was it wrong of me to come?"

"No. Not at all."

"Truly, I had nowhere to go."

"Of course you should have come to me."

The look of anguish in her face made his heart twist. As much as she rebelled against her father, she adored the man. He couldn't imagine the pain it had caused her when Martin had set her out. Her mother, fortunately, was a woman less prone to dramatics. Thank God she had helped Joelle, otherwise God knew where she and the baby might be now.

His baby. Again, his gaze was drawn to her abdomen. He stared at it in fascination.

My baby. It sounded so strange tumbling around in his mind.

"Are you certain?" he asked.

She gripped her hands together in front of her belly. "What are you saying?"

What *was* he saying? He knew Joelle well, and to his knowledge, she'd never lied to him. Still, he had to be sure. "Was there anyone else, Joelle? Could the child be anyone else's?"

Her eyes widened. She clutched her hands together so hard her knuckles turned white, and she shook her head vehemently. "You know there wasn't! You were my only lover. The only one!"

She heaved out a sob, and guilt flooded through him. Not once in all the years he had known her had she given him a reason to distrust her. God, he was a bastard. He strode to her, pulled her into his arms, and spoke to her in French, the language they used when they were most intimate. "Shh," he murmured as she clung to him, shaking. "You're safe now."

The sun had long since dipped beneath the horizon in a glorious purple-streaked sunset, and Kate had finally closed Becky's tasseled pink curtains against the encroaching darkness.

Kate and Becky had finished with the three dressmakers after Kate had stood in the center of the room for hours being poked and prodded as people discussed her shape and size and coloring as if she were a horse at the market. Becky hadn't been put off in the slightest by Kate's late arrival, for she'd arrived only moments after the modistes.

Becky was elated with the results, and the seamstress had promised Kate's first batch of clothing within a few days. Even Kate couldn't repress a little shiver of anticipation as she imagined herself dressed in the beautiful fabrics and fashions that Becky and the women had discussed.

A footman poked his head in the door and asked permission for Master Reginald to dine with Lady Miranda this evening. Flustered by the invitation as well as the delivery of it, Kate had given her permission.

Sitting up, Becky reached out her good hand and squeezed Kate's shoulder. "Come. It's almost time for dinner. You *will* come to dinner with me."

"I can't. Reggie—"

"Of course you can," Becky said sharply. "You and Reginald have been taking your meals here with me, which was perfectly acceptable whilst I was bedridden. But now Reginald shall dine with Miranda, and you shall dine with the rest of us. I will not allow my sister-in-law to eat with the servants."

"Becky—"

Becky raised her hand. "Kate, I won't hear another word. Understand me when I say again that you aren't a servant anymore. You're the sister-in-law of a lady, and that lady doesn't wish it to be bandied about that her sister dines in the kitchens."

Kate shook her head. "You don't care a whit about that. You said scandal couldn't touch you."

Becky grinned. "You know me too well. You are correct, of course—if someone dared to whisper about such a foolish thing, it wouldn't bother me. But I truly do wish for you to come with me. As my sister as well as my friend."

Kate hesitated. She wasn't certain she could face Garrett tonight—not after what had happened between them this afternoon. But that was cowardly, wasn't it? She'd have to face him sometime.

She'd never been accused of cowardice, and she wouldn't start now.

"I just regret that your lovely cream silk dinner dress hasn't arrived yet." When Kate was silent, Becky said, "Kate? Please come to dinner with me. It'll just be the four of us—Garrett, Aunt Bertrice, you, and me. Surely by now you can't find us all so very daunting."

Just then, Becky's new lady's maid, Josie, exploded into the room, looking fit to burst with gossip.

Becky glanced askance at Kate and then nodded patiently at Josie. "Out with it, then."

"Oh, Lady Rebecca. Well, you mightn't have heard, milady, but there was a beautiful and elegant lady come to see His Grace just after the seamstresses arrived."

"Oh? Really?"

Josie approached the bed, her face pink all the way to the edges of her cap. "Well," she said breathlessly. "The lady is Belgian."

"Is that so?"

"And," Josie said significantly, "she's heavy with child. *Very* heavy."

Becky frowned, and Kate's heart began to stutter. She looked back and forth from Becky to Josie.

Josie leaned forward. "The lady has informed His Grace that the child is his."

Kate stared straight ahead as pain squeezed like a fist in her heart. She felt Becky's eyes on her.

"Mere gossip," Becky said sharply, her voice barely audible above the roar rising in Kate's ears. "For shame, Josie. You ought to know better than to spread such rumors."

"But, milady, I swear it is the truth. Nell was polishing silver in the corridor, and she heard their conversation, clear as day."

Becky sighed. "Leave us." She hesitated and then said, "But return if you hear anything else, do you understand?"

Kate watched the girl leave, then turned to Becky, blinking hard. It was all she could do to keep from bursting into tears.

She shouldn't be reacting like this. Lord help her, she shouldn't be reacting at all.

"Kate, my dear friend," Becky murmured. She grasped Kate's hand. "It means nothing. Even if what she said is true, if the child is Garrett's, it means nothing."

"But it does," Kate responded in a rasping voice. It shouldn't, but it did.

It hurt. The fact that Garrett had lain with a woman in Belgium. The fact that he hadn't been as careful to ensure the lady didn't conceive as he had been with Kate. The fact that the lady had come back to him. Garrett's honor would compel him to care for the child. And the lady, too.

She could practically feel his affection for her seeping away to be replaced with renewed care for this woman, whoever she was.

The pain tightened, hardened like a lump of coal in her chest, with a thousand thorns of jealousy pricking at it. She tried to rein in her raging emotions, to no avail. She'd never known she possessed a jealous nature.

"Perhaps you should sit," Becky said softly.

She wasn't even aware she'd risen. Slowly, she lowered herself back into the chair, gripping its soft pink velvet arms.

What right did she have to be possessive of Garrett? For heaven's sake, she had no claim on the man. But tell that to the rage tingeing her vision. Tell that to the angry thorns tearing at her chest.

She ground her teeth.

"I was right," Becky sighed. "I knew it."

Kate blinked through the haze to look at her.

Becky awkwardly swung her legs over the edge of the bed, her robe hiking up to reveal her pale, slim calves.

"You are madly, passionately, and desperately in love with my brother."

As much as she commanded it, no denial would rise to Kate's lips. She could only stare bleakly at Becky, knowing that even if she did manage to mumble something, it would sound false. She was a terrible liar. She shrank back into the chair, remembering Becky's warning in the carriage on the way to Calton House.

"I know exactly what you're thinking, Kate. And you can stop it right now."

Kate's eyebrows pinched together. "What am I thinking?"

"You're thinking your love is impossible. Unattainable. Well, you are wrong."

"What are you saying?" Kate breathed.

"I've had a great deal of time to think, lying on this bed these past days. I finally understand you, Kate. And I understand my brother. And I see clearly what you both need."

Kate didn't dare ask what that might be.

"Each other," Becky said firmly.

Kate groaned.

"You see, you've disregarded a crucial—perhaps the *most* crucial—element of this equation."

"What's that?" Kate whispered.

"You aren't taking into account where my brother's affections lie. You don't feel you're deserving of Garrett's love, and that's why you aren't able to comprehend what he feels for you."

Kate shook her head.

"You see, Kate. I believe my brother is just as madly in love with you as you are with him." She paused. "I have changed my mind since Kenilworth. William and his servant said you seduced Garrett—"

Kate let out a gasp.

"—but," Becky continued, "now it has come together for me. You didn't seduce Garrett. You and my brother seduced each other."

"No," Kate groaned. She hurt all over, inside and out. Air pressed in on every inch of her body, crushing her. Shrinking her. It was all too much. From the appearance of this woman, to what had occurred between her and Garrett earlier today, to what Becky had discerned from her no doubt obvious, abominable mooning after her brother, Kate felt smaller than a toad and ready to leap away, burrow beneath a lily pad, and hide from everyone forever.

Becky knelt before her, her face glowing. She took

Kate's hand in her own. "Listen to me, Kate. You and my brother are perfect for each other. Do you hear me? Perfect."

"Please, Becky..." she breathed.

Becky stood, pulling Kate up with her. "You must be strong, Kate. Now, let us prepare ourselves for dinner. Let us go see for ourselves who this mystery woman really is."

Aunt Bertrice met Garrett in the corridor as he finished speaking with the housekeeper, giving orders to prepare a room for Joelle and her maid and to have someone set an extra place for dinner.

"Yes, sir, I'll see to it immediately." The housekeeper curtsied and turned away.

Aunt Bertrice raised a brow. "What's this?"

Well, he couldn't very well make a secret of Joelle's condition, so he laid it out in the plainest terms for his aunt. "A woman from Belgium has come to see me, Aunt. She is with child, and I believe it is mine."

Aunt Bertrice's eyes narrowed. "You intend to keep your doxy in residence at Calton House?"

"No. She's a French lady of good birth. A widow. And since she will be a guest in my house and carries my child, I expect to see you offer nothing but kindness to her."

Aunt Bertrice's lips thinned. "Garrett, this is shockingly improper."

"She is to be welcomed into this house," Garrett said. "As any member of our family would be." Instantly, Garrett regretted not giving his aunt this speech regarding Kate as well, for he'd witnessed the way she regarded

Kate with narrow, distrustful eyes. In a way, he understood his aunt's suspicion. Fisk had frightened Aunt Bertrice like nothing else in her life, and because of that, she was loath to trust his sister. Of course, the fact that Garrett had faith in Kate should be enough—but his family members no longer trusted his judgment, and rightly so. He'd forced his entire family to take Fisk into their circle, and look what had come of that.

"May I meet this... lady?" Aunt Bertrice asked.

"Of course you may. But only if you behave."

"Gad, boy," Aunt Bertrice said. "I'm not a child, so you needn't treat me as one." As they neared the door, she asked, "Does she speak English? Or shall I have to communicate in French? Or Dutch, God forbid?"

"She speaks English very well. You will find her quite educated." He gave her a sidelong glance as they neared the door. "But you ought to speak to her in French. If I recall, you spent many years there and are quite fluent."

She raised her brows. "You've remembered more and more, eh?"

"I remember everything," he said quietly. Taking a deep breath, he shoved open the door.

"Garrett—oh!" Joelle lowered her head and dropped into a curtsy. "Forgive me."

"Madame Martin, this is my aunt, Lady Bertrice. Aunt, Madame Martin."

Joelle's blue eyes shone as she raised her head. "It is a pleasure." She looked from Garrett to his aunt. "The family resemblance is undeniable."

She curtsied again, and Aunt Bertrice inclined her head. "Madame Martin."

Joelle clapped her hands together. "Your accent—it is lovely. Do you speak French, Lady Bertrice?"

"I daresay it's a bit rusty, but yes, I lived in Paris for many years when I was younger."

"Paris? Ah, yes, that is my most favorite place on this earth!"

Aunt Bertrice's eyes glowed, and Garrett remembered how her demeanor changed whenever she spoke of Paris. She became wistful and dreamy—altogether unlike herself. Garrett had never doubted that the best years of his aunt's life had been lived in Paris.

"It is my favorite place as well," his aunt said, and then she launched into flawless French. "Have your travels taken you to Paris, Madame Martin?"

Joelle switched to French as well. "Yes, I lived there briefly with my husband before the war."

Garrett strode to the sidebar to pour himself some brandy while the women talked. By the time he'd raised his glass to his lips to take the first sip, they were seated beside each other on the sofa, their heads close, deep in conversation. He might have smiled, if…He shook his head, feeling like a bastard for admitting it to himself. A part of him wished to see Kate's belly big with his child. Not Joelle's.

He downed a generous swallow of brandy, savoring the burn as it slid down his throat.

Kate trailed behind Becky as she led the way downstairs. They were to meet with Garrett, Aunt Bertrice, and the mystery woman in the drawing room before progressing to dinner together. Kate felt awkward and shy and ungainly, and altogether uncomfortable in her too-large green dress. She couldn't comprehend how she'd ever bear this night. How she could face Garrett after the revelations of this afternoon and the revelations to come.

The child is his...the child is his. The words Josie had spoken in Becky's bedchamber sloshed and bubbled around in her stomach like a bottle filled with water and soda and shaken into an angry, frothing sea.

They followed a footman into the drawing room. When he announced them, Garrett rose from his chocolate-brown armchair, and Lady Bertrice bobbed up from her position seated on the sofa. "Oh, my! Is it time for dinner already?" She scowled at Garrett. "Why did you say nothing?"

Garrett didn't answer. Instead he stared at Kate for a long, agonizing moment, all kinds of indecipherable emotions seething in his blue eyes.

"What is—" Kate began, but Lady Bertrice cleared her throat loudly, and Garrett wrenched his gaze from Kate. He took a step forward and held out his hand to the second occupant of the sofa, offering to help her to rise.

Garrett's Belgian lover. Heavy with child. Kate dragged her gaze upward from the bright yellow skirt covering the woman's large, rounded belly.

She was lovely. With blond, bouncing curls tumbling to her shoulders and a pale oval-shaped face tinged with pink and offset by pouting red lips and blue eyes. She turned to smile and curtsy at Becky, and Kate caught a glimpse of her profile. Her chest tightened, and when the lady murmured a greeting, Kate gasped.

Everyone's gaze shot to her, but Kate couldn't see anything but the woman standing in the center of the room.

People spoke, but all she could hear was her renewed heartbeat clanging like cymbals in her ears.

She stared wide-eyed at Garrett's mistress...and Willy's mistress. Garrett's pregnant paramour was the woman Kate had seen her brother tupping in Bertie's cottage.

Chapter Seventeen

Kate had escaped, mumbling something about a headache and excusing herself from dinner. She ran upstairs and flung herself onto the enormous bed in the Ivory Room, clutching her knees to her chest and rocking back and forth on the ivory satin counterpane.

Eventually, it occurred to her that she could be wrong. There were many blond ladies in the world, even many blond ladies with foreign accents, and the fact that this one had exactly the same texture and color of hair as Willy's mistress could be sheer coincidence. And Kate hadn't seen the woman's face in Bertie's cottage, only her profile.

As for her body, she'd only seen Willy's mistress's rounded backside and one plump thigh, so short of asking this lady to strip naked, she could hardly judge. But the fact that she was so heavily pregnant was... unexpected, to say the least. Kate couldn't imagine any man would so violently ram himself into the body of a woman that close to her delivery date.

Then again, she couldn't have imagined Willy doing any of the things he'd done to Garrett and his family.

Willy's mistress had seemed to enjoy how rough he'd been to her. Everything Kate had seen when she'd peered in the window that day failed to reconcile with the innocent-faced lady she'd seen in Garrett's drawing room.

Ultimately, she possessed no proof that the lady in the drawing room was Willy's mistress, and yet something about her made her believe—believe down to her bones—it was the same woman. While her mind streamed reasons she might be wrong, her gut told her she wasn't.

Still, there was no proof. If she accused this woman, would anyone believe her? Her story would sound too fantastical to be true. And if Becky knew how besotted Kate was with Garrett, surely most of the household knew as well. Would they attribute her accusations to spiteful jealousy? Because Lord knew, at this moment, spiteful jealousy wasn't a foreign emotion to her.

Could the intensity of her jealousy be clouding her reason?

Even Garrett—the soul she most trusted—couldn't be trusted to look at this objectively. If he'd truly bedded the woman, then he must possess some affection for her. The truth would hurt him. He wouldn't want to believe it.

A knock sounded on her door, and she looked up in surprise. It was too early for dinner to be over, surely. "Who is it?"

"It's Becky."

Kate clung tighter to her legs. It would be beyond the pale to turn Becky away now. "Come in."

Becky entered and lowered herself gingerly on the edge of Kate's bed. "I begged off dinner early. I told them my arm was paining me."

"Is it?"

"No more than usual." After a brief silence, she said, "I didn't expect you to run away like that, Kate. It was unlike you."

"I know." Kate looked away, toward the window. "I'm sorry. I couldn't help it."

"I understand." Becky's voice was gentle. "Would you like to hear more about her?"

Kate swallowed. She did and she didn't. She wanted to know everything, to understand, but she didn't want to see or hear or discuss that woman ever again in her life.

"Yes," she choked out. Then she squeezed her eyes shut in fear.

"Her name is Joelle Martin. She's from Belgium, as Josie said." Becky took a breath. "Garrett has made it clear he believes the child is his."

Should she tell Becky her suspicion? It would hurt Becky terribly. How could she knowingly hurt her friend? Especially if she were wrong. Becky would hate her. They all would.

But she wasn't wrong. She *knew* she wasn't wrong.

"Kate?" Becky murmured, squeezing her arm. "Please don't despair. Garrett was concerned for you—he wanted to call the doctor to check on you—in fact, I rather thought he'd prefer to come to you himself, but I told him I was certain you'd be well in the morning and I convinced him to wait."

"I'll—be all right." Kate opened her eyes. Goodness—

she'd been so caught up in her despair she had forgotten all about Reggie. "What time is it?"

"Past eleven."

She scrambled off the bed. "Oh, dear. I must go fetch Reggie."

"I received a note from Miss Dalworthy at dinner. She was hesitant to wake you due to your headache, but she said Reginald had fallen asleep with Miranda upstairs and asked if it would be all right for him to stay for the night."

"He should be with me."

"Kate." Becky's expression turned sober. "You ought to let him rest."

"He has nightmares. He's so easily frightened."

"I know," Becky said. "I also know Miss Dalworthy is well-equipped to manage such things. In any case, I told her that if Reginald woke or began to cough, she was to bring him straight to you."

Kate paused, her hand on the door handle. There was no reason to drag Reggie down here at this hour—except for the comfort she'd glean from having him close. She dropped her hand. "Thank you."

Becky smiled. "What are sisters for?"

Kate tried to return the smile, but it went flat. Sisters were there to care for each other. To soothe when one was in pain. To support and encourage.

Not to accuse the mother of her brother's baby of being her husband's mistress. Kate rubbed at her temple as pain stabbed through it.

"Did Garrett...did your brother...how did he...?" She wanted to know how Garrett looked at this woman. How he behaved in her presence.

Becky sighed. "He was very polite to her, Kate, and quite solicitous. But there was something in the way he treated her that I couldn't quite put my finger on. In truth, he seemed more interested in ensuring you were all right."

"Did you like her?" she asked quietly.

Becky gave her one-shouldered shrug. "She was quite sweet-tempered. Aunt Bertrice pronounced her 'fetching.' But I don't know. I suppose I'm not as willing to believe her claims. Perhaps it is because of what happened with William, but I doubt if I shall freely bestow my trust on anyone ever again."

"You trust me."

Becky nodded. "I do. I've known you for months, though."

"Two months. That's not very long."

Becky pulled her black shawl more tightly across her shoulders. "Long enough. Especially given what we"—her gaze flickered to the gold-trimmed ivory wallpaper—"experienced together."

Kate remained silent for a long moment. She'd changed. A month ago, she would have blurted her suspicions right away. But her accusations would horrify Becky, and that alone made her hold her tongue. She wasn't willing to risk their friendship for a suspicion that might be a product of her overwrought, jealous imagination.

"I trust you, too, Becky. You're a good friend to me." The best she had ever had.

Becky smiled. Her smile, like the rest of her, was naturally pretty, and it sent a flush of something sweet through Kate. From the moment they'd met, she'd secretly dreamed of becoming close to Lady Rebecca. And now they were friends in truth.

Friends didn't gossip. They didn't plant seeds of suspicion in each other before knowing the facts. Before she opened her mouth, Kate must find proof of Joelle's relationship to Willy. She wouldn't send this house into chaos without cause, nor would she risk the fragile but important bonds she'd forged here. Before she accused Joelle, she needed to be more certain.

Kate remembered returning to Bertie's cottage after she'd seen Willy and the woman there the first time. How she'd seen the woman's undergarments lying about. She remembered those undergarments—blue silk stockings, ribbons of coquelicot and forest green, lacy drawers of powder blue and white. If she could search through the woman's luggage, she might find some of those garments... and then she'd have proof—at least enough proof to convince herself.

Tomorrow. As soon as Joelle left her room tomorrow, Kate would search it.

The door clicked shut behind Aunt Bertrice, and she stood just inside the library, her arms crossed over her ample bosom. She still wore the primrose dress she'd worn to dinner, and a dyed primrose feather stood up from her elaborate hairdo as if sprouting from the back of her head.

"You should marry her."

"What?" Garrett sputtered to his aunt, who'd just let herself into his sanctuary without knocking.

The night had been damn long, starting with Kate fleeing, continuing with his sister's early departure, and ending with his enduring hours of feminine discourse—in French—between his aunt and his... and Joelle. Finally, after midnight, they'd separated and he'd escaped to the library to think.

He was worried about Kate. Someone must have told her about Joelle. Damn them. He'd have preferred to speak to her himself. But, then again, what would he say? Putting himself into her shoes, he could only imagine the horror that must have surged through her at the sight of his pregnant ex-lover. She probably hated him now. She should hate him now. It was damned thoughtless of him not to have gone to her first, to explain. Garrett swallowed the remainder of his port.

He'd go to her now, if he wasn't such a coward.

"I'm dead serious," Aunt Bertrice said flatly. "It is the honorable thing to do."

Garrett narrowed his eyes. "I am not so certain of that."

"Well, I am." She swept deeper into the room and lowered herself into one of the plush leather armchairs. "I believe it is the perfect solution. Keep her here until the child is born, and then take her to London. She is a lady and will bear the duties of a duchess with aplomb. You will have your heir. And—" she tapped her fingers on the arms of the chair, "—I rather believe it will finally put to rest the scandal of your divorce."

Garrett raised a brow. "How's that?"

"Well, everyone will understand. You went away to Belgium and during your years there you fell madly in love with a ravishing Belgian beauty."

Garrett's lip curled as he poured more port into his tumbler. "I thought it was already clear that during those years Sophie fell in love with Tristan. I fail to see how my affair with Joelle could have anything to do with it."

"Of course it has something to do with it." His aunt waved a hand. "You're a man. Sophie is a woman. The world will be much more understanding of it happening to you. And it will help that Joelle is so very young and lovely."

"Ah. So you think I should send the message to society that I chose to discard Sophie for the younger and more nubile Joelle Martin?"

"Well..." Aunt Bertrice must have seen the rage building in his eyes, for she chose to retreat rather than pursue the madness of this rationale. "Not exactly."

He released a breath. "Aunt, before we continue this absurd line of conversation, let me state the facts. I haven't yet decided what to do with Joelle."

"Marry her," his aunt said shortly.

He rotated his glass in his hand, staring at the ruby-red liquid swirling in it. Joelle would like rubies. Now he was rich enough to afford them. "You don't know Joelle as well as I do."

"I fail to see why that should make a difference," his aunt snapped.

He thumped his glass on the table and gave his aunt a hard look. "The woman is ambitious. Let me be as blunt as possible: I wouldn't be surprised if she came running the moment she discovered I was a duke."

Aunt Bertrice's lip curled. "What, exactly, is so wrong with ambition, Garrett? We would all still be heathens if it didn't exist. Ambition created civilization."

"Ambition is selfish."

"Bah. I see true affection for you in her eyes."

He sighed, knowing she spoke the truth. He saw it, too.

There was no denying he and Joelle possessed a special fondness for each other.

But love? Did she love him? Christ, did he love her? Months ago, when he'd told Sophie about Joelle, he said he wasn't certain whether he loved her. But that was before he met Kate.

"And what of the child?" his aunt asked.

Garrett tilted his head. The child was of primary importance, but it was so like Aunt Bertrice to save its well-being for her final argument.

"You wouldn't want him fatherless."

"He—or *she*—will not be fatherless," he ground out. "Whatever might ultimately occur between Joelle and myself."

"If you marry her, he will have a father in truth. He will be legitimate. He will never have to bear the stigma of bastardy."

Garrett shook his head. He didn't savor the idea of fathering an illegitimate child—God knew the world was harsh to the illegitimate. However, God help the soul who spoke ill of any of his children, legitimate or not.

It would be easier for the child—*far* easier—if his father were married to his mother. To ensure the child's happiness and security, the clearest solution was to marry Joelle.

Garrett stared at the sleek rosewood surface of his desk, knowing his aunt studied him carefully. Waiting for him to come to the same conclusion she had—that marriage to Joelle was the only answer. The honorable answer.

He'd been so careful to prevent conception with Joelle. As careful as he'd been with Kate. He wasn't a complete fool, though—he knew nothing was guaranteed. Each and every time they'd lain together, they'd taken a risk. And they'd lain together many more times than he had lain with Kate.

Christ, for all he knew, he could have gotten Kate with child this very day.

"There's something between you and the Fisk girl, isn't there?"

He looked at his aunt blankly. "The Fisk girl?"

"Yes." She waved her hand. "Don't be dense, boy. You know exactly who I'm talking about. That over-tall, gangling Katherine Fisk."

He'd never associated Kate with her surname. Not once. He didn't like the sound of it. "Katherine James"—what her name would become should he marry her—sounded much better. Much more correct.

"I'll thank you for not speaking ill of Kate, Aunt," he said through tight lips. "Never forget. She saved my life, and Rebecca's."

Aunt Bertrice's lips twisted. "I seem to be constantly reminded of that fact," she said with a slight sneer. "It seems the both of you will spend the remainder of your lives fawning over her for it. Seems to me her actions were born more of self-preservation than heroism."

Garrett's fingers twitched. He curled them into fists atop his desk. "Watch yourself."

His aunt's eyes flicked from his face to his hands and back again. She shook her head. "So that's the way of it, eh? You're besotted with the girl."

He stared at her. He refused to allow her to drag him into this discussion. It was already clear what she thought of both Kate and Joelle, and where her wishes lay.

"You were wrong about William Fisk, Garrett. Do not

make that mistake again," she warned. "You nearly ruined this family with your blind trust. We are just beginning to pick up the pieces. Do not risk it again. Don't let another Fisk lead you astray."

His fists tightened over the smooth, cool wooden surface. A part of him knew his aunt could be right. Hell, his gut had screamed at him to trust Fisk almost as much as it screamed at him to trust Kate.

Yet he trusted Kate regardless. Nobody and nothing could convince him she was anything like her older brother. He grimaced at his aunt. "Thank you for your concern, Aunt Bertrice. And for your advice. I'll be certain to take your words—all of them—under consideration." He took a deep breath. He'd never given his aunt an order, but he was the head of this family, and if he wished to preserve any semblance of a decent relationship between them, she must leave. Now. He glanced at the door and then back to her. "You are excused."

Her mouth dropped open. For a moment, she gaped at him. Then she rose, straightened, and inclined her head at him. "Very well. Good night, boy."

She turned, and in a flurry of yellow silk, headed toward the door, the feather swaying atop her head.

The door slammed behind her, and he stared at it for a long while. A deep late-night silence shrouded the library, and despair flooded through him, heavy and thick, bonding his body to his chair. He poured himself another glass of port, raised it to his lips, and threw it back.

Kate made him happy. Just being with her, beside her, touching her, speaking to her, made him feel whole. Real. With Kate, he became a human being again rather than the confused shell of one.

He wanted Kate. He sank his forehead into his hand. Why the hell couldn't it have been Kate?

Kate stood in the corridor in a defensive stance, her fists clenched at her sides, staring at Joelle's door. Joelle had slept in the Yellow Room—the bedchamber Becky had at first intended for Kate. It was a charming room, with tall windows looking out over the gardens. Even though they'd awakened for the past week to a ground frozen solid, the gardens remained lovely to gaze upon. It had not snowed yet, but Kate thought it might any day. Lady Miranda had come to their room earlier to fetch Reggie to play and said she was "simply dying for it to snow, because then we shall go sledding, and Papa will take us for a ride on the sleigh."

Kate sighed. She stared at the solid wood door. Joelle Martin had left her bedchamber to walk the grounds with Garrett, Lady Bertrice, and the children, and her maid had gone belowstairs on an errand for her mistress.

This was Kate's chance.

She needed proof. For herself, as well as everyone else. If the undergarments she'd seen strewn across the floor of Bertie's cottage were in Joelle Martin's luggage, that would be enough. If she found any evidence relating to her brother in Joelle Martin's personal items, that would be even stronger proof. Either way, if she found anything, she would go to Garrett and Becky right away, and she'd tell them everything she knew, and, as painful as it would be for all of them, everything she'd seen.

Someone might catch her as she searched, and that would be a terrible embarrassment, but it would be worth it for the chance to stop Garrett from making a mistake as enormous as his mistake of trusting her brother.

When she'd awakened early this morning, it had occurred to Kate that Joelle Martin's baby might not be Garrett's. It could be Willy's. Joelle Martin could be carrying Kate's niece or nephew. If Garrett knew that, what would he think?

She cast a glance up and down the corridor, finding it silent and empty. Two resolute steps had her positioned before Joelle's door. She grabbed the handle and turned it.

Quickly, she slipped inside and pushed the door shut behind her. Pressing her back against the wooden planks, she released a ragged breath and gazed at the interior of the Yellow Room. Pieces from Joelle's seemingly extensive wardrobe lay strewn across the unmade bed, over the chairs, and on the floor. Resisting the impulse to gather everything up, fold it carefully, and place it where it belonged, Kate wondered how Joelle's maid occupied her time. Wasn't her mistress's clothing her responsibility? How could it be that no one had made the bed? Had they refused the services of a chambermaid? Probably the woman's only task was to ensure Joelle always looked absolutely beautiful. A task which she succeeded in too well, Kate thought bitterly.

Perhaps Joelle didn't care about neatness, although outwardly she was the epitome of elegance. Compared to her, Kate felt as awkward and unkempt as a newborn calf on unsteady legs. Inside, she felt even worse. Her jealousy had hardened into a dark lump of poison that had grown overnight like a rampant tumor. Earlier this morning, when they'd met on the stairs, Kate had to look away from Joelle quickly, so acute was her fear that darts might shoot straight from her eyes into the lovely woman's unsuspecting satin-covered heart.

It struck her that Joelle was as untidy as Willy's mistress, because she *was* Willy's mistress. She had to be. With every minute that passed, Kate doubted herself less.

A quick scan of the room didn't reveal any of the items Kate had seen lying about in Bertie's cottage, except for a similar pair of common white stockings. Those could belong to anyone, though. They weren't as distinct as some of the other lacy articles she'd seen in the cottage. Kate stepped forward, picking her way over the obstacles of undergarments, shoes, and hats strewn across the floor.

She studied the bed. The damask counterpane was green, with dozens of darker green stripes embroidered with jonquils traversing its length. The sheets were green, too, and a half dozen yellow and green pillows, meant to be arranged carefully at the head of the bed, were scattered carelessly on the floor.

Lamps, their bases painted with jonquils matching the bedcover, were nested within piles of hairpins and cosmetics scattered over the mahogany tables set on either side of the bed. Kate wondered how someone could create such untidiness in the space of less than one day.

Nothing incriminating, though, seemed to be within the vicinity of the bed, so Kate turned to the tall wardrobe.

Just as Kate placed her hand on the knob of the wardrobe door, she heard a click. The dark lump of poison within her tumbled frantically as she slowly turned to the Yellow Room's threshold.

Joelle Martin stood there, the pink dark in her cheeks, her lips parted. She blinked her wide blue eyes at Kate in surprise.

"Why are you in my room?" she asked in her husky, accented voice.

Chapter Eighteen

Angry heat surged through Kate. She narrowed her eyes at the other woman. Whatever had prevented her suspicions from gushing out of her last night popped free like a cork.

"I'm looking for something."

Joelle cocked her head. "What are you looking for?"

"Something to implicate you."

"Implicate?" Joelle repeated slowly, as if she were unfamiliar with the word.

Kate realized she was clutching the knob of the wardrobe, so she unclenched her fingers, dropped her stiff arm to her side, and turned to fully face the Belgian woman. "Right. Implicate. Something to prove that you were my brother's mistress."

The confusion on Joelle's face deepened, and a furrow appeared between her brows. She looked perfectly innocent, and for a moment, Kate hated her. She wished she possessed the talent to lie as smoothly as Joelle.

"Your brother? I have heard he recently perished. I am sorry. But he was married, was he not? To Lady Rebecca."

"Yes," Kate said. She met the woman's confused gaze. "But up till the day he died, *you* were his mistress."

Joelle's jaw dropped, and her eyes widened. "I do not understand what you are saying."

Her innocent performance did nothing to placate Kate; instead it roused her ire. "You lived in the cottage near Debussey Manor. I don't know for how long... but you were engaging in carnal relations with my brother."

Joelle gasped. "Of course I was not!"

"Oh, yes, I think you were," Kate snarled, unable to keep the venom from her voice.

"I think you are mad!" Joelle retreated into the corridor. Her gaze darted to the right and left, searching for someone to protect her from the crazed woman who'd invaded her bedchamber.

Rage bubbled up in Kate, mingling with the resident lump of jealousy, softening it, making it easier to choke up the words she'd wanted to blurt last night when she'd first seen this woman. "And now you are trying to fool Garrett and his family, aren't you?" She stalked toward Joelle. "Tell me, is that really his child you carry? Or is it Willy's?"

Joelle's face turned beet red. "How dare you accuse me of these things!" Now standing in the center of the passageway, she held her hands over her rounded belly and twisted her fingers nervously, as though she feared that Kate might attack her child. But Kate knew the truth—the woman twisted her hands out of guilt.

"I know it's true." Kate paused in the doorway, an arm's length from Joelle. If she took half a step, she'd be the perfect distance to punch the shorter woman in the nose.

Joelle shook her head. "You are wrong, Miss Fisk. You have mistaken me for another woman."

"No." Kate's voice lashed out like a whip. "Why won't you admit the truth? You know you'll be caught eventually."

"There is nothing to catch. I tell you, you have mistaken me for another!"

"How dare you," Kate growled. She took two steps forward and stopped, now face to face with the shorter woman. She stared down her nose at Joelle. "How dare you take advantage of this family!" she hissed. "How dare you lie and scheme and present your innocent, sweet face to them. How dare you show that face to poor Lady Rebecca, who was so terribly hurt by what you and my brother did to her. I know what lies underneath all that sugar, Joelle Martin. A heart as black as my brother's was!"

"What's this?"

Kate whipped her head around to see Lady Bertrice scowling at them from the other end of the corridor. Joelle burst into tears, and Kate returned her furious glare to the scheming woman. "Such brilliant acting," she grated out with a sneer. "You should be on the stage."

"Oh!" Joelle sobbed, clutching her distended abdomen. "Oh! Oh!"

Lady Bertrice strode toward them. "What the devil are you doing?" she spat at Kate.

Kate had had quite enough of trying to be polite to the older woman. Lady Bertrice had made up her mind to dislike Kate from the moment they'd met. "I'm asking Mrs. Martin some questions," she said without looking at Lady Bertice.

"About what?"

Still, Kate kept her focus on Joelle. "About her involvement with my brother."

"What on earth are you talking about?"

"Oh! Oh!" Sobbing, Joelle rocked back and forth, hugging herself. Kate glared at the real tears streaming down the woman's flushed cheeks. She clenched her fists at her sides, though she'd have much preferred to slap the woman across her pink-flushed cheek. Only the fact that Joelle carried an innocent babe kept her from doing so.

Lady Bertrice slid her arm around Joelle's waist. "Hush, child."

Joelle flung her shuddering body into Lady Bertrice's arms. The old woman looked at Kate through narrowed eyes. "She is utterly terrified. What have you done?"

Kate crossed her arms over her chest and glared right back at Lady Bertrice. "I've demanded the truth, that's what I've done."

"Please," Joelle whimpered. "Please. I must…sit. I feel faint…"

As she ushered Joelle into the Yellow Room, Lady Bertrice glared at Kate over her shoulder. "Go to your room. I shall deal with you later."

Becky and Kate took their dinner in Becky's bedchamber, neither of them desiring to spend hours of strained politeness in Joelle Martin's presence. They used Becky's broken arm as a convenient excuse, though they were both certain everyone knew the true reason they declined to have dinner in the dining room.

They hardly spoke over their roasted partridge, for Becky seemed more withdrawn and melancholy than usual, and Kate brooded over the afternoon's events. She'd gained nothing today but the further enmity of both Joelle and Lady Bertrice. As usual, she'd made a mess of things. It was a poor repayment to Becky, who'd been such a good, kind friend to her.

After they finished eating, Kate retired to the Ivory Room, where she tried to read a bit to a very tired Reggie, who'd spent most of the day outside in the blustery wind with Garrett and Miranda planning the rebuilding of Garrett's tree house. Kate envied the three of them.

"Reg?" she murmured after a few pages, noticing his eyes had drifted shut. "Reggie?"

No answer. She stroked her knuckles across his soft, rounded cheek as he breathed deeply in slumber. He seemed so happy here. So healthy it brought tears to her eyes. There was always someone to play with, someone to offer him a kind word or a hug. Everyone, from Garrett himself to his daughter and down to the scullery maids, had taken a liking to her little brother.

If only that were the case for Kate. But their dispositions were like night and day. While Reggie was shy and sweet, Kate was a brash, outspoken termagant. The way she'd shrieked at Joelle—it was unforgivable. She slumped against the slatted wooden headboard, closing her eyes in despair. She'd been so angry, so jealous and full of spite and fear of the future, she hadn't been able to contain her temper.

She slipped into an uncomfortable slumber against the

headboard, with the candle beside the bed still burning. Sometime later, the sound of the door opening had Kate surging up in the bed. Lady Bertrice, dressed in a purple robe and a green bandeau and looking somewhat like a newly picked turnip, stalked inside with such determination that Kate placed a protective hand over her sleeping brother's shoulder. She glanced at the clock on the fireplace mantel and saw that it was almost two o'clock in thc morning. The fire had died and thc room was ice cold.

She'd slept for longer than she'd thought. Turning her gaze back to the older woman, she realized she should have expected this. Lady Bertrice had said she'd deal with her later, but Kate had pushed the inevitably uncomfortable encounter from her mind.

"I told you I'd come."

"You did," Kate agreed in a low voice. She didn't want to wake Reggie.

Lady Bertrice cast a glance at Reggie and lowered her tone as well. "We need to talk, Miss Fisk. I want you out of this house."

Kate blinked at her.

"You needn't look like a confounded owl. I said I want you gone. Both you and your brother."

"Does His Grace agree?"

"He will." Lady Bertrice shrugged. "Well, he does, but he hasn't the heart to cast you out." Her blue gaze narrowed. "I, however, do."

"Why?" Kate whispered.

"Because you carry your brother's blood in your veins. Unlike my nephew, I have learned from my mistakes. I, like the rest of us, trusted William Fisk because he was Garrett's friend. Well, I certainly learned my lesson. I shall never trust anyone so freely again. Especially if he or she bears the name 'Fisk.'"

"But I am nothing like my brother. The death of his twin altered—"

"*And* you are a wrench in my nephew's happiness."

"What do you mean?"

"Your presence infuses the duke with guilt. He believes himself in debt to you, just as he believed himself in debt to your brother because he was the man who 'rescued' him from his fate in Belgium. And now my nephew feels responsible for you and Reginald because you were rendered helpless by William Fisk's death."

Drawing her thin robe across her chest, Kate flung her legs over the edge of the bed. "I'm not helpless. As long as he is with me, Reggie isn't helpless either."

Lady Bertrice sighed. "Just like your older brother, it seems your greatest natural talent lies in infiltrating and taking advantage of our family."

Kate blinked to try to soothe the sting in her eyes. "It wasn't my intention to infiltrate or take advantage of anyone. Your niece and nephew are the kindest people I have ever known. They have been too kind to me and to Reggie."

"*Too* kind," Lady Bertrice agreed. "My niece and nephew's greatest failure is their inability to judge people adequately. People of our prominence and reputation are most vulnerable to people like you."

"What do you mean?"

"People who try to take advantage of our trusting natures. Of our money and position."

"You're wrong about me," Kate said in a low voice.

Lady Bertrice hissed out a breath. "I will not allow it to

happen all over again. I will not watch idly as another Fisk tears my family apart—not this time. I want you gone, Katherine. You are all that stands in the way of Garrett's happiness. I cannot bear to watch you ruin everything."

"I still don't understand."

"He will marry Joelle Martin."

The skin on Kate's cheeks tightened.

"He will marry her before it is born," Lady Bertrice continued. "That way, the child will be born legitimate. And if it is a boy, God willing, Garrett will have his heir."

"He...plans to marry? Joelle Martin?" The world seemed to reel around Lady Bertrice's stout frame.

He never promised you anything, Kate. He never offered. Never said he loved you...

Deep in her heart, Kate had believed actions spoke louder than words, and Garrett's actions had constantly spoken of his love, his desire, his feelings for her. But perhaps she'd been wrong, and Garrett didn't care for her. He'd enjoyed speaking with her, and perhaps he'd desired her. He said they needed time to sort it out. But never, not once, had he given her any verbal confirmation that he wanted more.

Lady Bertrice's lips tightened. "However, Joelle is so terrified after your cruel outburst today, she's in such a poor humor she is threatening to leave Calton House, as heavy with child as she is. It was all Garrett could do to convince her to stay. She should be preparing for the impending birth, not fleeing to the Continent because a common English trollop frightened her."

Kate was stunned, frozen, too devastated by this news to respond to the trollop comment. She didn't care if a hundred people chanted "trollop" to her before an audience consisting of the king himself and all the noblemen of England. All she cared about was that Garrett was marrying. Not her. Not even Sophie, the woman who'd held his affection since he was a boy. Not anyone good, or honest, or pure. No, he planned to marry Joelle Martin. Willy's mistress.

Did he love her?

"I...don't believe you," Kate whispered.

Lady Bertrice squared her shoulders. "You'd best believe it, because it is inevitable. The child will require a father. My nephew knows this. His child's mother is a lady, and propriety demands he marry her. It is the proper thing to do."

Kate stared at the older woman. Her lips were pinched into a tight line, her eyes narrowed. But deep grooves lined her forehead. Worry wasn't an alien emotion to Garrett's aunt. Despite her knowledge that Lady Bertrice had never trusted her, Kate believed she wasn't an evil or malicious person. Kate was convinced that no strains of evil ran in the James family.

Those traits ran strongly in Kate's family, though. Lady Bertrice knew that, too. Ultimately Kate couldn't fault the older woman for her distrustfulness.

Lord, why hadn't she seen it earlier? Of course Garrett would marry the mother of his child—his honor would demand no less. If there was any chance the child was his, Garrett would do anything to give it a family and to save it from the wretched stigma a bastard must carry for life—the stigma Reggie would always carry.

Kate had fooled herself. Distracted herself with Joelle's possible treachery. Her heart dove to the vicinity of her toes as she realized what she must do.

She must leave this place. Lady Bertrice was right. She

couldn't continue to take from this family. She couldn't spend her days mooning after Garrett. Whether Joelle was innocent or guilty, Kate couldn't bear to watch Garrett marry her.

Yet if Joelle *was* guilty of sleeping with Willy and lying to Garrett about the paternity of her child, then Garrett would never marry her, even to save the child from the label of bastard. If he discovered the truth too late, after their marriage . . . Kate almost couldn't bear to think of it. It would be yet another betrayal for him to endure. It would destroy him.

She must help him. She must do whatever she could to find proof—if there was proof to be found—of Joelle's liaison with Willy.

She had only one remaining hope. At Kenilworth, she might find some evidence to confirm Joelle's deceit. It was an enormous risk, for she might turn up empty-handed, but what choice did she have? If she failed, Garrett would marry Joelle. If she remained at Calton House, Garrett would marry Joelle, and worse, Kate would be forced to watch, helpless, as it happened.

Lady Bertrice dug her hands into one of her voluminous pockets and drew out a small blue silk purse, which she thrust at Kate. "This is for you."

Kate stared at it. "What for?"

"Should be enough to get you home, and a bit extra."

"I don't want your money."

Lady Bertrice arched her brows. "I don't wish you out on the streets freezing to death. I am well aware you are lacking in funds. You have taken money from Rebecca for your wardrobe. Why not take this from me to ensure a safe journey home?"

"Because Lady Rebecca offered me clothing from the kindness and generosity in her heart," Kate shot back.

"Don't be a fool, girl. Perhaps I am not so noble, and I might be coldhearted, but I am no villain. My thoughts are for the well-being of my family. For all involved in this debacle."

"Lady Rebecca would not approve of this."

"Lady Rebecca is a child. She's using you as a shield to protect her from the pain resulting from her mistakes, and you know it."

Stunned at Lady Bertrice's insight, Kate took a step backward. Her backside bumped the bed.

The older woman's blue eyes softened. "I will not deny how helpful you have been to my niece. But there are certain hurts she must eventually face, and to do so, she must stop hiding behind your suffering."

Kate bowed her head. "I did not mean—"

Lady Bertrice sighed. "I imagine you did not. Likely you were simply pulled along by the tide of Rebecca's guilt. However, that does not excuse the confusion you have caused Garrett. Nor does it excuse the deplorable way in which you spoke to Joelle."

Kate raised her head. "I will leave," she whispered, her voice slow, slurred as if she'd imbibed a gallon of ale. Each word was nearly impossible to utter. Each word sucked at the little remaining strength she possessed. She was so afraid. She was terrified of leaving Garrett with Joelle, of his marrying her. She was petrified that she might never find proof. That she'd have to live forever merely suspecting that Joelle had lured the man Kate loved into becoming her husband.

"Good. First thing in the morning, I'll have the coachman drive you and Reginald to Skipton. There's a stage-coach that leaves there each Wednesday morning bound for Sheffield and thence to Warwickshire."

Kate nodded, trying to steady herself against the devastating pain rushing through her. The thought of Garrett marrying Joelle was like a poisoned blade piercing her chest.

He never offered you anything, Kate. He never mentioned marriage. Not once.

He would marry Joelle. Not her.

Kate closed her eyes in despair. Had she forgotten what had happened to her own mother? It was utter folly for a woman of her class to become involved with an aristocrat.

She'd been such a fool.

The child. Think of the child. If Garrett married Joelle, he'd be saving it from Reggie's fate. And yet she could only imagine the extent of Garrett's anger should he discover that his wife was treacherous, that she'd slept with his enemy, maybe even pretended Willy's child was his.

Better a bastard than that. Not only would Garrett be miserable, the rest of his family would suffer as well. Including the child.

Kate doubted she'd be able to remain standing if it wasn't for the small shred of hope that she might find Garrett's proof at Kenilworth. That would keep her upright until she arrived home, at least. And then, if there was no proof...

She couldn't face that now.

There had to be proof. If she had to find a way to travel to Belgium and locate the proof there, she would do it. She would do whatever it took.

"Very good." Again, Lady Bertrice held out the purse. When Kate didn't take it, she tossed it to the bed, where it landed at Reggie's feet, the coins inside clinking. Reggie didn't move. He slept like a log, like a healthy little boy should sleep.

With a sharp nod, Lady Bertrice turned, her purple robe billowing, and swept out of the Ivory Room.

Kate stood for a long moment, chewing her lower lip, staring at the door.

Before she left, she had to see Garrett. She couldn't just leave him. Without his confirming what Lady Bertrice had said. Without trying to warn him. Without saying good-bye.

It was after two in the morning. Surely he was abed by now, but she'd wake him. She'd agreed to leave Calton House in the morning. This was her last chance.

She pushed her feet into the warm slippers Becky had given her and tiptoed down the long, dark corridor to the opposite end of the house and paused at the tall double doors leading to Garrett's bedchamber. She'd passed outside his bedchamber before but had never been inside.

Kate stared at the doors, shudders rolling through her. She was so afraid of facing him. Terrified she'd break down, go to her knees, beg and plead with him to turn from Joelle and take her instead. Her pride was a very fragile thing at this moment, like a tiny spider's web shimmering in the rain, easily destroyed by an impatient hand.

Taking a deep breath, she raised her hand to the handle and turned it. Well oiled, it made no sound, and neither did the hinges as she pushed open the heavy door.

The room appeared cavernous in the dimness. The only

light originated from the fire still burning in the grate of a magnificent marble fireplace, its face shimmering with a pearly gleam in the flickering, inconstant glow.

Kate's eyes gradually adjusted, and she made out a group of chairs clustered around the fireplace, and what looked like a writing desk on the far side of the room facing a window perhaps as tall as her and twice as wide. Her gaze traversed the space until it rested on the bed. The dark bed curtains were drawn tight, and she couldn't see Garrett at all.

Thick carpeting absorbed any noise she might have made, so she crept forward on silent feet until she could touch the slick braided rope edging the bed curtain. She grasped the heavy material and drew it aside.

Garrett lay in bed. Blankets covered him halfway up his naked chest—the muscles and deep bronze tone of his skin apparent even in the limited light. As always, her breath caught at his beauty.

But then she beheld the delicate forearm draped across Garrett's shoulder. Kate's hand clenched at the edge of the bed curtain as her unwilling gaze trailed down the arm, revealing more and more of Joelle, dressed in a thin white nightgown that clung to her abundant breasts and rounded belly. In the midst of a fitful sleep, Joelle twitched, groaned softly, and pressed herself tighter against Garrett.

They were together. Sleeping together.

Kate had never slept with Garrett, not once.

Perhaps she didn't need to speak to him after all. Perhaps their speaking days were over.

Their touching days were over, too. And their kissing days. Their lovemaking days.

Kate dropped the bed curtain. On leaden feet, she left Garrett's room and plodded back down the corridor to the Ivory Room.

She went to the window, leaned against the frame, and stared into the darkness. Although the Yellow Room's window did possess a more desirable prospect of the gardens, Kate had loved the view this window offered. She'd spent hours here, gazing through the glass at the sloping roof of the stables, the comings and goings of the horses and stable boys, and the wintry landscape of the lands beyond. Gently, reverently, she traced the panes of glass with her fingertips and whispered good-bye to each one.

Turning away from the view for the last time, Kate discarded her thin robe and climbed into bed beside her sleeping brother as cold pierced through her thin nightgown and gooseflesh broke out across her skin.

"Well, Reggie, sweetheart," she said softly. "Looks like we're going home."

She closed her eyes against the tears.

Chapter Nineteen

Waking from a troubled dream, Garrett opened his eyes to see Joelle's wide blue eyes studying him. Every muscle in his body went stiff, and in an instant he was fully awake. He surged up. "What is it? Why are you in my bedchamber?"

"I came very late last night. I-I was not feeling well, and your presence, it comforts me."

"What's wrong?"

"I believed the baby was coming."

Garrett scrambled off the bed. "Are you certain? Hell, isn't it too early for this?"

"No... no. There were pains but they went away." She cast a tentative smile at him. "Your comfort made them go. Thank you."

Something about the way she was smiling at him... *no.* Usually after their liaisons in Belgium she left quickly so as not to rouse her father's suspicions. The few times they'd actually slept together he'd awakened to insatiable passion for her.

Now...there was nothing. In fact, waking next to her had the opposite effect. He was furious that she had invaded his bed. He didn't want her here.

"Well," he said roughly, pushing a hand through his sleep-tangled hair. He took a few deep breaths to calm himself. She'd merely come to him for comfort; she didn't deserve his ire. "It was the warmth that stopped the pains?"

"Yes," she said demurely. She looked up at him from beneath her golden brows. "Your warmth."

"Well, then, I shall order hot bricks placed in your bed throughout the night from now on. Those should warm you adequately, too." When she didn't answer, he strode to the door of his dressing room. "Excuse me."

He snapped the door shut behind him.

The struggle to balance his desire for Kate against his duty to Joelle and the child was about to kill him. There was no honorable answer. If he married Joelle, he'd relegate Kate to a far inferior position in his life, one she didn't deserve. If he married Kate, he would be evading his obligations to Joelle and the innocent baby she carried.

His instincts suffered no such qualms. They screamed at him to take Kate and forget Joelle. God. He stood in the center of his dressing room, and his skin literally crawled with the wrongness of waking beside Joelle Martin. How could he marry her? How could he even entertain the thought? How could he possibly marry one woman when it was another woman he wanted in his bed?

And yet, how could he condemn his own innocent child to bastardy?

There was a knock on his dressing-room door. Pushing his hand through his hair again, Garrett answered roughly, "Yes?"

"It is me, Garrett," Joelle said quietly. "Someone is knocking."

Frowning, he yanked open the dressing-room door. "Who is it?"

"I do not know."

Whoever it was knocked again, and Garrett's gaze skimmed over Joelle. For the first time he noticed that she wore a nearly translucent dressing gown, her brown nipples standing out from beneath the pale, shimmering material.

Hell, she'd been trying to seduce him. Looking away, he sighed, and it struck him that since she'd reappeared in his life, not once had he thought about her in a carnal way. In Belgium, they'd hardly been able to keep their hands off each other.

"You're not decent, Joelle."

"I am not," she agreed in a whisper.

"Go into my dressing room and stay there until whoever it is goes away."

"Yes, Garrett," she said humbly.

"And then go back to your room and put on some clothes."

She nodded and disappeared into the dressing room. Garrett pulled a robe over his shoulders and went to answer the door. "Yes?"

It was a footman carrying a candle followed by a pair of travel-worn men. "Sorry to disturb you, Your Grace," the footman said, "but there's been an emergency."

"What is it?"

One of the men stepped forward. "We're from the Grandfield Quarry, Your Grace."

"Yes?"

"There's been an accident." The man hesitated.

A fist tightened in Garrett's gut. He'd spent so much time focused on the affairs of his family, once again his other responsibilities had fallen by the wayside. He'd trusted the men he'd hired to manage any potential problems, but he hadn't overseen them as much as he should. And now something had gone wrong.

Garrett cast a glance at his closed dressing-room door. "I'll dress and meet you in the entry hall in five minutes. You can explain more on the way." Garrett turned to the footman. "Get these men something warm to drink and have my horse saddled."

"Yes, Your Grace."

After dismissing Joelle, Garrett hurriedly dressed in riding clothes. When he went downstairs, he found his aunt already awake. He left Joelle in her care, making her promise to send him a message should anything happen with her or the baby, and then he and the two men rode like demons to his granite quarry north of Melton.

"Mama?"

Kate gripped Reggie's hand as their mother slowly rose from the chair by the fire and turned to face them. The kitchen looked and smelled as it always did, with the crisp aroma of turpentine wafting from the freshly scrubbed counters, something bubbling in the big pot on the stove, and a sparkling clean flagstone floor. Kate was relieved to see Mama's grief over Willy hadn't seemed to interfere with her duties. Still, Kate stood with every nerve on edge, poised to snatch Reggie up and flee if her mother came after her with the poker again.

"Katherine?"

Though the kitchen hadn't changed, Mama herself had. She looked as if she'd aged fifteen years in the past few weeks. The gray streaks in her hair had widened, and deep lines furrowed her forehead and bracketed her mouth and eyes.

Kate and Reggie stood still, staring at their mother, who paused by the fire, returning their gazes. Finally, she spoke. "I thought I'd never see you again."

"Well..." Kate tried to smile, but the effort failed miserably. "We've returned."

Reggie slipped his hand from Kate's. "Mama?"

"Reginald, I think you've grown." Their mother pressed the back of her hand to her mouth. "You look like such a gentleman in those clothes."

Reggie stepped up to Mama, slipped his arms around her waist, and pressed his cheek against her stomach. "I missed you, Mama."

Awkwardly, she patted his head, still staring at Kate.

In the ensuing silence, Kate clenched her hands at her sides, still wary, still afraid that Mama would turn her away.

"I buried William," Mama finally whispered.

Lowering her gaze to the floor, Kate nodded.

"He's with Warren now."

"That's what I told him, Mama. Just before he..." Her voice dwindled.

"You are the only children I have left," Mama said miserably.

Kate couldn't find words to answer her. All three of

them stood in silence for long moments, Kate at the door, Reggie embracing Mama's waist, Mama's hands atop his blond head.

Finally, Mama glanced at the stove, where something simmered lazily. "I must have known you were coming, because I boiled some mutton. Are you hungry?"

"Yes, Mama," Kate said soberly. "We've been traveling all day with hardly a bite. We're starving."

The days passed slowly. Mama and Kate lived under the strictures of an unspoken truce: If neither mentioned Willy or the events surrounding his death, they could live together with some measure of mutual respect. Kate suspected that Mama understood she had attacked her unfairly when they'd told her of Willy's death, and she seemed to want to make up for it by treating Kate with more civility than ever before.

The morning after they arrived, Kate wore her old apron tied over the now-tattered green dress. Just in case she found Garrett his proof, she'd tucked the purse containing the remaining coins from Lady Bertrice into the pocket of the apron.

Reggie had awakened with a fever this morning, which worried her. Carrying him upstairs, she deposited him before the kitchen fire so Mama could watch him while she was gone. She left two books of nursery rhymes at his side.

Mama turned her sharp, dark eyes on her. "Where do you intend to go, Katherine?"

"There's something I must do, Mama. I'll be back in an hour or two. Will you watch Reggie for me?"

Mama simply nodded, leaving Kate to gape at her in

surprise. Had Mama truly accepted her evasive answer and left it at that? Without demanding more details or accusing her of being an irresponsible hoyden?

Something about Willy's death and the events surrounding it had changed her mother, Kate realized. She was no longer a naughty child in her eyes—she was a woman. Mama's equal.

She took the road to Bertie's house, for Kate rather thought she'd never take the shortcut again. Though Bertie had been properly buried in the Kenilworth cemetery, she'd recognize the clearing where she'd found him, remember the black gaping hole in his forehead...

She blinked away the awful memories as she drew up to the cottage. Using the key she'd taken from Mama's heavy keychain, she unlocked the door. It squealed on its hinges as she pushed it open. She took a deep breath and looked around. Despite the general state of disarray, the cottage's interior looked harmless enough.

Stepping inside, she shut the door to block out the frigid wind. Then she pulled off her mittens and tucked them in her coat pocket. She could search more thoroughly barehanded.

Directly before her, Bertie's bed, a secondhand piece from one of the manor's bedchambers, took up the bulk of space in the small room. Its linens were in disarray and covered in dust, as if someone had leaped straight out of bed and ran out the door, never to return. To the left of the bed, a stone fireplace with a pot over it occupied the corner, emanating a rank smell.

A small, rough-hewn table and two chairs were placed between the fireplace and an alcove holding an array of tools, dry goods, and cooking necessities. On the other side of the bed stood an old wardrobe with tarnished door handles. Garments—feminine garments, for the most part—and a few porcelain cosmetics containers lay scattered on the floor.

The abandoned garments wouldn't do Kate any good now—Joelle would never claim them. Kate needed indisputable proof.

Kate started at the wardrobe. Quickly rifling through the shelves, she found nothing but various items of unfolded men's clothing packed inside. Joelle had probably wanted Bertie's things out of sight, so she or her maid had stuffed them in here.

Kate searched the table next. A moldy loaf of bread sat on its center, surrounded by soiled dishes. In the corner beyond was a shelf of books, consisting of a Bible and other religious texts that had belonged to Bertie. She flipped through each one, searching for loose papers, but there was nothing, except one sheet written in a shaky hand. It was the beginning of a letter written by Bertie to his daughter.

Her heart pounding painfully for the dear old man, she returned the books to where they belonged and quickly went through the other items stacked on the shelf. She found a dish and blade Bertie used for shaving, a boiling pot, and dry food supplies.

Kate stooped to look under the bed, and she threw back the stale-smelling sheets. She searched the cubbyholes of a free-standing cabinet beside the fireplace. A thin layer of dust covered everything, and by the time she'd searched everywhere, her heart ached and she was filthy.

With a sigh, she lowered herself onto one of the chairs, leaned her elbows on her knees, propped her chin in her dirty, frozen palms, and stared glumly into the cold fireplace. Tears pricked at the backs of her eyes. She was tired and cold and lonely. She missed Calton House. She missed Becky. Most of all, she missed Garrett.

How desperately she missed him. How difficult it was to keep her bottom stuck to this chair rather than stand up, sprint all the way back to Yorkshire, and throw herself into his arms.

Suddenly, something caught her eye. Something white, glinting amid the fireplace coals.

Kate lunged to the fireplace and fell to her knees on the ragged oval rug. She clawed through the coals and ash, blackening her hands.

Her fingers found it, ruffled through it. A charred stack of papers. At once she saw the scrawl of a pen beneath the blackened ash.

"My Sweet Love Joelle," read the salutation.

"Oh, Lord," Kate murmured out loud. Tears of victory streamed down her face. She'd recognize Willy's handwriting anywhere.

Part of the mountain at Grandfield Quarry had collapsed, and several men had been buried in an avalanche caused by the engineers' failure to create proper supports for the areas left weakened by the quarrying.

Two full days passed before the men were dug out. Incredibly, some had survived in a pocket of air, but they'd lost five workers. Garrett went to visit each of their families to express his condolences, and by the time he returned to Calton House, five days had passed. Garrett rode home, feeling old, feeling somber, and all he could think about was seeing Kate. Holding her. Feeling her soothing hands on his body. Hearing her comforting voice.

He'd ached for Kate every day he was gone, and the ache had not only beset his mind, but also affected his body. His chest felt heavy, his muscles tight, his limbs stiff. He seemed to have forgotten how to form a smile.

He needed her.

After he'd seen to his horse, however, it wasn't Kate who met him at the door. It was his aunt and Joelle, who threw herself into his arms. Her stomach had grown in the few days of his absence. Gently, he pushed her back, trying not to grit his teeth.

"I missed you very much, Garrett," she whispered with shining eyes.

"How are you?" he asked.

She gave him a soft smile. "I have been well. Aunt Bertrice has been very kind. We have spent every day together."

Aunt Bertrice? It seemed they'd become quite friendly. Garrett frowned over Joelle's shoulder at his aunt, who shrugged at him, her eyes twinkling.

"Forgive me." He took another step back. "But I'm dirty from traveling, and—"

"Of course," Joelle said warmly. "Please, do go change. I have ordered a bath for you."

Garrett paused, feeling his eyes narrow. "Have you?"

Joelle nodded. "I hope you will not think me too bold, Garrett. I did believe you would be tired from your journey."

"Yes." He felt awkward, unsettled. He glanced again at the staircase. All he wanted to do was get away and go to Kate. God, he missed her. "Thank you, Joelle." From somewhere within him, he mustered a smile. "I'll go now. Will I see you at dinner?"

"Of course. I have ordered pheasant for dinner. Aunt Bertrice said it is your favorite."

Grinding his teeth, he strode up the stairs and down the corridor. Anticipation flushed his skin, made his blood race. He knocked on Kate's door, and when there was no answer, he turned the handle. He knew well enough that to enter a lady's room without her invitation was a terrible breach of propriety, but he also knew that Kate cared for propriety about as much as he did—which was to say she didn't care at all.

The door glided open. The Ivory Room was spotless as usual—and empty. As if it had not been occupied for a while. After a few moments standing in the vacant room, he strode to the door between the Ivory Room and Rebecca's bedchamber and knocked. His shoulders stiffened when his sister called from the inside, her voice ragged, "Who is it?"

"It is your brother."

He heard a dramatic sigh. "Come in."

He strode into his sister's room to find her still abed. "Did I wake you?"

"No. I was awake."

"What are you doing, then?"

Another sigh. "Sulking, I suppose." Wearily, she rose to sit upon the edge of the bed. "Welcome home, Garrett."

He frowned at her. "Where is Kate?"

"Oh, Garrett..."

Something clenched in his stomach at the tone of her voice. "What?"

"She's gone. Didn't you know?"

Blood began to race through his veins. "Gone? What do you mean?" He stepped menacingly toward his sister. "What are you saying?"

Rebecca clutched her splinted arm to her body. "Don't you care?"

"Of course I care!"

"Then why don't you know she's gone? She's been gone for days!"

That shocked him as thoroughly as if she'd punched him in the solar plexus. With her good arm. "What?"

Awkwardly, Rebecca rose on unsteady feet. He was too bewildered to think to help her. When she spoke, her voice was unnaturally shrill. "All you care about is your beautiful Joelle and that bastard child she carries. You don't care that Kate's mother might have already killed her with a... with a *damned* fireplace poker!"

Garrett stared at his sister, aghast, as she stalked up to him and stabbed a finger into his chest. "This is *your* fault!"

"I don't know what you're talking about, Rebecca. You know I was called away." He pushed his hand through his hair. "There was an emergency—"

"Did you trouble yourself to say good-bye to her? To tell her where you were going? To reassure her that that Belgian woman hadn't stolen your affections?" His sister sneered. "No, of course you didn't. You haven't spoken to her at all since Joelle arrived, have you? You've avoided her altogether, you selfish, horrid man."

He shook his head. He still didn't understand. "When did she leave? Why did she go?"

Rebecca blinked hard. "She didn't say why. But I think I know. Because Aunt Bertrice told her you were going to marry Joelle." His sister turned away in disgust. "And you don't even love her. I know you don't."

"Rebecca—"

"You love Kate."

You love Kate.

Rebecca stomped to her writing desk. She opened the drawer and withdrew a sheet of stationery. Stomping back across the room, she thrust it at him. "Read."

She watched him, clutching her still-healing arm to her body, as he unfolded the parchment, his heartbeat pounding in his ears.

Dearest Becky,

You are the best friend I've had in my entire life. More than anything, I hate to leave you. Thank you for all that you've done for me. I hope that someday you will find it in your heart to forgive me for leaving you without a good-bye. But you see, I am a terrible coward and couldn't bear to wake you.

Be happy, dearest Becky. And please, write to me at Debussey Manor. I will miss you very much.

All my love,
Kate

Garrett lowered the letter to his side and sank into one of his sister's effeminate pink chairs. She'd left him. Without saying good-bye—without even a note. He sat in silence for several moments, trying to gather his senses, which Kate's letter had just shattered and sent flying.

"I cannot believe she's gone," he finally murmured.

Rebecca, who still stood where she'd handed him the letter, whirled around to face him, her eyes cold blue steel. "Yes, she's gone. She gave up on you—on all of us. She's left us. She's gone. She's returned to—to that awful place."

His sister visibly shuddered.

Kate was gone. He'd never told her about his feelings for her. He'd never had a chance. She'd had nothing to hold on to when Joelle arrived, and as he'd struggled to claw his way out of the mire of confusion Joelle's reappearance had tossed him into, she'd given up on him. She'd left him.

He should have gone to her. Reassured her. Told her how Joelle's arrival had disoriented him, how he was trying to find the solution that would work best for all of them.

He'd abandoned her first. He'd treated her as if she were beneath them all. As if she were a servant—or his doxy, to be discarded the moment a true lady demanded his attentions.

Rebecca spun away from him, pressing her hand to her face. "Just go away, Garrett," she said with a groan.

As he dragged his lethargic body from her room, he heard her whisper, "Fool."

Her hands shaking, Kate wrapped her fingers around the crumbling edges of the papers and pulled them out, spilling black ash over her skirts.

Only bits and pieces were still intact, for the edges of the stack had burned completely away. But, as was common with thick stacks of papers, its center had been too dense and the fire too cool to burn it.

Carefully, Kate peeled away the top sheet, which, other than the amorous salutation, was charred beyond recognition. She blinked. There it was. Willy's dark, bold writing.

"Use these funds to come to me. Come right away." On the next line was part of the word *"Kenilworth."*

She peeled that paper away.

". . . everyone witnesses him slowly going mad. Everyone fears him. It is just as I'd planned."

Quickly, she turned the pages. Letters, all of them written from Willy to Joelle. Proof, and more proof. Together, they painted a picture of two people embroiled in a deep, dangerous deception. Two people with different motivations but similar goals: money and power.

She went through the papers again, trying to understand what Joelle and Willy had done and why they'd done it. Kate supposed Joelle had no knowledge of Willy's murderous intentions, for he never mentioned them, but his plans to steal Becky's and Garrett's fortunes was revealed in great detail. It was clear, from his words, that Joelle had supported him in this endeavor, and that they planned to escape together to France when all was said and done.

One of the last letters was fully intact.

My Sweet Joelle:

I know you are angry with me, sweeting, but it had to be done, you see. The ruse was up, because S. discovered my most incriminating papers . . . all of them! If only I knew she kept a copy of my key! The only way I could attain some measure of success was by professing my—false, you understand—love and devotion for Lady R. I fled with Lady R to Gretna and we married. Please understand, sweet Joelle, she has three thousand a year. Three thousand! I care nothing for this girl, for she is exactly that—an insipid child who will do anything I say. You have my most heartfelt promise: As soon as I can, I will leave her to her own devices and come to you. Then you and I shall take all that I have earned and see the world as we planned. We will buy a grand house in Paris and live like princes.

I will come to you soon, my sweet precious love. Until then I shall remain ever faithful and true,

W.F.

Joelle was just the kind of woman Willy would have adored. A delicate, feminine flower on the outside, a shrewd, ambitious schemer on the inside.

Yet many things still remained unclear. What had Joelle planned to do about Garrett? About her baby? Had Willy known about the child when he wrote all these letters? Whose baby was it? Willy's or Garrett's?

The letters didn't offer the complete story, but they gave enough of one. Without a doubt, Joelle had been Willy's mistress. She'd colluded in his efforts to destroy Garrett.

This would hurt Garrett terribly, and Kate's heart constricted at the thought. But he'd want to know. He wouldn't want to be kept in the dark.

More important, she wanted him to know.

The mail coach came through Kenilworth this afternoon. If she hurried…

Holding the charred letters in the crook of her arm, Kate picked up her skirts with frozen fingers and ran all the way to Kenilworth.

Chapter Twenty

Marry her."

"No."

Aunt Bertrice huffed out a breath. "Time runs short, boy. You could be ruining your life—the *child's* life—by delaying this decision."

He knew that, damn it. Garrett smacked his hands down on the desk. "I am busy, Aunt. Did you have something specific you wished to discuss with me?"

"Yes. This." Drawing a sheet of paper from her pocket, she slapped it upon the shiny wood surface.

He stared down at it. "What is that?"

"It's a special license from the Archbishop of Canterbury. It arrived today. Just now."

He ground his teeth. "How, pray, did you obtain it?"

"Does it matter? This document legally states that you are free and clear to marry Joelle Martin whenever and wherever you please."

"Did you forge my signature, Aunt?"

Gripping the edge of the desk, she bent toward him until their noses were an inch apart. "I am thinking of what's best for you! For your child and for your family. That is all."

"Well, thank you for your consideration," he pushed out. "But I still haven't made a final decision regarding Joelle." *Or Kate.*

And God knew, he didn't have much time. According to the doctor, she might go early. She could give birth any day. Any moment.

After a fitful night's sleep spent worrying about Joelle and agonizing over Kate, Garrett awakened the next morning to Miranda nudging at him, her cheeks flushed. "Papa! It has snowed. Look! Look outside!"

He rose, tugged on his robe, and allowed her to lead him to his tall bedchamber window. Sure enough, overnight, the world had turned sparkling white. It was more than a dusting—several inches of snow covered the ground. It must have snowed all night long, but the morning had dawned clear, and sparkling melted drops already slid from the stable eaves.

After he stared at it in silence for several moments, Miranda breathed, "Isn't it just lovely?"

Garrett smiled. She sounded so much like Sophie.

His smile froze on his lips as something occurred to him. Weeks ago, whenever he'd thought of Sophie, a piece of him had felt mangled and raw, as if a wild animal had attacked him and left him bleeding.

The pain had ended when he'd met Kate. That night on the blanket, when they'd eaten dinner together outside with their fingers like "barbarians."

She'd doctored the wounds his divorce had caused. She'd healed him. Made him whole.

"It is very lovely," he told Miranda somberly.

"Will you come outside with me, Papa? Can we go sledding?"

"Yes, darling. I'll take you outside. Go get dressed and meet me in the entry hall." He chucked her beneath her dimpled little chin. "We'll play for a while then go inside and have a warm breakfast."

She scampered off, leaving him looking after her. When he turned away, heaviness descended over him. A new piece of him was torn and bleeding, and this time he didn't know how to fix it. Maybe if Kate were near…

He dressed and shaved himself quickly—he still was uncomfortable making use of a valet—and by the time he went downstairs, Miranda and Rebecca, both of them wearing mittens and thick coats, awaited him. He raised a brow at his sister. "Are you coming?"

"I suppose." She gave him a tight smile. "It is the first snow of the season, after all. I shouldn't want to miss it."

"Are you certain it'll be all right? Your arm—"

"I'll be careful," she interrupted. "Just steady me if we encounter any ice, will you?"

"Of course."

The three of them linked arms and went out to the front drive, descending the ice-encrusted stairs with utmost caution.

They remained outside for longer than he'd anticipated. They built a snowman, had a gentle snowball fight, and he pulled them about on the sled.

"Your Grace!"

It was the butler, and Rebecca raised the snowball she

was poising to aim at Miranda. "Ready to join our battle, Jenkins?"

Jenkins stiffened. "Er...no." He turned to Garrett, who had knelt to rub his wounded thigh—the cold always made it ache. "Sir, I've come outside to inform you—"

Rebecca *tsked*. "Don't say you're scared, Jenkins. We won't pummel you too hard, we promise."

Garrett glanced at Rebecca. Her cheeks were flushed, and so were Miranda's. Despite their differences in coloring, for his daughter was blond while Rebecca was dark, they looked the same, like part of a family. They were a family, he realized. He wondered if he fit with them. For a fleeting moment this morning, he'd felt as though he had.

"Your Grace," Jenkins said stiffly. "It's Mrs. Martin. Her child, sir..."

Garrett's eyes widened. "Is she...?"

Jenkins tilted his head. "Yes, sir. Exactly."

"Are you certain?" Garrett's heart began to race.

"Yes, sir. Lady Bertrice has informed me that it is time."

Garrett was already moving toward the house, taking long strides, his feet making deep impressions in the snow. "Help Lady Rebecca return safely to the house," he called to Jenkins over his shoulder.

In the entry hall, he kicked off his sodden shoes and yanked off his gloves, hat, and coat, leaving them all in a pile on the shiny parquet floor.

He bounded up the stairs, taking them three at a time, and finally barreled into the Yellow Room.

"Joelle!" he exclaimed as she, her maid, Aunt Bertrice, and two other servants who were crouched to pick up items strewn about the room looked up in surprise. He turned to Joelle, who lay tucked beneath the blankets. "Is..." He took a deep breath, brushed the hair out of his face, and tried again. "Is it time?"

"I think, yes. I have not had a baby before this, so... it hurts a little..." Suddenly, Joelle's face went pale. "Here it comes again. Ah..."

He lunged to the bed, reaching for her as she reached out to him, her face contorting in pain. She grabbed his hand, and with power he didn't know she possessed, proceeded to squeeze the blood from his digits.

This woman—his one-time lover, his companion and only friend during the years of his exile in Belgium—was going to have his baby.

"Isn't it too early for the baby to be born?" he asked no one in particular.

"Early, but not dangerously so," said one of the nearby women in a gentle voice.

He looked up at his aunt, who stood on the opposite side of the bed. "Why didn't you tell me as soon as her symptoms appeared?"

Aunt Bertrice's lips twisted. "Relax, boy. It will still be many hours yet. She's only just begun to labor."

Joelle's grip on him relaxed. "I did not know for certain if it was real this time. It just began..."

Garrett's heart pounded in his ears. "I must call the doctor. Stay here."

"Yes, Garrett," she said in a small voice.

Bending down, he gently touched her cheek. "I'll return shortly."

As soon as he left her bedchamber, he realized belatedly that he could have remained at Joelle's side and ordered a servant to fetch the doctor. Or maybe Aunt Bertrice had already summoned the doctor. He didn't know. Regardless, it was probably improper for him to be by her side.

Nevertheless, a nervous, edgy energy coursed through him, and he doubted he could merely sit passively. He grabbed the first footman he saw by the shoulders and somehow managed to relay his command. And then he proceeded to prowl the corridors of Calton House, telling anyone and everyone he saw to prepare for the imminent delivery of his child. He found himself pausing at Kate's door, and his rampant heartbeat stalled. God, he missed her.

"Garrett."

He spun around to face his aunt. "I've called the doctor."

She nodded. "Good. And I've called the vicar."

His racing heartbeat stalled.

Christ. His time had run out.

An hour and a half later, Garrett stood by Joelle's bedside once more. Sweat bathed his face as he gazed at the vicar, who stood on the opposite side of the bed. The ceremony had ground to a halt while Joelle suffered through another of her birthing pains.

Holding Joelle's hand, Garrett allowed his gaze to skim over the others in the room. Jenkins stood as witness with Aunt Bertrice. A white-faced Miranda sat in the chair beside Aunt Bertrice, wringing her hands in her lap, and Dr. Barnard stood on the other side of the bed, quietly watching the proceedings.

He wondered why his daughter wasn't more animated. Then again, Miranda was an intuitive child. She seemed to know things...perhaps she had deciphered how this decision tore him apart.

The vicar took a deep breath as Joelle's pain subsided and her hand relaxed in his own.

"Shall we continue?"

"Yes," Joelle said in her husky voice. She hadn't seemed the least bit surprised when Garrett had appeared in the room with the vicar at his side. Aunt Bertrice had likely warned her. Or perhaps the two of them had schemed together to call the man here. He couldn't know.

Garrett closed his eyes wearily. This was a most inauspicious start to a marriage. "Yes, please go on."

Joelle squeezed his hand and smiled up at him encouragingly, and the vicar adjusted his spectacles. "Repeat after me, if you please, Your Grace." He cleared his throat to complete Garrett's part of the vows. "'Till death us do part, according to God's holy ordinance; and thereto I plight thee my troth.'"

"'Till death us do part, according to...'" Garrett paused, turning toward the door as it opened. The vicar released an impatient breath as Rebecca stepped in, her face drawn and pale.

She closed the door behind her, turned back to the crowd staring at her, and straightened her spine, looking directly at Garrett. "Forgive my interruption," she murmured. "Please. Continue."

Garrett had forgotten what he was supposed to say. Seeing his sister's stricken expression sent truth careening through him.

He closed his eyes and pictured Kate's beautiful, trusting face tilted up to him at the waterfall.

He didn't love Joelle. He didn't wish their child

condemned to a lifetime of illegitimacy, but marrying the woman he didn't love at the expense of the woman he did couldn't be the answer. It would condemn himself, Kate, and Joelle, too, to a lifetime of unhappiness.

He needed Kate. He wanted Kate. He wanted to marry her. He wanted her beside him forever. He loved *her*, damn it.

He glanced down to look at where he still clasped Joelle's swollen fingers. Slowly, he dragged his gaze up her arm and to her oval face, contorted in the agony of another labor pain.

He shook off her hand as if it had singed him and looked up at the vicar. "Forgive the inconvenience," he said, the words scraping over his dry throat, "but there will be no wedding today."

The vicar's eyes widened. Joelle groaned. Behind him, a woman gasped. Aunt Bertrice, most likely.

Garrett turned on his heel and left the room, brushing past a Rebecca whose eyes glowed with triumph.

He escaped to the library and formed a plan. He'd wait until the baby was born, make certain both mother and child were well. He'd explain everything to Joelle. He'd ensure she and his baby were well cared for, of course. Though he couldn't marry its mother, the child would receive all the advantages of its high birth and never want for a thing.

As soon as everything was settled here, he'd ride to Kenilworth and fetch Kate. He'd been an ass to her. He'd hurt her. He'd do whatever he could to make up for it.

Finished making his plan, he raised his brandy glass to his lips but set it down abruptly when the door to the library flew open. Rebecca paused at the threshold. Her raven hair had fallen from its pins and hung in a sleek fall to her waist, and smudges of black stained her white muslin skirts. Tears streaked her cheeks.

"Rebecca, what—?"

"I sent Tom off with a letter for Kate, and he returned with these. Kate sent them from Kenilworth." With glowing eyes, Rebecca held up a sheaf of half-burned, blackened papers in her good hand. She stalked up to Garrett and slammed the papers on his desk, sending ashes fluttering all about. "Read them."

Aunt Bertrice appeared just behind Rebecca, wringing her hands. She appeared as pale as Rebecca had earlier. "Rebecca, what is the meaning of this? You're utterly filthy!"

Both Garrett and his sister ignored her. Garrett stared at the singed papers blackening his desktop.

"What are they?" God, did he want to know?

"Letters." Rebecca angrily swiped a fresh tear from her cheek. "From William Fisk to Joelle Martin. She tried to burn them, but as you see, she didn't fully succeed."

Aunt Bertrice gasped. "That's impossible."

Garrett flipped through the papers, reading quickly, his breath growing short. A cold sweat broke out on his forehead.

As if from a distance, he heard Aunt Bertrice and Rebecca speaking in low voices.

He couldn't hear what they said—it was just a jumble of words, indistinguishable above the roaring in his ears. He was reading instructions from Fisk on how Joelle should poison him with opium, should she have the need.

Fisk using endearments for Joelle that made Garrett's stomach roll with nausea.

Fisk laughing about the money he'd stolen.

Fisk talking about Garrett's ruin.

Fisk promising Joelle a life in France, both of them rich as Croesus from Garrett's money.

Fisk making slanderous remarks about Rebecca.

Fisk imagining what he'd do to Joelle in bed when next they met.

Garrett raised his eyes. Aunt Bertrice leaned against the wall, looking pale and haggard. Rebecca stood stiffly on the other side of his desk. She'd crossed her arms over her chest, and a muscle worked in her jaw. She was otherwise utterly still, as if she'd banished all emotion. He realized this was just as devastating news to his sister as it was to himself.

Dropping his gaze, Garrett read the last letter. When he was finished, he let it slide from his fingers. It dropped back onto the desk with all the others.

He rose abruptly, collected the papers, as uncaring as Rebecca had been about their staining his clothing, and stalked past his sister and aunt. They rushed after him as he strode to the Yellow Room and threw open the door.

"Everyone out." His voice was raw. After one glance at his face, nobody questioned him, even the doctor. They simply scattered as he moved to the side of the bed to watch Joelle dispassionately as her body spasmed with pain. The last person to leave gently shut the door, leaving them alone.

When she relaxed, he held up the letters. "Why, Joelle?"

Her wide eyes blinked at the charred papers and then moved to him, her gaze, as always, ever so innocent. "What are you talking about?"

"No more pretending," he grated out. "These letters are from William Fisk to you. Tell me why you did this. What you wanted from me."

"Garrett..." Her voice dwindled, and her eyes flicked back and forth guiltily. She looked like a trapped animal with nowhere to run. He had her, and she knew it. "I love you."

"Do not make me angry, Joelle."

There was enough of a warning in his voice for her to try a different tack.

"Those..." She waved her hand weakly at the papers he held out. "I do not know what they are."

"Yes. You do."

"They are not mine."

"They're addressed to you."

"I am certain they are forgeries."

"I know Fisk's writing well. When he was my agent, I became very familiar with it. I have no doubt those letters were written by him."

She tore her gaze from his. Her body quivered and trembled beneath the flowery bedclothes.

"Did he pay you to keep me in Belgium?"

Silence.

He took her chin between hard fingers and turned her head so she faced him. "Answer me."

She groaned softly.

A hint of violence rumbled in his tone. "Do not make me threaten you."

"Yes," she whispered, squeezing her eyes shut.

"He paid you?"

"Yes," she said again. She switched to the more

comfortable French. "At first...he paid me to keep you with me in Belgium."

Garrett dropped the letters to his side. All those years. As soon as he'd saved the funds to return to England, they'd disappear, and she spoke of thieves in the area. Or she'd beg help for a sickly person she'd met. Or she needed something essential for her family. Or...

God, it was her all along. She and Fisk had conspired to keep him in Belgium, away from his family and from his life in England, all those years.

He blinked hard and stared down at her as she succumbed to another spasm of pain. When it was over, he growled, "Look at me." When she turned her wary, exhausted gaze to his, he asked, "Is the child mine?"

She didn't answer.

"It is your choice how you'd like this to proceed." Ice hardened his body and encrusted his voice. "I will throw you out into the snow, or you can bear this child in my bed in my house. If you lie to me, know it will be worse for you. Much, much worse."

He meant every word. No more would he be seduced into trust by that innocent expression. She had been in league with Fisk.

True fear bloomed in her eyes. "I do not know if it is yours."

For a brief moment, he stood there, unable to move, staring down at Joelle through a screen of red. The blazing rage crawled under his skin, prickled in his blood.

Blindly, he turned and strode out of the room.

A knock sounded on the library door. "Come in," Garrett barked.

He'd been sitting in one of the armchairs facing his desk in solitary silence for several hours. He'd read through Fisk's letters again and again, each time a bit more calmly. An hour ago Rebecca had come to show him the quickly scrawled letter Kate had written, explaining that she'd seen Joelle with Fisk in the caretaker's cottage at Debussey Manor but hadn't seen her face and wasn't absolutely certain it was Joelle. Kate had begged their forgiveness for not telling them right away, but said she felt she needed proof before she could share her suspicions with Garrett and his sister.

Rebecca had left him with Kate's letter and had taken some of Fisk's writings—the most damning ones—to show to their aunt.

Garrett looked up as the door handle turned. As soon as the doctor's face appeared, Garrett smacked down his tumbler of brandy so hard, liquid splashed over the lip of the glass and onto his hand.

"What?" he demanded. "What news?"

Dr. Barnard carefully shut the door behind him. Then he turned to face Garrett. "It's a girl, Your Grace. A touch early, I daresay, and she's very small."

"Healthy?"

"Yes, sir. Very healthy indeed. Perfect in every way."

Garrett released a breath, but his fingers remained wrapped around the glass like a lifeline. "And her mother?" The question came out as a snarl.

Dr. Barnard flinched, but then he nodded. "She is tired, but quite well. She's young and strong, and she'll be up and about in no time."

"May I see them?"

"Of course, Your Grace."

By the time the doctor had finished his sentence, Garrett was out the door. At Joelle's bedchamber, he pushed past the maid standing guard and threw open the door. At least six feminine gazes shot in his direction and gasps erupted from all corners of the room.

Just inside, he reeled to a stop. Joelle lay in the bed with fresh snowy linens tucked round her. Aunt Bertrice stood on the opposite side of the room. Rebecca stood beside his aunt, reaching her hand toward a tiny, blanket-wrapped bundle held by one of the maids. They all looked at him in surprise.

"Forgive—" He cleared his throat. "Please forgive my abrupt entrance."

"Garrett..." Aunt Bertrice looked strained. Repentant. Ash stains, nearly as dark as those covering Rebecca's dress, stained her pelisse.

Garrett stared at the gurgling bundle in the maid's arms.

"Might I...?" He swallowed and took a tentative step forward.

"Of course, Your Grace," the woman murmured.

It felt as if he was walking through pudding. The maid met him in the middle of the room. Garrett reached forward, and she gingerly placed the tiny bundle in his arms.

The babe was light as a feather. In awe, he stared down at her. All he could see was her tiny round face. Her eyes were open in slits, a hint of blue peeping through. A dusting of light brown hair tufted at her crown and disappeared behind the blanket folded over her head. She had a pug nose as small as a button, and tiny pink lips rounded into an O.

It was impossible to tell whether she was his or his enemy's.

She closed her eyes, puckered her lips, and made little smacking noises. Sensing a presence beside him, he looked up to see an unfamiliar woman curtsying. "I'm Mrs. Cauley, Your Grace. The child's nurse. I do believe she's hungry, sir."

Garrett frowned. "Oh. Of course." He gently handed her to the nurse, who took her and then bustled out.

After the door clicked shut behind them, he turned slowly toward Joelle. As much as Fisk, this woman had had a hand in his years of hell. Unlike Fisk, she'd faced him as she'd manipulated him. Yet he must control his rage, for she was a woman, and she'd just endured eight hours of laboring with a child. A child whose paternity was uncertain.

He clenched his teeth against the fury surging through him. She'd been through an ordeal. As much as he wanted to grab her and throw her out of his home by the scruff of her neck, some semblance of gentlemanliness remained inside him, because he simply couldn't. *Not yet.*

Joelle looked as though she'd survived a battle. Dark circles ringed her eyes, and her normally shiny, bouncy hair hung in limp strands around her face. Her lips were white.

"Garrett?"

He held his arms tense and straight at his sides. "I thought to name the child Charlotte. However, if you had any other ideas—"

"No," Joelle interrupted listlessly. "No ideas. Charlotte is very good."

On the fringes of his vision, Garrett saw Aunt Bertrice

and Rebecca hovering in the corner. Aunt Bertrice wrung her hands. He looked up at her. "Get out. All of you."

Rebecca ducked her head at him, her eyes sparking a challenge before she straightened her spine and marched out. Her face pale, his aunt herded the remaining servants from the room. Garrett returned his steady gaze to Joelle. Her eyes followed Aunt Bertrice as she bustled the maids out and then followed behind them.

"Tell me how it began," he said as soon as the door clicked, leaving them alone.

She licked her lips. "I am so very tired," she said in a small, weak voice.

"I don't give a damn."

"Please, Garrett—" Fright edged her voice, but it was false. If she'd spent that much time with Fisk, then there was a steel in her she'd never shown to Garrett. He'd no longer treat her like a porcelain doll.

"You will talk. You will tell me everything." The threat was evident in his voice, in his posture. If she didn't speak, he'd wring the truth out of her, every word, every confession. Yes, she'd just labored for eight hours, but she'd done so in his house, under his protection. That protection was about to end, and she knew it.

"I am not a bad woman." Her blue eyes gazed up at him, entreating. "I care for you. Deeply. We have shared too much for me to be indifferent."

"Be that as it may," he ground out, "I require information. *Now.*"

After a moment of silence, she gave a slight, fearful nod.

"How did it begin?"

"He came to me," she whispered. "Early in 1819. He

said..." She took a weary breath and closed her eyes. "He said I could be rich someday if I did exactly as he said. He was very convincing, and it seemed so easy."

Garrett clenched his teeth. So even that first day—when he'd seen her in the fields staring at him—she'd had an ulterior motive. "What did he tell you to do?"

Her gaze skittered away from him.

"Look at me, Joelle. What did he tell you to do?"

"Seduce you," she whispered.

"And in return?"

"He paid me each time, with bonuses when I took money from you, and he promised me more. Much more." She looked up at him imploringly, rising on her elbows. "It was not a hardship, Garrett. I liked you very much."

His lip curled. "When did you take him into your bed?"

Thank God he didn't love this woman. Thank God he hadn't married her. If either had been true, every word out of his mouth would have been sheer torture. Instead, he was grim, determined. He wanted information, and he wanted it now. Because he was leaving at dawn tomorrow. He was going to Kenilworth to return to the woman he did love but had driven away.

"He did not come often—he was in England—"

"When?" he bit out. "When was the first time?"

"In 1819."

Garrett blinked hard. He would not give her the satisfaction of seeing him lose his tight grip on his emotions. She didn't deserve it.

"He loved me, Garrett!" she sobbed. "And I loved him."

"He married my sister, Joelle."

"He had no choice, do you not see? He would have lost

everything if he did not marry her. And now he is dead, and I am lost. I came to you because I had nowhere else to go."

"Were you aware of his intentions for my family?"

"He sent me letters from England to tell me how he planned to take his due from you."

Garrett's gaze hardened, and Joelle hastened to explain, her eyes feverishly bright. "He took from you only because it was the only way for him to receive compensation for the death of his brother." She pressed a trembling hand to her breast. "I saw his sadness. He...he was very bereft, even many years after Waterloo. He did deserve recompense for his suffering. You are so rich, it is not something you would have noticed. He needed that money. He deserved it!" Her voice shook, not with animosity, but with devotion to William Fisk and his pain.

"Did he come to Belgium this past March?"

"Yes. He was there in March and into April."

"Did you engage in carnal relations with him then?"

"I...Yes."

"So you cannot know the identity of the child's father," he said flatly.

"As I said, I do not know for certain." Again she closed her eyes, and her voice took on a pleading quality. "But I feel she is yours."

He would never know. No one would. Charlotte could be his, or she could be his enemy's. Yet Garrett had spent the past days believing it was his child she carried. A sharp, piercing pain of loss slammed into Garrett's chest, sending residual waves of anger cascading through him.

Could he simply discard the child because she *might* belong to another man? A dead man?

Charlotte was innocent. Garrett, Joelle, and Fisk were the guilty parties. There was no question that Garrett had bedded Joelle. He had taken the risk, accepted it. And now he must accept the consequences. The child was his responsibility now, regardless of her parentage.

In addition, if Charlotte was Fisk's, then that meant she was Kate's niece. Of all the remaining members of the Fisk family, Garrett knew Kate would wish to care for her. Kate belonged with him, and that fact only solidified his knowledge that Charlotte did as well.

Charlotte was his, by law and by right.

"Please, Garrett," Joelle whispered. "My father will not accept us. I have nowhere to go...I will end in the poorhouse."

"Don't think I'd allow that fate to befall my daughter," Garrett said harshly. "I will always provide for her."

Joelle winced. "I trust that you will care for the child," she said in a small voice. "You are the most honorable man I've ever known."

"That honor doesn't extend to you, Joelle," he said. The frigid tone of his voice flooded the room, sending a chill through it. Joelle trembled at the sound.

"William...he made very grand promises to me," Joelle whispered through white lips.

"Ones you couldn't resist."

"Yes. It is true. But—"

"And when you returned to England, you went straight to him, didn't you? Not to me."

"It is not what you think."

"What, then?"

"My father did force me to leave, but William, he sent me the money to come to England. I went to him because I feared you," she said, her voice a near whisper. "I feared that you would discover that I knew him, and you would be angry with me."

"But after his death you had nowhere else to turn."

"Yes," she whispered. "When he did not come to me, I went to Debussey Manor and his mother was there. She said he was—" Tears welled in her eyes. "He was murdered. I did not know where else to go but to you. I had nothing more than the money required to bring me to Yorkshire."

"And then you became seduced by the idea of being a duchess."

"That is true. Aunt Bertrice—she is so kind. She helped me to see that I could be what I always dreamed, and that you were the man who could give it to me." Crystalline tears seeped from both of her eyes. "I am sorry, Garrett. I cared greatly for you, but William... we understood each other. He was so ambitious, so strong. I... loved him."

"You were the same." *Ruthless, ambitious, avaricious...*

"Yes." Her chest heaved. "We were the same."

Garrett gazed at her through narrow eyes. His hand gripped the bedpost like a vise. "Were you aware I was in Kenilworth?" he asked, his voice hard. "Did you know I killed him?"

Joelle gasped. "No, that is impossible," she said through her sobs. "You were here. He told me you were at Calton House."

"He lied."

She shrank away from him, weeping harder, cowering deeper into the bed, gripping the bedclothes in pale hands. "No."

"He planned to murder my sister and then he intended to murder me."

"No." She shook her head adamantly. "No, you are wrong. William desired revenge, but he wanted your money only. He was not a murderer."

"You're wrong, Joelle."

"You lie." Tears streaked down the sides of her face. "He was no murderer!"

Slowly, he straightened. He didn't have the time to hold this lying, deluded creature by the hand, comfort her, and make her understand. He simply didn't care about her anymore. She wasn't worth it. He had more important things to occupy his time.

"You must rest," he said coldly. "You've had a trying day."

"You killed him." Her entire body shook with the force of her sobs. "You killed my William."

"Goodnight, Joelle." He turned and strode from the room. When he shut the door against the sounds of her cries, her presence melted from his heart and disappeared from his emotions. Joelle Martin was simply a ghost from his past now. A memory. A mistake, yes, but not one he would punish himself for or waste his time regretting.

He'd made bigger mistakes. And now, nothing mattered but his need to make things right.

Chapter Twenty-one

As he'd planned, Garrett rose at dawn. He'd scarcely slept—his mind was too entrenched in his need to rush to Kate. Too late, he realized it would have been better for him to leave last night as soon as he'd pulled the truth from Joelle.

He paused at the door to the Yellow Room but then passed it and stopped at the next room. As quietly as he could, he turned the handle and opened the door. On the narrow bed set against the far wall, Mrs. Cauley shifted, turned, and released a prolonged snore.

Next to the bed stood Charlotte's cradle. Careful not to wake Mrs. Cauley, he walked up to it and stared down at her. She slept, completely still but for the rise and fall of her tiny chest.

Her coral lips, round face, and pale skin reminded him of Miranda. Unlike Miranda, however, she'd always be regarded as his bastard. A pang of pain shot through him at that thought. Closing his eyes, he vowed never again to think the word "bastard" in conjunction with Charlotte. Nor would he accept it from anyone else.

She was his daughter now, and she'd be loved, cared for. He'd make certain she experienced the carefree childhood that all children should have. He brushed his fingertip over the soft, plump curve of her cheek. "I'll be back soon," he promised in a voice lower than a whisper.

He turned and glanced at the wall separating this chamber from the one next door, and the softening he'd felt in his chest in Charlotte's presence instantly went hard and cold. Before he'd given it a second thought, he'd left Charlotte's room, his feet led him to the Yellow Room, and his hand was turning the door handle.

The bed was made, and someone had tidied the room. Aunt Bertrice sat beside the bed, her head bowed, her hands clasped in her lap. Garrett's brows snapped together, and he closed the door behind him, gazing at his aunt in question.

Aunt Bertrice looked up. She didn't seem at all surprised to see him. "She's gone."

"I don't understand."

With trembling hands, Aunt Bertrice pulled her robe tightly across her chest. "She was going to leave regardless. She couldn't remain here. Not after what she did. None of us would allow it."

"She just gave birth." Garrett hadn't been thinking that far ahead, only that he must go to Kate.

"She is strong and young, and the birth was an easy one. She was tired, but eager enough to go. I gave her the use of a carriage to Leeds."

"But..." He gestured to the door behind him. "She didn't take Charlotte."

"She had little interest in her baby, compared to..." His aunt's voice dwindled, and understanding dawned.

"You paid her off."

After a moment of silence, Aunt Bertrice said, "Yes. Yes, I did."

"How much?"

"It is of no import."

"How much?" he ground out.

"Oh, what does it matter, boy?" Aunt Bertrice waved her hand in the air. "It was five thousand pounds, on the written condition that she never intrude upon our lives again."

A muscle twitched in his jaw. He just stared at her.

"I know you wanted her out of your life, and so did I. Thank God you decided at the last moment not to marry her. Thank God Katherine sent those letters." She tightened her fists over the edges of her robe. "Thank God none of you listened to me when I would have led you all astray. So focused was I on the evil of the Fisk name, I didn't see a new evil when it stared me in the face. I was so easily willing to trust when I promised myself I would never do so again. I so confidently believed I was the one who wouldn't be duped this time, and yet I was the most trusting of us all. If you had listened to me, I would have blindly led you into a lifetime of regret and misery."

"You—" Garrett began, but she shushed him.

"I owe this to you. To all of us. It was the least I could do."

He shook his head helplessly. She'd given Joelle years'

worth of her own income. The woman didn't deserve it. "I don't blame you for what happened."

"You should," she said darkly. "I was a complete ninny. And I will be the first to admit that her *Frenchness* seduced me." She sounded disgusted with herself. "To think that I encouraged you to marry someone who was in league with that villain William Fisk..." She shuddered, and her knuckles whitened over the fabric of her muslin robe.

"You were doing what you thought best. There was no evidence to give you any indication of her guilt." He let his gaze rest on the bed, the relief washing through him surprising in its intensity. "I'm glad she's gone," he admitted.

"I am, too." Her eyes glistening, Aunt Bertrice looked toward the window where the impending dawn cast a pale gray light into the room.

"You will miss having someone with whom to share your stories of France."

Harshly, she rubbed a hand across her eyes. "Not at all."

Her melancholy washed over him. Taking a few steps forward, he bent down and kissed her forehead. "I'm leaving, Aunt Bertrice."

"I know," she sighed. "You're going after Katherine Fisk."

"Yes."

"I'm glad, Garrett. I'm neither stubborn nor stupid enough to keep from admitting my fault in this. I was wrong about Kate. I can see that now. It is clear to me that from the beginning she has had all our best interests in mind." A tiny smile flitted across her lips. "You should marry her, if that is your wish."

He tilted his head in acknowledgment. "I'll return soon."

"I wish you the best, my dear. And take her to Gretna Green. If you don't have a special license, I daresay that is the most expedient place to marry."

"I daresay that's very wise counsel, Aunt."

"I always come round, Garrett. Eventually."

Reggie's fever had worsened by the time Kate arrived home from sending Willy's letters, and in the ensuing days, his condition became serious. Kate wouldn't leave his side, so Mama was the one to go to Kenilworth to fetch the doctor, whom Kate paid with the remaining coins from Lady Bertrice.

The doctor said it was influenza and that Reggie was at great risk due to his weakened lungs. Kate refused to believe the man's dire predictions, and she refused to give him any of the awful prussic acid he prescribed. Reggie hadn't consumed any prussic acid at Calton House, and he'd fared better without it.

She bathed Reggie with cool cloths, fed him warm broth, gave him the lemon bark infusion the old cook used to brew, and read to him. She did everything she could to comfort him, to ease his breathing, to soothe his heated skin.

On the third day of the fever, it raged at its highest, and she'd finally coaxed Reggie into a fitful slumber. The air, heavy and reeking of Reggie's illness, shrouded her so thickly, she could hardly breathe, and with a glance at Reggie to ensure he slept, she stepped out of their tiny chamber. As soon as she closed the door behind her, she sank against it and stared miserably at the lumpy, white plastered wall across the corridor.

It was early November. Joelle's babe was due soon. By now, Becky might have received the burned letters. But was it too late? Had Garrett already married Joelle? Kate's eyelids grew heavy, and she allowed them to sink. It didn't matter whether Garrett was married. She must stop pining for him. Married or not, he was far away and lost to her. Her life was as it was meant to be: here at Debussey Manor with Mama and Reggie.

"Katie?" Reggie's reedy voice filtered through the door, and Kate instantly righted herself and went inside.

When Reggie turned to her, his eyes were dark and serious but no longer held the sheen of fever. He'd kicked off the blankets, and sweat ran in rivulets down his cheeks and plastered his nightgown to his chest.

"Oh, Reggie." She laid a hand over his damp, cool forehead and bit back a sob of relief. "Are you feeling better, sweetheart?"

He nodded. "A little. I'm hungry."

Kate closed her eyes. *Thank God*.

Two more long days passed before Kate dared to leave Reggie alone. That afternoon, she planned to clean Bertie's cottage, close it up for winter, and carry the dusty linens back to the house to be washed. The task had been put off for far too long. As Kate tugged on her mittens, Reggie, who was curled up on the chair beside the fire, looked up. "I'm well today, Katie. May I go with you?"

"No, Reg," Kate said soberly. "I shall be gone a while, and I don't want you out walking in this cold. Not so soon." He'd been up half the night with a hacking cough, and the thought of his illness returning had caused a stone of fear to settle in her stomach. She smoothed the skirts of the green dress from Calton House, now stained with the ash and dirt from her last visit to Bertie's cottage.

When she finished her duties today, she would set aside what little pride she retained, and she would write Becky to beg her to take Reggie for a week or two. Calton House seemed to be the only medicine that could truly cure him.

"But Katieeee," he whined.

She looked at him in wide-eyed shock. Could it be true? Was her agreeable, sweet baby brother arguing with her?

"I want to!" He stamped his foot on the floor. "I am tired of this place!"

"No."

He grabbed the book in his lap and flung it across the room. It slammed into the wall then landed on the floor with a smack, its pages ruffling open.

Her jaw dropped. "Reginald Fisk! What on earth are you doing?"

"I want to go with you!"

"Well, you cannot, and that is that." She stared at him in bemusement. Was this behavior a product of loneliness, of missing Calton House, of fear for his health, or was he merely getting older and more prone to outbursts?

She knelt before his chair. "Sweetheart, I'll be back before dark. We'll play a game of backgammon, all right?"

A single tear carved a path down his cheek. "But I want to go."

She gathered him in her arms, holding him tight when he resisted. "You cannot, Reg. It's too cold, and it'll make your chest hurt."

"But I want to!" Two more tears spilled down his thin cheeks.

"Shh, sweetheart. I know. I know, Reggie." She rubbed his back, soothing and petting him. He'd been so happy, so healthy, at Calton House. In their last days there, she'd allowed him to go off for hours at a time, comfortable that he wouldn't be overcome by a coughing fit or an attack of asthma.

When his tears subsided, she kissed him on the cheek and rose. "If I don't go soon, I won't return till after dark, and then we won't be able to play backgammon at all," she said gravely.

He didn't answer her, just stared forlornly at the cast-off book on the floor. She scooped it up and handed it to him. "Here, finish your book. Mama will be down soon." She kissed him again. "Be good."

"Yes, Katie," he mumbled, but he wouldn't meet her eyes.

Just then Mama entered the kitchen, a frown deepening the creases on her forehead. "What is all this commotion?"

"It's nothing. Reggie was upset but he is fine now."

He set the book aside, propped his chin in his palm, and gazed unhappily into the fire. Mama eyed Reggie for a moment, then she gestured at Kate. "Come into the larder with me for a moment, Katherine."

"Yes, Mama." With a trailing glance at her brother, she followed her mother into the small, empty room leading from the kitchen. Kate remembered the fat sides of beef and mutton and the fowl that always hung in this tiny, windowless room. She shuddered. She'd always avoided this place. Now the room was empty and clean, but it still carried the faint odor of raw meat, and she stayed away out of long-ingrained habit.

Once she passed through the door, Mama told her to shut it. Kate did as she was told then gazed at Mama, nearly overcome by curiosity. Her mother turned from one of the shelves, holding up a midsized packet in her hand. She smiled. "Beefsteaks."

"Oh?"

"Mr. Templeton brought them early this morning—you were downstairs with Reginald." Mama turned the packet over in her hand. "I wonder what I shall make with them. I could stew them, or make a beefsteak pie. Or perhaps I shall simply fry them with some butter."

"It all sounds equally delicious to me, Mama," Kate said quietly. Mr. Templeton was a widower butcher from Kenilworth who often visited her mother. Kate liked Mr. Templeton. He was a jolly, red-cheeked old man, the kind of man who would take great joy in bouncing a ruddy grandson on his knee. He possessed a friendly, outgoing personality—an excellent foil for her mother's stern one—and was always very kind to Reggie.

Her mother gave her a wary look, and Kate's heart sank. "That wasn't what you brought me in here for, was it?"

"No." Mama turned away again and reached for something on the counter. "Mr. Templeton also brought the post. You have received a letter from Yorkshire."

Kate's heartbeat quickened, but when she saw the seal broken on the stationery, her chest clenched. "You opened it," she said flatly. "You read it."

Mama released a harsh breath. "Don't give me that look, girl. The fact of the matter is, I am worried for you.

I do not know what happened to you in Yorkshire, and since you are unwilling to speak to me about much of anything—"

"You have no right to read my letters!"

Mama's nostrils flared. "You are my daughter. My child. My responsibility."

Kate snatched the page from her mother's hand, and with a glimpse at Becky's flowery script on its front, clapped it to her chest. "It's mine. It belongs to me."

"I did it for your own good, Katherine."

"You care nothing for my good."

"How can you say that?"

"You tried to kill me with the fire poker!"

Mama staggered backward until her hip collided with the countertop. "I would never hurt you." Her voice was strained. "You are my daughter. My only daughter."

Biting her tongue to stop the venomous, angry words from spewing out of her, Kate wrenched her gaze away from her mother. She was too furious to see straight, to think. Her fingers trembled over the smooth surface of the stationery.

Clutching the letter like a lifeline, she closed her eyes and slowly regained control of her faculties. Becky, her dear friend, had finally written to her. What had she said? Had Kate's proof of Joelle's deception arrived? Had it come in time to stop Garrett from marrying Joelle?

Finally, she opened her eyes and spoke to her mother, her voice flat. "I've never been good enough for you."

Mama tilted her head, her gaze lowering to the parchment pressed to Kate's chest. "Read that letter, Katherine. Then we shall talk."

Kate unfolded the paper and read.

My Dearest Kate,

It is with great heaviness of heart that I write you this morning, for as my pen scrawls across this paper, Joelle Martin is laboring with her child. Worse, Garrett and the vicar are in her room with her. Oh, Kate, Garrett marries Joelle as I write this!

Oh, dear Kate, all I can think about is you. How much I miss you and how much it will hurt you to read this letter. How I wish I could be there to comfort you. As much as it pains me to write these words, I feel it my duty to inform you of these events, for you are my dearest friend, and you deserve to hear the news from me before you hear it from someone who loves and understands you less.

I must end this quickly, because Tom will leave for the village to meet the mail coach soon, and I wish to make certain he takes this letter with him. I hope he will bring back a letter to me from you as well...

I will write more tomorrow, I promise. For now, please remember how much I miss you, dearest sister. God bless you and keep you, dear Kate.

Remember me,
Becky

Kate couldn't move. She just stared down at the words blurring into black streaks on the page.

The burned letters hadn't yet arrived at Calton House when Becky had written this. Kate was too late. Garrett had married Joelle while she labored with his—or Willy's—child.

But surely by now the letters had arrived. Poor Garrett. Kate's fingers curled, crumpling the stationery in her fist. He must have been devastated to learn of his new wife's treachery. What had he done? How had he reacted?

She closed her eyes.

"Katherine?"

Kate had forgotten she was in the larder; forgotten Mama was there with her. She looked up at her mother, unable to hide the bleakness that had descended over her like a shroud.

Her mother's lips were pinched. "You love him? You're in love with the Duke of Calton? You have had intimate relations with the man, haven't you?"

Mortification churned in Kate's gut, rendering her speechless. She tightened her fist over the crumpled letter.

Mama sighed. "I knew this would happen."

"You don't know me at all," Kate said, her voice tight.

"Oh, but I do, Katherine. I know you very well." Mama took a small step forward, her eyes softening. "For you see, you are just like me."

Kate couldn't deny that. Her actions in the past weeks proved her mother's words.

"You were always so full of life," Mama continued, "of irreverence, of the sheer joy of living. I was the same way at your age. I defied my parents, and I mocked prudence at every turn. But, you see, in doing so I ultimately ruined myself. All my desires, hopes, and dreams for a happy, fulfilling life were carried away on the heels of my recklessness.

"From the moment you were born, I saw so much of

me in you. I knew that if I didn't root you in modesty and reserve, you would make the same horrific blunders I did, and you would be ruled by your emotions rather than good sense. Led by your heart rather than your mind."

Mama stepped closer. Gently, she peeled Kate's fingers open, took the crumpled letter, and set it on the counter. Turning back to Kate, she laid a hand on her shoulder. "Did you engage in carnal relations with the Duke of Calton, Katherine?"

Whatever pride Kate retained had crumbled to dust and blown to the four winds. "Yes," she whispered. "Yes, I did."

"All of my efforts were for naught, then."

"Yes, Mama. Everyone in our family has always known that your efforts to mold me into a lady would never succeed. From the moment I was born, my wayward nature was set in stone."

"It is not your fault. It is mine."

Kate gave a hopeless shake of her head.

"I should have realized the impossibility of changing a person's essence. I could not drive your spirit out of you just as my father couldn't drive it out of me. It took the unkind effects of love to subdue me. First it was your father. And then..." Mama took a shaky breath. "Lord Debussey relit the fire within me, but once again, I was incapable of wisely judging his purpose. I didn't know until too late that he would use it to burn away the remaining shreds of my spirit."

While Kate and Willy and Warren had been growing up, they had feared discussing their father in their mother's presence. Though the three of them were madly curious, any mention of their father elicited an icy fury in their mother. But Kate was a woman now, and no longer afraid. She deserved to know about the man who had fathered her.

"Tell me more. Why did you defy your family to marry Papa? Why did he leave us?"

Her mother's lips twisted. "He never loved me, Katherine. I thought he did—he was ever so dashing, and he showered attention on me as if I was the only girl in the world. But the truth was that he thought if he eloped with me, he'd become part of a fine family and his deepest desire would come to fruition: He'd marry into riches and people would treat him like a gentleman."

Mama described him as Becky might someday describe Willy. Even as boys, he and Warren had desired nothing more than to be recognized as fine gentlemen.

Mama bowed her head. "After we married, the unthinkable happened. My father disowned me. He never spoke to us again and wouldn't allow us in the house. We were forced to leave Birmingham. As soon as we settled at Kenilworth..." Mama's voice broke, but then she forged onward. "Your father took a mistress. Several, perhaps. After he got me with child for the second time—that was you, Katherine—he lost interest in me altogether. When you were small, I woke up one morning and he had gone. No good-bye. No note. I knew he had tired of me. I wasn't at all surprised."

"Where is he now?" Kate whispered.

"I don't know, nor do I worry about it any longer. It is far better to live alone than with a man who despises you, for it wasn't his departure that leached away my spirit, it was his antipathy." Mama shook her head. "But I failed to learn from my mistake. Fifteen years later I repeated it."

First Kate's father and then Lord Debussey. Mama never had experienced true love, not as Kate had, at least for fleeting moments.

But perhaps she deluded herself, as her mother had deluded herself into thinking first her father loved her, then Lord Debussey. Perhaps Garrett had been just as false in his admiration of Kate. Look at how quickly he'd turned away from her once Joelle Martin had swept back into his life.

"Are you with child, Katherine?"

"No, Mama," Kate said dully. "I'm not with child."

Some of the tightness in Mama's shoulders eased. "Good. You don't want to bring another bastard into the world."

"No, I don't."

"Katherine, look at me."

Slowly, Kate raised her gaze to her mother's frowning face.

"It is over."

Kate nodded.

"You must forget him."

"I know," she whispered. "But how?"

"I will help you. I have experience in such matters. You've one advantage over my most recent debacle—your beloved doesn't live in the same house."

Kate choked on a sob. She had become her mother, after all. She had traveled the same heartbreaking path, after telling herself for years that no matter what, she would never make the same choices Mama had made. That she'd never allow anyone such power over her, that she'd never suffer, never disgrace herself. Yet she had done it all.

Her mother's hand moved from her shoulder to cup her

cheek. "There is still a future for you, Katherine. If you are not pregnant with his child..."

"I'm not."

"...then you can find a good position elsewhere. Somewhere better than this lonely old pile. Lady Rebecca clearly adores you. She will make you an excellent reference."

"No, Mama. I will stay here. This is where I belong. With Reggie, and with you."

Pressing her lips together, Mama nodded. "If that is what you want."

"It is."

Mama's fingers tightened on her cheek. "Katherine, you must understand. Every harsh word I said to you, I said because you were my daughter and I loved you. I loved you and I did not want you to suffer as I have."

Kate was twenty-two years old. She thought it rather late for her mother to be telling her she loved her for the first time in her life. But as she stared at the woman facing her, she saw that her mother was getting old. Deep grooves furrowed her forehead, her eyelids hung heavy over her dark eyes, and lines bracketed her mouth. And the expression on her face, beneath all the bitter years of loneliness and rejection, was sincere.

Clearing her throat, Mama dropped her hand to Kate's shoulder and patted it. "You were to clean Bertie's cottage today, weren't you?"

Kate nodded.

"You'd best get on with it, then. The afternoon is upon us and darkness comes early these days." Mama paused. "And hard work goes a long way in taking the pain away."

"Yes, Mama." She turned away but then hesitated and turned back. "Mama?"

"Yes?"

"Don't read my letters again."

With that, she took Becky's letter from the counter, tucked it into her pocket, and walked out of the larder.

After so many days of sitting at Reggie's side in their tiny room, the crisp, cool air of late autumn felt cleansing. Kate turned her face up to the pale gray sky and breathed deeply as the heels of her shoes crunched over the icy bracken.

She'd been such a fool with Garrett. She'd told him in the beginning that she offered herself freely with no expectations, and she'd failed to keep her word. Not only that, but he'd told her outright that anything between them would be impossible. He'd never promised her a thing.

As she'd always done, she'd plunged in headfirst. She'd thought she'd seen feeling for her in his eyes, in his face, in his actions. Because of that, she'd allowed herself a glimmer of hope. She'd allowed herself to dream that he loved her, too.

It didn't matter. She'd lived in a dream land for a short time, and now she'd returned to the life she was meant to lead. *This* was her life, and life was what one made of it. She refused to allow hers to be wretched and full of misery and pain as her mother's had been.

Reggie was on the mend, and that in and of itself was reason to rejoice.

It was over between her and Garrett. He was the bronze god from her pool at Kenilworth Castle, and he didn't belong in the real world. He was a fantasy. An unattainable dream.

Kate unlocked the cottage door and pushed it open. As before, it was as if she walked into a block of ice, only today was even colder than the last time.

The ashes she'd pulled from the fireplace on her previous visit had stained the rug and scattered onto the flagstones. Haphazard piles of clothes—Bertie's, Joelle's, and probably Joelle's maid's—lay strewn on the bed and the floor. A layer of dust covered everything, and the place reeked of rotten food.

Kate found some coals and started a fire. Pulling off her mittens, she held her red, chapped hands out over the flames, reveling in the warmth seeping through her fingertips.

Sighing, she rose and set a pot to heat over the fire for the scrubbing she'd do later. As the water heated, she took the broom from the pantry leading off the kitchen area and swept up the loose ashes. Warmed by the activity, she shrugged out of her coat and laid it on the bed. Uncaring that her hair had half fallen out of her cap, she rolled the rug and left it near the door so she could take it home to beat. Kneeling before the fire, she removed the warmed water, dipped a cloth in it, and began to scrub the table.

The door squeaked on its hinges, and Kate's heart leaped into her throat. Slapping the wet cloth to her chest, she spun around. Her eyes widened until she thought they might burst from her skull.

"Garrett?"

Chapter Twenty-two

Kate stared at the big, broad man looming over the threshold. His blond hair brushed the fine black wool covering his shoulders. His narrow blue eyes focused on her. His fists were clenched at his sides.

"Kate."

A familiar shudder rolled through her as he said her name. She would never understand how he did that—made such a simple, one-syllable word sound so important, so vital.

"What are you—?"

In two strides he stood in front of her. He hooked his arm around her waist and pulled her tightly against him, pressing the wet cloth between their bodies. Before she could say another word, his lips descended on hers.

Reality crashed into her with such force it left her gasping.

This man was an illusion. He wasn't for her. He was a

vision in a pool, something to dream about, never something to hold on to. And he was married.

She pressed her fists—one of them still clutching the soiled cloth—against his chest, and with all the force she could muster, she thrust him away. "Stop!"

He stepped back, but he didn't let her go. The warmth of his fingers seeped through her bodice, heating the skin of her waist.

"Why?" It was more a growl than a word. He stared down at her, intensity rolling off his body in hot waves that washed over her in a torrent that muddled her mind.

"Why?" she echoed. "Why?" There were so many things to list, she didn't know where to begin. So she uttered the first coherent thought that she could pluck out of the deep mire of reasons. "Because this is Bertie's house."

"I don't care."

He yanked her to him again, but she flattened her hands against him, pressing the wet cloth against his chest, holding him at bay.

"You should be at Calton House with your family. Not here."

"*You* are my family."

He hovered over her. His lips were so close, she could feel the warmth of his breath on her lips.

"You're . . . a . . . duke."

"I know. God help me." His hands tightened over her waist. His lips brushed over hers again, and she trembled in his arms. There were more reasons, so many more, but with him so near, warming her to the core, her thoughts melted like butter. Every time she tried to pluck one of them to use to make him go away, it slipped through her fingers.

"I'm filthy," she said desperately.

Pulling slightly away, he arched a brow. "Do you think I care?"

"Your coat. I will soil it." She already had, she knew, with the damp, dirty cloth she pressed against it.

"Kate."

In one giant rush, she remembered why she couldn't be near him. Why she didn't want to be near him. She burst into tears.

"You're married!" she sobbed, glaring at him through her blurring eyes. What was his purpose in coming here just days after he'd married Joelle Martin? How could he? How *dare* he storm in and once again disrupt the world she was finally righting after he'd turned it upside down?

He frowned. "What?"

"I know you never promised me anything." Angrily, she swiped a tear from her cheek. "I have finally admitted to myself that you are far beyond my reach. I don't care what she's done. I don't care if you've left her. You're *married*."

"No, Kate—"

"Why did you come here? Why?" She tried to wrench her body from his grip, but he held her firm. "Let me go!"

"No."

"You shouldn't be touching me! It's wrong!"

"No, it isn't." He yanked her closer. "There's nothing—"

"Let go of me!"

"I'm not married, Kate."

"Yes you are! Becky wrote to me—she told me everything."

"You were misinformed. I never married Joelle Martin."

"Becky wouldn't lie to me."

"I'm not married, Kate."

She frowned, thoroughly confused and still unable to control her tears. "She said Joelle was in childbed, and you were marrying her as she wrote the letter, and the vicar was in the room and—"

"I love you."

"—she was so appalled that you would..." Her train of thought withered. "What did you say?"

"I love you, Kate. I don't love Joelle. I never have."

"What?" she asked stupidly.

"I want to marry you."

"What?" It seemed to be the only word remaining in her vocabulary.

"I want to marry you. I would this moment, if I could. I should have married you weeks ago."

She blinked at him.

He framed her face in his big, callused hands. "Listen to me. I was a fool. After that day at the waterfall, I knew I wanted to make you mine. I knew long before then, really, but it wasn't until that day that I could finally admit it to myself.

"When Joelle arrived, I was confused. I knew I loved you, but I felt responsible for her condition, and I felt it my duty to do right by her and the child. I never wanted to marry her. I wanted only you. But I was a damned fool and never told you. I allowed you to live without knowing, allowed you to think I preferred her to you. But I never did, Kate, not for a moment. Ever since I laid eyes on you at that pool by Kenilworth Castle, there has never been anyone else for me. No one."

"But you slept with her!"

"I did not."

"I saw you." She blinked hard. Why was he lying to her? Why was he doing this? She balled her fists against his chest.

He looked angry, then confused, then angry once more. "God...you saw that."

"Yes!" She jerked away, and this time he dropped his hands and allowed her some distance.

His eyes boring into her, he spoke quietly. "There was one night she came to me without my knowledge, and when I woke, I saw her there and asked her to leave. I didn't allow her into my bedchamber after that. I don't desire Joelle."

God help her. She believed him. She shook her head. "There are too many things...we are too different. I am a housekeeper's daughter..." Her voice dwindled as the myriad reasons came flooding back to her. Even if Garrett wasn't married, even if he hadn't slept with Joelle Martin, there were a thousand reasons for them to stay apart.

"That is why I hesitated, too. I'd torn your family apart. I'd hurt you. You deserve better, Kate. But I would kill any man who touched you. I can't let you go."

"You must."

"I was a fool to let you go once. I shouldn't have waited so long to come after you." He stepped forward and took her hand, stroking the top of it with his thumb. "I never want to touch anyone but you. I never want to make love to anyone but you. Never." With his big, warm hand still engulfing her frozen one, he reached up with the other to stroke the tangled hair dangling from her cap.

"Sophie," she whispered.

Dropping his hand from her forehead, he frowned. "What about her?"

"Sophie is the one you love." Her voice was flat, raw. "You told me yourself. You love Sophie, and you always have."

He shook his head. "Kate, you don't—"

She grabbed his wrist and thrust it away. "No," she said harshly. "Your sister confirmed it. Becky said Sophie was lovely and elegant and wonderful. She said you love her." She firmed her trembling lower lip as she stared at him. "But you see, I can't be your second choice. I won't. I'm too proud. I know that pride is one of the seven deadly sins, but I cannot help it. I won't be second to Sophie, or to Joelle, or to anyone—"

"Joelle is gone from my life forever. And you're not second to Sophie."

"But I am."

He shook his head. "I will always care for Sophie. She is my daughter's mother, and we will always be friends. But I no longer love her."

"How can I believe you?"

"I stopped loving her the moment I started loving you." When she didn't respond, he said, "That second day at the pool. When you asked me to trust you. When you looked at me with those honest, open eyes and gave yourself to me."

Slowly, he lowered himself to one knee, gathered her hands in his, and bowed his head. "Marry me, Kate."

She gazed at him. Her mouth was dry as a desert.

"Reggie?" she croaked, staring down at him. Reggie was her last line of defense. If Garrett rejected her brother, then there could be nothing between them.

"He'll be ours." Garrett took a breath. "Miranda will be a part of our lives, too. And Charlotte." He gazed up at her. His blue gaze studied her, sought her acceptance, her approval.

"Charlotte?"

"Joelle's child. Joelle is gone, but Charlotte is mine now, as is Miranda. And I can only . . . beg you . . . in hopes that you and Reginald will be mine as well." His voice shook as he continued, but he pressed on. "Please, Kate, make me whole again. Please be my wife."

She stared at him for a long moment. His ice-blue eyes, his broad shoulders, his curling tufts of streaked blond hair. How beautiful this man was, how powerful. He was a duke of the realm. And yet he knelt before her. Her, Katherine Fisk, the plain, unimportant daughter of a housekeeper.

"This is my world." She gestured at Bertie's mussed cottage—at the dirty bundle of linens, at the soiled rug, at the bucket of soapy water. "This is the only world I have ever known. It is safe. Your world is different. It is dangerous. It . . . it can hurt me."

"I feel the same way," he said quietly. "After so much time in a world more like yours than the one I belong to, I'm relearning how to exist. It is a slow process. I won't lie to you and say it isn't painful or difficult, because at times it is both. But I know I will be stronger with you beside me." He looked up to her. "We will help each other."

His expression was so vulnerable, so humble. Suddenly, it struck her that she could destroy him with a word. She held the power—all of it—in her hands.

Yet she could no more destroy this man than she could herself.

She knelt in front of him and took him into her arms as his arms closed around her. "Yes, Garrett. I'll be your wife."

This time when his lips touched hers, nothing in the world could have stopped her from kissing him back.

They took Reggie, whose health had continued to improve with Garrett's arrival, with them to Scotland. Mama made no effort to keep her son at Debussey Manor. She feared caring for him without Kate, but more than that, she couldn't say no to Garrett. He was a duke, after all, and Mama could scarcely speak to him, so full of awe had she become in his presence. When he'd told her he intended to marry Kate, her only response was a stuttered expression of disbelief. And when Garrett had promised her a small house in Yorkshire for her personal use, she went pale and though her mouth moved as if she intended to answer, no words emerged from it.

Together, Kate, Garrett, and Reggie traveled to Gretna Green, the same place where Becky had married Willy. In a trembling voice, Kate repeated the words the minister recited, Garrett pressed a kiss to her lips, and suddenly, they were truly married.

The day after the wedding, they began the journey back to Calton House. A few days later, they rattled down the final stretch of the country road that would lead them to Calton House, and Kate gazed at Garrett from beneath her lashes as the carriage bounced along.

She loved him with a frightening intensity that continued to grow, though she'd thought that was impossible.

She adored everything about him, from his curling blond hair to his big, masculine feet. From the gentle way he looked at her to his gruff laugh when he played a game of cards with Reggie.

Yet she feared what was to come. Everyone would know the truth about Willy, her inferior birth and status, her father and mother. Kate knew what society would think of her. It would say she was a greedy, fortune-hunting trollop who'd taken advantage of the mad hero of Waterloo. She was terrified, but she could do nothing but brace herself for the inevitable scandal and remind herself that she could withstand anything as long as Garrett and Becky stood by her side.

Garrett handed the cards to Reggie to shuffle, then leaned forward and took her hands in his own.

"Sophie and Tristan are at Calton House, Kate."

She stared at him. They'd been married for all of three days and already it would begin. Swallowing hard, she pushed a response from her tight throat. "I see."

"It was our plan all along for them to arrive a few weeks before Christmas so we could share the holiday festivities with the children."

She nodded and turned away to look out the window as the stark, wintry land passed by. Would Sophie and Tristan despise her? Would they think her undeserving of the honor Garrett had bestowed on her?

Garrett continued to hold her hands, his big thumbs pressing gently into her palms. He made no promises, no guarantees, only reassured her with his touch.

Reggie fidgeted beside her. He had grown more excited as the hours passed, and he asked Garrett endless questions about the tree house and Miranda and school and toys and London. He even asked questions about baby Charlotte, which Garrett couldn't answer in detail, for Kate had learned he'd left Calton House when the child was only a few hours old.

Finally, the carriage drew to a jerking halt, and from her window, Kate saw the familiar gleaming Ionic columns of Calton House. A footman opened the door and helped her out onto the front drive. The day was unseasonably warm, almost springlike, and the sunshine warmed her shoulders through her coat. Within a second, Garrett appeared by her side. He took her hand in his own, and Reggie jumped out and reached for her other hand.

They lent her strength—just as they had the first time she'd arrived at Calton House. Only now she was the duchess, the mistress of this place—as absurd and impossible as that thought was—and at the top of the stairs, Becky stood beside Lady Bertrice. Kate's heart thumped in her chest in a combination of pleasure at seeing Becky again and trepidation about seeing Lady Bertrice.

Just as it had on their first arrival, the journey up the stairs seemed to take forever. With each step, Kate had to remind herself to be strong.

Finally at the top, they stopped to face Becky and Lady Bertrice. Garrett released her hand but stood beside her, tall and bristling with pride. After a moment's pause, Becky enveloped her in a warm, one-armed embrace. "Oh, Kate," she breathed. "You've come back to us. I am so very happy."

Kate held her friend tightly. "I missed you, Becky."

"And I missed you, my dearest sister."

"How is your arm?"

"It grows stronger every day."

When Becky released her, Kate mustered her courage and slowly raised her eyes to Lady Bertrice, bracing herself for her biting tongue. She nearly stumbled backward when she saw the expression on the older woman's face. Her eyes were lowered in an expression of humility and coated with a glistening sheen of tears.

Reaching out, she grasped both of Kate's hands and curtsied. Kate gazed at her in openmouthed shock.

"Well, you needn't look so surprised," Lady Bertrice said crossly. She impatiently scrubbed at her watering eyes. "I was proven wrong, you know. And forgive me, but I am rather glad that my nephew followed the correct course despite his old ninnyhammer aunt's rantings." She looked beyond Kate's shoulder at Garrett and gave a sharp nod. "Well done, boy."

"Aunt," was all Garrett said, but Kate detected a faint wryness in his tone.

An hour later, Kate stood awkwardly in the unfamiliar space of Garrett's bedchamber. The maid had just finished with her hair, and with a curtsy, had left her alone. Earlier, Reggie had eagerly ventured off with Becky to meet Gary, Tristan's son. As he'd walked away, Kate had seen his cheeks flush a healthy pink. It was part of the miracle of Calton House.

Kate had discarded the borrowed green dress for the last time and now wore a red silk dress that the dressmaker had delivered during her absence. She turned around slowly, taking in the way the new dress clung to her body, the way the skirts swished gently around her ankles.

It was time to face the world as the Duchess of Calton.

She remembered the rabbit she'd saved from Warren

and Willy, how its tiny heart had fluttered in fear against her fingers. She felt just as frightened and timid as that rabbit, but also just as ready to bare her teeth, bite down hard, and then run for her life.

The door opened, and Kate spun around. She opened her clenched hands when Garrett appeared in the doorway. His gaze roamed her body, and he smiled in approval. "It is just as I imagined."

"What is?"

He shrugged. "It always—even from the first day—angered me to see you in clothes so far beneath you."

She tilted her head, confused. "How do you mean?"

"I suppose I always knew you were meant to be a duchess."

"Meant to be a duchess?" She gave an unladylike snort. "I wonder whether the day will ever come when I hear myself referred to as a duchess and I don't feel like pointing at the closest female and asking, 'Are you certain you don't mean *her*?'"

"It will come," Garrett said confidently. "After all, if I can be a duke..."

"It's different, Garrett. I know you forgot about your position for many years, but you were born to be a duke. I was born to be a maid."

"No. You weren't."

Pressing her lips together, she bowed her head and nodded.

"You were born to be with me. Just as I was born to be with you."

Without raising her head, she looked up at him through her lashes. "Do you truly believe that?"

"I do." His voice was flat, but with a forceful edge that pierced straight through her haze of self-doubt.

She stood silent for a long moment, savoring his declaration. He believed what he said. He believed in her, and knowing that, how could she not believe in herself?

"I brought something for you." Standing before her, he opened his hand. A gold chain and a cluster of red gems lay in his palm.

"What...?"

"I hope you will accept this as a wedding gift." He grasped one end of the chain and lifted it, stretching the glittering gems into a straight line. "These were my mother's rubies."

"It's lovely, Garrett, but why didn't you give it to Sophie?" It didn't make sense. As his first wife, Sophie would have been the one to inherit his mother's jewels.

He frowned, then shrugged. "I never thought of it. I don't even think she knew of its existence. Perhaps, somewhere deep down, I always knew it would belong to you. Will you wear it?"

"I...of course I will."

She stood motionless as he clasped the chain at the back of her neck, his callused fingertips scraping against the sensitive skin just below her hairline.

Kate touched the smooth facets of the gems lying in an arch just below her collarbone. "Thank you."

"Are you ready?" he asked, his voice soft.

Kate closed her eyes then opened them and gave him a lopsided grin. "Ready as I ever expect to be." Renewed nervousness leaped across her skin like fleas, and she clutched her hands together to keep from scratching her arms.

"Rest easy. It's just Sophie and Tristan. They are friends."

"Mm. Yes." *Friends*. Kate couldn't comprehend how he could be so blasé about Kate's meeting his ex-wife and her current husband. Yet there was an underlying tension in his tone as well as in his stance. Was he just as wary as she was? Was he trying to hide it?

He stepped closer and took her hands in his own. "You look as if you're going to jump out of your skin, Kate. If you want them to go away, I'll tell them to leave this house and stay with Sophie's parents until you are ready."

"No." She smiled at him again. "I must stand tall. I must be brave."

"You're the bravest woman I know."

"But this is just the beginning, isn't it?"

He nodded gravely. "And we will face it together, as we will face everything that is to come."

Lifting her chin, she linked her arm in his, and they walked down the long passage to the opposite corner of the house.

At the door to the salon, Garrett paused. Reaching up, he nudged her chin until she faced him.

"Remember how much I love you." He touched his soft, warm lips to hers. They clung together for the briefest of moments, then he let go, grasped her hand, and opened the door.

A man dressed in a sharply tailored tailcoat rose instantly. He held his hand out to help up the woman who sat beside him on the crimson chaise longue. As she and Garrett stepped into the room, Kate glimpsed the man's crisp white cravat and waistcoat, starkly contrasting with the black of his tailcoat and pantaloons.

She'd recognized him immediately, for she'd met him once before. Tristan, Lord Westcliff, had come to Debussey Manor in the spring in a quest for information about Willy. He was the person who had told them that Willy hadn't died at Waterloo as they'd thought but was alive and living in London.

The woman rose. She wore a white dress of silk or perhaps satin, elegant in its simplicity. Her resemblance to Miranda was evident in her hair, her complexion, and the shape of her face. Until now, Miranda had always struck Kate as the girlish likeness of Garrett, but she saw now that the child was truly a product of both her parents.

Unbidden, unexpected tears pricked at Kate's eyes, and she struggled for a long moment to regain her equilibrium. When she did, Tristan bowed. "Garrett. Your Grace."

Sophie followed suit, and Kate belatedly realized that the "Your Graces" were meant for her, not Garrett.

She curtsied at them both and stammered a greeting but then wondered if she'd addressed them correctly—the words had vanished from her memory as soon as they emerged from her mouth. She winced, her lips twisted, and she squeezed her eyes shut. "Forgive me. I don't believe I'll ever become accustomed to 'Your Grace.' Please, you must call me Kate."

Sophie smiled, and sweet relief swept through Kate, because Sophic's smile wasn't anything like one of those horrid false smiles she used to see plastered on the faces of the ladies who came to parties at Debussey Manor long ago.

"I hope you will call me Sophie, too," she said quietly. She pressed the back of her hand to her cheek—her flame-red cheek.

Kate blinked at her. Was Sophie—the ever so beautiful and perfect Sophie—as uncomfortable as she was?

Suddenly, Kate's shoulders felt much, much lighter.

Garrett, standing beside her, squeezed her hand. He took a breath, puffing out his chest a little. "We are glad to see you both. Can I offer you some refreshment?"

Sophie's gaze swung to Garrett, and she blinked her light brown eyes owlishly at him.

Tristan chuckled. "I see your manners have come round in the past few months."

"No." Garrett frowned, then shrugged. "I suppose it is because I lack anything further to say."

"Ah, I see." Tristan cleared his throat. "Nothing for me, thank you."

They were all embarrassed and uncomfortable. These fine gentlemen and this beautiful lady were just as human as Kate was. Just as flawed, and ultimately just as perfect.

She could do this.

Kate looked at Sophie, who stood quietly, her eyes not focused on anyone in particular, her cheeks rosy. Then she glanced at Tristan, who looked at Garrett expectantly, his eyebrows making dark pointed arches high on his forehead.

There was no need for Kate to look at her husband. The tension cascaded off him, invisible but easily detected by everyone in the room. In spite of all his attempts to soothe her nerves before this meeting, now he bristled. He braced his feet and clenched his fists as if prepared to attack at the slightest provocation.

"Have you seen what Garrett has done to the tree

house?" Kate asked, her voice shattering the uncomfortable silence.

Tristan, Garrett, and Sophie all looked at her. A fine line appeared between Sophie's brows. "Tree house?"

Kate nodded vigorously. "Yes, indeed. There is a small house in one of the oaks beyond the gardens. Garrett said the three of you played in it when you were children. It was in poor repair, but he and Miranda and my brother Reginald have braved the weather to rebuild it. I believe it is finished, for they have called upon Lady Rebecca and me to help with the final trimmings."

The color in Sophie's eyes deepened. "Oh..." She looked up at her husband. "Do you remember it, Tristan?"

Tristan's eyebrows descended until they reached a more natural position. "Vaguely. I remember disliking being cooped up in the place."

"Well, of course," Sophie huffed, but her eyes twinkled like polished bronze. "You would force Garrett and me to hang sheets in the door and in the windows and promise not to peek while you roamed around the grounds for hours to bury your treasures."

"Treasures!" Kate exclaimed, squeezing her husband's hand in encouragement, for he still stood puffed up like an overanxious bodyguard. "What kinds of treasures did you bury, Lord Westcliff?"

"Well, rubies, of course. Like the ones you're wearing now—" Kate pressed her fingers over the rubies. "And emeralds and diamonds, and piles of gold doubloons."

Garrett shook his head. "That's not quite how I remember them..."

"Indeed not," Sophie agreed. "I remember rusty nails, buttons stolen from the housekeeper, and if we were lucky, an occasional penny coaxed from one of the footmen..."

Garrett led Kate to the sofa opposite the chaise longue Sophie and Tristan had been sitting on, and the four of them sat. Kate listened to them reminisce about the tree house and the madcap archaeological expeditions Tristan used to take Garrett and Sophie on across the extensive grounds of Calton House.

Sophie grinned at something Tristan said, and Kate saw a hint of the hoyden Garrett had told her about. For the briefest of moments, she could imagine this elegant woman climbing the rope ladder to the tree house.

A deep feeling of contentedness swelled within Kate. These were real people, not icy statues of perfection. They were not people to either fear or place on a pedestal. They were people she might someday grow to love as part of her family.

Eventually, Tristan changed his mind about refreshment and asked for a drink, and when he and Garrett moved to the sidebar, Sophie and Kate rose as well. Kate clasped her hands behind her back and walked toward the window, Sophie at her side.

The blue-and-green-striped curtains were open, and the window looked out over the great lawn fronting Calton House. Kate pressed her hand against the pane, its warmth at odds with the wintry landscape outside. The grass was pale; the trees barren of leaves. Everything was silent and still. Yet the sun beat down on it all, melting the remaining bits of ice that had hidden in shady corners since the last snowfall.

"Thank you for meeting with us this afternoon,"

Sophie said quietly. "I know it was soon, but Tristan and I were so eager to make your acquaintance."

Kate didn't quite know how to answer that without confessing her own trepidation, so she remained silent.

Sophie gave her a faltering smile. "I also wished to welcome you to our family."

Kate gave her a curious look. "Did you?"

"Yes." Sophie's expression softened. "I didn't want to hide away, or encourage you in any way to think I might be any kind of a threat to you. I hope we shall become friends."

"Really?" Kate couldn't contain her surprise. "In all honesty, I rather expect all of society to shun me, and frankly...well, I expected you to be at the head of the pack." She winced and bit her lip. "Please forgive me for being so blunt. But it is the truth."

"I understand. And I am grateful that you're so forthcoming." Pink crept over Sophie's cheeks once more, and she clasped her hands in front of her. "I will try to make myself plain as well. You must understand that despite the fact Garrett and I were married once, we were separated for over seven years, and during that time we both changed too much to rebuild a marriage. Yet we did not change so much as to lose the fraternal affection we hold for each other. It is an unconventional relationship, for certain, and one that continues to cause raised eyebrows everywhere I go. I have grown weary of it, even after just a few months." She sighed. "But I feel that since you are his wife, it is important for you, above all others, to understand."

"But how can that be?" Kate asked incredulously. "How can you fall *out* of love?"

Especially with Garrett? She didn't—couldn't—understand anyone growing apart from Garrett. She knew with complete certainty that her love for him would remain steadfast, soul-deep, until the day she died. He was the only man she would ever love.

"I found someone else. I belong to Tristan now. And though it has happened very quickly, I'm glad Garrett has found someone as well."

Kate stared at her.

Sophie unclasped her hands and reached for one of Kate's. "You've nothing to fear from me, I promise you."

Kate gazed into the other woman's clear amber eyes, and she knew that Sophie had spoken from her heart. She sighed, and with the sigh, the remaining fear and self-doubt floated from her body.

"Thank you for saving him." Sophie squeezed her hand. "For being honest and good. Between Becky and Aunt Bertrice, I heard everything that happened. He is lucky—so lucky—to have found you."

Kate turned to look out the window once more. "There will be a terrible scandal. Everyone will think me unfit to be a duchess."

"Yes, there will be a scandal." Bringing Kate's hand up, Sophie pressed it between two of her own. "Not only that, but you have become embroiled in the scandal of our divorce—the scandal that will occupy the gossips for months to come. We must all be strong. Remember, you have Garrett beside you and the rest of us bolstering you from all sides. Becky, Aunt Bertrice, Tristan, and me. Together, we can overcome whatever they throw our way."

Sophie's soft hands cradled Kate's hard, callused ones.

How strange to marry into a family such as this one. They were so blue-blooded, just a tiptoe away from royalty. A month ago, this would have been unthinkable. But now, unbelievably, it wasn't so impossible to imagine all of these powerful people uniting behind her. Garrett and Becky had already proven that they would.

"You're a James now, Kate," Sophie murmured. "No scandal will touch us. Together, we shall prevail."

Chapter Twenty-three

The day after their arrival at Calton House, Kate and Garrett sat side by side on the nursery sofa and hunched over baby Charlotte, whom Kate held cradled in her arms. Reggie and Miranda played with toys on the opposite side of the room.

Kate touched a fingertip to the baby's tiny, pink lips. "She's so perfectly lovely."

Garrett smiled down at Charlotte, and she gazed at him, blinking her deep blue eyes in recognition. "She is."

Looking up, he glanced at the older children playing, and then back to Kate. "These are my children," he said quietly, so they couldn't overhear. At that moment, Reggie and Miranda laughed loudly, and Miranda rocked back on her heels, clapping. "I always wanted children when I was young," he continued. "Happy children. I never thought I'd be so blessed."

Kate stared down at sweet little Charlotte. Though she

believed she'd never have the opportunity, she'd always wanted to be a mother. She had been one already, truly, for Reggie had always belonged to her. Now she suddenly had a daughter, too, in Charlotte, and a second daughter, in the precocious, compassionate eight-year-old Miranda, who would spend half her time with them and the other half with Sophie and Tristan.

Her family. Kate's heart opened and accepted it, swelling with love for the three children who now belonged to her. Reggie, her half brother, the son of her mother and a marquis; Miranda, her sweet and observant stepdaughter who would perhaps teach her more about being a lady than anyone; and innocent baby Charlotte of unknown paternity, abandoned by her birth mother for five thousand pounds.

Kate turned to the man who'd brought them together. Her husband. Her duke. Her god, deposited in Kenilworth by a lightning bolt directly from Olympus.

Tentatively he reached out to touch her stomach just below Charlotte's tiny body. "Perhaps we will be blessed with more."

"Would you like that?"

His palm flattened over her bodice. "Yes, I would. I'd like it very much."

She suddenly realized that she might be able to give him something no one else had. A legitimate son. An heir.

"Ah, Kate." Garrett leaned forward to kiss first her forehead and then the baby's. "I know you're loath to part with her," he murmured. It was true. Ever since she'd first seen Charlotte, she'd scarcely let her go except to sleep or to be fed. "But will you walk with me awhile?"

"Yes, of course." In truth, she was eager to go outside, for despite the fact that Christmas was only a few weeks away, the weather was extremely favorable for the season. All the snow had melted, and the bright shaft of morning sun piercing through the crack in the curtains held the promise that today might be even warmer than yesterday.

They gave the baby to her nurse, and Kate donned one of her new walking dresses—a white, pink-dotted, and beribboned muslin. Once dressed, she went downstairs where Garrett awaited her in the entry hall.

Garrett smiled when he saw her and held out her gloves. "Your new dresses suit you."

Taking the gloves from him, she frowned. She rather thought she loved the dresses somewhat more than she should, but they were so lovely, and they fit her more perfectly than she could ever have imagined. "Do you think so?"

"I do." Taking her arm, Garrett led her into the sunshine. "Rebecca chose well."

"No doubt I shall find some reason to roll about in the mud and ruin them all by the year's end."

"I hope you do." He grinned. "And then we will buy you more."

They strode in silence through the grounds, past the octagonal gazebo, and over the Palladian bridge. Kate turned her face to the sun, allowing its warming, healing rays to soak into her upturned cheeks, uncaring that it might make her brown as a heathen.

When Garrett turned her down the path marked by a pile of stones half-hidden by weeds, Kate asked, "Are we going to your waterfall?"

"Our waterfall," he corrected, helping her over a jumble of twigs. "I thought we could have a picnic."

He spoke no more until the sound of roaring water filled her ears, and when they turned the final curve in the path, the falls thundered before them—a white wall of water strengthened to a torrent by the thaw.

"Oh!" she exclaimed. For on the small lawn facing the pool across from the falls lay a blanket, and atop the blanket sat a basket. The same basket and blanket he'd brought to their first rendezvous near the bank of her pool.

"You kept them," she said in amazement.

"Yes." He slid a glance at her, then looked away. "I found them where we'd abandoned them at the pool before we left Kenilworth. I couldn't let them go."

Gripping his arm tighter, she blinked back her swelling emotion. She'd never known it was possible for a man to possess such a heart.

He turned to her and drew her into his arms. "I'll never forget that night."

She slipped her arms under his coat and around his back, feeling muscle and sinew beneath her fingertips. She stared into his blue, blue eyes. "Neither will I."

He led her to the blanket. This time, she realized, she would have no qualms about sitting on it. He smiled, and she smiled back at him as a sweet understanding washed over her. Her confidence increased by leaps and bounds hourly. Every time Garrett looked at her with that stormy look in his blue eyes. Each time he touched her or whispered a word into her ear.

"You're so beautiful when you smile," Garrett said.

He'd always liked it when she smiled. Even on that first night...She closed her eyes, remembering what he'd said: *Your face lights up when you smile. Each time you've smiled, since that first smile you gave me yesterday, I've ached for wanting you.*

"Do you still ache for me?" Her stomach clenched hard as soon as the words left her lips. Running her teeth over her lower lip, she stared up at him.

They hadn't yet lain together as husband and wife. Reggie had slept with them at the inns they'd stayed in between here and Gretna, so physical contact had been nearly impossible. Last night after coaxing Reggie to spend the night away from her for the first time in his life, Kate had slept beside Garrett in his bed, but she'd been so exhausted from the day's events that she'd fallen asleep as soon as her head touched the down pillow.

"Always. Every time I lay eyes on you, I burn for you."

His fingers trailed up her body, and she felt the press of every one of them through the layers of fabric between them and her skin. His palms came to the sides of her head, cradling it for a long moment before he dropped his hands. Hooking his arms behind her knees, he lifted her and gathered her close. He carried her the few steps to the blanket and gently laid her down.

She gazed up at him looming over her. She watched his tender expression as his fingertip trailed over the bones of her face as if to memorize every detail. As if he was in awe of her.

Slowly, his mouth descended to hers, at first soft and tentative, but Kate wrapped her arms around him and tugged him closer. She brushed her tongue along the seam of his lips, coaxing him to open.

When he did, instinct took over. He shuddered beneath her hands, and his heat seeped through the fabric of his shirt. They sank into the kiss, making up for the weeks of lost intimacy. All that mattered now was that they were here, that they were together with nothing to keep them apart any longer.

Kate kissed his lips. She kissed the features of his face, the scar above his eyebrow, the shell of his ear, the dimple in his chin. He kissed her jaw, her neck, the slope of her nose, the line of her bodice. She touched him all over, irritated by the fabric of his shirt blocking her fingertips from his skin.

When she fumbled at the buttons of his falls, he raised his head and gave her a searching, assessing look. "Here?"

"Yes. Here. Now."

With a soft groan, he relented. His hand curled around her calf and then traveled up her leg, lifting her skirts.

"So soft," he murmured. "So sweet."

In one swift movement, he was over her, his shaft nudging her. Instantly, she went from warm to boiling hot. Ready and open for him. She'd wanted him so badly and for so long, every inch of her body clenched in anticipation.

"Now!" she whispered. Gripping his shirt in her fists, she arched her body toward him.

He slid home in one deep thrust. All the way inside her, he paused for an infinitesimal moment, and both of them shuddered together.

Then he began to move. He took her with hard, commanding thrusts. Heat coiled deep within her. She was hot and pliant, possessed by the man she loved just as she possessed him. He made her his, and she made him hers. Forever. Wholly and completely, they took each other.

"Kate," he ground out. "Kate."

Hard and untamed, he claimed her like a wild animal claimed its mate. His hands tangled in her hair, pulling it free of its pins. She tore at his shirt, demanding the heat of his skin against her hands and lips.

The crash of the nearby waterfall swept over them, roared through their blood, bound them together and made them one. The coil inside her tightened and compacted, and then it exploded like a thousand bubbles bursting beneath her skin. Nothing existed but the screaming pleasure roaring through her. They came together, surging heat pulsing between them.

The surge slowly subsided, like a receding tide after a storm. Garrett dropped onto his elbows and then rolled to the side, gathering her in his arms and holding her against him.

"God, how I love you."

"You came inside me," she whispered, overwhelmed by the sheer bliss of feeling him lose himself deep within her.

"Yes." He stroked her hair. "I will never again give you anything but my whole self."

She could stay here forever, locked in the comfort and safety of his embrace.

"I am a duchess," she announced drowsily, some time later. It was the first time she'd said it out loud. She *was* a duchess now. It no longer seemed so foreign, or so impossible.

"My duchess," he said. "Forever."

"Forever," she repeated, smiling to herself.

Neither of them relinquished hold on the other. Clinging to her husband, Kate nearly fell asleep to the soothing sound of his heartbeat and the crashing of the falls, but eventually, he shifted, rising to one elbow. He gazed down at her. "Are you hungry?"

She grinned. "Of course."

"There's roasted chicken and wine." His eyes flashed at her. "And almond tarts…I can't guarantee they taste like clouds, though. They're not Cook's specialty."

Anything would taste like a cloud to her this moment, Kate was certain of it. She sat up, adjusting her skirts around her. She glanced at Garrett as he rummaged around in the basket.

"Oh, no!"

"What is it?" He stopped in midaction, a furrow appearing between his brows.

"I've made ribbons of your shirt!"

He laughed. "Good."

"But…what will they all think?"

His lips cocked in a smile. "That you can't keep your hands off me?"

"That's scandalous."

"Trust me, my love. You're my wife. They're not going to expect you to remain chaste."

Heat crept over her cheeks. "Oh, Lord."

He tore off a piece of chicken and raised it to her lips. "Here. Eat."

"Always wanting me to eat," she grumbled, but she took the succulent piece of chicken from his fingers and licked away the juices. This time she recognized the desire in his expression as he watched her tongue flick over his fingertips, and she grinned as a sweet feeling—a confident feeling—rushed through her.

They fed each other chicken and took sips of wine.

Garrett had turned away and was drawing the almond tarts from the basket when Kate saw the creature slithering on the grass near the blanket. She reached out to Garrett and squeezed his knee.

"What...?"

"Snake." She gestured toward it with her chin, her heart drumming in her ears.

It was an adder, a big one with a bold, black zigzag stripe down its back. Not two feet from the edge of the blanket, it raised its head and stared at them. Its eyes were red, with a vertical slit pupil.

Garrett put his hand over hers, gently pushing it away. Slowly he made to rise, but before he could move, the snake seemed to nod at them. It turned away and slithered into the brush, finally disappearing into a crevice in the sheer face of the cliff covered by the wild garlic.

"It's gone. How odd to see one this time of year," Garrett mused, staring after it. "They hibernate in the winter. Perhaps the unseasonable weather brought it out." He turned back to her, and a line of concern deepened in his brow when he saw the stricken expression on her face. "Are you all right?"

"Yes." Relief filled her, so acute she could hardly speak. The snake had left them alone. He had decided they weren't worth his trouble, and he'd gone back to his winter den. She smiled at her husband, certain it was a sign. There would be no more snakes in their lives. "I...I'm more than all right. I'm...happy. He won't bother us anymore, you see?"

"Yes, I do see," Garrett said quietly. "I don't think he'll come back." He brushed his thumbs over her cheeks, and she recognized that stormy look of desire in his eyes. "We'll take the tarts home."

She nodded, and he leaned forward to place a gentle kiss on her lips. "We still haven't made love in a real bed," he murmured. "I should like to try it."

A delicious shiver ran up her spine, spreading tingles through her limbs. "So would I."

"Then we'll go straight to our bedchamber," he said. "And we'll take our tarts and eat them afterward in bed."

She wrapped her arms around him and buried her face in his chest. "It will be perfect," she breathed. "Because I'll be with you, and there is nowhere I'd rather be."

It's not over yet!
After years of heartbreak,
can Lady Rebecca learn
to trust in love?
Turn the page for a
sneak peek at the next tale
of passion and romance from
Jennifer Haymore.

A Season of Seduction

Available in mass market in
October 2010.

Chapter One

London, 1827

Tonight I will be his.

Becky closed her eyes as a maid sprinkled rosewater on her hair. Though she'd known the gentleman for nearly a month now, they remained strangers to each other. She knew nothing of his past, his family, or his origins, and he knew nothing of hers. When they were together, they spoke only of the present and lived in the moment. She preferred it that way. Nevertheless, there was something about him that made her yearn to dig beyond his hardened shell and discover what lay beneath.

Hypocrite. She certainly didn't want him delving into her soul. There was a part of her she'd locked tight long ago and must never reveal. Not even to a lover.

As long as she kept that vulnerable part of her safely guarded, tonight would set her free. Jack couldn't hurt her—she wouldn't allow that to happen. He *could*, however, release her from the lonely prison that had held her captive for the past four years. He could make her feel alive again.

"You're thinking about something, Becky. I see it in your face."

Becky opened her eyes. Cecelia, Lady Devore, stood in the center of the room wearing a simple white muslin dress, her hands clasped behind her back. Becky met her friend's gaze in the mirror.

"Yes," Becky admitted. "I am."

The edges of Cecelia's lips curved, and her eyes took on a knowing gleam. "Tell."

Becky glanced at the maid and dismissed her with a small movement of her hand. The girl capped the bottle of rosewater, then set it on the table, curtsied, and went away.

When the door clicked shut, Becky said, "I think tonight is the night."

"Do you?" Cecelia's voice was soft. Knowing. "You've grown fond of our Mr. Fulton, have you?"

Resting her crooked arm on the smooth surface of the dressing table, Becky wiggled her fingers. The last two fingers on her left hand tingled often, and she'd grown to take comfort from the sensation. The tingling was a part of her, like her bent, deformed arm, and it reminded her of a period in her life she'd do well not to forget. "It's not that I've grown fond of him, per se. I've grown fond of…parts of him."

"Ah. Parts you wish to become more intimately acquainted with."

Becky's cheeks heated. "Well, yes, I suppose you could put it that way."

Cecelia's renowned bluntness extended to matters

most people kept to themselves. That was one attribute of her friend that had originally drawn Becky when they'd met during the Season earlier this year. She found Cecelia's matter-of-fact approach to mankind's baser nature equally refreshing and shocking. Despite their months of friendship, she still blushed often in the other woman's presence.

Seeing her discomfiture, Cecelia's expression softened into one of compassion. "I am pleased for you, Becky. It has been so long."

"Yes. It has." It had been four years since she'd last lain with a man. She'd been so eager with her husband—eager to learn and eager to please. She had reveled in every touch they'd shared. Until things had turned sour.

"Too long," Cecelia said.

"You are spoiled, Cecelia. Many widows never touch another man after their husbands die."

"Well, that is their loss. I lost my husband the same year you lost yours, and as you know, many men have warmed my bed since." Cecelia shrugged. "I shall offer no apologies for it. I love men."

Becky arched her brows. "Really? I wouldn't say so. As a whole, I'd say you're rather cynical about the male sex."

Cecelia laughed lightly. "'Tis true. I daresay men are most appealing when they're in my bed naked and occupying their mouths with pursuits other than talking."

Tiny hairs prickled on the back of Becky's neck. When they'd last met, Jack had kissed her, and the erotic touch of his lips had sent electric bolts shooting through her body, reminding her that no matter how long she kept it confined, her innate passion would never disappear.

"You're ready, Becky."

She released a shaky breath. "I'm not certain."

Cecelia laid a hand on her shoulder. "I know it is what you want. Whatever should happen between you and Mr. Fulton tonight, you're well equipped for it."

In the past few months, Cecelia had drawn her outside the tight confines of her loving but protective family. Late one night after a few glasses of wine, Becky had confessed her secret desires to her friend, and Cecelia had taken it upon herself to candidly teach her all about how a widow should properly manage an affair—from the seduction to the culmination to what must take place afterward. She was as ready as she'd ever be.

"I feel so heartless." Staring into the mirror at Cecelia, she ran a fingertip along the smooth neckline of her pink satin dress. "It feels wrong to approach such intimate topics so... easily. So carelessly."

Cecelia shook her head firmly. "You mustn't feel that way. I believe this is one of the weaknesses of our sex—we often become so overwrought in matters of carnal love that we are unable to see them for what they are."

"And what are they?"

"Simple fleshly pursuits. Completely separate from matters of the heart."

"But there must be an overlap." Becky thought of her brother's love for his wife. In the four years of their marriage, they'd only grown more in love and more affectionate with each other.

"Sometimes there is," Cecelia admitted. "But it is generally not the case. It is a rare specimen of a man who allows his carnal desires to trickle under his skin in such a manner." She smiled and waved her hand. "Yes, yes, your brother is one of them. But one need only survey the men of our class to prove my hypothesis."

Becky tried to return her friend's smile. "You are probably right. Never fear, Cecelia, I will remember everything you have taught me. My heart will remain uninvolved. Whatever becomes of the time I spend with Mr. Fulton, I shall possess fond memories of all that we will share."

She hoped she was telling the truth. She *wanted* to be telling the truth. Yet she was terrified, for though she'd tried with all her might to heed her friend's warnings, she worried that Jack Fulton had already melted away a chunk of her armor and had begun to burrow beneath it.

Drawing on the gloves the butler had just handed him, Jack glanced at the Earl of Stratford. "Everything in place?"

Stratford nodded, then cocked a blond brow at him. "I feel it imperative to ask you one final time: Are you certain about this course? I am not personally acquainted with the woman, but she comes from a formidable family. If they were to discover that you planned it..."

Jack raised his hand. "Easy, man. I'm no fool. No one else knows."

Stratford was the only man in London he trusted. Jack had returned three months ago after a twelve-year absence from England to discover most of his childhood acquaintances had matured into weak, foppish creatures.

Stratford, on the other hand, was neither weak nor foppish. In the past weeks, Jack had learned a little of the man's past. Like Jack, the earl had lost someone—a woman—when he was very young. That experience had clearly done much to form the man he was today—he was well known in most circles as a profligate rake. He was the kind of man the mamas of the *ton* warned their innocent daughters about.

Stratford nodded, and together they walked through the front door of the earl's townhouse. The sun shone brightly through the haze, but an icy wind whipped leaves and rubbish down the street, and Jack pulled his coat more tightly about him. He glanced at his friend.

"I need this," he said quietly.

Stratford paused, his hand on the stair rail. "I know."

"It is the only way. I don't have much time. I'll not escape from England with my tail between my legs this time."

"Of course." Stratford's tone was mild. His gaze slid in Jack's direction. "I'd choose a different course. But I am not you."

"No," Jack said tightly. "You are not."

The earl shuddered visibly. "I have no desire to be shackled to anyone. Ever."

Neither had Jack, until he'd seen Lady Rebecca—*Becky*. He'd first glimpsed her a month ago at the British Museum. He'd followed her at a distance, observed how she'd clutched her arm to her chest as she studied the Egyptian artifacts in studious silence while her companions gossiped and chatted amongst themselves. A part of him had softened. Standing apart from the others, she looked fragile and distant. She was beautiful. Delicate. Seraphic. But something about her, some dark edge he couldn't quite place his finger on, reminded him of himself.

She was a duke's sister, he learned. She'd been a

victim of a carriage accident just after she was widowed at the tender age of eighteen, which explained the way she'd guarded her arm so carefully at the museum. Though four years had passed since the accident and the loss of her husband, her family still hovered over her and protected her virtue as though she were a virgin debutante.

As Jack learned more about her, understanding dawned. She was the answer to his dilemma.

He'd discovered that Cecelia, Lady Devore, was a bosom friend of his target. Fortunately for him, the lady had been one of Stratford's conquests, and they remained on civil terms. Stratford had arranged an introduction, and upon meeting Jack and hearing of his interest in Lady Rebecca firsthand, Lady Devore had given him a once-over with a cunning gaze and had agreed to discuss the prospect of a meeting. The next day she'd sent a note naming a date, time, and place—a small, currently unoccupied townhouse she owned in Kensington.

He'd seen Lady Rebecca four times. Lady Devore had chaperoned their first meeting, but they'd met alone since. They'd dined, they'd played chess, they'd talked late into the night. She had played the pianoforte for him while he'd watched raptly, his body hardening at the way her lips parted, allowing the pink tip of her tongue to peek out, as she focused on the notes.

He was tired of being teased. He was tired of shaving away her layers of shyness. He knew she wanted him—he witnessed it when her eyes followed him across a room, when her breath caught as his fingertips grazed her cheek. He'd kissed her two nights ago, and she'd responded with breathless passion. She was ready.

More important, he was running out of time. He would be married—or dead—by Christmas.

Tonight would seal their future.

Tonight would be the first night of the rest of his life with Lady Rebecca Fisk.

THE DISH

Where authors give you the inside scoop!

From the desk of Dee Davis

Dear Reader,

The American Tactical Intelligence Command (A-Tac) is an off-the-books black ops division of the CIA. Hiring only the best and the brightest, A-Tac is made up of academicians with a talent for espionage. Working under the cover of one of the United States' most renowned think tanks as a part of Sunderland College, A-Tac uses its collegiate status to keep its activities "eyes only."

I suppose my love of academia is in part responsible for the creation of A-Tac. I graduated from Hendrix College in Arkansas. A small liberal arts school, the campus is dotted with ivy-shrouded buildings and tree-covered grounds. So although I moved my fictional Sunderland to upstate New York, it's still very much Hendrix that I see as I write. And like Nash Brennon (the hero of DARK DECEPTIONS), my degree is in political science. Although, unlike Nash, I have never worked for the CIA or taught in the social sciences.

But I have been in love. And I know how easy it is to let things get in the way. To let fear and distrust rule the day. To let a twist of fate stack the cards against finding happily-ever-after. Thankfully my situation was never quite so dire, but I can understand how Annie Gallagher feels when her path crosses Nash Brennon's again. Eight years ago, he betrayed her in the most basic of ways, and now they find themselves on opposite sides of a dangerous game. Annie with a desperate mission to rescue someone she loves, and Nash charged with stopping her—no matter the cost.

To get some insight into my world as a writer—particularly as the writer of DARK DECEPTIONS—check out the following songs:

"When I'm Gone"—3 Doors Down
"Into the Night"—Santana (featuring Chad Kroeger)
"Fields of Gold"—Sting

And as always, check out www.deedavis.com for more inside info about my writing and my books.

Happy Reading!

Dee Davis

♥ ♥ ♥ ♥ ♥ ♥ ♥ ♥ ♥ ♥ ♥ ♥ ♥ ♥ ♥

From the desk of Jennifer Haymore

Dear Reader,

When Katherine Fisk, the heroine of A TOUCH OF SCANDAL (on sale now), entered my office for the first time to ask me to write her story, I realized right away that she wasn't like one of my normal heroines. She was obviously of the lower orders, dressed in plain brown wool and twisting her hands nervously in her lap. Still, there was something about her dancing brown eyes that intrigued me, and I asked her why she had come.

"I'm in love," she said simply.

I laughed. "Well, that *is* what I write about. But tell me about this man you love."

"Well—" She swallowed hard. "He's a duke."

"Hmm." I studied the calluses on her hands, evidence of a life of hard work. "That makes it . . . difficult."

"I know," she sighed. "But there's more—much more."

"All right," I said. "Tell me."

I was already feeling doubtful, and I hesitated to encourage her. Don't get me wrong. I mean, I love Cinderella stories—but this girl really didn't look like a match for a duke. Plus, she didn't look like she could pay me what my last client had (my last client was a duchess, and she was loaded).

"Well . . . I think he wants to kill my brother."

I tapped my pen against my desk. A servant girl besotted with a duke intent on killing her beloved brother? Impossible, but also . . . "Intriguing," I said, "but you're making this difficult, you know."

"I know." She clasped those calloused fingers tightly together. "There's still more. There's the matter of the duke's wife . . ."

Well, that was that. I rose, intending to politely show her out. "I'm so sorry, Miss . . . Fisk, was it?"

She nodded.

"Miss Fisk, I'm sorry. If the man is already married, there's nothing I can do for you—"

"Oh, he isn't married!" Her brow furrowed. "Well, I don't think he's married . . . But he has a wife." Her frown deepened. "At least . . . he had a wife, but . . ."

I lowered myself back into my chair. "Okay. You're

going to have to start from the beginning. Tell me everything. Don't skip any detail."

She nodded, took a breath, and began. "When I first saw him, he was naked . . ."

And that was how it began. With a servant and a naked, married (or not!) duke seeking retribution from her brother. By the time Miss Fisk finished telling me her story, I was so hooked, I had to put pen to paper and write the entire, wild tale, and, believe it or not, I offered to do it pro bono. I'm usually pretty mercenary about these things, you see, but I figured if I pulled it off, at the end Miss Fisk would be more than capable of paying me, and quite handsomely, too.

I truly hope you enjoy reading Katherine Fisk's story as much as I enjoyed writing it! Please come visit me at my website, www.jenniferhaymore.com, where you can share your thoughts about my books, learn some strange and fascinating historical facts, and read more about the characters from A TOUCH OF SCANDAL.

Sincerely,

Jennifer Haymore

♥ ♥ ♥ ♥ ♥ ♥ ♥ ♥ ♥ ♥ ♥ ♥ ♥ ♥ ♥

From the desk of Rita Herron

Dear Reader,

I've always loved small towns. They feel homey and friendly. Everyone knows everyone else, trades recipes, and watches over one another's children. A small town is a safe place to raise a family.

But have you ever noticed that there seems to be one news story after another about the man or woman next door in those small towns who turned out to be a serial killer? Then there's the soccer mom who killed her husband. Or the man who slaughtered his family.

I've always been fascinated by this idea and it occurred to me one day, what if I took it one step further? What if brutal killers are living among trusting people in small towns . . . and they're not the scariest and most dangerous hidden element? What if there are demons, too? An entire world of them who live underground and mingle with the normal citizens.

And nobody in town knows about those demons . . . except, of course, for the local sheriff, Dante Valtrez . . . who is one of them!

There, I had my setup. But that wasn't enough. I needed to get into the heart of my hero and heroine.

Having a degree in Early Childhood Education, I've always been intrigued by the effects of parenting and society on young children. Our parents teach us to be nice, to follow the rules, to respect others and not to be naughty. But what if my hero wasn't taught that behavior as a child? What if he was taught to be naughty, to be evil? What if Dante Valtrez was raised by demons?

But even if Dante was a demon, I wanted him to be a hero. Like his brothers Vincent in INSATIABLE DESIRE and Quinton in DARK HUNGER, he has both good and bad in him (don't we all?), so he struggles with his own evil side throughout his entire life.

But how to showcase this struggle between good and evil? And then it occurred to me—what if he had to choose between killing a little girl to earn the acceptance of his fellow demons and doing what he knew was right and being forced out of the only community he ever knew? I chose to have Dante put to the ultimate test at age thirteen because that's the beginning of adolescence, a confusing time when a boy changes from a child to a man. This is a pivotal moment for Dante, because he's so torn at the sight of the little girl and her happy family, something he secretly craves, that he can't kill her. He fails the demon test because his humanity surfaces.

From that point on, Dante can't go back. But he doesn't fit into the mortal world either or think he deserves love. Still, he becomes determined to protect innocents from the monsters who raised him.

But Dante has suffered a painful childhood and has been tortured, He does deserve love, and the romantic in me had to find the perfect woman to give him that love. And who else could possibly save Dante but the one he was supposed to kill? The little girl he saved as a child who becomes the woman who wants to destroy all evil through her work?

Romance, suspense, murder, demons, family issues, secrets—this story is chock-full of them all. I hope you'll enjoy the surprise twist at the end and the final installment in the Demonborn series, FORBIDDEN PASSION—out now!

Rita Herron

"You should stay away from me."

Garrett took a step closer to Kate, close enough to feel the sweet heat cascading from her body. She smelled of cinnamon and pine.

She stood her ground. "I don't fear you."

"I'm dangerous."

"Perhaps," she breathed. "But not to me."

"Associating with me will only bring you pain."

"How can you say such an awful thing?"

"I have that effect on people."

She reached out and brazenly placed her hand flat on his chest, scorching him through the thin linen of his shirt. "So be it. But no matter how much pain associating with you might bring me..." Her words dwindled as he pressed his palm over her hand.

She stared at his hand engulfing hers on his chest. Raising his other hand, he touched one finger to the soft skin beneath her chin and pressed upward, forcing her to face him.

"Tell me what you were going to say."

Her eyes shone, and she blinked. "I'll never regret it."

Bending his head, he touched his lips to hers.

"Jennifer Haymore's books are sophisticated, deeply sensual, and emotionally complex. With a dead sexy hero, a sweetly practical heroine, and a love story that draws together two people from vastly different backgrounds, A TOUCH OF SCANDAL is positively captivating!"

—Elizabeth Hoyt, *New York Times* bestselling author

Please turn this page for praise for Jennifer Haymore...

PRAISE FOR *A HINT OF WICKED*

"Full of suspense, mystery, romance, and erotica... I am looking forward to more from this author."

—Las Vegas Review-Journal

"A clever, provoking, and steamy story from an upcoming author to keep your eye out for!"

—BookPleasures.com

"Haymore is a shining star, and if *A Hint of Wicked* is any indication of what's to come, bring me more."

—FallenAngelReviews.com

"Debut author Haymore crafts a unique plot filled with powerful emotions and complex issues."

—RT BOOKreviews Magazine

"A unique, heart-tugging story with sympathetic, larger-than-life characters, intriguing plot twists, and sensual love scenes."

—Nicole Jordan, *New York Times* bestselling author

"Exhilarating... a thrilling historical."

—Midwest Book Review

"Complex, stirring, and written with a skillful hand, *A Hint of Wicked* is an evocative love story that will make a special place for itself in your heart."

—RomRevToday.com